B60

TRAITORS

D0778296

TRAITORS

BY ANDREW SNADEN

BARBOUR
PUBLISHING

© 2004 by Andrew Snaden

ISBN 1-59310-145-7

All rights reserved. No part of this publication may be reproduced or transmitted for commercial purposes, except for brief quotations in printed reviews, without written permission of the publisher.

Churches and other noncommercial interests may reproduce portions of this book without the express written permission of Barbour Publishing, provided that the text does not exceed 500 words or 5 percent of the entire book, whichever is less, and that the text is not material quoted from another publisher. When reproducing text from this book, include the following credit line: "From *Traitors*, published by Barbour Publishing, Inc. Used by permission."

Cover illustration: Douglas Miller

Cover photo © PhotoDisc

This book is a work of fiction. Names, characters, places, and incidents are either products of the author's imagination or used fictitiously. Any similarity to actual people, organizations, and/or events is purely coincidental.

Published by Barbour Publishing, Inc., P.O. Box 719, Uhrichsville, Ohio 44683, www.barbourbooks.com

Our mission is to publish and distribute inspirational products offering exceptional value and biblical encouragement to the masses.

ecpa Member of the
Evangelical Christian
Publishers Association

Printed in the United States of America.
5 4 3 2 1

To Mom, who challenged me to write.
To Dad, who gave me something to write about.

ACKNOWLEDGMENTS

I want to thank my wife, Mary, and daughter, Sarah, for their support and encouragement. Also, thanks to Wanda Dyson for her insight, and to Jamie Cain for editing, line by line, and making this a better story.

PROLOGUE

C rouched on the rocky Seattle beach, FBI Agent Sam Perkins paused as he reached for the plastic blanket covering the corpse. The crisp early spring air, the salty tang of the ocean, and the complaints of the seagulls all seemed real enough, but the body had to be a dream, had to be someone other than Paul.

"Want me to do it?" the Seattle police detective standing over him said.

"No."

Sam tightened his arm muscles to keep his hand steady and pulled the blanket back. Vacant eyes bore into him, knocking him backward onto the smooth stones. He clenched his teeth and fists, holding back screams of rage.

A hand rested on his shoulder. "It's your partner, isn't it?" the detective said.

Sam turned his moist face toward the sea. "Yeah."

危险 خطر
ОПАСНОТЬ

ONE

Yuri Davidov peered at his cards through a cloud of cigarette smoke. Queens full of aces—a full house. He looked over his cards at Tony Heng, a skinny Asian gangster whose uncanny string of luck had just run out. Yuri tossed a packet of money to the center of the table. "That's your thousand plus two. Want to count it?"

One of Heng's bodyguards reached for the money, but Tony waved him off.

"I trust you, my Russian friend. After all, according to my uncle we're business partners now, aren't we?" Heng's thin lips spread into a toothy grin.

Davidov narrowed his eyes. "So I've been told."

Heng touched his chin and pondered the cash in the center of the table. "Such a large bet. Perhaps I should fold?"

"I'd expect as much from you."

Heng grinned. "Ah, a taunt. Is it because you have a strong hand or because you're bluffing? Russians like to bluff, don't they?"

Yuri put his cards facedown on the table and tapped them. "It'll cost you two thousand to find out."

Heng reached into the pocket of his designer jacket and pulled out a wad of cash. He peeled off twenty one-hundred-dollar bills and threw them on the table. "Finding out is worth two thousand. You Russians like to bluff; we Chinese like to gamble. Let's see what you have."

Yuri flipped his cards over. "Full house."

Heng cursed. "And all I have is two pair."

Yuri took a turn at grinning as he reached for the pot.

"Hold on," Heng said and laid down his cards. "I have two pair of fours. I believe four of a kind beats a full house." Smiling, Heng scooped the discards into the deck along with his four of a kind and pushed the deck to Yuri. "Your deal."

Davidov tightened his jaw and balled his hands into fists. "You cheating scum! I discarded a four. There are four fours in a deck, not five."

Heng's eyes darkened. "No one calls me a cheat!"

"I'll do more than call you a cheat." Yuri growled, reaching across the table. He froze midtable when Heng's hand darted into his coat. *The punk is actually going for his gun.* Yuri snatched his own pistol from the small of his back and leveled it at Heng.

But Heng continued to draw his weapon.

خطر

In an apartment across the street, Special Agent Ali Marcoli pressed her earpiece to her ear. "Sam, you better listen to this. Davidov just caught Heng cheating at cards."

Sam Perkins turned from the telescope at the window and rushed to the table. He picked up an earpiece and fit it in. "Not good."

At the crack of the gunshot, their eyes locked.

Perkins jumped to his feet. "Call for backup. And stay put."

Ali opened her mouth, but Sam bolted out the door of the apartment before she could utter a word. She pulled out her cell phone, made one quick call to Seattle police and another to the FBI, then headed for the door. Stay put? Not a chance.

She dropped down the building's worn wooden steps two at a time and burst out onto the street. Ali squinted her eyes against the hot July sun. She'd left her sunglasses upstairs. Ali looked left, then right—no sign of Perkins. She bit her lower lip, trying to decide what to do.

Two Asian men, Heng's bodyguards, popped out of the building across the street, one bald and the other with close-cropped hair. They looked up and down the street while they talked, then Baldy went to the left while Brushcut went to the right.

Where is Heng? Ali wondered. He never went anywhere without the bodyguards—unless he didn't need bodyguards anymore.

If they split up, it could only mean one thing. Davidov had shot Heng, and to save their own skins they had to find and kill Davidov.

Perkins must have seen Davidov come out the front door and followed him. What Sam didn't know was that one of Heng's bodyguards was on his tail.

Ali needed to act fast. Sam would be defenseless if the bodyguard surprised him from behind. Which one should she follow? Ali put herself in Davidov's place. If she'd just blown away a crime lord's nephew, which way would she run? Most likely toward the downtown section and get lost in the Independence Day festivities.

Ali shadowed Baldy from the opposite side of the street.

The heavyset man peered into the window of each business and poked his head down each alley. After two blocks the bodyguard ducked into an alley.

Ali heard sirens echoing from the way she'd come. The police would go to Heng's apartment, but she needed them here. She reached for her cell phone then realized Sam could be dead by the time she made the call.

The rookie FBI agent cut across traffic, using her badge as a shield. Adrenaline coursing through her, she followed Baldy into the alley where tall buildings on each side washed it in dimness.

Halfway down the alley Sam struggled with two men, Baldy and Davidov. Ali reached for the Glock tucked in her hip holster and paused with her hand on the grip. She couldn't fire when the three men were wrapped up with each other. Ali sprinted toward them and shouted, "FBI!"

Baldy released Sam, who continued to struggle with Davidov, and turned to her, his lips twisted into a grin. A couple inches shorter than she, but with beefy shoulders and sledgehammer fists, Baldy presented an imposing image. Ali whipped out her weapon and trained it on the man. He grinned and held open his hands. "I'm unarmed. A man wouldn't need a gun to take me."

"Shoot him," Sam grunted then tumbled with Davidov to the ground.

Baldy put himself between Ali and the two men fighting on the ground. He continued to advance. "Shoot," he said. "But if you miss, or if the bullet goes through me, who will you hit?"

Baldy was right, and Ali knew it. She holstered the Glock, then turned her body sideways. She held up her hands loosely and beckoned Baldy to take her on.

"Don't be a fool, Ali," Sam shouted. "Shoot him."

"It's okay. I can handle this," she said. Like a cat, she focused on Baldy's advance. He moved in a classic martial arts position—one hand high, the other low. If he got a direct hit, she'd suffer for it. But behind her waited a great equalizer.

Baldy ran forward, swinging fists and throwing kicks. Ali shuffled back until only six feet separated her and the flying sledgehammers. She sidestepped a kick and grabbed an empty metal trash can. When he punched, Ali held up the can and felt his fists thud into it. Howling in pain, Baldy shook his hands. Ali threw the trash can at him, and as his hands went up to knock it away, she side-kicked Baldy's right knee. His leg buckled, and Ali fired two quick snap kicks to his chin. He rocked back and forth on his heels then dropped like a sack of potatoes.

Ali looked over at Sam, who now had one knee in Davidov's back while he handcuffed him. He shook his head as Ali rolled Baldy onto his chest, cuffed him, and then rolled him again.

Perkins hauled the lanky Davidov to his feet, then shoved him up against the brick wall of the building, patting him down but finding no weapon. Ali spotted Perkins's gun off to the side, picked it up, then walked it over to him. Perkins grudgingly took it and shoved it into his holster.

"What happened?" she asked.

"I had my gun on this idiot, who didn't see fit to tell me that your guy was coming up behind me. He kicked me in the elbow, and I dropped the gun. Next thing I know, the Asian guy was on me. Davidov tried to run, so I grabbed him, and then you showed up. I guess I should say thanks."

"It would be nice."

"I told you to stay put."

"Would you have?"

Perkins rubbed the back of his hand across his sweaty brow and smiled. "Nah. Thanks."

"You're welcome."

"So what's your story?"

"I called for backup like you said, then I followed you to the street. No sign of you, but I saw Heng's bodyguards looking up and down the street. They split up, and I followed this one figuring if Davidov was on the run, he'd be heading toward downtown."

"Good thinking." Perkins turned to Davidov. "You and I are going to have a little chat."

"I'm not saying anything until I speak with a lawyer."

"Assuming you live that long," Perkins said.

Davidov's eyes widened. "What do you mean?"

"Well, there were four people in Heng's apartment. One bodyguard is out cold after meeting my partner, who happens to be the Pacific Northwest ladies kickboxing champion, and the other is off looking for us. You're here, which means the gunshot in the apartment was for Heng. I'm pretty sure he's dead, and you're in big trouble with his uncle. If you want any kind of break at all, now is the time to start talking."

"I want my lawyer."

"Fine. We'll put you in the general population of the local jail, and you can call your lawyer. Maybe Heng's uncle won't care that you shot his nephew. You'll probably be okay in there. In fact, maybe we'll have you released on your own recognizance and see how you fare."

Beads of sweat popped out on Davidov's forehead. "It was self-defense."

"Sure it was."

"Really. Heng was cheating at cards, and I called him on

it. He went for his gun. I got mine out first, figuring he'd stop when he's staring down a barrel, but he just kept drawing. I had to fire."

"Uh-huh. So where's your gun now?"

Davidov went silent.

Perkins chewed on his lower lip. "You've got a real problem here. I don't believe you'd leave anyone—dead or alive—with a weapon. I figure you took Tony's and ditched it along with your gun. Now, I had a good eye on you the whole time you were outside, so that means they're in that building. The only way you can prove Tony was armed is to tell me where the guns are. Am I right?"

Davidov looked away.

Perkins turned Davidov's face to his. The man's angular features were in a state of panic. "This is a onetime offer. I give you my word we'll do our best to keep you alive if you cooperate with us. We'll even do what we can to back up your self-defense claim."

"How?"

"You have witnesses," Perkins said.

"Yeah, but they work for Heng. They're never going to tell the truth."

Perkins glanced back at the moaning form of Heng's bodyguard. "Don't be so sure. Knowing Heng, it won't be long before there'll be a way to convince our friend it would be in his own best interest to talk."

خطر

Loud voices fueled by a well-liquored lunch crowd made quite a din. Josef Grachev shouldered his way through the bar crowd, ignoring the pounding music to peer toward the back booths. The strapping Russian mobster spotted the lithe form of Billy Heng in a booth against the oak-paneled back wall. At a nearby table were four men, three Asian and one white—Heng's bodyguards. Grachev had brought his own, two men built like NFL linebackers. Like him, they were former KGB, and if trouble started, they knew how to take care of it.

He crossed the bar, ignoring the welcoming looks young women cast at him. In his midforties, Grachev looked more like his late thirties with his dark, handsome features.

While his men took position at the table across from Heng's men, Grachev seated himself in the booth opposite his counterpart. He waved away the waitress who started toward him.

"We have a problem," Heng said in a soft voice.

Whereas Grachev's voice was excessively masculine, Heng's was almost feminine. What the Triad saw in him, the Russian couldn't understand.

"No kidding." There was no trace of an accent in Grachev's voice. He'd spent a lot of time in the States, during and after the KGB era.

"My nephew is dead."

"He probably deserved it," Grachev said.

Heng's eyes darkened. "He was my brother's only son. He did not deserve to die. What should be done, that is our concern."

"Well, Davidov has been with me a long time. I'm not about to just shoot him."

Heng stood. "Then it seems we have nothing to talk about. Maybe we will just carry on our business without you."

"Sure, you do that. Go back to smuggling people into the U.S. in those rust buckets that you call ships. How many did the Coast Guard intercept last year? All but four, I believe. Not one shipment has been intercepted using our freighters.

Is your nephew really worth that much?"

Heng lowered himself back into his seat. "Are you saying nothing should be done? We are to continue trusting you when your man shoots one of ours? Are you willing to give up the healthy fees and additional cargo we pay you for using your ships to protect one murderer?"

Grachev tapped his fingers on the table. They were getting a lot of cash and drugs from the Triad for delivering would-be refugees from the Far East in Russian container ships. The Coast Guard wasn't as willing to stop and search Russian-flagged vessels as they were the boats the Triad had been using. "Well, what does your man say?"

Heng's expression relaxed a bit. "He says Davidov was cheating at cards. When Tony caught him, Davidov got angry, pulled his gun, and shot him."

Grachev clenched his jaw. There was no way Davidov would have just shot Tony. Something had to have happened. He hated being lied to, especially to his face. "I'd like to talk to your man myself."

Heng smiled. "That is no longer possible."

"What do you mean?"

Heng shrugged his shoulders. "He failed in his duty to protect my nephew. I do not tolerate mistakes."

"You just made a big one."

Heng lifted his eyebrows. "What's that supposed to mean?"

Grachev shook his head in disgust. "You've given the FBI the leverage they need with the bodyguard they have in custody."

危险

خطر

ОПАСНОТЬ

TWO

THURSDAY, JULY 4

D o you think we should feed him?" Ali said, pointing at Jimmy Lo sitting in the adjoining interrogation room.

Sam glanced at his watch. "Hmm. Seven o'clock. Nah. It's not our fault his lawyer is taking so long. Look, show me how you did the kick."

"Sure," Ali said. "Crouch down on one knee, then snap a kick sideways toward your opponent's knee." Ali crouched down and fired a kick at his leg, stopping an inch from his kneecap. Perkins jumped back, a grin on his face.

"Whoa, you're good. Let me try."

Ali grabbed a chair and placed it in front of him. "If you don't mind, I'd rather you practiced on a chair for your first time. Aim for the top of the leg."

Sam crouched down, shifted his weight to one knee, and shot his leg out. The kick threw him off balance, and he fell against the wall that contained the one-way glass. The glass rattled from the impact just as the door to the room opened.

"Knock it off, you two," said Assistant Special Agent in Charge Arthur Conners. The dark-haired man shook his head at Sam. Squarely built, Arthur Conners led the task force investigating the alliance between the Russian and Chinese gangs.

Ali held out her hand and helped Sam up from the floor, and the three of them looked through the glass at Jimmy Lo. He stared back at them, though he couldn't see them. The rattling of the one-way glass reminded Lo that they were watching.

"Do we really need this guy?" she asked.

Conners tapped his pen on the worn, wooden table he was seated behind. "Yeah. The U.S. Attorney's Office isn't about to give Davidov immunity if his story can't be corroborated."

"Aren't they being a bit fussy?"

Conners shrugged. "It's their call. We can't really blame them. If we give Davidov immunity and it turns out he did not shoot in self-defense, imagine how that would play in the media."

Sam glanced at his watch. "It's sure taking his lawyer long enough to get here."

Conners looked at his own watch. "Well, Lo's had five cups of coffee. Maybe his bladder will encourage him to open up once his lawyer gets here."

Ali and Sam both chuckled. Lo had stopped all interrogation by requesting a lawyer. To show what good guys they were, they kept providing him with coffee. As for letting him use the washroom, well, they'd get to that when they got to it.

The door to the room opened, and an agent stuck his head in. "Lo's lawyer is here."

Ali and Sam both looked at Conners.

"Go to it, guys."

Sam followed Ali into the hallway. Ali raised her eyebrows at Lo's lawyer. The man was easily as tall as Perkins, well built, and, though Ali had expected someone of Asian descent, white. Sam stepped even with her.

"I take it you're Mr. Lo's lawyer," Sam said.

"Chuck Springfield." The lawyer held out a massive hand.

Sam shook it, and Ali thought the two men squeezed hands just a tad longer than necessary, testing to see who had the stronger grip.

"Sam Perkins," Sam said finally. "This is my partner, Ali Marcoli."

Ali extended her hand and was surprised when Springfield took it gently. It was a nice change; most guys tried to break it to prove their virility.

"So you want to question my client?" Springfield asked.

Sam nodded.

"Did you read him his rights?"

"Yep," Perkins said. "And no sooner had I said 'Do you understand your rights?' than he asked for his lawyer."

"Okay," Springfield said, "let's go in and talk."

Sam held open the door, and Springfield entered the interrogation room ahead of Ali. Perkins shut the door behind them. Springfield took the hard metal chair next to Lo.

"Hi, Jimmy," the lawyer said. "Chuck Springfield. The firm sent me down to represent you."

Lo looked up from the table, loosely shook Springfield's hand, and grunted.

"Now, Jimmy, these agents are going to ask you some questions. I'll let you know if it's okay to answer them." Springfield looked up at Sam. "Ask away."

Perkins put his foot on a chair and leaned toward Lo. "Davidov said Heng was drawing his weapon and he had no choice but to shoot. Is that right?"

"Don't answer that," said Springfield.

Both Ali and Sam turned their eyes on Springfield. "Why not?" Sam said. "We're not asking him to incriminate himself."

"You're asking him to place himself at the scene of a crime. As far as I can tell, my client hasn't committed a crime."

Lo looked up and smiled.

"Actually, he has," Perkins said. "He assaulted both Agent Marcoli and myself."

Springfield shrugged. "Minor charges."

"He also interfered with Agent Perkins while he was making an arrest."

Springfield looked over at his client. "Did you?"

Lo shook his head. "I saw him beating on the other guy in the alley. I thought it was a mugging. I just went in to help."

Springfield looked up and smiled. "A perfectly reasonable explanation."

"I need to go to the washroom," Lo said.

Perkins shook his head. "Later."

Springfield straightened in his seat. "You're not going to deny my client washroom privileges?"

Perkins shrugged. "No one forced him to drink five cups of coffee. He can hold it until he answers some questions."

Springfield clenched his jaw. "I want to speak to your superior."

Ali could see Sam was itching for a fight, but she had learned long ago you catch more flies with honey. Not only that, but something about Springfield bugged her. He looked like anything but a lawyer. "Let him go to the can," she said.

Perkins's eyes flashed but then softened. If they were going to work together, he had to trust her. The fight in the alley had gone a long way toward building that crucial trust.

"Sure," Sam said. "Let's go."

Lo stood, his hands shackled. Springfield rose to his feet as well.

"You're staying here," Ali said to the lawyer.

Springfield pulled at the lapels of his suit coat. "Where my client goes, I go. I don't want him coming back here black and blue because he slipped in the washroom."

"Then no one goes," Perkins said. "Because it's not going to be two against one in the restroom."

The lawyer exhaled sharply. "Surely you aren't saying. . ." He threw up his hands. "Well, then she can come."

"Oh, please," said Ali. "We aren't a bunch of schoolkids here that everyone has to go and hold each other's hands. I assure you, Mr. Lo won't be any more black and blue than he already is."

Lo's hand went to his bruised chin. Ali smiled at him, reminding him that she, a woman, had bested him. That trash can trick was something an old Scottish boxer taught her. "Maybe Mr. Lo would like me to accompany him instead."

Lo shook his head quickly. "No, that's okay. I'll go with him," he said, nodding his head toward Perkins.

Springfield sat down and shrugged his shoulders. "He just better come back the way he left."

"Whatever," said Sam as he guided Lo out of the interrogation room.

"Would you like a cup of coffee?" Ali asked the lawyer.

"No thanks." His eyes gave her the once-over, and his tongue peeped out and licked his lips.

Ali contained her irritation. She wanted to put Springfield at ease, and giving him a lecture on leering wouldn't do that.

"You're very attractive for an FBI agent," he said.

Ali flitted a coy smile. "Why, thank you."

He smiled back. "You're welcome. Maybe after we're done here, we can get a drink or something?" He drew out the word *something*.

"It's a possibility," Ali said. She had had her doubts about Springfield, and now all the warning lights and sirens were going off. "So, being a criminal lawyer, you must really keep up on the case law."

Springfield leaned back in his chair. "I try. Why do you ask?"

"Well, you sure scared my partner."

Springfield lifted his eyebrows. "I did?"

Ali took the seat across from Springfield. "Sure. You see, Perkins is old school, a dinosaur. He still believes you can deny suspects the washroom and slap them around a bit. He doesn't even know about last week's Supreme Court decision on Barkman. That's why I jumped in and got him to take your client to the washroom. The Supreme Court's made it clear that a suspect's constitutional rights extend to basic human comfort. Barkman got off of bank robbery because they didn't feed him for twelve hours. There was no way I was going to let Lo walk because we didn't let him go to the washroom."

Springfield chuckled. "Well, you're one smart cookie. I can see I'm going to have to be careful around you."

Ali grinned. "I went to law school, too. I still keep up." Her cell phone rang, and Ali flipped it open. "Yes. Okay. Excuse me."

"I'll be here," Springfield said.

Ali left the interrogation room and entered the observation room, where Conners was sipping coffee with a broad smile on his face. "I think we just got a big break."

"What?" Ali said.

He handed her a police report. Ali glanced at it and smiled. "Just the leverage we need. Does Sam know about this?"

"No. I'll show it to him when he comes back with Lo. This would go a lot better if we could get at him without his lawyer. I think we could shake him up pretty good."

"That's easy," Ali said.

"How?"

"Arrest the lawyer."

危险
خطر
ОПАСНОТЬ

THREE

Former CIA agent Jonathan Corrigan awkwardly crouched and kept his breathing calm. An adrenaline rush could make his hands unsteady and be fatal to his objective. It had been a long time since he'd done this, but it was like riding a bicycle —you never forgot. But this was more than a bicycle ride. There were high stakes, and failure just wasn't an option.

An early evening cool ocean breeze pushed some of the July heat off his back. His stomach complained a bit from being bent over, but he ignored it. It had never been the same after he'd been shot. His left leg ached, too, thanks to the second bullet. He couldn't bend it completely, so it put him on an awkward tilt. Fortunately his partner let him lean against her, helping him keep his balance.

Everything was stacked up against Jonathan, but ten years in the CIA had taught him how to overcome obstacles. He held his hands at the ready, his index fingers locked. He focused on blocking out the crowd. It was just him and her now, and they would not be denied victory.

A pistol cracked and Jonathan rolled his fingers along the cow's teats, squeezing the milk into the stainless steel bucket below. The crowd in the stands of the Bellingham Fourth of July Fair erupted in cheers as Jonathan and nine other local farmers milked away.

He'd practiced for a couple weeks, and he and Bonnie were like a well-oiled machine. His hands moved in a steady rhythm while the Jersey cow happily munched on hay lying on the ground in front of her. The pail filled with the warm, foamy milk and cream.

"Jonathan, he's ahead of you," the sweetest voice in the world called from the stands. His wife, Laura, was his backup. She'd brought binoculars and was keeping a close eye on the only competitor Jonathan wanted to beat, his brother, Danny, who was milking the cow next to him.

Breaking discipline, Jonathan glanced over at Danny. The muscle-bound Seattle police officer had his Jersey flowing milk like she was a fire hydrant. Ten years away from the farm put Jonathan at a decided disadvantage against his brother. He couldn't lose. Not in front of his lovely wife, and not to Danny.

"Sorry, Bonnie," Jonathan whispered to the cow. "This might hurt a bit." He turned her teat on a right angle and shot a stream of hot milk, catching Danny Corrigan in the side of the face. His brother howled and wiped at the milk.

Jonathan turned his face away in time to avoid the retaliatory strike. Milk soaked the back of his head, but he'd broken Danny's rhythm. The crowd, taking up the rivalry, began to cheer for him.

He feverishly worked Bonnie's teats, and the milk level climbed up the pail.

"Keep going," Laura shouted. "He's catching up again."

Jonathan's hands could go no faster. He just hoped it

would be enough. The milk continued to climb; it was just below the ring, only another quarter of an inch. The pistol fired, and Jonathan fell back off the three-legged milk stool onto his rump, shaking his head. His brother held his hands high over his head accepting the crowd's polite applause. At least they'd wanted Jonathan to win.

Danny stepped over to him, milk still dripping from his face, and held out his hand. "Need help up, old man?"

Jonathan chuckled, then grabbed the cane that lay on the ground next to him, and let Danny help him to his feet. The crowd roared and Jonathan waved, then limped over to the grandstand while Danny went to collect his trophy.

Jonathan shook hands with the crowd as he climbed the stairs. Laura waited for him at the end of the tenth row along with Danny's wife, Rita. He pushed out his lower lip in a childish pout when his gaze met hers. Laura stood and held her arms open. "Come and cry on Mommy's shoulder."

"You bet," Jonathan said and buried his head on his wife's shoulder while she patted the back of his damp head. He took in a deep breath of her hair, wanting the moment to last forever. *Mommy*. It was more than just an affectionate term; Laura was three months' pregnant with their first child.

Their road to marriage had been a rocky one. They'd dated for over a year before his treachery led to a two-year separation. Jonathan spent every day of those two years loving the woman he'd betrayed, and only God's grace—and a national crisis caused by Laura's late father—had thrown them back together. Though Jonathan's mother wanted them to wait to marry, neither of them would have it. Both in their midthirties, they wanted to get their new life on the road as soon as possible.

Now, a year later, everything was perfect. Well, almost.

Whenever Laura placed her hand on her belly, there was sadness in her eyes. Jonathan knew she wanted her mother with her, but that was impossible. Alice McIvor was in prison for conspiring with her husband, Harrison. Jonathan had tried to get her out, but so many national security issues were involved that even he didn't have that kind of pull.

Hearing footsteps, Jonathan and Laura turned to see Danny trotting up the stairs holding a gold trophy in his massive hands.

"So I guess pizza later is on you, my older little brother," Danny said.

Jonathan held up his cane in a warning gesture. "Watch who you're calling little."

Danny was indeed the larger of the Corrigan boys, beating Jonathan's six-foot-one-inch frame by three inches. Danny was also more muscular, but the hard work of his dairy ranch kept Jonathan fit. If push came to shove, Jonathan had no doubt he could whip his younger brother.

Danny looked over at his wife and smiled, then his face clouded. "Where's the girls?"

"They went with Roxanne to go on the rides."

"What, they didn't want to watch their old man teach these farmers a lesson in how to milk?"

Rita shook her head. "I'm afraid hanging around with their teenage aunt appeals to little girls more than watching a bunch of guys relive their glory days milking cows."

Danny faked disappointment then grinned.

Laura rubbed her stomach. "I don't think I'm going to make it until pizza. I could really use some ice cream right now."

"At your service, ma'am," Jonathan said, taking a short bow. "Anyone else?"

Rita held up her hand. "I wouldn't mind a cone."

"Danny?" Jonathan said.

"I'll come with you. I want to check on the girls."

"Sure," Jonathan said.

Danny handed his trophy to Rita and followed Jonathan down the wooden steps. The arena was being set up for barrel racing next. With any luck they'd be back in time before it finished.

"You don't want to check on your girls; you want to check on Roxanne."

"You bet. I've never seen a girl attract more boys without trying in my whole life."

"She sure is pretty," Jonathan said. "I hate to think what would have happened to her if Mom hadn't rescued her."

Danny shuddered. "I know what happens on the streets, and she's one fortunate girl to have caught Mom's eye. Speaking of Mom, when does she get back?"

"Couple of days. Nice to see her take some time for herself."

"Your moving onto the farm has taken quite a load off of her."

The two brothers worked their way through the crowd toward one of the concession stands. Four lines grew from the colorful building, each containing at least ten people.

"Tell you what," Danny offered. "I'll check on Roxanne and the kids while you wait in line."

"Good plan."

While Danny waded through the crowd in search of their adopted sister and his own two preteen girls, Jonathan took position behind two chatterbox teenage girls. He leaned on his cane, taking some of the weight off his leg. The midday heat reminded him of his time stumping through the deserts of the Middle East. Those days were long gone. His injuries and fame precluded him from ever serving as a field agent again.

The chattering stopped. One of the girls, a bouncy redhead, focused on his face. "You're. . ." She scrunched her forehead.

"Jonathan Corrigan," her slim, blond friend finished. "You saved the kids from those bombs, right?"

He smiled politely. "Yeah, but keep it quiet."

The redhead looked at his cane. "You can go ahead of us."

"I don't mind waiting in line," Jonathan said.

A trucker turned around, recognition lit up his face, and Jonathan found himself ushered to the head of the line as word was passed down that the local hero was waiting in line. There was no point in arguing. Maybe it was time to grow a beard.

Jonathan bought his cones, hooked his cane on his arm, and made his way back to the grandstand. Just as he reached the entrance, a hand gripped his elbow. He pulled his elbow free, sending the tray of vanilla cones to the ground. Jonathan whipped his head around to face two men in dark suits and dark glasses.

"Mr. Corrigan," one of the men said, "come with us."

خطر

A folder tucked under his arm, Sam opened the door and followed Ali into the interrogation room.

Jimmy Lo rested his cuffed hands on the table, a sheen of sweat on his forehead. "Where's my lawyer?"

Ali bumped Lo's chair on her way to the opposite end of the table. He spun his head around and glared at her, but all she showed him was her back. She sat down, propped her feet on the table, and leaned back. Sam positioned himself a few inches behind Lo.

Lo twisted and looked up at Sam. "My lawyer. Where's my lawyer?"

"You really want your lawyer?" Ali said. Since Ali had

flushed the rat, Sam decided to let her take the lead.

"Yes," Lo said.

"Tell me, Jimmy," Ali said. "This is the first time you met Springfield, right?"

"Yeah."

A sly grin crept across Ali's face. "Who hired him? Your boss, Billy Heng?"

"I'm not talking to you without my lawyer."

Ali swung her legs off the table, and the chair's front legs clunked to the floor. "Okay, you can have your lawyer."

"Up you get," said Sam. "We'll take you to your lawyer."

Lo looked up over his shoulder at him. "Up? Where are we going?"

"To the cells so you can visit with your lawyer."

Lo's bowling-ball forehead crinkled. "I don't understand."

"Your lawyer isn't a lawyer," Ali said. "I mentioned a recent Supreme Court case that even the worst criminal lawyer would know was a fake, but your 'lawyer' never batted an eye. Springfield was here to make sure you didn't talk before you went to the cells."

"Wonder what they had planned for you when you went down there?" Perkins said.

Lo shook his head.

Sam opened up the folder and tossed a few pictures over Lo's head onto the table. He looked over at Ali, whose grin told him all he needed to know about Lo's expression. The pictures of his fellow bodyguard's bullet-riddled, waterlogged body had their effect.

"The Coast Guard found him out in Puget Sound," Ali said. "Seems a pod of orcas were playing with the body. I guess your boss didn't count on that. Anyhow, that's what Billy Heng has planned for you. I'm sure he's got someone in the cells ready to silence you."

Sam moved from behind Lo and took the seat next to him. "It's time to play *Let's Make a Deal.* Behind curtain number one is a short holiday with the general prison population where you end up dead. But if you cooperate, you can pick curtain number two. It's gotta be better than curtain number one."

Lo looked over at Ali. "Curtains? What's he talking about, curtains?"

"Yeah, Sam, what's this curtain stuff about?"

Sam looked up at the ceiling. "You're younger than I thought. It's an old game show where contestants picked a curtain and won whatever prize was behind it. Sometimes it was good, but sometimes it was a stinker." He leaned toward Lo. "You already know what's behind curtain number one, and it stinks. So, do you want to try for curtain number two?"

Lo shook his head. "I'm—I'm not sure."

"Of course, he could always pick curtain number three," Ali said.

Lo looked over at Ali, hope emblazoned on his face. "Sure. What's curtain number three?"

Ali grinned. "We let you go and fish your body out of Puget Sound later."

Lo gulped and looked at Ali. "Curtain two, it keeps me alive?"

"Yes," Ali said, "it keeps you alive."

"If I talk, they'll—"

"Kill you," Ali finished. "They're going to kill you whether you talk or not. If you talk, at least we'll give you a chance."

"Make up your mind," Sam said. "Take the deal and live, or stay silent and end up silenced."

Lo took a deep breath while he looked up at the ceiling. "I'll talk."

خطر

Jonathan squared off to face the two men. He let the cane slide down to his hand and tightened his grip so it would be ready to use. "Why would I come with you?"

Both men reached into their suit jackets and flipped open their identification.

"CIA." Jonathan sighed. "Of course. What do you want?"

"Mr. Corrigan," said the man whose wallet had identified him as Robert Branch, "the director himself has ordered us to transport you to Langley. This is an urgent matter."

Jonathan pushed his cane against Branch's midsection. "I'll tell you what's urgent. My wife is pregnant and a fussy eater. At this moment, she's willing to eat an ice cream cone, but that could change while we talk. Now, because of you I have to hurry and get her another one. You guys tossed me out of the game; I'm not going anywhere."

Branch eased the cane out of his stomach. "Mr. Corrigan, we have to insist. This is a matter of national security."

Jonathan looked up at the sky. "National security." He leveled his eyes at Branch. "It's always national security. It was national security that covered up that mess here in Bellingham. People should've gone to jail for that."

"I know nothing about that," Branch said. "I just know the director said we have to get you to Langley ASAP."

"And if I refuse?"

Both men shifted uncomfortably.

"What? Are you going to drag me through this crowd and take me by force? These people won't even let me wait in a line for an ice cream cone. How do you think they'll react to the CIA taking their local hero into custody? You'll be lucky to get out of here with the clothes on your back."

"And that's if you get past me."

Jonathan turned to see Danny walk up.

Both agents took in Danny's build but didn't flinch. They'd been trained just like Jonathan and likely could handle themselves. What they couldn't handle would be the crowd that would jump into the melee.

"Who are these guys?" Danny said.

"CIA. They want to take me to Langley."

"Do you want to go?"

"I want to get Laura an ice cream cone."

Danny reached into his back pocket and flipped open his badge. "The CIA doesn't operate on domestic soil, but the Seattle police do. Take a hike, unless you want to duke it out right here on the fairgrounds. After we give you a whipping, we'll have the Bellingham police lock you up."

Branch sighed. "Mr. Corrigan, I'll be honest with you—"

"Oh, come on," Jonathan said. "The CIA and honesty are mutually exclusive terms. We all know that, so don't even waste your breath. Come on, Danny, let's get some more ice cream."

The brothers left the CIA agents standing dumbfounded.

"Do you think you should call Langley and see if it's important?" Danny said, while he and Jonathan headed back to the concession stand.

"It doesn't matter what it is. Even if I trusted them, which I don't, I promised Laura I'd never work for the agency again. I promised her the life of a farmer. I betrayed her once before and thought I'd lost her forever. I won't do it again. Nothing they can do will make me go back."

"But with the way the world is right now, are you sure you can keep that promise? Face it, Jonathan. You were in Middle Eastern counterterrorism. If they need you, that's what it's about."

Once again the people waiting in line insisted he go ahead, and Jonathan was thankful. Laura's maternal appetite was frustratingly unpredictable, and time was of the essence.

"There's lots of agents. It can't be so important that they need a broken-down guy like me. They'll make do."

"What if they can't?" Danny said, as Jonathan took the cones from the girl at the concession window.

"They'll have to." The adventurous little boy in him champed at the bit to be in the field again, but the soon-to-be father felt mortal. Before, Jonathan had nothing to live for. Now he had everything to live for.

خطر

Sam Perkins leaned against the wall and sipped his coffee. Ali sat at the table across from Yuri Davidov and pushed a document toward him. Lo's statement cleared the Russian of murder; now they could work on turning him.

"Ever watch *Let's Make a Deal*?" Ali said.

Davidov shook his head. "No. Should I?"

"Yeah, you should have," Ali said and explained the game show to Davidov. "This document grants you immunity and a new life if you cooperate. It's your curtain number two. We can get the U.S. Attorney's representative here in a flash and make it all legal."

"What about the other curtains?"

"Curtain one," Sam said, "is we charge you for killing Heng and assaulting me and turn you loose in the general population. But that's not really on the table."

"Why not?"

"Because we don't want you. For you, it's pick curtain number two, or you get curtain number three."

"What's three?" Davidov said.

"You don't want it," Sam said. "Pick curtain two, we put Grachev in jail, and you get a new life."

"Believe me," Ali said, "you really don't want to see curtain number three."

Perkins suppressed a smile.

Davidov tilted his chin. "Maybe I do. What is it?"

"We'll just turn you loose," Ali said, "and then start taking bets as to how long you'll live."

Perkins took the seat next to Davidov. "So tell us about this unholy alliance between Grachev and Heng, and live."

Davidov drummed his thick fingers on the table.

"What's this?" Ali said. "Feelings of loyalty to Grachev? His partner Heng has already killed one bodyguard and was trying to kill the other. What makes you think Grachev will be any different?"

"We go way back," Davidov said, his voice barely above a whisper. "I can't believe he'd kill me."

"Maybe he wouldn't," Ali said. "But do you think he can stop Heng from taking you out? Do you think he's going to blow this whole alliance just to save your skin?"

"Josef can protect me."

Perkins groaned. "I thought we were dealing with a smart guy. Guess I was wrong." Perkins opened up his wallet and tossed twenty dollars on the table. "Okay, Ali, he lasts six hours, tops."

Ali pursed her lips, reached into her blue jeans pocket, and pulled out a handful of bills. She peeled off a twenty and tossed it on top of Sam's. "You've got a bet. I think Davidov is street-smart. I think he'll make more than six but less than twelve."

Davidov stared at the bills on the table.

Sam took a notepad from the inside of his jacket pocket

and started writing. "Okay, I've got zero to six, and you've got more than six to twelve. I'll ask around and see who else wants a piece of this."

"What are you guys doing?" Davidov gasped.

Sam stood and opened the door. "Welcome to curtain number three. You're free to go. We've got Lo, and he's ready to cooperate."

"Lo knows nothing."

"Says you," Ali said. "Get out of here. We haven't eaten yet, and it's already well past dinner." She turned to Sam. "I can't believe we blew the Fourth of July for this clown."

"No kidding." Sam moved over to Davidov and grabbed his arm. "Up you get. We're done."

"Wait a minute," Davidov said. "Give me a few minutes to think."

"I don't think you understand," Perkins said. "We're done talking. You're free to go. Get out of here. You've wasted our time."

Perkins had to give Ali credit. Inside she must be thinking he was crazy, but her expression gave no hint she didn't disagree with his course of action.

Davidov fired a stream of Russian at them. It didn't sound nice.

Ali shot a stream of Russian right back, and Perkins cocked his head sideways. Davidov tensed like he'd been punched.

"You speak Russian?" Sam said.

"A little," she said. "It was offered as an elective at the university, so I thought, why not."

"What did he just say?"

"Loosely translated, he threatened to rip our guts out and let the dogs of the streets eat them."

"No kidding. What did you say?"

Ali smiled coyly. "It wasn't very ladylike."

"No," Davidov said. "It wasn't."

"Good," Perkins said. "Now get out of here."

Davidov stood slowly. "You're serious?"

"Absolutely. I was supposed to spend the day at the fair with some friends, and you messed it up. I don't ever want to see you again." He grinned. "Chances are, I won't. Go." He pushed Davidov toward the door.

Davidov glanced over at Ali, but her face was set like flint.

"No joke? I can leave?"

Perkins nodded his head.

"What if I want to stay?"

"Sorry, pal," Sam said. "You chose the wrong curtain."

Hesitantly, Davidov walked out the door, and Sam and Ali followed him. "Take a left down the hall," Sam said.

They escorted the Russian mobster to the lobby of the federal building. As soon as they passed the security checkpoint, Perkins took hold of Ali's elbow. "This is as far as we go."

Ali easily picked up on his plan. "We should at least walk him to the door."

"Are you crazy? What if the sniper misses and hits one of us?"

The word *sniper* grabbed Davidov by the collar. He turned toward them. "You know there's someone out there, and you're going to let me walk out?"

"We don't know anything," Sam said. "But I'm sure Grachev and Heng know where you are by now. I doubt they'll be stupid enough to try something in front of a federal building, but I'm not taking any chances. Even if the sniper just gets you, the mess is terrible. I'm wearing new pants."

Davidov looked toward the door but didn't move. He looked back at them. "If you knew there was a sniper, you'd have to tell me, right?"

"If you're so sure your buddy Grachev isn't going to kill you," Sam said, "and he can stop Heng from sending you for a swim like he did Lo's buddy, what do you care? It's what *you* know that matters. It's what you know Grachev will do. Now get going. I'm hungry."

Davidov turned to the door, but it was like his feet were bolted to the floor. He turned back toward them again. "Okay, we can make a deal."

"Smart guy," Sam said.

The Yuri Davidov they followed back to the interrogation room walked like a broken man. His shoulders were stooped over, and his walk lacked purpose. He was about to betray a lifelong friend, and it had to be eating at him. Perkins held no sympathy for the man. Davidov was involved in drugs, prostitution, extortion, and who knows what else. He deserved everything he got, and he'd never get what he deserved because of the deal they would make.

But it was worth it. Sam's stomach still roiled at the memory of the sight of his partner on the beach. Grachev had killed him—there was no doubt in his mind—and Davidov was the first big crack in the Russian mobster's armor.

They resumed their places in the interrogation room.

"I'll get Moody," Ali said.

A moment later, she reappeared with Ian Moody of the U.S. Attorney's Office. The stout attorney pushed back a wisp of dark hair as he sat next to Davidov and explained the plea agreement. "Now remember, Mr. Davidov," Moody said, "this deal is only valid if you cooperate fully. Do you want to discuss it with a lawyer before you sign?"

"No," Davidov said and signed the document.

Smart move, Perkins thought. After what Heng had tried

with Lo, a lawyer would be the last person Davidov could trust.

Moody scooped up the documents and left the room.

"So," Perkins said, "who killed Newberg?"

Davidov tensed. "Who's Newberg?"

Sam rushed Davidov and slammed his fist on the table. "He was my partner, you scumbag, and I know Grachev had him killed."

"I don't know what you're talking about."

Sam looked at Ali, who shook her head sadly.

"Back to curtain three?"

"Yeah," Sam said. "You promised full cooperation, Yuri. Get out of here."

"Wait," Davidov said. "Maybe I know something."

"Something?"

"Okay, I know what you want to know, but until I'm sure you're going to keep your end of the deal, I'm not saying anything about that."

"Of course we're going to keep our end of the deal," Sam said. "We're the government."

Davidov smirked. "Yeah, right. As soon as I'm in my new life, I'll talk about Newberg, but not before. We can talk about anything else."

Sam retreated from the table and took a deep breath. Davidov was smarter than he looked. "Okay, we talk about Newberg when you're relocated. Until then, why don't you tell me why mortal enemies now get along."

"Mutual benefit," Davidov said. "We have a good distribution network for drugs and prostitution, and the Chinese have a good supply of both. Josef figured both groups could make more money working together than apart. He called a truce, met with Heng, showed him the numbers, and next thing I know, we're working with the Triads instead of trying to kill them."

"So if the Chinese are supplying the drugs and girls, what are the Russians supplying?" Ali said.

"Ships. Up until the deal, the Chinese were smuggling people and drugs on rust buckets. They'd land in Canada and slip across the border because the Coast Guard kept intercepting them. The losses at the border were significant. Since the Coast Guard isn't as anxious to board Russian-flagged vessels at sea, we've been setting up container ships that can land here in Seattle."

"We can still search the containers at port," Ali said.

"Yes, but there are thousands of containers. There aren't enough people to search them all. Some drug losses are inevitable, as are human losses, but they're much lower coming in via our ships."

"Not to mention if the illegal immigrants land on U.S. soil they can claim refugee status and are protected by the Constitution," Sam said.

"Meaning hearings and the whole nine yards," said Ali.

Davidov nodded.

Ali leaned forward. "One thing I don't understand. These girls you bring over on the ships. Why would they want to come to the United States to live a life of prostitution?"

A cruel grin crept across Davidov's face. "They're told they're coming to work in restaurants or as domestic help. Once they get here, they're given no choice."

Ali curled up her lip, and Sam thought she might spit in Davidov's face. Fortunately she kept her cool.

"Okay," Ali said. "Let's get down to details."

"Then you'll put me in a safe house?"

Sam rubbed his chin. "No. I think you'll be going to cells first."

危险 خطر ОПАСНОТЬ

FOUR

Michelle Lee leaned against the wall of the cargo container. The air was stale and laced with the stench of human waste and vomit. A pair of wall vents near the roof provided them with fresh air and light. A hole in the floor took the human waste away, but the smell still came back up through it. She shared the container with at least fifty people. Everyone wondered how long they'd been at sea. Most agreed it was at least a month and America couldn't be much farther.

Good thing, too. More than a dozen of them were sick, and food supplies and fresh water were getting low. Michelle could tolerate the living conditions, but the ache in her heart for home was a constant pain. How could her parents have done this to her? Michelle knew the answer to that. The Chinese government only allowed one child per family, and that she was a girl made her a bitter disappointment from the beginning.

The final straw had come six months ago. A strange man dressed like everyone else—but white—visited the village. He told them about Jesus, the Son of God who had died for them, for her. His words were like water, quenching a parching she had always felt. She gave her soul to Jesus and forever put a rift between herself and her parents. Five months later, some men came to the village, gave her parents money, and Michelle found herself on the ship.

Someone slumped next to her. "Have you got any food?"

There wasn't enough light from the small hole to make out a face, but Michelle knew it was Kit. She'd already been to America and got sent back. "Ho said we should speak English."

"Ho is up front. Have you got any food?" Kit said in Mandarin.

Michelle clenched her jaw. "No."

"You're a Christian. You wouldn't lie, would you?"

"I'm not lying." Michelle had some rice hidden, but she hadn't lied. She was saving it for a young man who was ill. The rice really belonged to him. "Please, speak English."

"I told you, Ho is up front. He can't hear us."

"I want to speak English. Ho said the better I speak English, the better job I get. I might even get to look after children. Wouldn't that be wonderful?"

Kit's hand touched Michelle's chin. "You're way too pretty to work with children."

"What does that mean?"

Kit laughed.

خطر

The early morning sun warmed Josef Grachev's face as he leaned on the Russian freighter's rail. He stared eastward, where the Washington State coastline would be if the ship weren't over two hundred miles out. Spending the night on the ship had put him in a foul mood. Josef liked his luxuries, and even though he'd kicked the captain out of his cabin, it was Spartan compared to his Seattle home.

Sophie's hands kneaded his tense shoulder muscles. "Josef, relax."

He shrugged her off. "I can't relax. It's because of that idiot Heng we're stuck on this ship. All I can think about is killing him."

"That would cause more trouble, yes?"

Josef clenched Sophie's chin in his hand squeezing until she winced. "Sophie, I've told you before, don't think. I keep you for one thing only. If I wanted more, I'd get a woman with brains."

Her eyes fell. "Sorry."

Josef pushed out a deep breath and shook his head. He first laid eyes on Sophie when she stepped off the freighter that brought her from Russia. If he hadn't known better, he would've sworn Marilyn Monroe had been reincarnated in Sophie. Josef had decided to keep this one for himself.

A door opened, and Billy Heng stepped out onto the walkway, a broad smile on his face. "Good morning."

Grachev kept his expression neutral. "Good morning."

"Any news?"

"Not much," Grachev said. "We think Lo turned. Our people saw the U.S. Marshals escort him from the building. I guess it was to be expected after you killed his partner."

"Why didn't your people kill him?"

Grachev shook his head. "Because you said he doesn't know anything. I'm not going to kill a federal witness unless I have to."

"Did any of your people follow them?"

"All the way to the airport. They got in a chopper, so there's no telling where they took him."

"And Davidov? Has he turned?"

"I don't know," Grachev said. "He never came out of the building, which is a good sign. I'll be able to find out for sure."

"How?"

"A sacrificial lamb."

"What does that mean?"

"Never you mind," Grachev said. "Until we're certain, though, we'll stay here, out of the Coast Guard's reach. They wouldn't dare board a Russian vessel in international waters." Grachev looked out to sea, where he could make out another freighter steaming toward them. *It will do,* he thought.

خطر

Jonathan opened the gate, and the cows filed through on their way to pasture. Normally milking was done by farmhands, but Jonathan had given them the day off. He wiped the sheen of sweat off his forehead as he watched the cows take the trail through the wooded area surrounding the house and barn to the field beyond.

Farming wasn't as exciting as spying, but it wasn't as dangerous either. Sure, the odd cow dumped manure on his boot, but it sure beat getting shot at and running for your life.

His running days were over, he thought as he picked up his cane. The doctor said it was a miracle he could walk as well as he did. Jonathan had to agree. A bullet to the stomach and one to the leg, and all he had to show for it was a slight limp. He probably didn't need the cane, but he'd grown used to it, and he liked the image it helped him project—the gentleman farmer.

He looked back at the log house. Normally Laura would be rocking on the porch making the odd snide comment, but she was helping a friend at the friend's computer store. No one knew computers like Laura, thanks in part to a master's degree in computer science from MIT. She'd helped her father write encryption programs for the military, and what she could do scared Jonathan.

He took a deep breath of the country air. Life was perfect. Or was it? Seeing those CIA agents had stirred something within—an old itch, a wanderlust. No, better not to go there. Maybe a ride on his new mare, Phelan, would help quench those feelings.

He headed toward the barn then stopped when their German shepherd jumped to his feet and barked furiously, straining at his chain. Rudy was an ex-police dog, a gift from Danny. Someone must have turned into the driveway, and judging from Rudy's raised hackles, it wasn't Laura. Two black SUVs wound down the long wooded driveway. Couldn't they take no for an answer? Was it the answer he wanted to give?

Rudy was frothing now, so Jonathan walked over to the garage and stood beside him. The dog quieted down, but a deep growl rumbled in his chest.

The two vehicles pulled up in front of him, and all four doors of the first SUV opened. Six dark-suited clones with dark glasses bundled out and looked around, ignoring him and the dog. They say art imitates life, but life was imitating art as the six agents did their best to look like they were in a feature film. One of them spoke into his wrist, and Jonathan started to chuckle. He stopped chuckling when the back door of the second SUV opened and Conrad Bolton emerged.

He was dressed in blue jeans, Western shirt, and cowboy hat. Jonathan had never met Bolton, but he'd seen him on TV. And now the director of the Central Intelligence Agency was standing in his driveway. The tall, lanky man smiled and walked toward him. Jonathan took hold of Rudy's collar. It wouldn't do to have his dog attack the head of the U.S. spy agency. Likely one of the clones would try to shoot the dog and hit him instead. The dog tensed but held his place.

"Jonathan Corrigan?" the director said, holding out his hand.

Rudy went to all fours and exploded into a fit of barking, and the director snatched his hand back.

"*Mon ami,*" Jonathan spoke firmly to the dog. Rudy sat on his haunches and looked away as if he'd seen something more interesting.

"Well-trained dog," Bolton said. "*Mon ami.* French for 'my friend.' Does he know any English?"

"Afraid not," Jonathan said. "They don't like to use common words when they train these dogs in case someone accidentally gives an attack command. The guy who trained Rudy used French."

"I'll watch my tongue," the director said, extending his hand again. "I hope we can be friends."

Jonathan reluctantly shook it. "What can I do for you, sir?"

"As I think you know, we need your help."

"I think I made it clear yesterday that I'm out of the game. You guys gave me the boot, and I'm glad you did. I'd rather not have anything to do with the agency, especially after what happened in Bellingham."

"Can we walk a bit and talk?" the director said.

"I'd rather not," Jonathan said. If they talked, how much would his itch grow? Enough to make him break his word—again? "I'm afraid you came out here for nothing."

The director pursed his mouth. He turned around to his escorts. "Take a walk, gentlemen."

"Sir?" said the guy who had talked into his wrist.

"Take a walk."

The six men filed down the driveway out of earshot, as obedient as Jonathan's cattle. Bolton turned to him. "You had an asset in Lebanon. Goes by the name of Petra."

If a name could've gotten Jonathan's interest, that was the name. Jonathan looked after the agents walking toward the road. "Let's walk," Jonathan said and started toward the barn. The director followed him, neither man speaking until they were on the other side of the structure, out of the agents' line of sight.

"You're a careful man," Bolton said.

"If I'm going to talk about Petra, I'm not taking a chance on one of your guys reading lips or someone hiding out there with a shotgun microphone. What about him?"

"Your notes say he's highly reliable. Do you think that's still true?"

Jonathan leaned against the barn. "Absolutely."

"Why?"

"Because of his code name. Petra—the rock. That guy doesn't change."

"How do you know?"

"I know. That's all I'm going to tell you about him."

"Jonathan, I'm the director of the agency. If you can tell anyone about an asset, you can tell me."

Jonathan looked away for a couple of seconds, then turned his attention back to Bolton. "The last director of the CIA tried to kill me, my wife, and a good friend. You'll forgive me if I have a few trust issues."

Bolton tried to put a hand on Jonathan's shoulder, but he shrugged it off. "Jonathan, I'm not like Stone. I'm a straight shooter."

Jonathan set his cane against the barn and folded his arms. "Even if that's true, it doesn't make up for the fact that Stone has his freedom. He should be in jail."

Bolton set his jaw. "Technically you and your wife should be, too. It was messy all around, but we managed to contain it. Besides, everyone involved who lost property was compensated."

"You can't compensate people for being frightened to death," Jonathan said. "Money doesn't fix everything."

"No, it doesn't," Bolton said.

"And it sure can't make me trust you."

"I understand that," the director said. "And it seems your asset feels the same way. He sent us a message and said if we wanted more, he'd have to have a face-to-face with you, in Lebanon."

"Out of the question." Jonathan shook his head. "Like I said, my cloak-and-dagger days are over."

"Do you at least want to hear his message?"

Jonathan looked away. "No."

"Well, you're going to hear it. He said, 'Herod is coming to visit you. Rachel will weep again.'"

Jonathan felt cold. "No."

"Yes," Bolton said. "Someone is planning a strike in the U.S. against children on a scale the size of Herod's atrocity from the Bible. And the only person Petra will tell the details to is you."

Jonathan looked down at the ground. "Actually, it could mean a strike against just about any civilian target. Christians often refer to Herod's atrocity as the massacre of the innocents. That broadens the target area."

"Your asset is a Christian?"

Jonathan said nothing, but he was starting to get sick to his stomach. If Petra said it, it was going to happen. Whoever it was could hit anywhere, anytime, anyone.

"Well, will you help us?"

"I promised my wife I was finished, sir, that she'd never have to worry about me dying in some far-off country. I can't break that promise."

The director stepped closer to him. "Jonathan, I can understand your desire to keep your word to your wife, but have you considered that wherever they strike, she or someone you love might be there?"

Jonathan looked at the ground. "I broke my word to her once before. I can't do it again. Surely with your resources you can find a way. Nice to meet you, sir." He started back toward the house.

"We already tried to meet with him."

Jonathan stopped and turned. "And?"

"He said he'd only talk to you, because you're the only one he trusts to get him and his family out of Lebanon. No one else can do this, Jonathan."

Jonathan knew the director was right, but he couldn't forget those softly spoken words on their wedding night. His life was Laura now. He couldn't, wouldn't hurt her. And there was that other life, the child growing inside her.

"Jonathan, just think for a second. What if you got a call, heard that something happened to your wife that could've been prevented—how would you feel? I understand you're going to have a child. What if this 'massacre of innocents' doesn't happen until after your child is born? Your child is—"

"Enough!"

"Sorry, son," the director said. "This is critical, and if I have to play rough, I'll play rough. They tell me you're a Christian now. Well, how is God going to feel about you milking cows while innocent people die? We live in a different world, Jonathan. I can't take no for an answer."

Jonathan punted a pinecone into the woods. He couldn't say no, and he hated feeling trapped. Trapped by duty—on one side, his responsibility to care for his wife, to keep his marriage vows; on the other, the sense of duty that had driven him to serve his country in the CIA. The thought of losing Laura tore at his guts. Even if the chances of her being hurt were remote, someone would feel the pain he was feeling right now. Trapped. "All right, I'll do it. But I want something in return."

"What?" the director said.

"Oh, I think you already know," Jonathan said.

خطر

The container shuddered, and Michelle jumped to her feet along with everyone else who wasn't too sick to stand. They sounded like a flock of geese, everyone chattering at once with their theories. After a couple of minutes, it shuddered again.

"We have arrived," Ho announced in English. He had been after them the whole trip to speak as much English as they could and would only use Mandarin if absolutely necessary.

After about half an hour of shudders, the container lifted, and Michelle wondered if riding in an elevator felt like this. She couldn't help feeling a twinge of excitement about seeing America, despite Kit's veiled warnings about the future she faced. God had given her a new life; maybe now He was giving her a new home that shared her beliefs. She'd heard somewhere that America was full of Christians. It would be easier to live her faith here.

Michelle stumbled as the container thudded to a stop. A couple of minutes later, the steel doors swung open and fresh, salty air whooshed in. Everyone sucked in a deep breath and released it in a moan of satisfaction. Near the back of the container, Michelle stood on her toes but couldn't see over the heads in front of her.

"Move," a heavily accented voice commanded in English.

People up front began to shout curses. Angry voices in a

language she'd never heard before followed. Then the people in front of her started to move forward. Michelle helped a young man who'd fallen ill to his feet. With him leaning against her, she shuffled behind the rest of the group. Her heart plummeted when she saw where they were headed.

خطر

Laura Corrigan had to let the unexpected SUVs pull out of her driveway before she could pull in. Black vehicles, dark windows—her stomach sank to her knees. She had dreaded this day, and it had come. Jonathan was a Middle East expert, and his promise to his country was made before 9/11. It was only a matter of time before they asked him back.

She forced herself not to press the accelerator down and rush to the house. Too many critters inhabited the woods surrounding the Corrigan home. She clenched the steering wheel to stop her hands from shaking. What had they asked him to do? Had he accepted?

She parked her Buick Century outside the garage and sprang out. Rudy gave her a couple of welcoming barks, but she ignored him. Laura rushed into the house calling Jonathan's name. Silence answered.

"Oh no, Lord. Did he go with them?" She took a couple of deep breaths to calm her nerves. Her hand instinctively went to her belly. She left the house and headed for the barn.

She found Jonathan sitting on a hay bale, looking toward the corral. His head was bent down, praying. He turned to look at her, his face streaked with tears.

She'd assumed the black SUVs had brought a job offer, but maybe she was wrong. Jonathan had friends in the agency who were still in the field. Friends Laura never knew about, and now something had happened to one of them. The black vehicles had brought a different kind of bad news. She rushed over and threw her arms around his neck.

"Jonathan, what happened?"

He reached up and held her arm. "Nothing."

"Nothing? Government cars don't come here every day. You're crying. Did something happen to one of your friends?"

Jonathan gently pulled her arm from around his neck and guided her to his lap. Laura watched his dark blue eyes for a sign of what distressed him.

"I have to go."

Laura felt cold. It was déjà vu. Her mind flashed to another time, another place. It was her parents' house. FBI agents were tearing it apart, then Jonathan came to tell her everything she believed in was false. He was going to do it again. "Go where?" she whispered.

"I can't say."

She tensed and looked away. "You never stopped, did you?" She didn't want to look at him, to have him lie to her face, because she knew he'd lie. "You never left."

His hands were on her cheeks, turning her face to his. "It's not like that. I've been true to you, Laura, true to my promise. But something's come up, something no one expected."

Laura wanted to believe him, needed to believe him, but she couldn't. She pulled his hands from her face and stood. She walked a couple of steps before turning. "Why couldn't you just have told me the truth?" A tear escaped. "Did you think my love for you wasn't strong enough to take it?"

Jonathan stood. He held his hand out to her. "I swear I've had nothing to do with the CIA, and you just have to trust me that I wouldn't be going back if it didn't affect us all."

"Then tell me where you're going. How long will you be gone?"

"I can't tell you where I'm going, but it shouldn't be long."

Laura held her belly. Another tear matched the first. "Why do you torture me like this? I just can't. . .can't. . ."

Jonathan stepped toward her, but Laura spun and ran back to the house. He wanted to chase her but knew it would do no good. They'd had their fair share of newlywed spats. She needed time to cool off. He returned to his hay bale and his prayers.

A couple minutes later, he heard Laura walk up on him. *That was quick, Lord,* he thought. It usually took her an hour to cool down. Prayer really did help. Laura stood before him, hands behind her back. Her eyes were puffy, but anger seemed to have replaced tears.

"Is it dangerous?"

Now Jonathan wanted to lie. "It has risks."

"Will you be coming back?"

"Of course."

She stepped closer. "You're sure? You can swear right now that I won't be a widow, that our child won't be an orphan? You can swear that—right?"

Jonathan looked down for a couple of seconds and looked up at her. "No, I can't. But I—"

"Stop," she said. "No promises. When do you have to leave?"

"I've got a few hours. A jet is waiting for me at the airport."

"Good," Laura said. She produced their video camera from behind her back.

"What's that for?"

"If you die, one day I'm going to have a teenage girl. . ."

"Girl—you know already? How?"

"Never mind how I know," Laura said. "But one day she's going to start asking me all sorts of questions about her father. What was he like? What did he believe? Did he love me? I'm not going to answer those questions, Jonathan. You are. You're going to tell your daughter why you left us before she was born. You're the one who's going to try to make her understand. Not me."

She dropped the camera into his lap. "I'll drive you to the airport when you're finished." She spun and went back to the house.

Jonathan looked at the camera. *Daughter.* Though he would've loved a son just as much, he really did want a girl. And as he stared at the lens, reality hit him. "Oh, Lord, now I have an inkling how Jesus felt in the garden of Gethsemane. If there's a way out of this, please tell me, because I don't want to go."

危险 خطر ОПАСНОТЬ

FIVE

A li stepped out of the shower and wrapped herself in a bath towel. Normally she felt refreshed after a shower, but not today. Today she felt like retreating to the couch with a pint of ice cream. She stepped out of the bathroom and into the one bedroom of her tenth-floor apartment. Ali didn't have much space, but she had a great location.

She glanced at the clock on the dresser drawers. Eleven o'clock. Sam would be picking her up in forty-five minutes. The call had to be made. Actually both calls had to be made. It would be ten o'clock in the evening in Moscow. That call had to be made first.

She toweled off and slipped into her bathrobe then went to her computer and opened up her Internet browser. After a couple minutes, Ali had the number; she picked up her phone, punched in the number, and waited. She had hoped never to have to make this call. Three rings and a woman answered in Russian. Ali replied in the same language.

خطر

Friday lunchtime traffic was heavy when Sam pulled up in front of Ali's building. She was supposed to be waiting outside, but there was no sign of her. Like a pack of bleating sheep, horns sounded behind him. He and Ali were about to act on Davidov's first piece of information, and Sam didn't have time to waste looking for a parking spot. He activated the emergency lights in the back windows and under the grill of his LeSabre and double-parked.

Sam kept his face forward, not bothering to observe the obscene gestures of the drivers forced to drive around him. He drummed his fingers to the song on the radio. After a twenty-minute set of music, the radio went to commercial, and Sam remembered all the phrases his father used to recite about women being incapable of being on time. If this were a date, he wouldn't mind her being fashionably late, but this was work. He and Ali on a date. Not an unpleasant thought, but not likely to happen. *Not with this mug.*

His hand rested on the door handle to open it when he saw Ali emerge from her apartment building. She spotted the car and jogged over. A pleasant smell filled the car when Ali got in.

Sam glanced at his watch. It was already a few minutes past twelve. "We were supposed to meet at quarter to, right?"

"Yeah," Ali said. "I took a shower and kind of lost track of time. Sorry."

"Normally I wouldn't mind, but that ship will be in port soon. We need to be in position before then."

"I'll pay better attention in the future."

"You're in the big leagues, Ali. You realize losing track of time isn't a good excuse?"

"Yes. It won't happen again."

Sam glanced over at her. Her hair was still damp, and she looked straight ahead. Something didn't add up here. She was giving in way too easy. "You okay?"

"Sure. Why?"

"No reason."

Sam put the car into gear and hit the siren. The traffic was murder, and they needed to get to the port. He wove in and out of traffic and managed to make up for some of the time lost waiting for Ali.

He cut the lights and siren when they drew near to the dock. Concealed behind some cargo containers were five unmarked cars. He pulled up next to them.

Ten people stood in clusters near the cars. Six wore bulletproof vests, identifying them as Seattle police, and the other four had DEA jackets. Technically this would be a DEA operation. The FBI got the information, and the DEA would get the credit. Sam didn't care as long as they got the drugs and the confirmation that Davidov had indeed turned.

They got out of the car and walked over to the group. An athletic man crouched low at the edge of one of the containers, watching a container ship with binoculars.

"Hey, Sam," one of the DEA agents, a middle-aged man with close-cropped graying hair, said. "Glad to see you made it."

"Hi, Colin," Sam said. He glanced at his watch. "I thought the ship wasn't supposed to get in until one."

"Came in early," the DEA agent said, "but you haven't missed anything. They just started unloading. You got the warrant?"

Sam patted his pocket.

"Good."

Ali came to his side and handed Sam a bulletproof vest. He pulled it on.

"This is my partner, Ali Marcoli. Colin Lorenz, DEA."

Ali shook hands with the DEA agent. "Glad to meet you."

"So what's the plan?" Sam said.

"We think the target container is probably a few rows in," Colin said. "We're going to wait until it's exposed, board the ship, and search it. Once we confirm the drugs are in it, we'll impound the ship. That should hurt them a bit."

"No doubt."

"You got coverage on the other side of the ship?" Ali asked.

"Yeah," Colin said. "The Seattle police have a boat hiding behind a ship at anchor. It can get here in three minutes if they all decide to jump ship. We've got another team behind a container at the other end of the pier."

"So now we wait," Sam said.

"Yep," Colin replied.

Sam sat on the hood of their car, and Ali joined him. He looked over at her. She seemed to be somewhere else.

"Ali."

She looked at him. "Yeah."

"What's bugging you?"

She shook her head. "It's nothing. A woman thing."

"Hey, if you're not feeling good, go home. We've got enough help."

Her eyes flashed. "You'd like that, wouldn't you? Then you can write in your report that I couldn't perform my duty because I'm a woman. Nice try."

"That's not it at all. I know you can do your job. The way you handled Lo in that alley and then picked up on that phony lawyer knocked any doubts out of my mind."

"But if you had your choice, you'd prefer a guy partner, wouldn't you?"

Sam held up both hands. "I have no idea where this is

coming from, but I think you're a great partner. I know you'll watch my back."

Ali nodded her head but didn't say anything.

Sam decided his best course of action would be to keep his mouth shut. He passed the time looking out toward the sea while they waited.

"There it is," the DEA agent watching with binoculars announced about fifteen minutes later.

Both Sam and Ali slipped off the hood of the car and went over to the edge of the container.

Lorenz took the binoculars from the other agent and studied the container. "Yeah, that's it all right." He handed the binoculars to Sam.

Perkins peeked around the corner and focused on the container the crane operator was about to pick up. "Yeah, that's the number our source gave us."

Lorenz picked up a megaphone resting on the ground.

"Maybe you should let Ali do that," Sam said.

Lorenz cocked an eyebrow. "Want the FBI to get credit, is that it?"

Sam grinned. "Trust me on this one." He took the megaphone from Lorenz and handed it to Ali. "Give them the bad news."

A smile flitted across Ali's face. She stepped around the container and put the megaphone to her lips. "This is the FBI. Cease all activity and remain where you are. We are executing a search warrant for this ship." When she repeated it in Russian, all eyes were on her. She put down the megaphone and smiled at Sam.

"Cool, huh?" Sam said to Lorenz.

"No kidding." He lifted his radio and spoke into it. "Let's move."

DEA agents and police broke out of their hiding places and converged on the ship. Sam and Ali jogged behind them, preferring to let the police and DEA assault the ship. The crane operator ignored Ali's commands and continued to lift the container, swinging it toward the ocean.

"Great," Sam said. "They're going to dump it in the water."

"So," Ali said, "we call the Coast Guard to come and fish it out."

Sam stopped, and Ali followed suit. "These guys are professionals. You can bet they've got divers in the water ready to attach C4 to the container and blow it apart. By the time we get our divers in the water, there won't be anything left to find."

Ali looked up at the container and then squinted her eyes. "Can I see those binoculars for a second?"

"Sure," Sam said.

Ali raised the binoculars and focused on the container. "Oh no."

خطر

They drove to Bellingham airport in silence. Laura's emotions ranged from wanting to hold on to Jonathan and never let him go to pushing him out of the car. Part of her wanted to believe his protestations of innocence, that when he told her he had left the agency, he really had. The other part dreaded that their short marriage had been a sham. She shook her head. No, she couldn't believe that.

Laura only had one thing left to rely on: her faith in God. God had brought her and Jonathan together. She just had to trust Him that when this was all over, she would understand why her husband could go away on a secret mission while she stayed at home with their child growing within her. She had to believe that Jonathan had a good reason for breaking his promise.

Jonathan drove past the main terminal and stopped the car in front of a private hangar. Four dark suits stood out front. He shut the motor off and turned toward her.

"I—"

Laura held up her hand. "Don't say anything."

Jonathan nodded. He slipped out of the car and retrieved a small overnight bag from the trunk. Laura slid over to the driver's side. It wouldn't be too long before her belly would make that little maneuver difficult. She bit back tears. She wouldn't let him see her cry.

Jonathan came around and knocked at the window. Laura pushed the button to roll it down. He dropped a slip of paper on her lap. "If for some reason I'm not back by Wednesday, contact this address."

Laura clutched the paper and nodded her head. She didn't dare look at him.

"I'd like you to go straight home and wait for my message."

Message? Laura resisted the urge to look up at him. She nodded again. She had no plans to go anywhere else but home.

"If anyone asks, tell them I went to Boise to meet with an equipment supplier."

Laura looked up at him. "You want me to lie?"

He nodded his head. "Yes."

"Does that include your mother?"

"Especially my mother. It's bad enough for you to have to worry about this."

Laura looked straight ahead. At this moment, she couldn't promise him anything.

"I love you." His voice was barely above a whisper.

His words tugged at her heart. Laura wanted to respond, but stubborn pride wouldn't let her.

Jonathan left the window and came into her vision when he walked toward the dark suits. She watched his retreating back, and Laura felt déjà vu again. Once before she had watched the back of a man she thought loved her walk away. That man had been her father. He'd wanted to hold her, ask her forgiveness, but she'd refused because she was too hurt to forgive. She choked back a sob. She'd never seen her father alive again.

"Not this time." Laura shoved the door open and jumped out of the car. "Jonathan!"

He froze and turned around. One of the suits put his hand on Jonathan's shoulder and said something to him, but the sound of jet turbines from behind the terminal drowned out the man's voice. Jonathan shrugged the suit's arm off his shoulder and rushed toward her.

Laura stood and let his arms enfold her. She buried her face in his shoulder and embraced him. "Don't you dare make me a widow!"

He didn't say anything, and Laura knew he couldn't. Wherever he was going made such a promise impossible to keep.

"I'll do my best," he choked out.

It was only a couple moments, but it felt like forever, standing in each other's embrace. The suit called to him, and Jonathan let her go. He held her chin in his hand. "Make sure you go home and wait for my message. Promise?"

"I promise."

He rested his hand on her belly, then looked up and smiled. He took both her hands in his. "Let's pray."

Jonathan spoke a sweet prayer to God, asking for nothing more than that the Lord would keep the three of them in His hands and, if it was His will, to bring them together again. The strength and assurance in Jonathan's voice comforted her. It reminded her that it wasn't just them; they weren't alone. God was close, and if she needed to trust in anyone, it was Him.

Jonathan let her hands go, kissed her softly on the cheek,

and walked back toward the suits. They disappeared into the terminal. Laura stepped back and leaned against the hood of the car. Less than five minutes later, she heard the roar of the engines, and a private jet soared into the sky. She never took her eyes off it until it disappeared into the east.

Laura drove home on autopilot. She'd been tempted to detour and cry on a friend's shoulder, but she kept her promise to Jonathan. She pulled the car up in front of the house and got out. Laura didn't feel like going inside, so she wandered down to the stable. It was Jonathan's favorite place. Laura curled up on a hay bale and allowed herself a good cry mingled with desperate prayers.

She woke to the sound of Rudy going nuts. She looked at her watch; she had slept two hours. At the sound of tires crunching on gravel, she sat up. It was a black-government-car kind of sound. Besides, if it were a car he knew, Rudy would have stopped barking by now. She scrambled to her feet. Maybe Jonathan had come back!

Laura ran from the barn, and her heart leapt with hope at the government car pulling up behind her car. God did work fast. Something had changed, and Jonathan didn't have to go.

The car's back door opened, and the passenger got out. Laura stumbled to a stop, and her hand went to her chest. "Mom."

خطر

"What is it?" Sam said.

Ali lowered the binoculars and handed them back to Sam. "There's a one-foot hole in the bottom of that container. I'm not sure, but it may be a drain for waste."

"Why would a drug container have that?"

"I don't think it's a drug container. I think it's for people."

"People! We've got to stop him from dumping it."

"You go tell Lorenz, and I'll go for the crane." Megaphone still in hand, she dug in her feet and sprinted toward the ship. Sam was in pretty good shape, but she knew she was faster.

She couldn't count on the DEA agents. They were more concerned with arresting the crew than with trying to get to the crane. The container would be in the water long before anyone climbed up there. Best to arrest the ones they could grab, because the crane operator wouldn't be going anywhere. But the people in that container would.

She charged up the gangplank, pushing past a DEA agent who was herding a crew member down.

"Hey, we've got all the help we need," he called after her.

She rushed onto the deck and positioned herself in sight of the crane's booth. The container was just moving over the edge of the ship. Ali drew her weapon and put the megaphone to her lips.

"Do not drop the container, or I'll shoot," she said in Russian.

The container paused. She couldn't make out his face, but Ali was sure the operator was considering whether she was bluffing. The thought of all those people trapped in the container made her sick. The container started to move again, away from the ship. Ali fired at the booth, and the round impacted just above the operator's head. The container paused again.

"Take him out!" Lorenz called.

Ali started to squeeze the trigger, but the clamps snapped open, and the container dropped into the sea. *I'll deal with you later*, she thought. Ali sprinted to the ship's edge. The container was still floating but listing at the end. The water had to be pouring in through that hole in the floor. She could see a Seattle police boat making its way to the ship, but it wouldn't make it in time. Those people were trapped inside, and someone had to open the doors.

Ali jumped, and just before impact she pressed her hands against her sides, pointed her toes downward, and entered the water like a banana. She blew air through her nose as she sliced through the water.

Ali kicked to the surface and then over to the container. She could hear muffled voices and hands pounding against steel. A couple more splashes indicated some DEA agents had joined her, but Ali didn't waste time looking back. Fortunately the hole was on the end opposite the one with doors, so the water filling in the back tilted the door end up.

There was a small lip running along the bottom. Ali hoisted herself up, but her wet shoes kept slipping off the thin edge.

"Stand on my shoulders," a voice gurgled.

She looked to her left to see Sam holding on to the lip. "I've got great buoyancy," he said with a slight grin.

Ali climbed up on Sam and reached the handle. Putting all her weight on him, Ali drew her weapon and fired, blowing the padlock apart. The handle was like a semitrailer's. Ali pushed it forward then yanked it up. She knew she must be drowning Sam as she pushed against him to pull the door open. If she had time, she would've cried at what she saw.

People piled out of the container and into the water. The Seattle police boat arrived but instead of swimming toward the rescuers, the Chinese people were swimming away. With the door open, Ali was able to hoist herself inside. She glanced back at Sam, who was spitting out water but otherwise seemed all right. He pulled himself inside after her.

The container was listing at about thirty degrees now. Near

the back, Ali spotted a pretty young woman helping a young man keep his head above water. The girl looked exhausted.

Ali slid down the floor of the container and took the young man from the girl.

"Thank you," the girl said.

The boy's arms hung loosely around her neck. Ali worked her legs like an eggbeater and kept the two above water. There'd be no way she could haul him up the container. It was listing more. They'd have to let the rising water lift them out.

Sam splashed in beside her. "Let me take him."

"I'm okay," Ali said.

Sam nodded. After what seemed like an eternity, the water was only a couple feet from the top of the container. With Sam taking the boy's one arm and her the other, they hoisted themselves and the boy out of the container. The girl followed.

"Stay," Ali said.

The girl hesitated.

"I can help you."

"Must go," she said.

Ali grabbed her arm but had to let go when the girl struggled and threatened to drag them all under the water. "You can't go. You have no idea what they'll make you do."

"I know what I to do," she said, her English broken and heavily accented. "Must go." The girl swam away.

"I can handle this guy if you want to go after her," Sam said.

Ali looked after the girl. "I'm too tired to fight her in this water. Maybe the cops will get her. I hope so, because I don't think she has a clue what's ahead."

危险 خطر ОПАСНОТЬ

SIX

M ichelle's arms burned as she swam toward the shore. The lady seemed nice, but Ho warned them that American police pretend to be nice until they catch you. Then they beat you and, if you're lucky, send you back to China. Some, he said, are never seen again.

The pier ran the length of the shore, and Michelle swam over to it. A few of the others were sitting on the cross timbers that supported the pier. Barnacles covered the supports, so she had to swim around until she found a ladder. Michelle climbed the ladder and stepped onto a crossbeam that stayed above high tide and had no barnacles. She lay on it and rested. The hot summer sun warmed her to the bone.

She looked out toward the ship. Michelle could see some more of her fellow travelers being pulled out of the water onto the police boat. If they decided to search under the pier, they would all be caught.

For fifteen minutes, the police on the boat scooped people out of the water until it was full, but then instead of coming toward shore, it started to move out to sea. What was going on? Michelle shuddered. Were the American police taking them all out to sea to drown them? No, that couldn't be right. They only had to leave them in the container if they wanted to drown them. They were probably taking them somewhere to beat them. She had to get away before any other boats came looking.

Michelle dropped back into the water and swam parallel to the pier, holding on to whatever wasn't covered with barnacles whenever she needed a rest. It seemed an hour before she reached the end of the pier and swam for the rocky shore. The bank was steep, and she was hidden from the view of anyone walking along the top of it.

Sitting on the back side of a rock so she was hidden from the ocean, Michelle let the sun dry her clothes. She had no idea what to do next. In a strange country, hungry, and barely knowing the language, Michelle knew she should be in tears, but tears wouldn't come anymore. She'd done her fair share of crying when they took her from her village. The missionary had said Judas took money to betray Jesus. Her own parents took money for her. The world was full of traitors.

She had to get some kind of job. This city, whatever city it was, had to have a Chinese community. Almost every city in the world did. Surely one of her people would help her find work washing dishes or waiting tables. She didn't care what kind of honest work she did as long as she got a place to eat and sleep.

Michelle got up from her resting spot and climbed up the rocky shore. Dry now, other than being Chinese, she'd blend in. Ho had given them Western clothes along with fresh supplies when they switched containers. Now only her speech would give her away.

She crossed a gravel area to a paved road. Should she avoid open areas? Surely the police would be looking for her. Probably best to stay out of sight as much as possible. Michelle jogged a hundred yards and took a side street between two warehouses. She walked along, keeping in the shadows of one of the buildings. Her spirits started to lift. Maybe America wouldn't be so bad; it was sure pretty.

She arrived at another crossroad. Poking her head around the corner, the way seemed clear. Michelle jogged across and again kept in the shadow of a building.

"Lost?"

She nearly jumped out of her skin. The word was in Mandarin. A heavyset man stepped from behind a container that looked like it held garbage.

"Yes," Michelle said, thankful to hear her own language. "Can you help me?"

"Yes," he said, flashing a grin, "I can help you."

خطر

Alice McIvor held her arms open, and Laura rushed into them.

"Mom." It was all Laura could say. Her mother pressed her head against her shoulder, and Laura just basked in her mother's embrace. She wanted the moment to last forever, but it was broken by a surly male voice.

"Here's your stuff," the man said and dropped a duffel bag on the ground. "Remember the deal." With that he got into the car, and it drove away to the sound of Rudy's furious barks.

Laura stepped back from her mother. "What deal?"

Her mother pressed her lips together. "Laura, I probably understand less about what happened than you do."

"Let's sit on the porch, and you can tell me all about it," Laura said.

The two women stepped onto the wide veranda fronting the house and sat next to each other on the swing. They held hands and put the swing in motion with a few gentle pushes.

"It was so strange," her mom said. "Just before lunch this man shows up from the U.S. Attorney's Office with a presidential pardon."

"A what?" Laura said, her mouth hanging open.

"I know, I can hardly believe it, too. It's conditional, of course. I can never talk about what happened with your father, and that's just fine with me if it means I'm free. Next thing I know, I'm on a jet."

Laura wrapped her arms around her mother, overjoyed at how God had answered her prayers when suddenly her stomach revolted. "Gotta go," she said and bolted into the house and headed for the washroom.

After emptying her stomach of breakfast, Laura sat on the edge of the bathtub. This wasn't morning sickness. This was the realization of what happened. Jonathan's mission was important enough to get the president of the United States to pardon her mother for treason. He'd traded his life—and their future—for her mother's freedom.

Laura slumped to the floor. Why couldn't she have been happy with the life God had given her? Why did she have to go on moaning about missing her mother? That must've been the leverage the CIA used to get him to go back: "Do this one thing for us, and we'll let your wife's mother go." Her mother was the message Jonathan had promised.

Fortunately her stomach was empty or she'd have gone back over the toilet. It was so much like Jonathan to sacrifice himself for her happiness. She held her belly with both hands. Her daughter needed a father more than she needed her mother. If only he'd told her, she would've begged him to stay.

Now it was done, and she felt empty inside.

There was a soft knock at the door. "Laura?"

"Just a second, Mom." Laura ran some cold water and washed her face. Nothing could ever hide the redness, but maybe her mother would interpret them as tears of joy. She opened the bathroom door to the concerned face of her mother.

"Are you all right?"

"Yes," Laura said.

Her mother looked down at her left hand and then looked up and smiled. "You're married, and I'll bet you're pregnant. Why didn't you tell me?"

Suddenly Laura felt like she could throw up again. The problem with procrastination is you can only put something off until tomorrow for so long before tomorrow becomes today. In all her letters to her mother, not once had she mentioned she was married, and for good reason. How do you tell your mother that you married the CIA agent who put her and your father in prison?

Laura thought the news media would do the job for her. After all, Jonathan had a high profile and his marriage normally would have attracted attention. But after he saved the kids, the media had asked what America could do for him. He asked the media to stay out of his private life. One tabloid violated that rule and paid a punishing price. After that, none dared. Their marriage only made the Bellingham papers, so her mom didn't know.

"Well, uh, I kept hoping that someday you'd let me visit you. I wanted to tell you in person." *Good idea, Laura, make it worse with another lie.*

"I never wanted you to see me in there," Alice said. "So when's the baby due? What's your husband's name? Where is he, at work?"

Laura took her mother's hand. "Maybe we should go back outside and sit down."

"Sure, honey. You probably should rest. You look pale as a ghost."

They started down the hall toward the door when her mother released her hand. Laura turned to her and saw tears running down her mother's smiling face. "I'm just so happy for you, dear. After everything that happened, I'm glad you found someone." She rubbed at her face. "Oh, I'm a mess. I need a tissue."

"I'll get you some," Laura said and headed for the bathroom. When she returned, her mother wasn't in the hall anymore. Laura headed for the outside door and caught the image of her mother out of the corner of her eye. Her blood ran cold. She stepped into the living room.

Her mother turned slowly toward her, holding Laura and Jonathan's wedding picture. The picture vibrated in her mother's hands. She looked from the picture to Laura. "How could you? How could you have married that. . ."

The rest of the words her mother must have learned in prison.

"Mom, you have to understand. Jonathan—"

"Understand what?" her mother said. "Understand you married the man who put your father and me in jail? That man ate at our table, became like a son to us, and all the time he was spying. Because of him"—Alice flung the picture frame across the room, and it shattered against the wall—"your father is dead."

Laura reached for her mother. "Mom, things changed. He—wait a minute." Laura straightened her shoulders and dropped her arms to her sides. "None of this is Jonathan's fault. You two made your own bed. You're the ones who decided to betray our country. No one made you do it. In fact, did you think even for a minute of what your actions did to me?"

Alice McIvor clenched her teeth. "If that. . .*man* hadn't turned us in, nothing would have happened to you. We would've been safely in another country."

Laura's hands started to shake. "Oh, that's great, Mom. Safely in another country. Did it ever occur to you that I love my country more than money, a concept that must be tough for you? And besides, it didn't work out the way you planned. You got caught, and I lost everything. I lost my name, my career, and I almost lost my life."

Alice McIvor froze. "Your life?"

"Sure. Did you think they'd leave me alone? As soon as they learned what Daddy did, they came looking for me, and they found me. Jonathan risked everything to protect me, and I'll love him forever for that." Laura was in full rage mode now. "And, Mom, here's something else to think about."

"What?"

"Jonathan has left on a mission for the CIA. It's one of those 'can't tell you where I'm going and can't promise I'll come back' missions. Do you know why he did it?"

Alice curled up her lip. "Because he can't stand to stay out of the game?"

Laura bit back a bit of her own prison language. "No. Since I found out I was pregnant, I've been moaning about how I miss you, so he accepted this one last mission to get you freed." Laura clutched her belly, and tears streamed down her cheeks. "I'm sorry, Mom, but losing my baby's father for you just isn't worth it." Laura staggered over to the love seat, collapsed into it, and buried her face in a throw pillow.

خطر

Sam and Ali headed right into the interrogation room where

the captain of the freighter, whose papers identified him as Ivan Zdanivsky, was sitting. A heavyset man with a bald head and meaty jowls, he looked unperturbed with his shackled hands resting on the table.

"Three of those people drowned, you jerk," Sam said and pounded the table. He grabbed the captain by his uniform jacket, yanked him to his feet, and drove him up against the wall. "The crane operator said you gave the order to dump the container in the water."

The captain shrugged. Sam cocked his fist, and Ali grabbed his hand. "Whoa, partner."

Sam gave Zdanivsky a shove and spun away, leaving him to the charms of Ali.

She guided the captain back to his seat. If Sam's burst of anger affected him, the captain didn't show it.

"Now," Ali said, "why did you order him to dump the container in the water?"

"No English," the captain said.

"Sure you can," Sam said. "The harbor pilot said you spoke pretty good English when he boarded."

Ali spoke to the man in Russian.

The captain exhaled. "Okay, I speak English. I did not tell him to dump the container in the water. He drinks. I think he was drunk when he did it."

"You want us to believe you let a drunk operate your crane?" Sam said.

"His father is important in Russia. I have to keep him."

"Well, keeping him may cost you your life," Sam said.

The captain shook his head. "I don't understand."

"This is Washington State, buddy. They have the death penalty here, and you caused three people to lose their lives. You're a murderer."

The captain shook his head vehemently. "I didn't cause deaths. You did."

"Excuse me?" Ali said. "If I remember correctly, we tried to stop your guy from dumping the container and then tried to rescue the people. If they hadn't kept swimming away from us, we could have saved them all."

"Your fault they swim away."

"That makes no sense," Sam said. He looked over at Ali, who looked up at the ceiling and then at him.

"Let's step outside."

Sam made sure he bumped Zdanivsky's chair before following Ali out the door. They stepped into the next room where Arthur Conners was watching the freighter captain through the glass.

"What is it, Ali?" Conners said.

"The captain's got a point about us causing the deaths," Ali said.

"You're kidding," Sam said.

"Think about it. If we can catch them before they touch American soil, we can send them back to China without any kind of hearing at all. These people know that. It's illegal to leave China without permission, just as it's illegal to enter the U.S. without permission. These people are facing punishment not only from their government, but also from the people they sold themselves to in order to get here. What would you do? Swim for the police boat, or swim for shore?"

"Shore," Sam and Conners said.

"Which means if we try to charge this guy with anything more than manslaughter, we won't have a chance. And frankly, I doubt we can get the captain at all. We can't prove he gave the order, and the crane operator *was* drunk. We can't even prove they knew what was in the container. I think when push comes to shove, all these guys are going to walk."

Conners leaned against the table and sighed. "I have to agree."

Sam rubbed his face. "Yeah, me, too."

"The really big question here," Ali said, "is why did Davidov give us the wrong container number?"

"He's in the next room," Conners said.

"Then let's ask him," Sam said.

Conners picked up the phone. "I'll get someone in here to watch Zdanivsky."

They waited a couple minutes before an agent entered the room and relieved them. The three FBI agents went down the hall, Conners stepping into the adjacent observation room while Sam and Ali entered the interrogation room. They found a very agitated Yuri Davidov sitting at the table.

"How dare you put me in a cell?" Davidov seethed. "If Josef gets to one of the other prisoners, I'm dead."

"Your fellow prisoners are FBI agents," Sam said. "I hoped that by putting you in a cell Grachev would think you hadn't turned. However, after what happened today, I think maybe we should put you in with the real prisoners."

Davidov looked at Ali, then Sam. "What happened?"

Sam sat across from Davidov staring at him until the Russian looked away. "Three people died, you. . ."

Ali filled in the blank for him with something in Russian.

Davidov sat back in his chair. "Hey, don't blame me. I warned you the crew was armed and might fight back. If some of your people—"

Sam reached across the table and yanked Davidov forward. "They weren't our people."

"So you shot the crew. Why get mad at me?"

Sam released him and looked up at Ali.

Ali walked around and leaned close to Davidov's ear. "Cut the garbage right now, or we'll send you back downstairs wearing a name tag. Why did you give us the wrong container number?"

Davidov straightened. "I gave you the right number. What's going on? What happened?"

Sam shook his head slowly. "Where did you learn to act?"

"I'm not acting."

"Tell you one thing," Ali said. "The deal's off. You promised to cooperate. Because you misled us, a container full of Chinese immigrants got dumped in the water and three of them drowned."

Davidov looked like he'd been slapped. "No. That's not possible. That container had heroin in it."

Ali pulled at her damp hair. "I don't jump into the ocean to save drugs. The container had people in it!"

Davidov shook his head. "Drugs. I was in charge of that shipment myself. I know the number for sure. Josef must have switched the containers."

"And why would he do that?" Ali said. "You telling me he'd risk killing all those people just to save some drugs?"

Davidov nodded his head. "A container of heroin is worth a lot more than a container of people."

"Well, if he had time to take the heroin out of the container, why didn't he just leave it empty?" she said.

Sam groaned. "Let's step outside."

They stepped next door to the observation room.

"This is getting ugly," Conners said.

"No kidding," Sam said.

"So?" Ali said.

"Let's look at it from Grachev's point of view," Sam said. "Two guys are picked up. Jimmy Lo is put into protective custody, but Davidov, Grachev's guy, is thrown in the cells, meaning the Chinese guy who knows nothing has turned, but your guy might not have. If your guy has turned, he's got enough to put you away for life, if you're lucky. You need to know for sure."

"Well, you'd know he turned once we showed up and searched the ship," Ali said. "You don't have to lose the drugs or people to find that out. Just take both of them off."

"Unless you want to make him useless," Conners said.

Ali put her hand to the side of her face. "Oh no."

"Right," Sam said. "We've got a witness who's responsible for three deaths, and we've given him immunity. Can you imagine what a defense attorney is going to do with that?"

"Well, if that's what Grachev was thinking, he isn't too smart," Ali said. "He should've realized we'd just ask the people in the container if they were switched and Davidov is good as gold again."

"He didn't expect those people to be alive. Remember, we all assumed it contained drugs and were just going to let it get dumped in the ocean."

"What a monster," Ali said. "But we do have the people. Let's talk to them."

Sam turned to Conners. "Why don't you give the INS a call and get us clearance to talk to the immigrants?"

"You got it," Conners said.

خطر

Laura jerked awake when the phone rang. She grabbed the receiver. "Hello."

"Hi, honey," Jonathan said. "I just called to make sure you got my, um, message."

Laura could hear the whine of jet engines in the background.

He was being cryptic, which meant the call wasn't private.

"I got it, Jonathan," Laura said. "But I don't want it. You don't need to do this. Just undo everything, and I mean everything, and come home." Laura had forgiven her mother, but she'd trade her in a heartbeat to get Jonathan back. There was no way she wanted to explain to her daughter that Daddy died so Grandma wouldn't have to stay in prison for treason.

"Um, honey, it's not that simple."

"Sure it is," Laura said. "Send the message back and come home."

"I'll explain everything when I get back."

Laura fought back tears. "Jonathan, please, just come home. I only want you."

"I love you," he said, and the connection broke.

"I love you, too," she said to the receiver.

خطر

Jonathan slipped the cell phone back into his jacket pocket. He stared out into the darkness as the plane sped away from the coast.

"Want something to drink?" a female voice said.

Jonathan kept his eyes to the window, not wanting the military stewardess to see his tears. "No thanks."

"Well, if you want anything, sir, just ask."

I want to go home.

危险 خطر ОПАСНОТЬ

SEVEN

S am and Ali were in a Bell 407 helicopter, cruising five hundred feet over Puget Sound out toward the Pacific. Sam sat next to the pilot, and Ali shared the back of the FBI chopper with Greg Fong of the INS. Sam took a handkerchief from his suit jacket and wiped his forehead.

"Don't worry," the voice of Max Shoaf, the pilot, said through the headphones. "The nice thing about a helicopter is you can land anywhere."

"It's not the landing that worries me," Sam said. "It's the staying afloat."

The pilot pointed to a switch. "No problem. I flick this and a compressed air cylinder under the chopper fills airbags on the landing gear—and voilà, we have pontoons."

Sam looked over at Max, and confidence was written on the pilot's face. "And what if you don't have time to hit the switch?"

The pilot grinned. "The water isn't too cold this time of year."

"Thanks."

They cruised on for five more minutes, and Max said, "There she is." He pointed ahead and slightly to the left.

Sam squinted and saw the shape of a navy supply ship. He turned around to look at Ali, and she nodded her head that she could see it. The helicopter slowed to a hover.

"What's the matter?" Sam said.

"All military vessels, even ones used by the INS, have a buffer zone. I have to make contact before we approach or some trigger-happy crewmen might open fire on us."

"In spite of the big FBI letters?" Sam said.

"The military is a nervous bunch right now," Max said. "If you aren't expected, don't try to visit."

Max hailed the ship. Once they were cleared, the helicopter moved on. The supply ship didn't look much different from a civilian freighter, other than some light armament and the usual military gray paint job. Max set them down on a helipad at the stern of the ship. A helmeted crewman approached the chopper in a crouch and opened Sam's and Ali's doors. He motioned for them to keep low when they stepped out.

The three followed the crewman away from the chopper and into the ship.

"Oh, that's nice for a change," Ali said, tugging at her earlobe. Though there was a constant hum, the ship sounded like a quiet forest compared to riding in the helicopter.

"No kidding," Sam said.

A uniformed woman followed by two armed marines approached them with her hand extended. "Good morning," she said. "I'm Lieutenant Commander Dougherty. Welcome aboard."

All three shook the woman's hand.

"Before I can let you proceed, I need to see identification."

Each of them dug out their identification folders, and the tall redhead examined each, comparing pictures to faces. "Fine," she said. "Follow me." They followed the lieutenant commander, and the marines followed them.

Dougherty led them through the maze of corridors deep into the bowels of the ship. Eventually they came to a door at the end of a hallway. Two refrigerator-sized marines in battle fatigues stood at the door. Both straightened to attention.

"We'd like to enter," Dougherty told them.

One marine took a ring of keys from his belt and opened the door, and they followed Dougherty into the room. Their marine escorts took position by the door, weapons held across their chests. The door closed and the lock snapped shut.

About forty faces turned toward them when they entered. Sam felt like he'd just entered a refugee camp, only at sea. Cots lined the walls, some people sitting on them, others standing, all looking like cattle waiting for the farmer to make his next move.

"They're all yours," Dougherty said.

"You guys really are serious about not letting them touch American soil, aren't you?" Sam said to Fong.

"Absolutely," the slightly built man said. "We'll hold them on this ship until transportation can be arranged back to China. So what do you want to ask them?"

"Ask them if anything unusual happened in the last two days."

Fong translated the question, and the group responded with general laughter. An older man stepped forward. Balding and tugging a long, scraggly gray beard, he looked like the typical older master in kung fu movies. He spewed off a string of Chinese.

"What did he say?" Sam said.

Fong smiled. "He introduced himself as Ho. He said it depends on your definition of unusual. He said being trapped in a container and then dumped in the ocean might be considered unusual. Can you be more specific?"

Sam looked back at Ali.

"They have to tell us, or it'll weaken our argument," she said. "I want to take a closer look at them."

"We'd rather you didn't, ma'am," one of the marines said. "The last thing we need is a hostage situation."

Ali smirked. "Most of them are emaciated. They're no threat. Besides, I can handle myself."

Sam looked back at the marine. "She can, believe me."

Ali walked into the crowd, studying faces.

Sam turned to Fong. "Tell them I'm interested in something other than being dumped into the ocean."

Fong interpreted his statement. Sam noticed they all looked to Ho to answer for them. So at least they knew who the leader was. Ho spoke to Fong.

"He said something might have happened, but he wants something in exchange," Fong said.

"What?" Sam said.

"You have to let us go," Ho said in English.

"Why am I not surprised you speak English?" Fong said. He looked up at Sam. "This man works for the smugglers. He's put in the container to prepare them for America." He turned his attention back to Ho. "There's no way we're going to let you go."

"We might," Sam said, "depending on what he has to say."

"Let's step outside," Fong said.

Ali joined them, and they went out into the corridor.

Fong's teeth were clenched. "There's no way we're going to release all of them. One, maybe; all of them, no."

"Look," Sam said. "We need this guy to bring down a major smuggler of drugs and people. We let them in, and after they testify, you guys can throw them out."

"It's not that easy," Fong said. "Every one of them will file a refugee claim. Because they've landed, each case will have to be processed at enormous expense. Some of them will escape and probably become a cog in the very machine you're trying to shut down. Promise them what you want, but don't expect the INS to deliver, because we won't."

Sam turned to Ali. "What do you think?"

"If we can get one to testify in front of the grand jury, it'll help our case a lot. There's got to be one of them willing to break out of the pack."

"Fine, let's go back in."

They reentered the room. None of the group had moved.

"This is the deal," Sam said. "We are willing to let one of you into the United States in exchange for testifying to what happened in the container."

Fong translated. None of them moved.

"You sure they understood?" Sam said.

"They understood," Ho said. "It's all or none."

"It's a deal," Sam said.

Fong stiffened but said nothing.

"Good," Ho said. "As soon as we've stepped on American soil, we'll tell you what happened."

Sam shook his head. "We need to know what happened first."

Ho pursed his lips. "I think if we tell you what happened, that's all you need for your purposes. You just turn around and walk out of here. No, we must be in America, or we will not talk."

"And how do we know when you get on American soil

you won't change your mind and say nothing?" Sam said.

"Once we're there, you can bribe us with a promise of being allowed to stay," Ho said. "Besides, I give you my word."

"Great, the word of a smuggler," Fong muttered.

Sam rubbed his face. "Fine. You've got a deal. We'll get started on the paperwork."

Ho bowed slightly, and Sam, Ali, and Fong stepped back into the corridor.

"What are you doing?" Fong said. "We're not going to let them land."

"That's what you say," Sam said. "You have superiors, and so do we. Ours will talk to yours, and they can decide."

"You know," Ali said, "there's another possibility."

"What's that?" Sam said.

"The girl who helped me save that kid in the water. I didn't see her in there, so she must've escaped. We find her, we have our witness."

"That's if she's still in the city," Fong said.

"What do you mean?" Ali said.

"If the smugglers didn't pick her up near the docks, they'll get her in Chinatown. When they escape, they always end up in Chinatown."

"Then let's go to Chinatown and see if we can find her before they do."

"We can try," Fong said. "But in all likelihood she's in the back of a truck headed to New York to work in the sex trade."

خطر

Michelle stretched, enjoying the softness of the bed. Never in her life had she dreamed such comfort existed. Although Ricky looked scary, he'd been the perfect gentleman. He helped her escape from the American police and took her in his car to his apartment. The first thing he did was cook her a bowl of rice and fish. After that he showed her how to use a shower. No wonder everyone wanted to go to America. Warm water that sprayed out from the wall—incredible.

After the food and shower, the exhaustion from the voyage overcame her, and Ricky let her have his bed while he slept on the couch. Now she could hear him moving about on the other side of the door. Michelle pried herself from the bed and got dressed. She opened the door, and Ricky turned to face her from the kitchen.

"Hungry?" he said in Mandarin.

"Yes," Michelle said.

Ricky took a ladle and scooped steaming rice and vegetables from a pot on the stove into a bowl. He handed it to her along with some chopsticks, then filled a bowl for himself and sat on the couch. Michelle sat in a chair across from him.

"You slept almost the whole day," he said. "How many died on the way over?"

"Some got sick, but none died."

"It's sure better now that they use the Russian ships," Ricky said. "Nine died when I came over five years ago."

"That must have been terrible."

Ricky shrugged. "It's worth it to get over here. At least here you eat every day and can own some nice things."

"What will happen to me now?"

Ricky scooped a mouthful of rice and swallowed it. "You'll probably stay with me for a couple days. They figure at least eight escaped. As soon as they find them, they'll take all of you to another city called New York. It's a huge place, lots of work. I envy you."

"Envy me?"

"Sure. I'm still working off my debt. With the money you

can make, you can be free of them in a couple of years."

Michelle lifted her eyebrows. "They pay lots of money to care for children in America?"

Ricky's chopsticks paused between the bowl and his mouth. "Children?"

"Yes. Mr. Ho said I'll get a job looking after children."

Ricky closed his eyes and shook his head. "So pretty and yet so stupid."

"Excuse me?"

He opened his eyes and set down his bowl. Ricky leaned toward her. "You're not here to work with children. You're here to work with men."

"Men?" Michelle set down her own bowl of rice. "How do I work with men?"

Ricky's forehead creased. "You really don't know, do you?"

Michelle just looked at him.

"You're going to be a prostitute."

Michelle sucked in a short breath. "I can't."

"You don't get a choice," Ricky said. "They bought you, they own you. If you go to the Americans for help, they'll only send you back to China. Once you get back to China, if you aren't killed, they'll just send you to another country, one not as nice as here. Take my advice: Do what they tell you to do, and eventually you'll be free."

"I can't. God says it's wrong to be with a man who's not your husband."

Ricky laughed. "Well, God isn't here, is He? They are. There's no point in fighting them. They'll force you, and you will end up doing what they want. You might as well enjoy it as much as you can."

Michelle was between the door to the apartment and Ricky. If what he said was true—and the churning in her stomach told her it was—then she had to escape. To where, she had no idea, but unlike Ricky, Michelle believed God was with her and He would show her a way out.

She picked up her bowl of rice and scooped up some with the chopsticks. She put the rice to her mouth then pretended to retch. "I'm going to be ill." She dropped the bowl, shot to her feet, started toward the washroom, but then charged to the apartment door.

"No, you don't!" Ricky shouted.

Michelle snapped open the dead bolt lock and yanked the door partway open before Ricky's hand reached around her and slammed it shut. He grabbed her shoulder and spun her around.

"You're not going anywhere."

Ricky had his body angled sideways to protect his groin. Instead, Michelle drove her heel down on the top of his foot. Ricky grunted and lifted his leg, and Michelle shoved him in the chest. Ricky tumbled to the floor.

She yanked open the door and ran down the hall to the stairwell, hearing Ricky's shouts and rumbling footfalls behind her. Michelle pulled open the stairwell door and darted down the stairs. She glanced over her shoulder and saw Ricky enter the stairwell one floor above.

"Lord, help me," she whispered over and over while crashing down the stairs and bouncing off walls before turning to go down the next level. By the time she reached the ground floor, she'd gained one level. Ricky's size worked against him turning tight corners.

Michelle slammed the steel bar of the fire exit door and stumbled into the alley. Turning, she sprinted to the street and pushed her way through the crowd. "Help me!" she cried, but most people just stared.

Ricky's voice called from behind. He was yelling something in English. A white man grabbed at her, and Michelle twisted free. She glanced over her shoulder and saw the crowd on the sidewalk parting for Ricky. He had his hand held up, something shiny in it—a badge. More people grabbed at her.

Michelle flailed her arms and screamed, but the crowd grabbed onto her, pushing her to the ground. She moaned and squirmed but couldn't break free, and then Ricky stood over her. "We could've been such good friends," he said in Mandarin.

"God, help me," she said.

"Didn't I tell you?" Ricky reached down and gripped her arm. "God isn't here, but we are."

خطر

Roxanne looked over at her adopted brother, Danny Corrigan, while he drove the van. If only she'd had brothers like him and Jonathan when she was growing up. Guys like that never would have left her to live on the streets. They would've come for her and dragged her home, unlike her parents. She wasn't sure if they even noticed she was gone. Roxanne shuddered at the memory of the three years she spent running with gangs. *Thank You, Lord, for bringing Sandra and her sons into my life.*

In the back of the Windstar, some other members of her youth group were laughing. They were going to meet teens from a sister church in Seattle to do street ministry downtown.

"You know," Danny said with a slight grin, "I'm not doing anything tonight. Want me to hang around and help you guys?"

"No," the teens said in chorus.

"Why not? I know the gospel. I can hand out tracts."

"Yeah, right," Roxanne said. "One look at you—everything about you screams cop—and everyone will run for the hills.

We want them to stick around."

"Okay, I get it." Danny chuckled. "Taxi service yes, street preacher no."

"That about sums it up," Roxanne said.

"But"—he glanced over at her—"you keep that cell phone with you, and if you kids run into any trouble, call 911, then call me. Right?"

"Got it," Roxanne said. It sure felt good to be cared about.

Danny slowed the van. "Now what's going on up there?"

To her right Roxanne saw a crowd around an Asian man pulling at an Asian teenage girl. "Looks like that guy is beating her up."

"And everyone just watches," Danny said. "Figures."

Danny punched the gas pedal, and the van surged even with the crowd; then he brought it to a stop. "All of you stay in here. I'm going to straighten this out."

Danny jumped out of the van and charged over to the clustered people. Roxanne lowered the window so she could hear what was going on.

"Seattle Police," Danny said, holding up his badge.

The Asian man took one look at Danny's badge, released the girl, and ran.

Like a tiger after prey, Danny chased after him. The girl sprang to her feet and ran in front of the van, stopping just before a passing delivery van flattened her.

Roxanne leaned her head out of the van. "Wait, we can help you."

The girl turned to her, her eyes wide, her chest heaving. "No one can help," she said in heavily accented English, then ran across the street amid a riot of horns and screeching tires.

"Want me to try to catch her?" Dave Cooper asked from the seat behind her.

"No, when Danny says stay put, he means it."

Two gunshots cracked through the air. Roxanne knew Danny didn't have his gun, meaning he was being shot at. Roxanne tossed her cell phone to Dave. "Call 911," she said before jumping out of the car and running after Danny.

She found him slumped against the side of a building near an alley entrance. She stumbled to a stop and dropped in front of Danny. His hand held the left side of his head. Blood flowed freely from his head down the side of his face.

"Oh no, you've been shot," Roxanne cried and dropped beside him.

"Not shot," Danny said and shook his head.

"Then what happened?" she said, her hands shaking while she dug in her pocket for some tissues.

"I poked my head around the corner, and when I saw the gun, I jerked back and smashed my head against the brick. I stunned myself a bit."

"So you're okay?" Roxanne said, moving his hand aside and pressing the tissue against the wound.

"Other than hurt pride and a pounding headache, yes." Danny took over the job of stanching the blood flow with the tissue. Sirens echoed in the distance.

"You called the police?"

"I got Dave to do it."

"Good." Danny got to his feet, and Roxanne put her arm around his waist and steadied him.

"How's the girl?"

"She ran off."

Two police cars screeched to a stop beside them. Four bulletproof-vest-clad police officers jumped out. "Hey, Corrigan," a lanky officer said. "What happened?"

"Hi, Neil. An Asian male was struggling with a teenage

Asian female. I chased him to this alley, but when I poked my head around, he took a couple shots at me. Banged my head ducking. He's about twenty-five, short dark hair, heavyset, wearing a black T-shirt, blue jeans, and red running shoes."

"You okay?" Neil asked. "Want an ambulance?"

"No, I'll be fine."

"Okay then, we'll see if we can find this guy."

Two more cars screeched up. Neil walked over, talked to the driver of one, and both cars sped off. He returned to them. "They're going to circle around back. We'll go in this way. I suggest you stop off at the hospital and get that looked at."

"Yeah, I'll do that," Danny said. "You guys just be careful."

"Count on it," Neil said.

The officers removed rifles from the trunks of their cars and then entered the alley.

Roxanne kept hold of Danny while they walked back to the van. Another car roared toward them, this one unmarked. It stopped quickly, and Sam Perkins, a friend of Jonathan's, got out along with a tall attractive woman and an Asian man.

"Hey, Sam," Danny said. "What brings you here?"

"We heard a report about an Asian guy attacking an Asian girl," Perkins said. "Roxanne."

"Hi, Mr. Perkins."

"Why would that interest the FBI?" Danny said. "Nothing else to do?"

"Can't really tell you why we're interested," Sam said. "This is my partner, Ali Marcoli, and Greg Fong here is with the INS."

"Hi," Danny said.

"We're particularly interested in the girl," Ali Marcoli said.

"I didn't really get a good look at her. I was too busy chasing the guy."

"I got a good look at her," Roxanne said. All eyes shifted toward her.

"What did she look like?" Ali Marcoli asked.

"She looked my age, seventeen, and about five nine, my height. Really pretty. Dark shoulder-length hair, a small nose, fine features. She was wearing a light blue tank top, blue jeans, and white sneakers."

"Are you a teenager or an undercover cop?" Ali said.

"A teenager with one brother who's a cop and another in the CIA. Well, used to be. You pick up things."

Ali looked at Sam Perkins. "CIA agent?"

"Jonathan Corrigan's sister."

"No kidding," Ali said and looked at Roxanne with different eyes.

"That sound like your girl?" Sam asked Ali.

"Yeah, it's her."

"Then we better find her before they do," Greg Fong said, "or we'll never find her at all."

危险 خطر ОПАСНОТЬ

EIGHT

Sitting on the balcony in his favorite deck chair, former CIA director Elijah Stone sipped a glass of wine and looked out over the lake that filled the back of his twenty-acre property in Virginia. Funny how bad things could turn out so good.

What a bind the CIA and the National Security Council found themselves in after Bellingham! To admit to the illegal operation of the CIA and his involvement in it would have required all sorts of public hearings.

Eventually it would come out that the country had been left completely defenseless. Since no one saw fit to tell the president in order to preserve plausible deniability, if it did come out, the man would look like an idiot. Poor man still didn't know. In any event, lots of heads would have rolled, so Elijah got to keep his. A healthy severance package combined with his savings allowed him to buy a quiet home in rural Virginia on a great little fishing lake. What more could a man ask for?

He clenched his teeth. Corrigan behind bars would be a start. Because of that renegade, America missed its opportunity to rule the world. No more having to ask the United Nations for permission. They could have done whatever they pleased, and no one could say a word. But no, for the love of that woman, he sold them all down the river. Now the same need for secrecy that protected him protected Corrigan.

His wife, Shelly, walked up behind him and started to massage his shoulders. "Elijah, you're all tense again. What's eating you?" She didn't know anything.

Stone looked over his shoulder. Tall and slender, even with gray hair, Shelly looked ten years shy of her sixty years. He looked back toward the lake at the setting sun. "Ah, just a lousy day of fishing. There's that one big trout. I hooked him again, but he got off."

"Just can't stand it when one gets away, can you?" Shelly said.

Stone thought of Corrigan again. "No, I guess not."

Off in the distance, they could hear the *whump-whump* of helicopter blades.

"Huh. Not often you hear a chopper flying this close to dark," he said.

Shelly stopped massaging. "I'm sure glad we don't have to worry anymore about it being the agency coming for you. I've got you all to myself now."

It was a statement, but Stone knew Shelly really meant it as a question. "Yes, you do, dear. My spying days are over."

The chopper grew louder until they could see its lights in the distance.

"Looks like it's going to pass right over us," Shelly said.

"If it does, I'll be calling a few friends at the FAA. At that height, he's going to rattle this place."

A spotlight lit up under the helicopter and strafed the

lake before settling on Stone's home. The chopper slowed and began to descend toward his large backyard.

"Oh, honey, you promised me!" Shelly shouted over the roar of the blades.

Stone got up from his deck chair with fists clenched. "And I kept that promise! I have no idea what this is about, but it better be good!" His actions and voice were angry, but only for Shelly's benefit. Every night when he laid his head on the pillow, and every morning when he woke up, Stone only thought about one thing: getting back into the agency. A helicopter landing at night had to be good news.

Stone turned and went inside the house, and Shelly followed. "Stay here," he said. "I'll go find out what this is all about."

She grabbed at his arm and turned him toward her. "Whatever they say, please don't go back."

Elijah held his wife's chin. "Don't worry. They probably need clarification on something that happened when I was director. If you didn't insist we turn the phones off after seven o'clock, they probably would've phoned."

"And we'd never get a quiet evening, with people calling you all the time for speaking engagements or solving some problem for them."

"Well, now they've had to drop in and visit us." He released her chin. "Don't worry. This probably won't take long."

Stone bounded down the stairs two steps at a time and reached the back door just as three solid raps sounded. He looked through the peephole then opened the door. "Rich, what's the meaning of this?"

Rich Lavigne, deputy director of Operations, stood at the door. The raucous noise from the helicopter died down as the pilot cut the engine's power. A gangly man in his late forties with horseshoe baldness, Lavigne extended his hand. "We tried calling, sir."

"And you didn't assume no answer meant I wasn't home?"

"We called your security company and confirmed that your alarm system wasn't activated."

"I see. Nothing ever changes. Well, come on in."

Stone closed the door and waved for Lavigne to follow him down the hall. After Lavigne stepped inside his study, Stone closed the solid oak door.

"Have a seat," Stone said, pointing to a chair in front of his executive-size desk. Stone took the high-back leather chair behind the desk. His study bore a remarkable resemblance to his former office at the CIA.

Stone folded his hands and touched his chin. "I'm assuming this is important."

"Yes, Director," Lavigne said.

"I appreciate the sentimentality, but I'm the former director."

A grin crept across Lavigne's face. "Not anymore, sir. Three hours ago, *former* Director Conrad Bolton was struck by a car resulting in a head injury. He's in a coma."

Stone leaned forward and knit his brows, showing the right amount of concern on his face. "That's terrible." *Now hurry up and say what I hope you're about to say.*

"As a result, the president—in consideration of these perilous times and upon the recommendation of certain agency personnel—has decided an experienced man should take charge until Mr. Bolton recovers or a permanent replacement can be found. That man is you."

A grin crept over Stone's face. "Would the agency personnel include you?"

Lavigne put his arms behind his head. "Absolutely."

"I knew I made the right move when I kept you out of the

Bellingham mess."

"For which I'm grateful. I would say that debt has now been adequately repaid."

Stone leaned back in his chair. "Yes, very adequately."

Lavigne clasped his hands together and placed them on Stone's desk. "Frankly, sir, the agency really needs you. Mr. Bolton is an adequate administrator, but in these times we live in, the agency needs a certain type of individual."

Elijah Stone placed his hands on his desk. "And what kind of individual would that be?"

"Someone more ruthless than our enemies, sir."

"I think you've found your man," Stone said. He felt a slight tremor of nerves in his stomach when he said it. Shelly would be none too pleased. She was in full retirement mode, but he wasn't. He so badly wanted to get back into the game. Sure, she'd pout, but their country needed him, and how could Stone possibly turn down the president?

"I suppose I should return with you to Langley immediately in order to get caught up," Stone said.

"That would be a good idea," Lavigne said. "But there's one briefing I think I should give you now."

Stone arched his eyebrows. "Yes?"

"Corrigan is back with the agency."

Stone bunched his hands into fists. "How did that traitor get back in?"

"One of Corrigan's assets contacted us with a terrorist alert. The asset would only deal with Corrigan, so Bolton recruited him. He's in Lebanon as we speak."

Stone curled up his lip. "Which means he's subject to my tender mercies."

Lavigne nodded his head. "That's right, sir."

"So Bolton was just hit by a car?"

"Yes, sir."

"Then I think I better be extra careful when I cross the street."

"Not a bad idea, sir." خطر

Jonathan sipped his coffee inside the Beirut café. Dressed in a light cotton shirt and pants, he was thankful Petra chose to meet in an air-conditioned building. Even at 8:00 a.m., it was getting hot. He yawned and took another sip of coffee. It might be Sunday morning in Beirut, but it was Saturday evening in Seattle, and his body wanted to go to bed.

Under any other circumstances, Jonathan would have enjoyed visiting Lebanon. During the times when the city wasn't being attacked by one side or the other, it was a beautiful place. Located on the Mediterranean Sea, the city used to be a vacation destination with pristine sandy beaches. The beaches were still there, but war had made sure the tourists weren't.

This was a simple mission. Meet with the asset, if the information is worth it, give him what he wants, and get out. A no-brainer. Except Jonathan didn't feel good about this at all. He was rusty, unfocused. When he first entered the café, instead of plotting alternate escape routes, he had let his mind drift back home to Laura and his unborn daughter. Just how did she know they were going to have a girl?

The thought of not returning home worked on him now as it had the whole trip from Seattle to Langley. So much so that Jonathan decided he would do this on his terms. It took presidential clout to get him what he wanted, and Jonathan felt much safer because of it.

Two spy satellites were tasked to watch him. If anything suspicious headed toward the café, Langley would call his cell phone and direct him to the best escape route. An escape car was parked at the back of the café. Should the bad guys give chase, Apache helicopters just outside the city could be there in five minutes with permission to use definitive force. If that wasn't enough, Blackhawks loaded with Special Forces were at the ready on a carrier in the Med. This was about as safe as a mission got.

The door to the café opened, and a powerfully built Lebanese man entered. Piercing dark eyes above a thick black beard gave one message: Best you leave me alone. When he spotted Jonathan, though, he broke into a broad grin, and the grizzly bear suddenly looked like a teddy bear. He stopped at the counter to get a cup of coffee then crossed the café and took the seat opposite Jonathan.

"Darryl," he said, using the name he knew Jonathan by. "How are you?"

"I've been better, Emile," Jonathan said. He took Emile's hand, and the two men spent a couple seconds seeing who would wince first. Jonathan chuckled when Emile broke off the contest.

"I believe this is the first time you've won," his Lebanese friend said.

"Farmwork makes soft men tough."

Emile raised an eyebrow. "You, a farmer?"

"A lot has changed. They pulled me out of retirement to meet you. Why couldn't you just have told someone else your information and left me to my cows?"

"Because I don't trust anyone else," Emile said, "especially when it comes to my family. It won't take the terrorists long to figure out where this information came from, and when they do, I want those I love far away from here. You've always kept your word. That's why I insisted on you."

"Then I'm going to be straight with you," Jonathan said. "It's not as easy as it used to be to just let someone in, especially if they're. . ." Jonathan took a sip of his coffee.

"Of Arab descent?" Emile said.

"Yes."

"So you can't help me, but I suppose you still want me to help you?"

"I didn't say I couldn't help you; I just said it wouldn't be easy. It depends on how solid and useful your information is and whether we can corroborate it. I might not be able to get you into the United States, but I can get you somewhere, probably Canada."

Emile straightened up. "Canada. Canada is full of ice and snow."

"You've been watching too many old movies on satellite TV. I live just south of the border, and southern Canada is no colder than where I live. There's a lot of resentment in the U.S. against people of Arab descent right now. Some people see any Arab as a Muslim extremist."

"But my family, we are Christians, not Muslims. There are many Christians here."

"I know that, but some people can't get past skin color and ethnicity. Trust me, you'd prefer Canada."

Emile gripped Jonathan's forearm. "I will trust you because I have no choice. God will not let me keep this information secret, so I will tell you, and you will do the best you can for me. Swear?"

"You have my word," Jonathan said.

"Okay," Emile said. "About a year ago, I took a job working security at the port. Many of my fellow guards smoke, so I take my break outside. I was sitting near a Russian container ship when I heard a group of men moving toward it.

Since I was alone and they were all carrying weapons, I felt it best to just stay put and watch."

"Men with guns in Lebanon—that's not unusual."

"No, but what they had was."

خطر

Elijah Stone sat back and watched the two large screens in the operations room. One focused on the café, and the other took in a broader area so they'd be able to identify any potential threats.

Lavigne placed a cup of coffee in front of him. "Still black with two lumps of sugar?"

Stone smiled. "Nothing's changed. Nothing at all."

Near the top left of the screen, two black cars moving at high speed came into view. The operator, Angie Sims, an attractive brunette in her midthirties, focused the satellite on one of the cars. Gun barrels could be seen sticking out the window. "Threat identified," Angie said. "Time to get him out of there." She reached for a phone.

"Not yet," Stone said.

Angie turned and looked at Stone. "Sir? The mission protocol is to remove him at the first sign of threat."

Stone sipped his coffee. "That was the old protocol."

خطر

Jonathan leaned forward. "What did they have?"

"They were guarding a wood crate about six feet long and three feet square. It wasn't that heavy. Two of them carried it onto the ship while the others kept watch. They never got off. The ship left port two hours later, in the dark."

"How many of them were there?"

"Six," Emile said.

107

"Definitely sounds suspicious, but your message made it sound like a bona fide threat."

"I know two of the men," Emile said. "Both are members of Hezbollah. They're always in the streets screaming "death to the American infidel" and the like. Many young people listen and are seduced by them.

"Also, I couldn't read the name of the ship because it was in Russian, so later I sneaked into the harbormaster's office and checked the log. There was no entry for that ship. It came in during the night and left before morning. Someone was paid off to ignore it."

Jonathan sighed. "How sure are you that America is the target?"

"They were talking about seeing the devil's nest. Whenever they speak of the devil, they mean the United States."

Jonathan nodded. "Yep, that would be us. So we've got an unnamed Russian container ship headed toward the United States with a suspicious box that could be anything, though if two of them carried it, it wasn't a nuke. How long ago did it leave?"

"Three weeks."

Jonathan bit his lower lip. "That means it's no longer in the Mediterranean. It could've gone out through the Suez Canal or Gibraltar. With the number of Russian vessels in the open sea, it's going to be tough to intercept it until it gets closer to the United States. We'll search every ship if we have to. Did they say anything else?"

"Well, it doesn't make any sense, but one of them joked about getting to see the needle in space before he went to Allah."

Jonathan's stomach churned. Needle in space. . .the Space Needle in Seattle. It made sense. The East Coast was heavily defended; because it took a lot of extra effort to sail to the

West Coast, the threat from sea wasn't considered as great on the West Coast. Seattle, his brother's home.

Jonathan stood. "Okay, I've got a car out back. Let's go get your family and get out of here."

They exited through the café's back door and got into the black Peugeot parked in the alley. Jonathan started the motor and shifted it into drive. "So how is your family?"

"They are well," Emile said. "My wife is sad to leave Lebanon but understands why we must. My daughter is excited because girls can wear what they want in the U.S. My son, he's going to be a bit of a problem."

"Why is that?"

"He's been listening to the hotheads in the streets. More and more he talks about unifying the Arab people. He doesn't understand that even if all our enemies were driven into the sea, we would just turn on each other. The war would not end."

"Will he come without a fight? I can't take him if he's not willing."

"He'll come," Emile said. "He is my son."

Jonathan slammed on the brakes, and they both lurched forward. A long black car blocked the exit of the alley. He slammed the car into reverse and floored it. Another black car entered the other end of the alley and roared toward them. Jonathan stopped the car and put it in park. He looked over at Emile. "Looks like you don't know your son as well as you thought."

A tear trickled down Emile's cheek. "No."

Once the Apaches showed up, Jonathan knew things would be different.

خطر

Angie stood and spun toward Stone. "Sir, we have to send in

the Apaches now if we're going to have a chance of getting him out of there alive."

Stone took a long sip of his coffee. "Who said anything about getting him out of there?"

She put one hand on her hip. "I don't understand."

"It's simple. They won't kill him because they want to know what he knows. That means they're going to take him back to their hideout to torture him." The thought brought a half grin to his face. "We'll track them with the satellite, and once they reach their destination, we'll be able to track who goes in and who goes out. This is an opportunity to gather an incredible amount of intelligence on these terrorists."

"What about Jonathan?" she said. "He'll be tortured. Possibly killed."

Stone walked over to Angie. He noticed she wore no wedding ring. Too bad she worked for the agency, but he never mixed his work with pleasure. He put his hand on her shoulder and forced compassion to his face. "Corrigan knew what he was getting into. These are perilous times. Sometimes sacrifices have to be made. But don't worry. We won't wait too long before we go get him."

危险 خطر ОПАСНОЮ

NINE

Roxanne Corrigan held hands with the other teens as they stood in a circle by the Seattle Center fountain. Singing at the top of their lungs, they had attracted quite a crowd. Their youth pastor, Kyle, gave the signal, and they stopped singing. He turned to the crowd.

"Ladies and gentlemen," Kyle said, "thank you for your kind attention. Please don't leave. We're not here to ask for money; we're here to give you something. The love of Jesus Christ."

At the name of Jesus, the crowd dispersed. Listening to kids sing about Jesus was one thing; listening to some guy preach about Him was quite another.

"Maybe we should've just asked them for money," Connie Wang said.

Connie, Roxanne's Seattle partner for the evening, spoke with a slight trace of a Chinese accent. Each Bellingham teen was partnered with a Seattle teen. Roxanne had a good feeling about Connie.

Roxanne chuckled. "No kidding. Well, at least they heard

the gospel in song."

"Okay, kids," Kyle called them to attention. Kyle stood over six feet tall and was lean and muscular. "Let's go tell them about Jesus, but let's tell them safely. Go in twos, and girls approach girls, guys approach guys. Any trouble, use your cell phones to call me or, if the situation warrants it, the police. Share Jesus, but share smart. Let's say a short prayer, and then we'll go.

"Lord," Kyle began, his deep voice resonating in the hot summer night, "there are lost sheep out there. Help us to reach the ones You want to bring into Your fold. Watch over us and bless us. Amen." He looked up at the group. "Go get 'em, gang."

Armed with gospel tracts, Roxanne and Connie turned and walked a few feet from the rest of the teens. Connie stood a couple inches shorter than Roxanne's five foot eight. The Asian girl had long, dark hair and a smooth, oval face.

"Where do you want to go?" Roxanne said.

"Let's work our way over to Chinatown. I've always had a burden to witness to my own people."

"Great idea. You know, if we take Fifth Avenue, we can hit Westlake Center on the way. Lots of teens hang around there on a Saturday night."

Connie tilted her head. "You know downtown Seattle?"

"Better than I'd like to. Used to live here."

"That's so cool," Connie said as they started walking toward Fifth Avenue. "I'd love to live downtown, but my dad works for Microsoft, so we live over in Redmond. Did you live in one of those tall apartment buildings?" She pointed at the city skyline.

Roxanne shook her head. "I wish. I lived on the streets."

"Get out of here! You were a street kid, like these kids?"

"Yeah," Roxanne said, not so sure how she felt about the

status being a former street kid gave her.

"Wow. You must have an exciting testimony."

"Not really," Roxanne said as they started walking again. "Living on the streets wasn't all I expected it to be. Always hungry, running from cops, having to steal, having to hook up with a gang for protection, but then having to do the gang's will to stay part of it. It's no life."

"Then why didn't you go home?"

"The streets were safer than my home."

"I don't understand."

"My former parents were drug dealers, and for all I know, they still are."

"No way."

"Yeah," Roxanne said. "All sorts of weird guys used to come around. A couple started hitting on me when I was fourteen. My parents were too stoned to notice. One night a guy came into my room when I was asleep and tried to, you know. . ."

Connie nodded.

"I screamed for help, but no one came. By that time I kept a knife in my nightstand, so I stabbed him. I thought I killed him. I ran away, and I ended up downtown. I ran into a group of kids about my age. Kurt was the leader. They took me in right away, became my family."

They crossed Denny Way to Fifth Avenue.

"So you found the streets better than home?" Connie said.

"At first. They treated me nice, and Kurt became my boyfriend. But it wasn't long before Kurt had me shoplifting for him, acting as a lookout when he broke into houses—B and Es, they called them, breaking and entering. That's how I got rescued from the streets. We got caught doing a B and E."

"Juvenile detention, huh?"

"Almost. But God had other plans. The cop who arrested

us was a really nice guy. Talked about Jesus a lot. Turns out he told his mother about me, and she applied to the court to become my guardian without my even knowing about it. One minute I'm thinking I'm off to jail; next minute I'm going to live at a farm in Bellingham."

Connie raised her eyebrows. "Why would she do that? She didn't even know you."

Roxanne shrugged. "Mom says God told her to take me in, so she obeyed. I figured she just took me in to score some points with her church or God, so I made the poor woman's life miserable. I'd swear at her, break stuff, run away. . . . She just kept on hauling me back. I finally realized no matter what I did, Mom wasn't going to let me go, that she really loved me. After all that, when she told me God loved me even more than she did, I couldn't resist. I gave in to Him."

She glanced over at Connie. Her partner's eyes were moist. "Wow."

"Yeah," Roxanne said. "Sometimes I wake up in the morning and pinch myself to make sure I really live in a nice home and not in some one-bedroom dump with eight other kids. I'm hoping tonight we might be able to do the same for some other kid."

"Me, too," Connie said. "Me, too."

خطر

Wedged between two bearded, gun-wielding men in the backseat, hands cuffed behind his back and a sack over his head, Jonathan realized no Apaches or Blackhawks were coming. What went wrong? Why didn't Angie spot them coming? He specifically requested her because she was the best and he could trust her. She was his friend—at one time more than a friend. It had to be a technical failure. Something had interfered with the satellite. It was the only explanation.

Jonathan felt sick for Emile. What would happen to him? He half expected they'd shoot his friend, but before they shoved the sack on, he saw that the remaining terrorists were just talking with Emile like they were all old friends. If he didn't know Emile better, he would've thought his friend gave him over. Not Emile. The man was as solid as they come. Then again, Laura thought the same about him when he betrayed her.

The car raced through the war-torn streets of Beirut for about twenty minutes before coming to a stop. Hopefully the satellite link had been restored and Langley was tracking where they took him; otherwise getting home would be his sole responsibility.

He heard the door to his right open, then felt a machine gun jabbed into his ribs. Jonathan slithered across the seat and stepped out into the hot Lebanon sun. Another rifle barrel in his back propelled him forward. He jammed his toe on a step, and his four escorts laughed.

"Shame on you for laughing at a blind man," he said in Arabic.

An uneasy silence followed, then a hand gripped his upper arm.

"I will help you," a soft voice said.

Islam had a few things to say about helping out the disadvantaged, and even though he was their prisoner, he couldn't see, and that put him up there with a blind man. Jonathan had managed to shame them.

Jonathan counted six steps, and they entered a building. Another twenty feet, probably down a hall, and another door opened.

"We're going downstairs," his guide said.

Jonathan stepped forward tentatively and found the first

step. Twenty-four wooden steps, each step about eight inches, which meant they went down sixteen feet. They went up about four feet entering the building, so the total descent equaled twelve feet, still a pretty deep basement. At the bottom he could hear a key inserted in a lock and a dead bolt snap open.

A brisk shove and Jonathan stumbled forward. So much for being nice to the blind guy. The door slammed behind him, and the dead bolt snapped shut. First things first. Jonathan leaned forward and shook his head like a bucking bronco until the sack slipped off. Complete darkness surrounded him. "You could have at least turned the light on!" he shouted at the door. Laughter and retreating footsteps followed.

Jonathan slipped off his shoes so they wouldn't snag the cuffs. Lying on the floor, he lifted his knees to his chest, ignoring the protests his old leg wound made. Arching his bottom up, Jonathan slipped the cuffs over his rear and then his legs. Feeling around the floor, he found his shoes. He put them on, got up, and enjoyed a good long stretch with his hands in front of him.

Shuffling carefully, Jonathan moved over to the wall. Unlike James Bond, he didn't come equipped with exploding buttons or a two-way radio in his teeth. Except for the clothes on his back, they'd taken everything from him before putting him in the car.

He edged along the wall, feeling it out with his hands. Two walls later, he found the light switch and flicked it on. A solitary bulb illuminated the room. Jonathan sighed. The room had four concrete walls and a concrete ceiling. This explained the twelve-foot drop. The room was a bomb shelter converted to a dungeon. He imagined the concrete ceiling was two feet thick. At least he didn't have to contend with the sweltering heat down here.

He moved to the steel door. The dead bolt was the kind that needed a key on both sides to open it. Made sense. If they used it as a bomb shelter, they wouldn't want anyone to be able to lock them in from the outside. There were also brackets for cross braces to fortify the door on the inside. He didn't see the braces.

Jonathan's first option was to pick the lock, assuming he could find something to pick it with and some bearded giant wasn't waiting on the other side of the door. He didn't like to give in without a fight, but he realized if he was going to get out of there, it would probably have to be with outside help.

Two sets of footsteps rumbled down the staircase. The dead bolt snapped, and the door opened. A short, bearded man entered, while one of the men he'd seen at the car hung back at the stairwell. The new man wore loose white cotton clothes over his heavy frame and grinned with crooked teeth.

"When Emile told us he was meeting with an American spy, I never in my wildest dreams thought it would be you." He stepped forward. "You may call me Hussein. Not my real name, of course, but a name you Americans like so much." He glanced at Jonathan's shackled hands. "Why are your hands in front of you?" He turned his head slightly. "Omar, why are his hands in front of him?"

Omar, younger and partly bald but built similarly to Hussein, poked his head in the room. "We put them behind him."

Hussein put his finger to his lips. "Very flexible for a retired agent."

Jonathan shrugged but said nothing.

Hussein spoke with an English accent, which meant he was probably educated in Britain and then returned to the Middle East to fight. Jonathan knew this man was dangerous; he possessed intelligence but was driven by revenge.

"So I take it Emile betrayed me."

"What makes you think that?" Hussein said.

"Usually you guys shoot traitors pretty much on sight. It looked like a meeting of old friends to me."

"Yes. Even though he is a Christian, Emile has come to understand the Arab people will only be free when Zionist pigs and American infidels are driven from our land."

Jonathan spat on the concrete floor. "That traitor. If I get my hands on him, I'll—"

"Oh, don't be so indignant," Hussein said. "Your job is to turn people into traitors. Isn't that what you were doing in that café? Trying to get Emile to turn on his own people?"

Jonathan looked up into Hussein's dark eyes but said nothing. In spite of how it looked, he didn't believe Emile betrayed him. It had to be the son. By giving the impression he thought Emile was a traitor, he hoped to convince Hussein that Emile's information was false, not worth dying for. If the CIA offered ransom, Hussein would never let him go if he thought Jonathan believed Emile.

"So which are you? Hezbollah, al Qaeda?"

"What I am is not important. What is important is we have the famous Jonathan Corrigan, sweetheart of the American people. Many of our people will be freed in exchange for you."

Jonathan laughed, turned, and walked to the back wall before turning again to face Hussein. "Not going to happen."

Hussein grinned. "I think once we release a tape of you to the American media and they show it on your television, the American people will scream for the president to give us whatever we want."

The thought of Laura seeing him on TV, shackled and in the hands of terrorists, made him feel ill. He couldn't let that happen. "That would be the stupidest thing you could do."

The grin fell from Hussein's face. "Why would that be?"

"Because the president went on record saying he'd never negotiate with terrorists no matter what the cost. As soon as you make my capture public, he won't be able to negotiate because he can't appear to be weak.

"If you're going to get anything at all from him, you'll have to do it in secret. Even then, he won't let any of your people go. He's not going to risk the media finding out he let terrorists go just to get a CIA agent back. I am expendable in this war."

Hussein reached behind his waistband and pulled out a gun. He rushed forward, placed the barrel against Jonathan's head, and pulled back the hammer. "Then I will send you back in a body bag."

خطر

Ali sipped a cup of coffee while watching the crowd moving along the street. They'd cruised Chinatown for over two hours on foot and by car. "Maybe this girl is smart enough to know the first place everyone will look for her is Chinatown."

"That's assuming she hasn't already been caught," Sam said.

"I hope not. Without her, we have no case at all. I can't believe not one of those people on the supply ship was willing to testify."

"The INS interviewed each of them alone," Sam said. "Offered everyone a chance at America, and not one would agree to talk unless they all got to land. The INS isn't willing to make that concession, and I guess they have the final say on this one."

Ali shook her head. "They do know Grachev had an FBI agent killed? I wonder how they'd feel if it had been one of their people."

Sam pulled the car into a parking spot. "Hopefully no different. I see their point. What if they admit them and none of them talk? Then they have all these people to process and we're no closer to nailing Grachev. We have to find that girl, that's all."

"You know," Ali said, "all the smells of this street are making me hungry. Want to eat?"

Sam rubbed his stomach. "Maybe some soup. It took a lot of work to get my weight down."

Eleven o'clock and the streets were full with tourists looking for a late-night meal or entertainment. They worked their way through the crowd and went half a block down to the Peeking Dragon. The artwork in the window depicted a purple dragon peeking through his fingers.

They entered a spacious restaurant with a symphony of smells that made her stomach growl. It was like most Chinese restaurants: an open floor plan with tables laid out in rows and booths lining the window facing the street. They slid into one of the booths.

Seconds later, a lithe Chinese girl no more than fourteen showed up with water, dropped off menus, and took their orders for coffee.

"I wonder how many of these people are illegals," Ali said.

"Isn't that a bit racist?"

Ali felt like she'd been slapped. She didn't like to think of herself as a racist, but she'd done what all racists do. She'd projected on the group her experience with a few.

Sam opened his menu. "Just because they're Chinese doesn't mean they're here illegally. Many of these people settled this area during the gold rush doing jobs no one wanted. They're still doing those jobs."

"I guess you're right. I'll have to be more careful about my assumptions."

The corner of Sam's mouth curled up in a grin. "Hey, don't

sweat it. I thought the same thing, but when you said it, I got to take the moral high ground. Fact is, all of these people are probably here legally. The smugglers move them out of Washington as fast as they can."

The girl returned with their coffee. "What would you like?"

Ali ordered a combination dinner, but Sam stuck with vegetable chop suey. The girl smiled, took their menus, and headed back toward the kitchen.

Ali looked out into the street, watching the faces as they went by. Some were close matches, but not her girl.

"We can walk around some more after we eat," Sam said. "But then I think we should look in on Davidov. I want to check out the place the U.S. Marshals have him."

"Good idea, but forget dinner because I think I just spotted her."

Ali jumped up from the table and charged to the door of the restaurant. She slowed before stepping out into the street so as not to draw attention. The girl was moving with the traffic on the other side. A steady flow of vehicles forced Ali to stay on her side of the street while keeping pace with the girl. If she would turn toward her, Ali could get a good look at the face.

"Is it her?" Sam said, catching up to her.

"I'm pretty sure."

"If she runs, do you think you can catch her?"

"As long as she doesn't get too much of a lead. I'd prefer to get good and close before we make our move. Let's follow her to the intersection, and with any luck we'll be able to cross over and grab her before she realizes we're following her."

Ali and Sam shadowed the girl from the other side of the street. At one point, the girl glanced across the street but gave no indication she saw or recognized Ali.

"It's definitely her," Ali said.

"Good. Now let's be careful. If we can get this girl to corroborate Davidov's story, we'll have Grachev."

When they reached the intersection, the light to cross was red. The girl paused then slowly walked away from them with the traffic.

"Doesn't seem to be in much of a hurry," Sam said.

The light turned green.

"Something's not right," Ali said, as they started to cross. A moving van rumbling past drowned out her words.

"What?" Sam said.

The girl started to jog.

"Oh, great," Ali said. "The moving van."

Ali dug in and sprinted after the lumbering van; Sam's feet thundered behind her. The van shifted a gear, and the rate Ali gained on the vehicle dropped. The girl started to run now, matching the van's speed. Ali reached the corner just as the girl jumped on the running board of the passenger side and held on to the extended mirror. Digging down, Ali pumped her legs, managing to gain a little bit of ground, but when the van shifted gears again, it easily left her behind.

Ali jogged a bit then stopped, panting. "She must've spotted us," she said when Sam caught up to her a couple seconds later.

Sam pulled out his cell phone. "Maybe Seattle police can stop the van and grab her."

Ali put her hands on her hips. "Somehow I don't think it'll be that easy."

危险 خطر ОПАСНОТЬ

TEN

Jonathan closed his eyes and let thoughts of Laura flood his mind. His last sight before heaven wasn't going to be some bearded terrorist. Closing out the gun barrel pressed against his head, he thought of the California beach they used to walk on. She stood before him, the ocean behind her, the wind sweeping her copper hair. *See you soon,* he thought. Just not in this world.

A click, but no shot. He opened his eyes. Hussein's thumb held the hammer back from striking the bullet.

Hussein lowered the hammer and stepped back but kept the gun trained on Jonathan. "I think they'll trade something for you. But even if they don't, I am sure you can provide us with useful information. Useful enough to make keeping you alive worthwhile."

Jonathan sucked in a deep breath and shook his head. "I'm retired. There's not a lot I can tell you."

Hussein smirked. "Yes, I read in the papers about your supposed retirement, and yet here you are in Beirut. I think you can tell us a lot. Starting with how you got here. I assume you didn't take a direct flight. Did you come in through Israel, or did you come in by an aircraft carrier?"

"Canoe."

Hussein grinned. "I've heard about your wit. I should pistol-whip you, but why? It just bloodies up a perfectly good weapon. We've learned a lot from the CIA over the last year, and one of those things is the benefits of nonviolent persuasion."

"Such as?" Jonathan said.

Hussein chuckled. "Do you like rock music?"

خطر

Michelle stayed crouched so the driver of the van couldn't see her. People stared at her as she passed. Probably not every day that they saw someone hitching a ride the way she was. The traffic light ahead was red, and the van started to slow. Michelle jumped off as it rolled to a stop. She squared her shoulders and walked with a swagger as she'd seen some of the teens do. It seemed to explain her behavior to the gawking pedestrians.

She couldn't stay in the open long; the police lady would be sure to call for help. Michelle walked half a block down the street and slipped into an alleyway. She really had no idea where to go next. Chinatown hadn't been much help. Anyone she talked to made it clear that the best thing she could do was return to the smugglers, that they'd get her sooner or later. Her own people treated her like she had a disease. Michelle had no one to turn to in this strange country.

She headed toward the center of the city for no real reason, other than there seemed to be more people to hide among. Like a phantom, she moved through the city, keeping mostly to the alleyways. A couple of times, she hid when she heard other people in the alleyway. Michelle might be from the country, but she wasn't stupid. People smugglers and police weren't the only ones to fear in a big city like Seattle.

Eventually there were no more alleys to hide in and Michelle had to enter a street. Lots of cars and people moved along it, and Michelle moved with them until she came to an open square. She crossed the street and looked for a place to sit. Her stomach rumbled from being on the run all day and the only food she had came from Dumpsters. On top of that, her feet were killing her.

"Found you."

Michelle spun to see Ricky.

"You've caused me a lot of trouble, Michelle."

She tensed, trying to decide which way to run.

"Go ahead, run," he said. "You're safe because there are too many people around. I won't chase you. But when you're running, remember this: I'm not the only one looking for you. At some point, you're going to cause us more trouble than you're worth. When that happens, you'll go back into that ocean with weights tied to your legs."

خطر

"Yeah, right, Jesus loves me."

"He does," Roxanne said to the teenage girl. She couldn't be more than fourteen years old, but she was wearing too much makeup, and her otherwise pretty face was pierced everywhere it could be.

"Sure. And He's God, right?"

"Yes," Roxanne said.

"That means He can see everything, right?"

"Right."

"Then where was He when my foster parents were smacking me around? If He could see it, why didn't He stop it?"

"Did you ask Him to?" Connie said.

The girl shifted her weight and put her hand on her hip. "Excuse me?"

"She's got a point," Roxanne said. "I lived on the streets, and I don't ever remember asking God to help me out."

"Well, I have," she said. "And so far no answer."

"What about us?" Roxanne said. "We're here, telling you Jesus loves you, and we want to help you."

The girl smirked. "How? Are you going to take me in, give me a safe place to live?"

"We'll take you to people who can," Connie said. "Our church has an outreach program for people just like you."

The girl's brown eyes went from Connie to Roxanne and back again.

"Thanks, but no thanks. I've had enough broken promises."

"So have I," said Roxanne. "But since I met Jesus, I've had a lot of promises not broken." She dug a pen out of her acorn-colored leather purse and wrote on one of the gospel tracts they carried. She held the tract toward the girl. "Here, this is my phone number. You change your mind, call me."

The girl looked at the offered tract like it would bite her.

"Take it," Roxanne urged.

The girl snatched it from Roxanne's hand, then turned and walked into the square at Westlake Center.

"And remember, Jesus loves you!" Connie called after her.

خطر

"Come on," Ricky said. "Come back with me. Before you know it, your obligation will be paid off and you'll be free to live in America any way you want."

Michelle shook her head. "I can't do what they want."

"Sure you can," Ricky said. "They'll give you drugs to make

it easy. You won't even care after awhile."

Michelle bit down on her lip to hold back the tears. People were all around her, and yet she was completely alone. *Jesus, where are You?*

"Michelle, believe it or not, I'm your friend. I'm trying to help you."

"Jesus loves you." The English words drifted to her from the street. Michelle looked around to see two teenage girls, one Chinese and the other white, calling after a third girl. She turned back toward Ricky. "I have other friends."

She walked toward the girls.

"They'll kill you," he called after her in Mandarin. "And they'll kill anyone who helps you. Is your virtue that valuable?"

She froze. His words held her in place like no shackles could. If she went to those girls, girls who knew Jesus, she'd be putting their lives in danger. The missionary man said Christians were brothers and sisters. Even though she didn't know them, they were her sisters, and she couldn't let harm come to them. She'd have to go back, but she wouldn't do what they wanted. They'd have to kill her first.

خطر

"That poor girl," Connie said. "I'll be praying for her big time."

"Me, too. Well, let's go to Chinatown. There should be a bus any minute."

The two girls headed toward the bus stop when Connie gripped her arm.

"What?"

"I think I heard someone yell something in Mandarin about killing someone."

Both girls turned toward Westlake Center. Roxanne's heart jumped into her throat. "It's her, the girl I told you about. The one who ran in front of the van. That guy was pretending to be a cop arresting her. He shot at my brother."

"She's walking back to him," Connie said.

"I don't know about you, but I don't want to lose two in one night. We've got to help her."

Connie called to the girl in Mandarin while they ran toward her. The girl paused and turned toward them. The man looked up at them and quickly melted into the crowd.

"What did you say to her?" Roxanne said.

"Jesus loves you."

"Seems to have worked on both of them."

They slowed to a fast walk and approached the girl. She reminded Roxanne of a bird with a broken wing: full of fear but unable to fly away.

"Jesus," she said in heavily accented English. "You know Jesus?"

"Yes," Roxanne said. "But we have to get out of here. There could be more of his kind around."

The girl's forehead crinkled, and Connie translated. The girl rattled off something back.

"She says we should leave her. We are in danger if we help her."

Roxanne pulled out her cell phone. "Then I better call my brother."

"The cop or CIA agent?"

Roxanne paused, and pursed her lips. "That's a good question."

"Cop. Police, right?" the Asian girl said.

Connie answered her.

The girl shook her head violently. "No police. If police come, I die."

"Why does she say that?" Roxanne said.

Connie chattered back and forth with the girl. When they finished, a tear crept down Connie's cheek. "Her parents sold her to smugglers after she became a Christian. The smugglers said she was coming to the U.S. to be a nanny, but she found out they're going to force her to be a prostitute. If she gets sent back to China, the smugglers might send her back here to pay her debt, but if she's not lucky, she'll be killed as an example."

Roxanne's stomach roiled. "Tell her I'll phone my other brother. He's not with the police. He can help. And ask her what her name is."

Connie translated. "She's adopted an English name. She wants to be called Michelle."

"Hi, Michelle," Roxanne said as she punched in her home phone number, then put the cell phone to her ear. It rang five times before the answering machine picked up. Roxanne clicked the phone shut. "No one's home. They probably all went to the airport to pick up Mom. Well, we can't stay here. Did you drive your car?"

"Yeah," Connie said.

"Want to take her to your place?"

Connie looked down at the concrete. "That wouldn't be a good idea."

"Why not?"

"Because it's obvious Michelle is here illegally. My parents would just turn her in."

"Are you serious?" Roxanne said. "Your parents are Chinese. Why wouldn't they want to help?"

"They resent the fact that they went through all the trouble to immigrate legally, but boat people force their way into the country and give all of us a bad reputation."

"But she didn't force her way here. She's been sold as a slave."

Connie shrugged. "They won't believe her. They're pretty cynical."

"Well, she'll have to come to my place then," Roxanne said. "If anyone can help her, Jonathan can. Will you drive us to Bellingham?"

"What about your other brother? Doesn't he think you're staying at his place tonight?"

"I'll just tell him I'm homesick for Mom. It's not far from the truth."

Connie pulled in the corner of her lip. "Okay, give me the cell phone, and I'll clear it with my parents."

خطر

Ricky stayed obscured in the summer evening crowd, watching Michelle and the other two girls. He cursed inwardly as Michelle left with the two Americans and got into a cab. He had to get Michelle back. Heng had made it clear that if he didn't bring the girl back, he'd have to pay the full price. That meant another five years of slavery.

He turned his attention to a girl with multiple piercings on her face. He'd seen one of the girls Michelle went with hand that girl a piece of paper. With any luck, the piece of paper could lead him to Michelle.

The girl stood with a group of five other street kids. Ricky walked over to them. "Hi!"

They all looked up at him with disdain.

He turned to the one who had talked with the teens. "The dark-haired girl. She gave you a paper. Can I have it?"

The girl laughed. "Get your own. I'm sure they'll be happy to push one on you."

"Fifty dollars."

The girl's eyes widened. "You got it." She dug it out of her pants pocket but held out her other hand. "Money first."

Ricky put the bills in her hand, and she gave him the paper. His heart leapt. There was a phone number written on it, maybe the dark-haired girl's. It would be nothing to get her address now. Then he would go and drag Michelle back if he had to.

خطر

Connie pulled her Honda Civic up in front of Roxanne's house. Light streamed out of the living room windows. "Good, they're still up," Roxanne said. "Wait here."

Roxanne got out of the car and skipped up the porch steps. Rudy's deep barks sounded from the other side of the door. "Just me, Rudy," she said, and the dog went silent. Once inside she crouched down and gave the German shepherd a big hug. "Hey, boy, how you doing?" Rudy answered with a couple big licks and a furious tail-wagging. He padded after her when Roxanne went to the living room.

Inside, Mom, Laura, and an older woman were all watching CNN. They were reporting something about the director of the CIA being in a coma and some other guy replacing him.

"Hi, everyone!" she said.

Her mom broke into a broad smile as she got up from her easy chair. "Hey, what are you doing home? Laura said you were spending the night at Danny's."

Roxanne hugged her mom. *Why am I home early? Oh, I just found an illegal immigrant and thought I'd bring her home.* "I missed you, and the girl I was paired with gave me a ride home."

Her mom released her. "That was nice of her."

Roxanne turned to Laura, who was lying on the couch. She looked pale like she did when morning sickness first hit. "How's the baby business going?"

Laura flashed a weak smile. "Pretty good."

Roxanne looked at the other woman. "Hi."

"Oh, sorry," Laura said. "Roxanne, this is my mother, Alice McIvor. Mom, my sister-in-law Roxanne."

"No kidding!" Roxanne said. "Great to meet you."

Alice smiled, but there seemed to be no life behind it. "Nice to meet you, too."

Like a line drive, it hit Roxanne that something was wrong. In fact the whole room seemed to be a battlefield at cease-fire. Laura had made it no secret that she wished her mother was with her. Instead of the joy Mom usually had after retreats, it seemed like someone died. Roxanne started to feel nervous.

"Where's Jon?"

Laura looked away as did Laura's mother.

"Business trip, dear," Mom said.

"When will he be back?"

Her mom turned to Laura. "Wednesday?"

"Uh, yes, if he isn't delayed."

Great. What a time for Jon to take off on business. Did she dare tell her mom what she'd done? Roxanne looked at her mother's tired eyes. Now probably wouldn't be a good time. "Um, any chance my friends can stay the night?"

"Oh, honey, this isn't something you should just spring on us. I'm beat from traveling. I'm really not up to having guests."

"I'm sorry. I called, but no one answered."

"We all went to the airport to pick up Mo—Sandra," Laura said.

"I sure hate to send them back to Seattle. It's past midnight. It's warm outside. We can bunk in the barn."

Mom sighed. "There's no way three teenage girls are going to sleep out in the barn. Grab the foam mattress and sleeping bags and cram them into your room."

Roxanne kissed her mom on the cheek. "Thanks."

"Just don't keep us up with giggling," Mom called after her as she headed to the door.

"We won't," Roxanne said as she pulled open the outside door. Rudy followed her outside, yapping and circling the car like a marauding bandit. "Quiet, Rudy," she said, and he moved to her side.

The driver-side door opened, and Connie stepped out. "Well?"

"Jon isn't here."

"So what do we do now?"

"Mom says you can sleep over."

Connie raised an eyebrow. "Does she know who's sleeping over?"

Roxanne pursed her lips. "I kind of left that detail out."

Connie looked heavenward. "Don't you think it's something your mom should know?"

"Sure. Maybe in the morning when she isn't too tired."

"Better give me the cell phone so I can let my parents know about the change in plans." Connie moved to the other side of the car.

Roxanne opened the back door, and Michelle climbed out. Rudy sniffed in her direction but stayed at Roxanne's side.

"Nice doggy?" Michelle said.

"Yeah," Roxanne said. "You can pet him."

Michelle furrowed her brow. "Pet?"

"Yeah, pet." Roxanne petted Rudy.

Michelle gingerly stepped forward and lightly stroked Rudy's head. The dog looked up at Roxanne.

"Mon ami," Roxanne said.

Rudy gave Michelle's hand a big lick. Michelle stepped

back and giggled like a schoolgirl.

Roxanne heard the cell phone click shut. She looked over at Connie. "Is it okay?"

"They're not happy about it, but yes."

Michelle petted Rudy again, and he responded with another lick. She clapped her hands together. "Doggy, doggy, doggy," she said in a singsong voice.

"You realize sooner or later someone is going to talk to her?" Connie said.

Roxanne took in a deep breath and let it out slowly. "Yeah."

"And how do you plan on explaining that she has the vocabulary of a three-year-old?"

Roxanne chewed on her knuckle. "Unless we tell them she's your cousin from Hong Kong?"

"That would be lying."

Roxanne looked toward the house. Where was Jon? "Don't worry about it. We wouldn't be the only ones not telling the truth around here tonight."

ELEVEN

SUNDAY, JULY 7

Sam slammed down the accelerator, and the LeSabre shot forward. He cut across three lanes of traffic to the Renton off-ramp. Horns blared, but he paid them no mind. "Anyone else get off?" he said to Ali.

She was looking over her shoulder. "No, but you got a fair number of hand gestures for that stunt."

"I'll try not to let it get me down."

At the end of the ramp, they merged with the light Sunday morning traffic. They turned left under the highway, worked their way to the on-ramp, and headed back onto the highway. "Any tails?"

"Still clear. If anyone was following, we've lost them."

"Good." Setting the cruise at sixty miles an hour, Sam settled in the seat for the drive up to Everett.

"I feel sick about that girl," Ali said.

"Yeah, it would've been nice to catch her. Right now Davidov is about as useful as water to a drowning man."

"Actually, I was thinking more about what kind of life

she's going to end up with once the smugglers catch her."

"That's assuming they've caught her."

Ali sighed. "Where else could she be? Seattle PD spent the whole night looking for her. She vanished without a trace. They must've gotten to her before we did. Hopefully she won't wash up on the shore over the next couple days."

Sam glanced over at Ali. "Have faith."

"Faith? Like in 'God will work everything out' kind of faith?"

"Sort of," Sam said.

He heard her shift in her seat. "You don't strike me as the churchgoing type."

"Really? Why?"

"Well, for one, it was your idea to visit the safe house this morning. Most church people try to avoid working Sundays. You've used the odd bit of flowery language in my presence."

Sam chuckled. "Well, if flowery language condemned a person, then I know plenty of churchgoing people who are in big trouble. But you're right, I don't go to church."

"So where's the 'have faith' comment come from?"

"Jon Corrigan."

He glanced over as Ali straightened in her seat.

"How do you know him?"

"We worked together once, and we still hang around a bit."

Ali's fingers drummed on the dash. "Wait a minute. Corrigan was shot by an FBI agent's gun. That wasn't your gun, was it?"

Like everyone else, Sam had been sworn to silence for reasons of national security. Usually it bothered him that the Bellingham incident was under a veil of official secrecy, but this particular moment, he was never so glad to be able to say, "I'm afraid everything surrounding those events is classified."

"Aw come on, you're kidding me."

He shook his head. "I open my mouth, and I go to jail. You want that? Your next partner might not be so kind to a rookie."

She settled back in her seat. "I guess not. So Corrigan is religious? A religious CIA agent?"

"I think he got religion after he retired," Sam said. "But he says God is on His throne and we just have to have faith that everything will unfold according to God's plan. Kind of comforting in a way."

"Whatever helps you sleep at night."

Sam glanced at her. Ali stared straight ahead, her jaw tight. He must have hit a nerve.

The rest of the trip to Everett passed quietly, with the occasional short exchange of words. They worked their way through the city with a stop at Starbucks, then continued to the suburbs before pulling up to a single-level bungalow on a quiet street.

The curtains parted as they walked up the sidewalk. They didn't have to bang on the solid wooden door; it opened by the time they got there. A linebacker-type with a handlebar mustache and muscles bulging under his black T-shirt opened the door, a handgun holstered under his arm.

"Agents Perkins, Marcoli," he said and stepped aside for them to enter.

"Good morning, Marshal Croin," Sam said.

The marshal's eyes were on the steaming hot coffee and the fresh blueberry muffins Ali carried.

"I think I'm in love," Dixon Croin said as he reached for one of the take-out cups.

"Huh," Ali said. "All these years I've been wearing perfume to catch a man's attention. Now you tell me all I needed to do was dab coffee behind my ears."

"Not just any coffee," a woman's voice said. Erin Klyne, the other U.S. Marshal assigned to protect Davidov, stepped into the hallway. Ali's height, Erin kept her blond hair cut military-style and her muscular frame indicated that she was into bodybuilding—big time. The female marshal relieved Ali of one of the five cups she carried. "For this lug, it has to be Starbucks."

Sam looked at Dixon. "Don't you two have a witness to protect?"

"You bet," Dixon said.

"Well, you're not going to be able to do it in the hallway."

"That's true," Dixon said and grinned.

They went down a short hallway and entered the living room to the left. Sparsely furnished with Salvation Army-type décor, the room wasn't much. Davidov occupied a tattered green recliner in front of a twenty-five-inch television set. Ironically, *Let's Make a Deal* was on. He looked up at them and flipped off the set. "I thought you guys were coming last night. I had my heart set on something good to eat. These two burn boiling water."

Ali handed Davidov his coffee and dug a muffin out of a bag. "Sorry. We ran into some trouble."

Davidov stiffened. "What kind of trouble?"

"Nothing that concerns you," Sam said.

"Did you find the girl to clear me?"

Sam grabbed a chair, dragged it across the floor, and sat across from Davidov. Ali stayed by the entrance to the living room. "No, we think they've got her."

"Then she's dead," Davidov said, as if Michelle were no more than a cat hit on the highway. "No one will believe me now. They'll think I tried to kill those people."

"I'm afraid that's right," Sam said.

Davidov's eyes widened. "So what now? You're not going to let them get me—are you?"

Sam shook his head. "We'll keep our side of the deal. But we can't tie up two sets of U.S. Marshals to guard you. What we want to do is bring a court reporter here tomorrow and get your testimony on paper, then—"

"No, no, no. I'm not signing anything until I'm relocated. If I sign, you'll have the document and you won't need me to testify, which means you won't need to keep me alive."

"Not true," Ali said. "Even with a sworn statement, we need you alive. Juries are reluctant to convict on depositions."

"Then why do you need it?"

"Because we're going to relocate you tomorrow," Sam said. "We want the deposition in case we find the girl. With it and her, we might be able to go to the grand jury and get an indictment without bringing you out of hiding."

"Hide me first, and then I'll sign."

"We can't. Only the marshals who relocate you will know where you are. If we bring a court reporter out to your new location, that's one more person who'll know where you are. It's not a great idea."

"I don't care. Hide me; then I'll sign."

خطر

Josef Grachev stood on the bow of the cargo ship with his lawyer, Ray Kuhl. Dressed down in pleated slacks and a golf shirt, the solicitor still managed to look like five hundred dollars an hour.

"I want to go home," Josef said. "I want to swim in my pool. I want to lie in my hot tub."

"Ah, come on, Josef. It's not that bad on board. The food's

good." Kuhl grinned. "And it can't be too painful having Sophie for company."

Josef curled his lip and looked down at Kuhl. "Steak every night eventually tastes like cardboard."

"Well, if it's variety you want, it can always be brought on board."

Josef sneered. "I think the fewer people who know where I am, the better. Besides, I can't bring a golf course here, can I? Do you know what this is doing to my golf game? My handicap was down to five."

"I know what jail will do to it," Kuhl said.

"Any news on a grand jury?"

"Nothing."

"And that's probably what they've got. Nothing."

"They have Davidov," Kuhl said.

"But he's useless because of the container, right?"

"There's still the risk some of the Chinese will testify they were switched."

Wind coming from behind him, Grachev spat into the ocean. "Heng swears none of them will talk. They know if they do, we'll kill their families back home and them, too, once we find them."

"There's still the ones who got away," Kuhl said. "My sources tell me Seattle police spent all last night looking for a Chinese girl at the request of the FBI."

"So even if they do find her, what good is she? Assume she talks. They can't prove she was in the container. She'll probably ask for citizenship in exchange for testimony. Some witness. Bought to corroborate an event she can't prove she witnessed. Surely you'd be able to destroy her on the stand."

Kuhl put his hand on Grachev's forearm. "I don't want this to go to a grand jury, much less a trial. Bad things happen once a trial starts. Other potential witnesses get bold and come forward when they see the big boss in chains. You really need to deal with this definitively."

"You mean deal with Davidov definitively."

"Yes," the lawyer said. "Kill Davidov and you can go home."

That's what Grachev liked about Kuhl. None of this garbage about I can't hear this or that. Then again, Kuhl had certain tastes that Grachev provided for, tastes that had been videotaped. They made the lawyer his puppet. He had lots of people like that, in high places and low.

"Any idea where he is?"

Grachev nodded. "I'll know soon."

"I'll look forward to reading about it in the papers," Kuhl said. "Maybe our next meeting can be on the golf course."

خطر

Laura kicked off the covers and sat upright on the edge of the bed. Nightmare after nightmare stole sleep from her. Most of them entailed Stone chasing Jonathan or her or both of them. She practically threw up when the news reported that the president had appointed Stone the CIA interim director. Didn't the president know the man was a nutcase? Worse, didn't the president know Stone would kill Jonathan as easily as look at him?

Thoughts of Jonathan sent her hand to her belly. How safe was she? Stone wouldn't dare try to exact revenge against her, would he? Laura shuddered. She'd have to make sure she didn't travel alone until Jonathan returned. *If he returns. No, don't think like that. He'll come home.* With Stone watching his back? Laura forced the bile down. She had to do something, but what? She looked at the Bible on her nightstand. And insignificant as it seemed, she knew that was all she could do.

Laura bowed her head and let God know how she felt, that she needed Jonathan, that their child needed him, and that she was going to trust God to bring him home. Then her prayers moved to Roxanne. That girl was up to something, and Laura needed to find out what. She finished praying and headed for the bathroom.

After a quick shower, Laura pulled on some blue jeans and a T-shirt. She headed downstairs and encountered her mother and Sandra in the kitchen, head-to-head over a cup of coffee. Both of them looked up when she walked in.

"Hi, Laura," Sandra said.

Her mother smiled but said nothing.

"Hi."

"I've just been getting to know your mother."

Laura went over to the counter and took a slice of dry bread out of a bag on the counter. Anything more than bread would have a short stay in her stomach. "That's nice."

"Amazing how God freed her from prison like that."

"He works in strange and mysterious ways."

"Yes," Sandra said. "All those strings Jonathan pulled to get her free and no luck, then suddenly the government just decides to let her go. Wonder what made them change their mind?"

Laura turned and looked out the kitchen window. It was going to be another sunny day. "Just glad they did."

"Quite a coincidence her release coincides with Jonathan going on a business trip."

Laura looked at her mother. Alice McIvor barely shook her head.

Sandra got up from the table and crossed over to her. She took Laura's free hand. "He didn't go on any business trip, did he?"

Thanks, Jonathan. Now I've got to lie to your mother, the

woman who's treated me like a daughter since the day she met me.
Laura took a deep breath. "Jonathan said if anyone asked, he
went to Boise to meet with an equipment supplier."

A tear rolled down Sandra's cheek. "If anyone asked? I'm
his mother, Laura. Where is he?"

Laura shook her head. "I don't know."

"But he's working for the CIA, isn't he?"

Laura nodded her head.

Sandra Corrigan swallowed. "Stone is in charge of the
CIA now. He hates Jonathan."

Laura's voice cracked. "I know."

"Oh, honey, I'm sorry." Sandra put her arms around her.
"This must be much harder on you."

"How do you think I feel?" her mother said from the
kitchen table. "I get out of prison only to find out my freedom
might cost my daughter her husband."

Her mother's self-pity put a stop to any tears. Laura released Sandra. "That's right, Mother. Make this about you."

Her mother leaned back in her chair. "I'm not making it
about me. I'm just letting you know I feel bad about this."

"Right. I think the words you used to describe Jonathan
yesterday were"—she looked at Sandra—"not very nice. Now
you feel bad about it. Nice try."

"I do feel bad."

Laura stepped around Sandra and stood in front of her
mother, hand on hip, foot tapping. "What? That he's gone, or
that it'll be awhile before you know for sure the man who
'caused' Dad's death won't be coming back."

Alice's head fell to her chest. Laura felt Sandra's hand on
her shoulder.

"Laura," Sandra said, "you need to calm down. That's not
what your mother meant."

She resisted the urge to shake off Sandra's hand. "You have no idea what she did to me."

"*She* is your mother," Sandra said. "Wherever Jonathan is, he's there because he wanted to bring you two back together. Don't let past hurts get in the way of what he wanted."

Laura looked down at her mother. How she'd changed! Before prison the woman Laura called Mom had a noble bearing that took years off her true age. The woman staring at the tabletop looked like she'd left sixty years of age behind, instead of it being in her near future. Laura felt an urge to reach down and stroke her mom's snowy-white hair. Her hand moved then, but something deep down grabbed it.

Thoughts of being torn from her sleep, the sanctity of her bedroom destroyed. Overnight, everything had been ripped from her. The aching loneliness of losing everyone she loved, years of feeling like a ghost moving through the world moved her hand back to her side. "I'm going for a walk."

Laura turned and brushed past Sandra on the way to the mudroom.

"Laura, you have to deal with this."

"Not right now, Mom."

"Mom?" she heard Alice McIvor repeat.

Laura paused at the entrance to the mudroom and turned. "That's right, Alice. I called her Mom. I've been calling her Mom since I got married, because that's who she is. My mother."

Alice looked up at her, eyes glistening. "Honey, what happened doesn't change anything. I'm your mother."

Laura heard the little voice that said, 'Don't say it,' but the words were well on their way. "No, you're the woman who brought me into this world. Nothing more. Sandra has treated me like a daughter since day one. You could take lessons from her." Laura continued on into the mudroom, slipped on a pair of loafers, and burst outside, slamming the door behind her.

Normally entranced by the beauty of the Corrigan farm, she felt blinding tears fill her eyes. She stormed off the porch and headed toward the barn. The horses were always good listeners.

Why, oh, why had she prayed for her mother to be freed? The woman deserved to be in prison for what she'd done. She put a hand on her stomach and fell into a slow walk. The answer was under her hand. Once she knew she was pregnant, Laura developed selective memory. She wanted her mother so badly that she only remembered the good times. Now that Alice was here in the flesh, all the anger and pain had come back. Laura had a lot of hurt, and at the moment, all she wanted to do was hurt back.

As she got closer to the barn, Laura slowed at the sound of voices. Roxanne was in there with her two friends. She turned to pass on the other side of the barn to avoid having to explain her tears, but Rudy poked his head out the door of the tack room and gave a short welcoming bark. "Great," Laura whispered.

Roxanne's head popped out after Rudy's. "Hey, Laura." The teen's smile dropped. "What's the matter?"

"Nothing," Laura said, wiping at her tears.

Roxanne turned around and spoke into the tack room. "Back in a minute." She walked over to Laura, her eyes searching. "You okay?"

Laura forced a smile to her face. "Yeah."

Roxanne put her hand on Laura's shoulder. The teen was four inches taller than she was. "So you always go for a morning walk with puffy eyes and a runny nose?"

"Sure, helps clear the sinuses."

"Uh-huh. Jon didn't go on a business trip, did he?"

"Of course he did," Laura said a little too quickly.

Roxanne dropped her hand. "You guys had a fight, didn't you? I might just be a kid, but I'm not stupid. The way all you adults have been acting, I knew something was up."

I wish that were all it was, Laura thought. "I had a fight, but it was with my mother, not Jonathan."

Roxanne lifted her eyebrows. "Your mom? Why? I mean, you wanted so desperately for her to be here, and now she is. What happened?"

"It's complicated," Laura said. "If you don't mind, I'd like to leave it at that."

Roxanne shrugged. "If that's what you want. But remember, I am your sister. Sort of. If you ever want to talk."

Laura smiled. Her relationship with Roxanne was a bit unusual. Technically the girl was her sister-in-law, but nineteen years separated them. She tended to see Roxanne more like a niece, although Jonathan treated her like a sister. "Sure. Speaking of talking, I'm a little confused about your friends."

Roxanne shifted her weight. "What about them?"

"Well, you mentioned something last night about Michelle being Connie's cousin from Hong Kong. You said that's why she doesn't speak very much English, right?"

"That's right. Why?"

"Then why does she speak to Michelle in Mandarin?"

Roxanne gnawed on the corner of her lip. "What do you mean?"

"The people in Hong Kong normally speak Cantonese. The people from mainland China speak Mandarin."

Roxanne looked toward the ground. "You speak Chinese?"

"It's a great language for encryption," Laura said. "I'm nowhere near fluent, but I can tell the difference between the two dialects." She put her fingers under Roxanne's chin and lifted the girl's head. "Michelle is from mainland China. What's going on?"

"It's complicated. If you don't mind, I would like to leave it at that."

Laura chuckled. "Nice try, kid. There's a big difference between a fight with my mom and a girl from mainland China sleeping in the house. I watch the news, Roxanne. She's from that ship the DEA raided, isn't she?"

"Yeah."

"Why is she here?"

Roxanne shrugged. "We ran into her last night when we were witnessing. A guy was hassling her, and she had nowhere to go."

"She's in this country illegally," Laura said. "We have to tell the police."

Roxanne shook her head and stepped back. "We can't. They'll just send her back to China."

Laura let her arm drop to her side. "Probably. But she shouldn't have tried to come here illegally. She's the author of her own misfortune."

Roxanne's face turned red, and she tightened her hands into fists. "She didn't try to come here. She was sold to smugglers by her parents and brought here against her will. They're going to force her to be a prostitute. If she goes back to China, they'll kill her. If she's lucky."

"She's probably lying to you."

Roxanne shook her head sharply. "She's not lying. The first time I saw her, some Chinese guy was pretending to be a cop arresting her. He would've gotten her, too, if Danny hadn't chased him."

Laura lifted her eyebrows. "The same guy who shot at Danny?"

"Yeah," Roxanne said.

Laura took a deep breath. *What to do.* "We can't keep her here forever. Sooner or later, the authorities are going to have to get involved."

"I know that," Roxanne said. "The reason I brought her here was because I figured Jon would know what to do."

"What do you think Jonathan can do?"

Roxanne shrugged. "Apparently plenty. It looks like he got your mother out of prison. Surely he can help out a poor Chinese girl—who, by the way, also happens to be a Christian."

Laura looked past Roxanne at the barn. She understood Roxanne's strong feelings to protect this girl. One thing Roxanne and Laura shared with Michelle was time spent on the run with no one to turn to. "Okay, we'll hide her until Jonathan gets home."

"Thanks," Roxanne said, throwing her arms around Laura.

"It's the right thing to do," Laura said. *Besides, now God has to bring Jonathan back, if not for my sake, for Michelle's.* Without the connections of a former CIA agent, her next stop would be China.

خطر

Pounding music from a boom box and powerful lights on stands battered him, but there was nothing Jonathan could do about it. They were on the other side of the room, and they'd shackled him like a convict. Leg irons and handcuffs connected with a chain gave him only enough movement to use the bucket they'd left for a privy. He couldn't cover his ears, and the three-foot chain tethered to his foot and the wall kept him from getting at the boom box and lights and breaking them to pieces.

The only protection he could give his ears was to lie on

the floor and press one ear against his shoulder. The discomfort, noise, and lights deprived him of sleep, which is what they wanted. Sleep-deprived people were more likely to talk.

The music wasn't even any good. The CD playing over and over again was some kind of rap artist. He would've preferred they pound on his head with a hammer rather than force him to endure that garbage. He laughed out loud. Jonathan had become his father. He remembered his dad telling him that rock music was nothing but a bunch of noise, and now he felt exactly the same way about the current generation's choice of music. But unlike his father, Jonathan knew he was right.

The aggravation soon pushed out the mirth of his thoughts. Agents were trained to endure torture, but nothing fully prepared someone for the real thing. The biggest enemy was despair. Hussein could do anything he wanted, and Jonathan had no power to prevent it. He had no control over his destiny. This was as close to hell as a human being could come in this world. He was completely alone, completely helpless.

No, that wasn't true. God had to be with him, because He promised to always be with him. But while he couldn't see God, any minute that madman could walk in the door and put a bullet in his head. Jonathan pulled at the handcuffs and pounded his feet against the wall then started to yell, just to hear something other than that incessant beat.

危险 خطر ОПАСНОПЬ

TWELVE

S am pulled onto Interstate 5. No one appeared to be tailing him. Ian Moody of the U.S. Attorney's Office sat in the passenger seat. He glanced in the rearview mirror. In the backseat sat the court reporter, a petite brunette named Jennifer Gray.

"He changed his mind?" Sam said. "He's willing to give his deposition?"

"Yeah," Moody said. "I guess the deputy marshals worked on him all night, freaking him out that the marshals who hid people were handpicked and could be trusted to keep their mouth shut. You couldn't trust a court reporter to do the same. He was putting his life in danger by insisting his deposition take place after relocation."

"Good. That way if anything happens to him, we've still got the deposition."

"So where's your partner?"

"Sick. Flu or something."

"Flu? It's summer."

"Allergies then. She really didn't say."

Sam did a few stunts to shake tails as they traveled up to Everett, but nothing indicated they were being followed. Even though they would be moving Davidov today, he saw no reason to ease up on security. "The exit to Everett is coming up. Get ready."

Both Moody and Gray checked their seat belts and braced themselves. Sam took the off-ramp then slammed on the brakes. The antilock braking system kicked in, and the pedal chattered as he maneuvered to the side of the road. The minivan that followed them down the exit ramp blasted its horn and shot past them. Several preteen girls wearing baseball caps stared as they passed.

"Not likely Russian mafia," Moody said.

"Unless they've taken to recruiting girls' baseball teams."

"Wouldn't put it past them," Moody said, "but I think we're safe today."

Sam guided the car through Everett, stopping at Starbucks before going on to the safe house. Two dark blue Caprices were parked on the street in front of the house. "Looks like the relocation team is already here."

"Guess we should've brought more coffee."

"Yeah," Sam said. He glanced in the rearview mirror at Jennifer. The pretty young woman could only be in her early twenties. "You understand that everything you hear in there is absolutely confidential?"

"Yes, sir."

"You never repeat it to anyone. Not to your coworkers, not to your mother, your priest, or whoever shares your pillow at night."

Her dark eyes flashed. "No one shares my pillow, and I can keep a secret."

"Okay. Just want to be clear."

"We're clear, sir."

"Then let's get this done."

They exited the car. Only midmorning, and the temperature had to be in the mid-80s.

Jennifer got her recording equipment from the trunk, and Moody balanced the tray of coffee in one hand and his briefcase in the other. Sam needed to keep both hands free in case the unthinkable happened. They walked up to the front door of the house. Sam surveyed the quiet street. Nothing looked out of place, but his stomach felt like a basketball game was going on inside it. No way anyone could have followed them. No way at all.

He rapped on the door and stood in front of the peephole. A couple seconds later, the dead bolt lock snapped open and a chain lock slid off its holder. U.S. Marshal Erin Klyne opened the door wearing a bulletproof vest.

"Ah, the coffee man."

"That'd be Mr. Coffee Man to you," Sam said. "Unless you want to go without."

Erin gave a short bow and stepped aside. "Please enter, Mr. Coffee Man, both you and your most worthy guests."

"You guys must be going stir crazy," Sam said as he, Moody, and Gray stepped into the house.

Erin lifted an eyebrow. "You think? We're still trying to figure out if it was me or Dixon who got us babysitting duty. Even transporting prisoners is better than this, although I prefer catching them." Erin locked the door behind them then took the tray of coffee from Moody.

"Look at it as sort of a mini vacation," Sam said as they headed down the hall.

"Well, next time I go on holidays, the safe house better

be on a beach in Mexico."

"If it is, I'll be doing the protection duty myself," Sam said.

"Don't worry, it'll never happen."

They stepped into the living room, and Erin set the tray down on a worn walnut coffee table.

Davidov sat in the recliner, but Sam's attention was focused on two older men in dark gray slacks, shirts and ties, and bulletproof vests. Both had short graying hair and humorless faces—the relocation team.

The men stood, and Sam extended his hand. "Sam Perkins, FBI."

"Jake Pannett, U.S. Marshals Service." The closest man shook his hand. Jake's weathered face was a collection of scars, and his grip was restrained. If he had wanted to, he could probably crush Sam's hand. This guy had to be ex-military.

"Hi," Sam said, releasing Pannett's hand.

"Terry Shaffer," the next marshal said. Terry looked more like a guy who spent his days golfing, but his grip was firm.

"Nice to meet you." Perkins pointed to Moody and Jennifer. "Ian Moody, Assistant U.S. Attorney, and this court reporter will remain anonymous for security reasons." After everyone shook hands, Sam added, "Now, I hate to be picky, but let's all exchange IDs."

"Wouldn't have it any other way," Pannett said. Everyone but Jennifer produced their IDs.

Sam turned to Erin. "Do you know these men as U.S. Marshals?"

"Yes."

He turned to Dixon. "Do you confirm this?"

"Yes."

Sam knew he was being a little overcautious, but after the phony lawyer incident with Lo, he wasn't taking any chances.

He glanced over at Davidov, who was looking a little nervous. "How are you doing?"

"I'm bored, too." He stood up and grabbed himself a coffee, then returned to the recliner.

"I'd like to feel sorry for you," Sam said over his own coffee, "but I won't. Just be glad we're keeping our side of the deal and not turning you loose. I'm sure Grachev has a bullet ready with your name on it, if he could find you. Ready for your deposition?"

Davidov nodded and used the remote to flick off the TV.

"Okay then. You've met Mr. Moody from the U.S. Attorney's Office before. He'll be asking the questions. This young lady is a court reporter, and she'll be recording everything you say."

Davidov looked up at Jennifer with a wolfish grin. "It's been a long time since I've seen such a pretty face."

"Hey," Erin said.

Davidov ignored her. "It wouldn't hurt if you told me your first name?"

Jennifer started to open her mouth, but Sam held up his hand. "You don't need to know that." He turned to Dixon Croin, who was also watching Jennifer. "Croin, how about a chair?"

"Yes, sir," he said with a smile on his face.

Sam made a mental note to bring a more matronly court reporter next time.

Croin brought in a kitchen chair. Jennifer set up her portable equipment while Moody sat on the edge of the couch closest to Davidov's chair and put his briefcase on the table. Shaffer and Pannett stood by the door to the kitchen, and Sam leaned against the wall near the entrance to the living room.

Moody looked over at Jennifer. "Ready?"

She nodded.

Moody pulled a black folder from his briefcase. "Start recording," he said to Jennifer. "This is the deposition of Yuri Davidov in the matter of the murder of FBI Special Agent Paul Newberg. State your full name."

"My name is Yuri Davidov. For the record, I am giving information in exchange for being safely relocated."

Sam had to hand it to Davidov. The deal was now part of the official record. No way they could renege and still use Davidov's deposition.

"Fine, Mr. Davidov," Moody said. "The U.S. Attorney's Office concurs that the government has agreed to put Mr. Davidov into witness protection provided he cooperates fully, makes truthful statements, and, when required to do so, testifies in court. Is that your understanding of the arrangement, Mr. Davidov?"

"Yes."

"Then let us begin. What is your relationship to Josef Grachev?"

"I was his right-hand man."

Moody removed an eight-by-ten photograph from his folder. "Is this Josef Grachev?"

Davidov looked at the picture. "Yes, that's Josef."

Moody handed the picture to Jennifer. "Please certify that this is the picture he identified as Josef Grachev."

Jennifer took the picture and wrote on it, then signed it and handed it back. The certification process was crucial; otherwise some defense lawyer would argue that the Grachev Davidov identified was someone other than his client. If for some unfortunate reason Davidov wasn't alive to testify, the court reporter could verify who he meant.

"What is Josef Grachev's business?"

"He owns lots of businesses. Nightclubs, restaurants, furniture stores."

"Thank you. What about illegal businesses."

Davidov grinned. Perkins wanted to offer to smash his teeth down his throat, but Jennifer would record anything said in the room.

"Drugs, prostitution, and people smuggling."

"Who supplies the drugs?"

"The Chinese."

"Which Chinese?" Moody said.

Davidov looked up at Sam. "You'll take me somewhere safe today, right?"

Sam nodded. "After we're done here, these men will relocate you. None of us will have a clue where you are."

"Okay. Josef gets the drugs from Billy Heng."

Moody dug into his folder and produced another eight-by-ten. "When you say Billy Heng, are you referring to this man?"

"Yes."

Moody went through the same procedure with that picture with Jennifer.

"How does Grachev pay Heng for the drugs?"

"Transportation services and cash."

"What kind of transportation services?"

"Grachev has connections in Russian shipping. He lets Heng smuggle people on Russian cargo ships in exchange for drugs."

"Is that all they smuggle on the cargo ships?"

"No, they smuggle drugs, too."

"You recently identified for the DEA and FBI a container that was supposed to have drugs in it, didn't you?"

"Yes."

"That container did not contain drugs but people. Did

you lie to the DEA and FBI?"

"No."

"You maintain that to the best of your knowledge drugs were in that container?"

"Yes."

"What kind of drugs were supposed to be in there?"

"Heroin."

"How do you explain the absence of the drugs?"

Davidov shrugged. "Josef must've suspected that I turned, and he switched the drugs for people."

"Why would he do that?"

"So you wouldn't believe me."

"And you truly had no idea there would be people in that container?"

Davidov shook his head. "None."

"Let's talk about the murder of Special Agent Paul Newberg, who was working undercover under the alias Derek Pausini."

Davidov shifted in the recliner.

"When did you first meet Agent Newberg?"

"Josef introduced me to him about a year ago."

"And how did Newberg come to meet Josef?"

"Newberg worked for one of Josef's dealers, Marty Rowland. He found out Marty was skimming and told Josef."

"When you say Marty Rowland, is this the man you mean?" Moody showed Davidov another photograph, then repeated the certification process when Davidov confirmed his identity.

"And Josef rewarded Newberg with Rowland's territory?" Moody said.

Davidov shook his head. "Not just for that. Newberg killed Rowland, too."

Moody looked up from his notes. "Excuse me?"

"Newberg killed Rowland."

He looked up at Sam. "Your undercover agent killed Rowland?"

Sam looked away for a second. "Newberg's report said it was self-defense."

Davidov scoffed.

"You don't agree?" Moody said.

"I was there. We went out on Josef's boat one night, and Josef confronted Marty. Marty said he wasn't skimming, but Newberg had proof. Grachev pulled his pistol to shoot Rowland, but Newberg said, 'Let me.' He shot Rowland twice and pushed his body into the ocean, then chucked in the gun."

Moody rubbed his brow. "You realize if you're lying our deal's off."

"I'm not lying. Why would I make up a lie like this? You want the truth, I'm giving you the truth."

Moody turned to Sam. "Any comment?"

Sam shook his head. "Our account is different." At least the official one; what really happened was a whole different matter.

Moody pushed out a deep breath. "Okay then. So according to you, Newberg killed Rowland. This is how Josef came to trust him?"

"Yes," Davidov said.

"And Newberg took over Rowland's territory?"

"Yes."

"And how did he do?"

"Grachev was really pleased. More money came in than when Marty had it."

"So what went wrong? How did Grachev uncover that Newberg was an FBI agent?"

Sam leaned forward. This was something he wanted to know, too.

"Grachev's accountant figured it out."

"The accountant?" Perkins said.

Moody shot him a sharp look. "I ask the questions, Agent Perkins. How did the accountant figure it out?"

"The accountant keeps track of the serial numbers on the money coming in and going out."

Sam started to feel nauseous.

"One day the accountant checked the money Newberg brought in. A bunch of the numbers matched the numbers of money the feds seized three years ago at the Mexican border. Newberg paid for drugs with Grachev's own money. Josef knew Newberg was working with the FBI or DEA."

Sam closed his eyes and shook his head. Poor Newberg.

"Who's the accountant?" Moody said.

Davidov shrugged. "I don't know."

"Mr. Davidov, our deal is contingent upon your full cooperation. What is the accountant's name?"

Davidov held out his hands. "I can't tell you what I don't know. It's a big secret. Only Josef knows who the accountant is."

"But the accountant figured out Newberg was undercover?"

"Josef told me the accountant figured it out."

"So Josef Grachev knew Newberg was a law enforcement officer before he killed him."

"Yes."

"And it was Josef Grachev who killed Newberg? Not someone else—perhaps you?"

"It wasn't me."

"You saw Grachev do it?"

"Yes."

"How do we know you're not lying? You were Grachev's

right-hand man. If he told you to, you would've done it—right?"

"Sure, but I didn't," Davidov said.

"Can you prove it?"

"Yeah."

"How?"

"Because of the way Newberg died. I had nothing against him; I even liked the guy. If Josef had told me to kill him, I would've just shot him, not put him through the horrible death Josef did. He took the betrayal personally, and because of that, he took care of Newberg personally."

"Stop recording," Moody said. He looked up at Sam. "Does this seem credible to you?"

Perkins nodded. The FBI's investigation concluded Grachev did the deed himself based on the mutilation of Newberg's body. The viciousness of the attack indicated it was a crime of deep emotion. Now they had an eyewitness's testimony.

"Okay then," Moody said. "We're all done. Marshals, please take Mr. Davidov into protective custody and relocate him." He turned to Yuri. "I strongly suggest you follow the marshals' instructions to the letter. When we lose a witness, 99 percent of the time it's because they do something stupid like phone a relative or get their picture in the paper. We'd like to keep you alive."

Davidov furrowed his forehead. "What happened to the other 1 percent?"

Moody smiled. "Occasionally we make a mistake. You're pretty important, so we've been extra careful."

"Okay, Mr. Davidov," Pannett said. "Let's get ready. Stand up."

Davidov got up from his recliner, and Pannett tossed him a bulletproof vest. "Put this on."

Davidov looked at the vest warily but slipped it on. "If no one knows I'm here, why this?"

Pannett tightened the Velcro straps on Davidov's vest. "We like to be ready for the 1 percent. Now this is how it works. I'll be on your left, and Marshal Shaffer will be on your right. Marshal Croin will take point, and Marshal Klyne will follow. You'll make a very hard target in the highly unlikely event Grachev knows where you are."

Davidov tilted his head. "If Josef knows where I am, then I'm dead."

"I'll check outside," Sam said, and went down the hall and stepped outside into a wall of sweltering heat. Being close to the ocean, Everett suffered from high humidity on hot days. Sam stripped off his suit jacket and slung it over his shoulder.

He walked halfway down the sidewalk toward the street then looked to the left. A few vehicles were parked along the street, but none with motors running or gunmen hanging out the window. He checked to the right and saw nothing amiss and returned to the house. The marshals were waiting by the front door with Davidov.

"Looks clear."

"Let's go," Pannett said.

As if they were guarding the president, the marshals made a human shield around Davidov. They moved out of the house and stepped lively to the lead Caprice. A gentle ocean breeze came up from behind and washed over Sam, giving him relief from the heat. Pannett opened the door for Davidov, and Yuri bent over to get in. Sam heard a spitting sound from the left and watched Davidov crumple to the asphalt.

خطر

Acting CIA Director Elijah Stone leaned back in the leather

chair and surveyed the office. Too bad Bolton wouldn't hurry up and die so he could remodel. Using Bolton's office felt like sleeping in someone else's bed. It was comfortable enough; it just wasn't his bed. It didn't have his personal mementos, pictures of him shaking important hands. The intercom buzzed.

"Director Lavigne to see you," the secretary's voice said.

Stone pressed the intercom button. "Send him in."

Lavigne entered carrying a file folder. "Director."

"Have a seat," Stone said, indicating one of the chairs in front of his desk.

Lavigne sat and placed the folder on Stone's desk.

"Let's hear what you've got," Stone said.

"Well, unfortunately these terrorists are smarter than average. They made their demands to our Beirut section chief instead of going to the media."

Stone cursed. "I was hoping they'd make a big public demand. Then the president would have to back up his nonegotiation stance, and it'd be his fault if Corrigan dies. I'm assuming the section chief disavowed Corrigan."

Lavigne nodded. "We're not admitting he's ours, but they made a demand anyway."

"What do they want?"

"They gave him five names."

"And what did the chief say?"

"He laughed and told them there'd be hockey in hell before anyone would be released."

Stone grinned. "And they left in a huff."

"No, they switched the demand to two million dollars. He told them he'd talk to us before giving an answer."

"Great. They would ask for the one thing we can give. Tell him to open with telling them he's not ours, but because he's an American, we'll pay a hundred thousand."

"For that amount, they may just kill him," Lavigne said. "How are we going to explain that to the president? Corrigan is a national hero."

Stone gritted his teeth. "He's a traitor; the president just doesn't know it. Tell the chief he can go five hundred thousand, but any more than that, he has to get back to us."

"We've also got the problem with Corrigan's wife. She knows he's on a mission. Sooner or later she's going to start making noise if he doesn't come back. It's not like she can't get a national audience."

Stone scratched his chin. "I think the best way to handle her is with the truth."

Lavigne raised an eyebrow. "The truth?"

"Sure. She knows the president's stance. If she goes public, then the president knows, and no one can do anything. If she keeps her mouth shut, she has our assurances we'll do what we can to get him out. Her best hope is us."

"Which is really no hope at all?" Lavigne said.

"I wouldn't say that," Stone said. "Sure, I hate Corrigan, but if we can get him out, we will, if only to avoid having to answer a whole bunch of questions on how we lost him. But my primary objective is still to get intelligence on as many terrorists as we can. The longer we drag this out, the more we learn about them."

"So, who'll call his wife?"

Stone smiled. "Oh, I'll take care of that detail. It'll be a pleasure letting Mrs. Corrigan know her husband is in the hands of terrorists. Anything else?"

"Yeah, and it's not good."

"What?"

"You know that brunette working the satellite surveillance?"

"I noticed her," Stone said.

"Well, since this mission was set up by Bolton, I did a little background checking on the participants. She and Corrigan have a history."

Stone slumped back in the chair. "Just what we need. A participant loyal to Corrigan. Any indications she's gone outside the agency?"

"None. In fact, she seems to be on board with the program."

Stone chuckled. "Maybe he dumped her back then and she's enjoying this."

"To be so lucky."

"I don't like to leave anything up to luck. Usual program—monitor her phones, e-mail, Internet traffic, the works. Have her followed. If she mails something, dig it out of the box. If she contacts anyone who might be an ally to Corrigan, cut off the communication."

"Yes, sir."

"Anything else?"

"That's it," Lavigne said.

"Okay then. Keep me posted."

Rich Lavigne got up and headed for the door.

"Wait a second, Rich," Stone said. "Initiate the same program for Corrigan's wife before I call her. She is quite resourceful."

危险 خطر ОПАСНОТЬ

THIRTEEN

S am dropped to the ground and drew his weapon. The marshals dragged Davidov behind the Caprice, a trail of blood following. It had been a head shot. Sam looked around in time to see Moody appear at the safe house's door.

"What happened?" Moody said.

"Davidov is dead!" Sam shouted. "Stay back and call 911. Tell them we've got a sniper and to cordon off the area. You two stay inside."

"You got it." Moody retreated into the house.

Keeping low, Sam charged across the yard and took up position behind a car parked in the neighboring driveway. He searched the street for the sniper. The gunman could have shot from anywhere. A roof, a tree, behind a car.

Footsteps charged up from behind him, and Pannett appeared at his shoulder. "The sniper's gone."

"How do you know that?" Sam said.

"Because it's standard protocol. Kill, then move. If he wanted more than Davidov, he would've kept shooting. He's done his job. He's moving now. If we're going to have any hope of catching him, we've got to get going."

Sam looked at Pannett. The marshal's eyes were like steel bearings. "How do you know this?"

Pannett's mouth formed a straight line. "Trust me, I know. Based on the wound, he was at our level, probably hiding behind a tree. My guess is he shot from three hundred yards. Since I didn't see any vehicle pull into the street after the shot, my guess is that right now he's cutting through yards to the next street where his escape vehicle is. This guy will have everything worked out. He probably figured we would stay hunkered down, afraid of another shot, which in turn gives him time to escape. If we guess which way and head him off, we have a chance. Left or right? Your call."

"Left," Sam said.

"Fine. You head back down and block off the entrance to the street. I'll go up and try to flush him to you. Hopefully we've got the right street."

"If not?" Sam said.

Pannett shrugged. "He gets away. Now let's go."

Sam charged to his Buick while Pannett jumped into the Caprice. The smoke of rubber billowed out behind the marshal's car as he did a U-turn and headed in the direction of the shot. Sam hit his lights and siren and surged forward. Of all the days to be sick, Ali had picked this one. *Ali picked this day to be sick.* A sickening thought flashed through Sam's mind. He pushed it aside for now. He wanted to catch the sniper who killed Davidov.

Sam reached the end of the street, and his tires screeched as he turned right. He floored the accelerator to the next street, and the car shuddered to a stop at the head of the street. Halfway down the street he could see a car speeding away from him. It all came down to a race between Pannett and the sniper's car to the other end of the street.

Taillights flashed, tires screeched, and blue smoke flooded from the fleeing car as it skidded sideways and stopped. Sam could see the flashing grill lights of Pannett's Caprice racing toward the sniper's car. Pannett stopped and jumped out of his car. He chased the sniper to the houses on Sam's left. Sam jumped back into his Buick and gunned it.

Ten seconds later he brought his car to a stop next to the sniper's car. He jumped out and ran in the direction Pannett had gone. A tall wooden gate at the side of a single-level house still swung on its hinges. Sam charged through it and into a small backyard just in time to see Pannett disappear over the top of a six-foot privacy fence.

Sam stopped, took a couple of deep breaths, and then sprinted to the fence. When he was six feet from the fence, two gunshots changed his plans. Sam put the brakes on and stumbled into the fence. No way he was going over that fence until he knew who had done the shooting.

"Pannett! You all right?"

"Yeah," the marshal called back, "but our suspect is gone."

"Great," Sam said. He grabbed a lawn chair and dragged it over to the fence. Sam stood on it and peered over. Crumpled on the ground lay a man in his midthirties, a pool of blood forming underneath him and a gun in his hand. "Gone?"

Pannett shrugged. "Well, he certainly isn't in our world anymore."

"What happened?"

Pannett pointed to a six-foot, black wrought iron gate with a locking mechanism. "I pulled him down from that gate. When he hit the ground, he pulled a gun. I didn't have any choice."

Throughout his career, Sam had been present at a half-dozen shootings. Some cops were despondent, some seemed to enjoy it, and Pannett seemed to think it was all in a day's work.

"I really would've liked to have kept him alive," Sam said.

"If I'd had a choice, I would've taken it, but you know this isn't like the movies. Kicking the gun out of the guy's hand doesn't work. He gets a shot off, and if I'm lucky, I spend the rest of my life with a colostomy bag. If I'm not lucky, I end up wherever he went."

"I know, I know," Sam said. "But with Davidov gone, our case against Grachev just went south."

"Davidov might not be dead," Pannett said.

"What?"

"He was breathing when I saw him last."

خطر

Ali opened the door to her apartment and dragged herself in. Maybe she should get a cat. Some days it would be nice to have someone to greet her, even if that someone's affection was totally contingent upon being fed and scratched regularly. Somehow in climbing the ladder, she had forgotten to make any friends. Acquaintances, yes, but no friends. Not the go-to-coffee-and-pour-your-heart-out kind of friends.

Funny, but Sam was probably the closest she had to that kind of friend. Ali let out a short laugh. "Yeah, I'm sure he'd be able to relate."

All Ali wanted to do was crawl into bed and die—she felt that bad—but she still had a phone call to make. She glanced at the wall clock, but it wouldn't matter what time it was in Moscow. She was to call anytime.

خطر

In the short time it took Sam to get back, the Everett police had already erected a roadblock at the head of the safe house's street. Safe house. What a joke that had turned out to be.

How had Grachev found it? Only six people besides him knew the location: the marshals, Moody, and Ali. Even Davidov didn't know because they blindfolded him before they took him out there. That left two possibilities. They had been followed, or someone was a traitor.

Sam shook his head. No. Everyone had been checked out.

But Ali didn't come today, did she? a little voice whispered in his ear. *Ali speaks Russian; isn't that convenient? What do you know about her?*

"Maybe not enough," Sam muttered as he pulled up to the roadblock. He flashed his ID and drove through to the safe house, where two more police cars were parked. Four officers were keeping back any onlookers. Croin and Shaffer still maintained a protective shield around Davidov while Erin Klyne crouched down beside him. Sam got out of the car and ran up to them.

"Is he alive?"

Erin Klyne was pressing a cloth against both sides of Davidov's head.

Croin nodded. "Yeah, but don't get your hopes up. One shot to the temple, in and out. Probably not much left in there. Just his brain stem keeping him breathing."

"Maybe not. You called an ambulance?"

"Yes," Klyne said. "Should be here any second."

Just then an ambulance appeared at the head of the road, and the police waved it through. It pulled close, and two paramedics jumped out and rushed toward them with their medical kits. "What have we got?" the first one said, a muscular black man in his late twenties. His partner, a thin white guy in his early twenties, relieved Klyne at Davidov's head.

"Head shot," Croin said. "It's not pretty."

"Okay, we'll take it from here."

The three marshals and Perkins took a few steps back to give the paramedics room to work.

"Did you catch the sniper?" Shaffer said.

"Yeah," Sam said.

"Good." Shaffer holstered his weapon, as did Croin. "After we work on him awhile, maybe we can turn him against whoever hired him."

"That's going to be a little tough."

Shaffer curled up his lip. "They're all tough at first, but he'll crack."

"He's not tough; he's dead."

"What? How?"

"He pulled a gun, and Pannett had to shoot him."

"Why am I not surprised?"

"What's that supposed to mean?" Sam said.

Shaffer shrugged. "Nothing."

"I want to know what you mean."

"You'll have to find out on your own. Pannett's my partner, and I've said too much." He turned toward the house.

Perkins grabbed Shaffer's arm. "And I'm an FBI agent investigating a crime. Withholding information from me is a federal offense. What is it about your partner I need to know?" Sam released him.

Shaffer kicked at the asphalt. "Well, it's not like you'd have any trouble finding out. I've been a marshal for twenty years. Only once did I shoot a suspect, and that was during an armed standoff. Pannett has killed eight suspects and wounded six in the last ten years. Before he was a marshal, he was a cop. I'm not sure about his record then."

"Why has he still got a badge?" Sam said.

"He's been cleared in every incident, all shootings justified. They can't fire him for doing his job. He just seems to get in the thick of it a lot."

"He better not have been trigger-happy this time," Sam said. "From the looks of things, Davidov is going to spend the rest of his life, however long that turns out to be, in a vegetable garden. I really could've used that sniper."

The black paramedic called to Erin. "There's antiseptic foam in the bag there. I suggest you clean your hands ASAP."

Erin dug out the bottle of antiseptic and rinsed her hands like Lady Macbeth trying to wash off the blood of her murdered husband. She got up and stood next to them, her lower lip trembling. "They talk about it in training, but it isn't the same."

Even in the hot sun, Erin's face was pale.

"You get used to it after you see a few," Shaffer said.

"Look, everyone back to the house," Sam said. "There's nothing more we can do here." He looked at Croin and nodded toward Erin. Croin nodded back and took his partner's elbow.

"I'll join you in a second," Sam said.

The three marshals walked back to the house, where Moody and Jennifer waited by the door. Hopefully they had listened to him and stayed inside while he and Pannett chased the sniper.

Sam crouched down next to Davidov and held out his badge to the paramedics. "Special Agent Perkins, FBI."

"Swanson," the black paramedic said. "Can you move back, Agent Perkins? We've got a patient to save."

"Keeping him alive won't save him. Give it your valiant best, but when you get to that hospital, make him look dead—a sheet over his head and the whole nine yards."

"I can't do that."

"If you want to save him, you will. The guy who ordered this hit will try again if he thinks this man survived. Get him to the hospital and log him in as John Doe, DOA. Pass on my instructions to the doctor; then as best as you can, be discreet about keeping him alive."

Swanson looked at his partner. "I don't know."

"Play it by the book then," Sam said. "Just keep this in mind. The next time you're picking up some kid's body off the streets because of an overdose, playing by the book kept the guy selling those drugs out of jail."

Swanson looked back at Perkins. "This guy being dead is that important?"

"No, this guy looking dead is that important."

Swanson nodded. "You got it. He died on the way to the hospital, which is probably what will happen anyway."

"You don't think he'll make it?"

Swanson shook his head. "Only thing keeping him alive is the brain stem. It just hasn't figured out yet that nobody else is home. We'll do our best, but short of a miracle, he'll be a true DOA."

"Do your best then." Sam stood and jogged to the house, where he found everyone assembled in the living room.

Erin Klyne rested on the couch next to Jennifer. The men were all standing and watching out the living room window.

"I think it best we keep the curtains closed," Sam said and herded the men aside while he pulled them shut. "The fewer people who know who's in here, the better." He turned to Erin. "How are you doing?"

She held up her hands. "What if he has something? What if I got it? What was I thinking?"

"You were thinking you wanted to save a life. We'll have his blood tested."

"Can you do that without his consent?"

"He's a witness in federal protection. Right now we're his

momma and poppa, but that probably won't matter pretty quick here."

"Why?"

"Paramedics doubt he'll make it."

"Not that he'd do us any good with what's left of his brain," Moody said.

"You got that right," Sam said. Deep down he hoped something was left of Davidov that could testify in court. "Here's where we're at. Davidov is as good as dead, but we do have his testimony." He turned to Moody. "Is it enough on its own?"

Moody shook his head. "Maybe for a grand jury, but we'd never get a conviction. We still can't get around the container, and the defense will make a big deal about not being able to cross-examine Davidov. We need another witness. The accountant he talked about would be nice."

"As long as Grachev is in hiding, it's going to be hard to get anything. We need to make Grachev believe he's safe, that he's accomplished his goal so he'll come out of hiding." Sam rubbed his face and looked at the empty recliner for a few seconds. "Okay, this is our story. Davidov refused to talk until he was relocated." He looked at Jennifer. "You got absolutely nothing. When you go back to the office, if anyone asks you, tell them the day was a complete waste."

Moody lifted his hand slightly. "Uh, Special Agent Perkins? Have you considered that one of us might be working for Grachev? If so, it's only a matter of time before he knows this lady has Davidov's deposition. How long do you think she'll live if that happens?"

Jennifer looked at Moody and turned pale.

"We'll have to put her in protective custody," Sam said.

"You mean like Davidov?" Jennifer said.

Sam scratched his chin. "Look, it's highly unlikely that

anyone here is a traitor. It's more likely one of us was followed."

"But you're not sure?"

Sam shook his head. "Not 100 percent—no."

Jennifer looked at each one of them as if she expected one of them to pull out a gun and shoot her. "Then I'll hide myself."

"You'd be safer in protective custody," Croin said.

Jennifer smirked. "You'll forgive me if I don't jump at that offer."

Sam pursed his lips then nodded. "It's probably best you hide yourself. I'm sure the marshals have a bunch of cash they were going to give Davidov to help set up his new life. They can give it to you. Pay cash everywhere you go."

"And how will I know when it's safe to come out?"

Sam took out his wallet and removed a business card. "This is my boss's number. He didn't know where Davidov was hidden. Call him in about a week to see what you should do. Besides, we should know pretty soon whether it was one of us."

"How?" Moody said.

"Well, we're the only ones who know Davidov gave a deposition. If one of us is working for Grachev, they'll tell him and he'll stay in hiding."

"Or they could say nothing in order to protect themselves," Moody said.

"I don't think they'd do that with Grachev as a boss," Sam said. "In fact, if it is one of us I expect that person will be disappearing soon. Seven people knew where he was, and there's going to be an intensive investigation of each of us. If there's dirt, the FBI will find it. If there's a traitor in our midst, it's only a matter of time."

"And what if Grachev just decides to play it safe and stay in hiding?" Croin said. "There'll be a cloud hanging over all of us."

Sam nodded. "That's true. And if Grachev stays in hiding, then whichever one of you it is, you better run and run fast, because my mission in life will be to hunt you down."

"Hey!" Croin said. "How do we know it's not you? Maybe it'll be us hunting you down."

Sam smiled. "You don't know it's not me, but I do. Now, you and Erin stay here with these two. Shaffer, why don't you and I take a look outside and see if our sniper left anything behind that'll help hang Grachev?"

"Actually," Croin said, "in Washington State he does have the option of lethal injection."

خطر

In the early evening, Angie Sims pulled away from CIA headquarters in Langley with a dark gray government-type car following her. There were two clones wearing dark glasses and dark suits in front. A lot of gray cars left CIA headquarters, so she paid it no mind until she turned right, and it turned right. She took a left at the next light, and so did the clones. Coincidence, possibly. But then again, maybe Stone found out about her relationship with Corrigan. Time to play it safe.

Angie pulled sharply off the street into a handicapped parking spot. She breathed a sigh of relief when the gray car kept going with neither occupant glancing at her. She waited a couple of minutes to see if they circled the block and passed her again, but they didn't.

Angie pulled out into traffic again, keeping an eye on the rearview mirror. No gray car, but when she turned left, a brown sedan with a lone male occupant turned with her. Angie made three more left turns, and the brown sedan stayed with her. The probability of someone making three more left turns to reverse their direction was too small for Angie's liking. This guy was tailing her, too.

She kept her eye open for another handicapped spot, pulled over, and let the sedan pass. She waited a minute, pulled back into the traffic, and in seconds the gray car was following her. No maybe about it. The only explanation was that Stone had found out about her and Jonathan, and he didn't trust her. A knot formed in her stomach. What were these guys' orders? Follow her, or worse?

She could head out to Norfolk where her parents lived. Her father used to command a destroyer, but heart problems had cut his career short. No. If their intentions were malevolent, she didn't want these guys anywhere near her father. He'd try to do something about it. The best person for this situation was a man she'd come to consider the brother she never had.

Angie drove through Langley until she came to a nice, middle-class neighborhood. The gray car and brown sedan switched off a couple of times, and currently the brown sedan tailed her. Halfway down the street she stopped in front of an older two-level home. Angie shifted the car into reverse, and her foot hovered over the accelerator in case they cut her off and tried to take her. The brown sedan passed by. A couple seconds later, the gray car appeared in the mirror and parked about two hundred feet back.

They were content to watch for now. They were probably on the phone trying to figure out who lived in the house. Angie wasn't a field agent, but she wasn't stupid.

She got out of the car and walked three houses down. There, Angie sprinted down a paved walkway between two houses, which connected the street to a cul-de-sac behind it. She could hear the roar of a motor. Her target house was two houses left of the exit. Angie charged to the house, ran alongside it, and banged on the basement entrance door. No answer. She prayed he was home and banged again. She could hear footsteps on the path.

"Open the door," she whispered. "Please don't be gone on one of your trips."

The footsteps were getting closer.

危险 خطر

ОПАСНОТЬ

FOURTEEN

S am stepped outside the house, followed by Shaffer, just as the paramedics loaded Davidov into the ambulance. Sam felt a jolt. A blanket covered Davidov's face. He was supposed to die en route, not at the scene. Sam rushed up to the attendants.

"What happened?" he said.

Swanson shrugged. "Can't keep mush alive. Sorry, Agent Perkins. He just didn't make it."

Sam kicked at the ground. "That's just great."

"Hey," Shaffer said, "even if the guy lived, it'd only be his body. A vegetable can't testify."

"I guess you're right. I just kind of hoped. . ."

Swanson lifted his eyebrows. "That a guy with a head shot would recover?"

"Yeah."

"That truly would be a miracle," Swanson said. "Well, we've gotta get the body to the hospital so a doctor can officially pronounce him."

Swanson climbed into the back of the ambulance, and his

partner closed the doors and hopped into the driver's seat. Sam and Shaffer watched as the ambulance quietly drove away. No need for lights and sirens now.

"Tough break," Shaffer said. "With him, you had a good chance of nailing Grachev."

"Oh, we'll nail Grachev. One nice thing about chasing criminals is they aren't the most trustworthy bunch. We'll get someone else to turn."

"I hope you do, but to be honest, after what happened to Davidov, it's going to be hard to convince anyone we can protect them."

"Only until we find the traitor. Let's see if we can find where the sniper took his shot from. Based on the bullet wound, it had to be from this side of the street."

They slowly walked up the street, paying attention to the ground. It was an older neighborhood, most of the houses in need of repair. Some yards were still kept up; others were threatening to return to the state they had existed in before the white man came to Seattle.

"Pannett figured the shot came from three hundred yards."

"Then it probably did," Shaffer said. "Pannett did two tours in Vietnam. He lost a couple of buddies to snipers, so instead of hating them, he became a sniper himself, for our side, of course. Wonder what's keeping him?"

"Everett police. They're going to want a few questions answered before they let him go."

"I'm sure he'll have the answers."

Sam looked at Shaffer. "You don't like your partner, do you?"

"I don't dislike him," Shaffer said. "We've just got different ideas on law enforcement."

"Do you think there's any chance he shot the sniper just on general principle that he hates snipers?"

Shaffer stopped and pursed his lips before shaking his head. "No, he'd never go that far. It happened the way it happened."

"Glad to hear it," Sam said. "It's tough enough nailing Grachev without U.S. Marshals shooting potential witnesses."

They continued down the street and came to one house with particularly long grass. Sam looked back to the safe house. "This has to be close to three hundred yards."

"Yeah."

Sam took out his handgun, ejected the clip, and crouched down in the grass. He aimed toward the marshal's car. "With a scope the shot is possible, but the angle seems wrong for the way the bullet went in and out. He had to have made his shot from the street."

"If he did, then why didn't we see him take off?"

Sam replaced the clip, then holstered his weapon and surveyed the vehicles parked on the street. Half a dozen older cars and a couple vans, one only fifty feet further down the road. He pointed to the older Chevy van with a terrible dark blue paint job. "Would you care if you lost that van?"

"No."

Sam removed his weapon, and Shaffer did likewise. "You hang back. I'll approach the van."

"Uh, you hang back. I'll approach the vehicle," Shaffer said. "I'm wearing a vest. You're not."

Sam nodded. Weapons raised, they approached the van. Because of the dark color, it wasn't readily apparent, but Sam could see that a foot-square section of the door panel looked removable.

Sam hung back ten feet while Shaffer sidled over to the van door. The marshal put his hand on the handle; Sam pulled back the hammer of his gun. Shaffer yanked open the door, and Sam fired.

خطر

Angie pounded the door again while looking to her left. Her breath came in short gasps. She wasn't a field agent. She didn't have any training for this kind of thing. Any second now they'd find her and do whatever they wanted.

She turned and pressed her back to the door, hoping against hope they wouldn't notice her as they walked past on the street. Her heart pounded like a jackhammer. *Oh, Duncan, why couldn't you be home?* Just as one of the men appeared in the corner of her eye, the door opened and Angie stumbled backward into strong arms. A foot reached around her and pushed the door shut.

"Angie, what's going on?"

Angie turned to face Duncan McIntyre. His blue eyes were bloodshot, and even though it was only seven o'clock in the evening, he looked like he just got out of bed. Though he wasn't far from fifty, Duncan was solid as a rock but not muscle-bound. He put his arms on her shoulders. "You're trembling. What happened?"

"I'm being followed."

"Did they see you come in here?"

"I don't think so."

Duncan cocked his head sideways. "You sure?"

"Pretty sure."

Duncan herded her into the sparsely furnished living room of his basement suite and sat her on the couch. He went to one of the windows facing the street and peeked through the closed curtains. "He's looking at the house. Probably heard the door shut. Now he's trying to figure out if he heard you coming in here or just someone coming home." A minute passed. "Not good."

"What?"

"He's on his cell. He thinks you're in here, and he's probably calling for backup. Looks CIA. Is he?"

Angie wrapped her arms around herself to ease the shaking. "I think so. I may have picked him up at headquarters, but I didn't notice him for a while. First, there was a dark gray car with two guys in it, and then a brown car with just one guy. They took turns following me."

Duncan kept watch on the street. "Any idea why?"

"I'm working the satellite surveillance for a Middle East mission. Stone is hanging the agent out to dry, and I think he just found out I used to date the guy. Now he doesn't trust me."

Angie could see the side of Duncan's face. His forehead furrowed. "Corrigan is the only spy you ever dated, if I remember correctly. He's retired, really retired. Why would he be in the Middle East?"

"An asset contacted us who would only speak to Jonathan, so Bolton convinced him to come back one last time. Jonathan would get what he could from the source, and Bolton would extract him at the first sign of trouble. But at the first sign of trouble, Stone was in charge. I informed him of the mission protocol, and he said there was a new protocol. He let whoever they were—probably Hezbollah—take him. We saw them enter a building in Lebanon on Saturday. We haven't seen him since." Angie wiped a tear from her eye.

"You still have feelings for him?"

"I'll always have feelings for him. I just couldn't go to the next level."

"You know he's married, right?"

"That's why he'll never know about my feelings. But I made a promise, and I intend to keep it."

McIntyre glanced at her with a lifted eyebrow. "What promise was that?"

"He specifically requested me for this mission, and he made me promise if the CIA hung him out to dry that I'd tell his wife."

Duncan chuckled. "I wonder what he expects her to do. Go to the press, I guess. Have you told her?"

Angie shook her head. "At first I thought Stone actually might know what he was doing. He said we could gain a lot of intelligence on the terrorists by watching who came in and out, and if we went in for Jonathan, that opportunity would be lost. No new terrorists have entered that building in the last twenty-four hours, and Stone hasn't made a move to get him."

"They might be negotiating," Duncan said. "They probably want one of theirs for one of ours. Things could be going on behind the scenes you don't know about. If I were Stone, I'd give up one of theirs, and as soon as they hand Corrigan over, I'd blow the building and kill them all."

"So I don't tell his wife?"

"You'd be violating your oath if you did, and risking prison. It's a federal offense."

"So I do nothing?"

"There's nothing you can do. By now everything connected to you is wired. Same for Corrigan's wife. The second you try to contact her, they'd break the connection."

"And what if Stone isn't negotiating? There've always been rumors in the agency that he didn't just leave to spend more time with his family. You should see him. He looks like Captain Kirk did when he got the *Enterprise* back. Whenever he uses Corrigan's name, he practically spits it out. I'm going to have to try to reach her."

"You will do no such thing." Duncan shook his head hard.

"Excuse me?"

"Angie, you're in over your head. You can't fight a man like Stone."

"Someone has to. I can't just let Jonathan die."

"Someone will." McIntyre took a deep breath. "Now there's three guys standing out there. Time for you to go."

"Huh?"

McIntyre let the curtain close and stepped over to the couch. He held out his hand. "Come on."

Angie took his hand. He helped her up from the couch and led her into his bedroom. "Hide in the closet. They'll be at the door any second now."

Angie started to speak, but he guided her inside the closet. Duncan crossed the room and pulled a gun from the top dresser drawer and came back to the closet. "No matter what you hear, stay in here. If anyone opens it other than me, shoot." He pushed the gun into her hands. Duncan started to close the door then stopped. "You don't have the coordinates of that building in Lebanon where they're keeping Corrigan, do you?"

خطر

Three slugs impacted the back of the driver's seat before Sam stopped firing. Shaffer had dropped to the ground. "It's okay," Sam said.

"What happened?"

Perkins pointed to the van. Shaffer got up and saw a sniper rifle on its tripod lined up with the removable steel plate. "I just saw the muzzle and fired."

Shaffer whistled. "I would've, too. So he left the murder weapon behind. Good thinking. If he got caught with this, he'd be off to Walla Walla."

"He couldn't have been thinking that clearly. He drew a weapon on your partner and found out the answer to life's great mystery."

Shaffer nodded and smirked. "That he did. The fact that

he left the van and weapon behind leads me to believe that even after forensics goes through this thing with a fine-tooth comb we won't know any more than we do now."

Sam walked up and peered into the van. He crinkled his nose. "Our shooter was a smoker." Sam pointed to a partly open curtain that separated the driver's section of the van from the back. "I'll bet he had that curtain closed when he opened the door to shoot. From three hundred yards, the darkness of the van would blend with its color, and the sun being behind it didn't hurt his cause any. We probably wouldn't have noticed the hole even if we were looking at it. Once he shot, he probably slithered through the curtain and out the front door. He would've kept low until he was out of our sight." Sam scratched his nose, irritated from the stale cigarette smoke. "I wonder what he smoked?"

"Let's check the ashtray," Shaffer said.

Sam dug rubber gloves out of his pocket and snapped them on. They walked up to the driver's door of the van, and Sam pulled it open. He leaned over the seat and pulled out the ashtray. He straightened and faced Shaffer. The marshal peered into the ashtray and stirred its contents with a pen.

"Interesting," Shaffer said.

"Either our shooter smokes two brands of cigarettes, or there were two men in this van."

"Meaning one is still out there." He started off toward the roadblock.

"Where you going?"

Shaffer stopped. "I'm going to tell the police there may be another suspect on foot."

"Don't bother," Sam said.

"Why not?"

"I've got my reasons."

Shaffer studied his face. "What reasons?"

"I'd rather not say at this time."

"Well, considering we don't know how these guys found Davidov, I think you should say at this time," Shaffer said. "Or I'm going to tell the cops to start looking."

Sam chewed on his lower lip while he considered Shaffer. "Even if you did work for Grachev, it wouldn't matter. The other guy is going to go back and tell Grachev that Davidov's dead."

"So will the papers."

"Yeah, but Grachev doesn't trust the papers. He'll trust his own guy. I need Grachev to feel safe, and if he's sure Davidov is dead, he'll feel safe."

"Unless he knows about Davidov giving his deposition."

Perkins nodded. "If he finds out about that, he'll probably stay in hiding. If he does, there'll be a cloud of suspicion over all of us."

"And if he doesn't know? If he does come out of hiding?"

"Then it wasn't one of us." *But it could still be Ali. She doesn't know about the deposition.*

"What now?"

"I'll get the FBI to do the forensics on this van; then I'm going to go to the hospital and order blood tests on Davidov so Marshal Klyne can sleep easy. I want Croin to let the court reporter use his car to go somewhere and hide. Make sure you give her the cash you had for Davidov."

"Don't you think it would be better if we just got a couple of different marshals out to take her into protective custody?"

Sam looked back at the safe house where Davidov had fallen. "I don't think she'd go for it, and I wouldn't blame her."

خطر

Director Elijah Stone hung up the phone with a grin on his

face. Not once during the conversation had he let on how much he was enjoying it. He came across all business, best interest of the country in mind. Of course, Laura Corrigan didn't believe him, but she got the message. Her husband was in his hands, and if she wanted him back, she'd keep her mouth shut. And he wasn't completely lying. They would get Corrigan back if the price was right—or if he was still alive when Stone decided to take out the terrorists and extraction was practical.

He leaned back in the chair and put his hands behind his head, then swiveled the chair to look out the window. Dusk was starting to settle in. Back home, the fish would be jumping and the birds performing their evening song. He preferred the view out of the CIA building much better. Some grass, some trees, but most of all, power. America was in tough times, and Stone knew what had to be done. His intercom buzzed.

Stone swiveled back around and pressed the button. "Yes."

"Director of Operations Lavigne," his evening secretary said.

"Send him in."

Stone's smile faded at the sight of Lavigne. The man's features were pinched, and his body language called to mind a dog waiting for the beating sure to come. Stone sat forward. "What happened?"

Lavigne took a seat across from him and looked away for a second. "The three agents who were following Angie Sims are in the hospital."

"What? How did that happen?"

"Sims escaped surveillance for a short time. One agent was pretty sure she went into the basement entrance of a house."

"Whose house?"

"It belongs to some old lady by the name of Ida Patterson."

Ida Patterson. For some reason, that name sounded familiar.

"And I'm assuming this old lady didn't take out three agents."

Lavigne shook his head. "No, the guy renting her basement suite did."

"And what's his name?"

"Duncan McIntyre."

Stone let his head fall back against the back of the chair. "Just great."

Lavigne raised an eyebrow. "You know him?"

Stone nodded. "He works for us—sort of."

"Excuse me?"

"Duncan McIntyre is an old Cold War spy. He was the kind of spy you'd give him the name and picture of a problem, and the problem would go away. He speaks Russian like a native and conducted most of his operations in the old Soviet Union."

"If I'm Director of Operations, why haven't I heard of this guy before?"

"He doesn't work for you. He works for intelligence."

"Intelligence?"

"Yeah. When the Cold War thawed, we had to call him back. He really only knows how to do one thing, and with Russia almost our ally, we can't have a guy like him running around. We reassigned him to intelligence and kept him on the payroll."

"Strange I've never run into him in the building."

Stone shrugged. "He only comes to work when he feels like it. If he does come in, it's usually only for a couple of hours. He'll read some Russian intercepts, write a report—usually a very useful one—and then leave. He spends most of his time at Fort Bragg helping a colonel buddy of his train Special Forces."

"That explains why he took out three agents without breaking a sweat."

"Oh yeah," Stone said. "When it comes to hand-to-hand, I don't know of anyone who can match him. What did he do to your guys?"

"One guy's got a serious concussion, and they'll have to do reconstructive surgery on his nose. Another has a broken knee and jaw. The last guy was lucky. He's only got a bruised trachea because McIntyre put him in a sleeper hold."

"Was Sims there?"

"I assume so," Lavigne said. "McIntyre told our guys that Angie Sims was his friend, that if anything happened to her the consequences would be severe."

"I didn't think McIntyre had any friends."

"Why do you say that?"

Stone pursed his lips. "Trust me, he's the ultimate loner. Why he'd care for this woman is beyond me."

"So what do we do about him? We can't just let this stand."

Stone leaned forward and put his hands on his desk. "Oh yes, we can. As much as I'd like to keep this Corrigan thing under wraps, I don't want to get into a private war with McIntyre. No more following Angie Sims. You can tap her phones and watch her e-mail, but stay away from her."

"This McIntyre guy is that powerful?"

"No," said Stone. "He's that dangerous."

危险 خطر ОПАСНОТЬ

FIFTEEN

L aura Corrigan dropped the phone back in its cradle and backed away as if Stone's venom could still strike her. Without ever saying it, Stone had made the situation perfectly clear: Keep quiet and do nothing, or Jonathan dies. She looked over at Sandra who had been watching her talk to Stone. Her mother was down the hall in the guest room, a place where she spent a lot of time.

"What's wrong?"

She slipped her hair behind her ear. "Nothing."

Sandra stood and walked over to her. "Nothing, nothing. You look like you just got the fright of your life."

Laura looked into her mother-in-law's eyes and started to open her mouth. *Tell no one,* Stone's voice echoed in her mind. "Really, it's nothing."

Sandra put a strong farm-woman's hand on her shoulder. "You're lying. It's about Jonathan, I can tell. You may be his wife, but I'm his mother. I went through a lot of pain to bring him into this world. What is it?"

Laura looked away. "I can't say."

Sandra's hand rested on Laura's belly. "Just imagine that little child in your womb is grown up and in trouble. You'd do anything to save her, wouldn't you?"

Laura nodded her head.

"Then believe me when I tell you that whatever you heard on that phone call, you can tell me, because I love Jonathan every bit as much as you do. I'll do whatever I have to. Now who was it and what did they say?"

Laura's legs felt rubbery. She shuffled to the kitchen table and sat down. Sandra sat across from her and held her hands.

"That was Stone," Laura said.

Sandra's grip tightened, and her eyes widened. "What did he want?"

"Jonathan has been captured by terrorists."

Sandra sucked in a short breath. "Oh, Lord, no."

"Stone said they're negotiating to get him back, but that if I do anything to make it public, he's as good as dead."

"Do you believe him?"

"Which part?" Laura shrugged her shoulders. "That he's trying to get Jonathan out? Maybe. I mean, he hates Jonathan, and the feeling is mutual. The man tried to kill both of us, and we cost him his career, or at least we thought so. It seems he's risen from the ashes. But would he let Jonathan die without trying to rescue him? That would be hard to cover up. Jonathan is a national hero. The question is, how hard is Stone going to try?"

"We need to pray about this," Sandra said. "We need to pray that God will keep Jonathan safe and soften Stone's heart."

Laura nodded her head in agreement. The two women bowed heads, and Laura listened as Sandra Corrigan poured her heart out to God for her son. When it was Laura's turn to pray she felt inadequate. She hadn't known God the many years that Sandra had. Would He listen to her? He had to. She wasn't just one person praying, she was two.

When they finished praying, Sandra fetched a box of tissues, and the two women made temporary repairs to their faces.

Sandra gripped Laura's forearm. "Laura, sometimes it doesn't seem like it, but there is a God. He sees what's going on here, and He's working. We just can't see it quite yet."

Laura nodded. "I know."

"For now we'll keep this between us, but if we don't hear good news soon, we have to consider calling in some favors for Jonathan. Agreed?"

"Agreed," Laura said. "If you don't mind, I think I'll go to my study. I've got a little work to do, and it might help take my mind off of this."

Sandra released her arm. "Sure, honey. And look, if you need a shoulder to cry on, keep in mind that mine's right here."

Laura stood and smiled. "I will. Mine's here for you, too, just in case you feel like you need a cry."

Sandra nodded. "I'll do that."

Laura went down the hall and then upstairs to her study. To most people, a study is a quiet room with a comfortable chair, desk, and a wall lined with good books to read. Laura's looked like a computer warfare center. She had six networked PCs so she could use their combined processing power, plus a couple independent workstations for tasks that didn't require so much power.

Working from home, she'd developed a successful business writing encrypted programs for business and industry. Right now she was so angry she wanted to turn her years of training at MIT and at her father's side against the CIA. She could start off with a denial of service attack and bring their Web site down. While they scrambled to bring it up, she could get into their main computers and wreak havoc.

Laura slumped into the swivel office chair in front of her computer monitor. As good as it would feel to strike back, she'd never forgive herself if, while the CIA was busy defending itself against her attack, America's enemies struck. Besides, the CIA wasn't the enemy; Stone was.

She rolled over to her desk and opened the top drawer. Inside was the slip of paper Jonathan had dropped in her lap. If he got in trouble, she was supposed to use the e-mail address. Whose e-mail was it? What was she supposed to say? Were things different now that Stone was in charge? Or had Jonathan feared that Stone might somehow recover control of the agency while he was away? Would the person at the other end of this e-mail address know what to do?

Sandra said God was working. Well, maybe this e-mail address was what He needed to get the job done. She tapped her space bar, and the computer woke from standby mode. Her firewall flashed a warning on her screen. For the last three hours, someone had been trying to hack into her computer.

Laura glanced at the firewall hardware between her computer and cable connection and smirked. "Not in this lifetime, whoever you are. And whoever you are, you picked the wrong day to mess with me."

Laura loaded up her antihacker software, which also happened to be her hacking software, and started to trace the Internet provider address of the hacker. Of course the first result was phony, but her software kept digging, chasing the hacker back to his den. If he were smart, he would unplug his Internet connection while he still had a chance. Laura grinned. She followed him right through his own firewall. Now she could really punish him. Her smile faded. She was in the CIA's system.

Of course it was the CIA. Along with Stone's threat came surveillance. Laura backed out of the agency's system. Later, when she calmed down, she'd send them an e-mail explaining the weakness in their system and how to fix it. *Wait a minute,* she thought. *These guys put Jonathan's life in danger.* For the sake of the country, she'd e-mail and tell them about the weakness. If they wanted to know how to fix it, they could hire her.

Laura looked at the e-mail address. It might hold the key to Jonathan's rescue, but she couldn't use it from home. She could go to her friend Olivia's business, PTL Computers, but they'd follow her there. They'd know she would be trying to send out an e-mail, and if they reacted the way they did the last time, Olivia's place would get wrecked.

Laura was beginning to see the wisdom in Sandra's words. She needed to let God work. "You've got until tomorrow morning," Laura said, "then I send this e-mail out. I know just the place."

خطر

Sam parked in the hospital's visitors lot and jogged up to the emergency entrance. Early Monday evening business appeared to be steady. Over a dozen people occupied the waiting room in various states of injury. Sam approached the admitting desk, which was occupied by a middle-aged woman with her dark hair tied back in a bun. The nurse peered over her glasses when he walked up.

"May I help you?" she said.

Sam held up his identification. "Special Agent Perkins, FBI. You have a DOA here who belongs to me."

The nurse raised her eyebrows. "Did the DOA have a name?"

"You mean there was more than one today?"

"Two. Which one is yours?"

"He should've been logged under John Doe."

"Ah yes, John Doe. That would be Dr. Everly's patient."

"Patient? The guy's dead."

"Patient sounds nicer than corpse, doesn't it?"

"I guess so," Sam said. "Could you get the doctor for me?"

"Certainly."

The nurse picked up her phone, punched a couple numbers, and her voice echoed through the hospital calling for Dr. Everly. Five minutes later, a sixtyish man approached. He had a shock of snow-white hair, a wizened face, and crooked teeth. "You paged me?" he said to the nurse.

She pointed to Sam. "The FBI is here about your John Doe."

The wizened face turned beet red. "You sure took your sweet time getting here."

Sam took a step back. "Excuse me?"

"A body like that is perfect for organ harvesting. We could've saved or improved at least three lives with his body, but we didn't know who he was or who could give permission. Now it's too late."

Sam looked over at the waiting room. All eyes were on him and the doctor. "I'm sorry. I got tied up with the shooting investigation. I came as soon as I could."

"Not soon enough," Everly said. "Look, we don't really have a lot of room to store bodies here. I'm assuming you're going to require an autopsy although cause of death is pretty evident. Our medical examiner has already dropped by. Do you want him to do it or one of your own people?"

"Our people will do it."

"Fine. Please make arrangements to pick up the body as soon as you can. For the record, though, we'd like you to identify him. Come with me."

Sam followed the doctor, who flew through the emergency room. The doctor opened the door to a room at the end of the ward and flicked on the light switch. A gurney with a white sheet draped over a body occupied it. He closed the door.

"It's okay," Dr. Everly said to the gurney. "It's the FBI agent."

A hand reached from underneath the sheet and pulled it back to reveal a pale body, and Sam jumped. "What's going on here?" Sam said.

"Sorry to frighten you," Dr. Everly said, "but I didn't want to say anything outside. This is Dr. Rimes, an intern at the hospital."

"I don't understand."

"Well, with a little makeup and rinse, we managed to make him look like your John Doe. Your John Doe is upstairs in intensive care. We needed a body to replace his in case someone started asking questions."

"Good thing, too," Rimes said. "Someone opened the door and peeked in here."

"Did he look at your face?" Sam said.

Rimes shook his head.

"Your John Doe's prognosis is quite good," Everly said.

Sam found a chair and sat down. "Let me get this straight. My John Doe, a guy with a bullet through his head, is alive and expected to recover?"

"Well, he won't fully recover," Everly said. "The bullet passed right through both eye cavities, so he'll be blind. But it missed everything important."

"This is a joke, right?"

"No joke," Everly said. "I've seen this before. Someone puts a gun to their head, has the barrel too far forward and at the wrong angle, and then wakes up alive and blind. It's a long shot—no pun intended—but it happens. That's how I got the idea to list him as an attempted suicide."

Sam thought back to the shooting. A breeze had started up just before the shot. At three hundred feet, a breeze could easily change the path of the bullet by an inch or two. Someone was watching out for Yuri Davidov. "Is he conscious?"

"No, and we don't expect him to be for quite a while."

"Who knows about this?"

"The two paramedics, Dr. Rimes and I, and the nurse up in intensive care. We'll have to tell the other nurse who comes on shift about it as well, because when he wakes up, he needs to know he's someone else."

"You trust these people?"

Everly nodded. "I do. We all share the same contempt for the drug trade."

"I'd like to see him."

"I'd rather you didn't," Everly said. "We've gone to a lot of trouble to make him look dead. Someone already peeked in this room. Might've been a staff member, might've been someone making sure he is dead. The best thing would be for you to just walk out of here, and we'll have the medical examiner's van pick up Dr. Rimes and take him to the morgue. I leave it up to you to inform them of what's going on. They get the dead kids after we do, so they should be cooperative."

Perkins stood and shook his head. "I have to hand it to you guys. You've done a terrific job."

"Well," Dr. Everly said, "we do expect the FBI to pick up the tab for your John Doe's medical care. And since we're a publicly funded hospital, a donation wouldn't hurt either."

Sam chuckled. "We've spent money on worse things. I'll see what I can do. Thanks again, guys."

Sam put on his best "life sucks" face when he left the hospital. He was pretty sure someone in that waiting room was watching and would go back and report it to Grachev. By tomorrow Grachev would be back on the streets thinking he was untouchable. Sam would let the Russian mobster believe just that, because while they waited for Davidov to wake up, they could try to find the accountant. With the accountant and Davidov, they could put Grachev away forever.

خطر

The door opened, and Hussein entered the room. He turned off the flashing lights on the stands and then leaned down and pressed a button on the boom box. The music stopped but kept on beating in Jonathan's head. Hussein smirked at him. "You don't like this music?"

Jonathan stood up. "It's not music; it's noise." His voice was no more than a ragged whisper.

"We agree on that," Hussein said. "Fortunately the walls and ceiling are so thick we didn't have to hear it upstairs." Hussein's hand hovered over the boom box switch. "Now, are you interested in sharing some information with us? We've got some nice lamb cooked upstairs and a cot, or would you rather hear some more?"

Deprived of sleep, the thought of a meal and a soft bed pulled at Jonathan's deepest desires. He remembered from college psychology that man's basic needs were food, water, and sex, and there was a lot of dispute over which came first. Jonathan could now tell the professor from personal experience that it was definitely food and water. He licked his parched lips and worked up a slight amount of saliva. "Thanks for the offer, but I'll have to pass."

Hussein hit the boom box button, and it felt like the man

slammed Jonathan against the wall. The terrorist stood and laughed while Jonathan leaned his right ear into his shoulder to protect it. After a couple minutes, Hussein turned it off.

"Why endure so much pain?"

Jonathan kept silent.

Hussein pulled his gun out of his waistband, cocked it, and then sauntered over to him holding the gun pointed downward. "You know, we offered to sell you to the CIA. Your director Stone says you don't belong to them, but he'll give us five hundred thousand American dollars anyway." Hussein stood inches from him. "For five hundred thousand dollars, I'd rather see you die." The gun started to move upward.

Stone's name was like a bolt of electricity sending adrenaline coursing through Jonathan's veins. How did Stone get in charge? It didn't matter. He was on his own. Time to leave. Jonathan slammed his forehead into Hussein's face. The gun fired into the floor, and Hussein collapsed to the ground.

Jonathan dropped on top of the unconscious terrorist and prayed for all he was worth that Hussein had the keys in his pocket. Shouts filtered down from upstairs. He checked Hussein's left pocket and caught a break—the keys. He found the handcuff key, but his hands fumbled it. Jonathan took a couple deep breaths to slow the adrenaline. Footsteps coming down the stairs. He freed one hand, fell forward, and grabbed the gun Hussein had dropped.

Omar charged through the door, his automatic weapon raised. Jonathan squeezed off a single shot from the handgun and caught Omar in the shoulder. The terrorist spun, and his machine gun skidded into the corner. More voices calling from the upstairs. He aimed the gun at Omar. "Tell them everything is all right, or you'll die."

Omar spat at him but missed. "I don't care if I die." He

opened his mouth to call upstairs.

Jonathan put the gun to Hussein's head. "Fine. Then he dies."

Omar's mouth stopped. Jonathan pulled back the hammer. Omar called upstairs, assuring them everything was under control.

Jonathan finished freeing himself from the restraints and tucked the handcuffs in his pocket. He went to Omar as fast as a man with a gimpy leg could and grabbed the three extra machine gun clips tucked in Omar's waistband.

Footsteps pounded down the stairs, obviously not convinced by Omar's assurances. Crouching against the wall, Jonathan stuck his hands around the corner and blindly fired three shots up the staircase. Feet charged back up the stairs. "Not so tough when the other guy's got a gun, are you?" Jonathan yelled after them.

Jonathan turned to Omar and pointed the gun at his mouth. The terrorist's face erupted in sweat, and his dark brown eyes opened wide. Rule number one when escaping, never let anyone live that you don't need alive. One hostage would do. He put pressure on the trigger.

Good rule. Blow him away, and send him to a Christless eternity. You don't work for them anymore. You work for Me. The hair on the back of his neck stood. Had he really heard that? Jonathan eased off the trigger.

"Get it over with," Omar said, his breathing labored. "Kill me."

Jonathan frowned. "No can do." But what could he do? He couldn't shoot them all in the shoulder. This went entirely against all his training as a former Navy SEAL. *Lord, I'll keep my ear open for suggestions, but Emile said a ship of terrorists is headed to Seattle. I really don't see any other choice. I have to get out of here and stop it any way I can.*

Jonathan went to the corner and retrieved the machine gun. Stuffing the handgun in his waistband, he shuffled over to the doorway. He slipped around the corner and kept the machine gun aimed up the stairway. The door at the top was open. He eased up the stairs. A board creaked, and a hail of bullets flew through the door at the top and embedded into the staircase's plaster ceiling. Jonathan opened fire at the open doorway as he retreated back down the stairs and into the room.

"Give up," a voice called down the stairs in broken English. "You can't escape."

Hussein moaned. Jonathan shuffled over to the terrorist and gave him a kick in the ribs. "Get up," he said.

Hussein shook his head and opened his eyes. He looked over at Omar slumped against the wall and sucked in a short breath. "Omar, are you okay?"

Omar nodded his head.

Hussein looked up at Jonathan. "I will kill you, American pig."

Jonathan pointed the gun in Hussein's face. "For now, just get up before I put you to sleep forever."

Hussein struggled to his feet, blood still dripping from his broken nose.

"You're going to be my shield up those stairs."

"Never."

"Fine," Jonathan said. "Then you can go back to sleep and I'll take him." He raised the weapon to strike Hussein across the face.

Hussein put up his hand. "No. I'll go."

"Let him take me," Omar said. "I'm dying anyway."

"Just lie still," Hussein said. "Help will come soon."

Hussein glanced over at Omar. Jonathan suspected these

guys were more than just fellow terrorists—probably brothers.

Jonathan slung the machine gun over his shoulder and pulled the handgun out of his waistband. He pointed it at Hussein. "Turn around and put your hands behind your back."

Hussein did as he was told, and Jonathan snapped the handcuffs on him. Jonathan grabbed a handful of thick hair at the back of Hussein's head and twisted hard. Hussein sucked in a short breath. The way you control a horse is by its head; a man wasn't much different. He put the handgun to Hussein's cheek. "Keep this in mind. You do anything to help them and I'll kill you, and then I'll come back and kill Omar. Understand?"

"Yes," Hussein hissed.

"Let's go." Jonathan shoved Hussein forward to the door. "Want to call up and let them know you're coming? They might decide to shoot first and mourn later."

Hussein nodded his head. "Don't shoot!" he yelled in Arabic. "He's aiming a gun at me."

Silence answered back. Hussein relaxed, and Jonathan twisted the terrorist's head to face him. Hussein was smiling. When he heard something metal hissing and clattering down the stairs, followed by the upstairs door slamming shut, he understood why. A moment later, his eyes and throat were burning in the cloud of tear gas that billowed from the canister.

危险 ОПАСНОТЬ
خطر

SIXTEEN

MONDAY, JULY 8

S am Perkins sat across from Conners in his office at the federal building in downtown Seattle. His boss was on the phone talking to the medical examiner in Everett. Faking a man's death was beyond the ability of one FBI agent, so Sam had to go to his boss for help.

Conners hung up. "Okay, the ME is faking a death certificate, and they've got an unclaimed body they can ship out, just in case Grachev's men are watching the morgue. We've got this thing about as secret as we can make it. Our big concern now is to find out how Grachev knew where Davidov was hidden. Either you were followed, or someone is dirty."

"I'd swear on my life I wasn't followed. I went through so many twists and turns each time I went out there that if there'd been a tail, I would've seen it. I even had Ali and Moody keeping an eye on the sky in case a chopper followed us."

"What about electronic surveillance? A transmitter on your car?"

"All the vehicles have already been gone through with a

fine-tooth comb. Nothing."

"Then someone's dirty," Conners said. "Any idea who?"

"Pannett's a good choice. He made sure the sniper would never talk."

Conners shook his head. "Couldn't be Pannett or Shaffer."

"Why not?" Sam said.

"They were the marshals who relocated Marty Rowland after we faked Newberg shooting him. If they were dirty, Rowland would be dead. The other two marshals?"

"I have a hard time believing Klyne or Croin were involved. They knew they'd be escorting Davidov to the car. I doubt Grachev could pay them enough to stand near a guy while a sniper takes a shot at him."

"They were wearing vests, and Pannett and Shaffer were closest to Davidov," Conners said. "I think we need to take a good look at those two. I'll have agents ripping through their lives. What about Moody?"

Perkins shrugged. "Unlikely. He's based in Washington, D.C. It's a stretch Grachev would have him in his pocket, but we should probably dig into him as well."

"I'll have to get clearance from the U.S. Attorney on that one, but considering what's happened, I don't think we'll have any trouble. Who does that leave?"

"There's the court reporter, but she didn't even know where she was going."

"Maybe she had a transmitter in her purse or something?" Conners said.

"She didn't even know she was getting this assignment until we showed up at the federal building. Hard to believe we'd pick the only dirty court reporter who just happened to have a transmitter in her purse, just in case she got picked to do the deposition."

"Still, we should look into her."

"I'd prefer we didn't right now," Sam said. "She's in hiding, and the investigation may inadvertently expose her. She's a material witness, and I don't even want to know where she is."

"Fair enough," Conners said. "Based on my math, that leaves you and Ali. I can't think of anything Grachev could do to turn you, not with how close you were to Newberg, so that leaves your partner."

Sam nodded his head.

"Where was she when all this was going on?"

"Called in sick."

Conners raised his eyebrows. "Doesn't that seem a little suspicious to you?"

"Oh yeah."

"So?"

"The way I see it, everyone we've talked about so far has enough information to convince Grachev to stay in hiding except for Ali. If any one of them is dirty, he'll stay wherever he is and that person will disappear. If he comes out of hiding, the only person who knew where Davidov was but doesn't know he gave his deposition—or is alive for that matter—is Ali."

"She's our number one suspect, isn't she?"

Sam nodded.

Conners reached for his phone. "I'll have her suspended pending a full investigation."

"Wait." Perkins held up his hand.

"What?"

"If she is dirty, then that means she's working for Grachev. I would rather give her more rope so that when there is enough to hang herself, she'll sing loud and long to avoid swinging from it."

"You're willing to work with a potentially dirty partner?"

"Absolutely. The best way to catch her is if she believes her cover is secure. Besides, if she's dirty, I want to be there to take her down."

"Okay, but in the meantime, I'm going do some checking."

خطر

Josef Grachev leaned on the luxury yacht's railing and watched the lights of the container ship dim as the yacht increased the distance between them. He resisted the urge to give the ship the one-finger salute. It wasn't that the crew treated him badly. In fact they treated him with almost royal deference, as they should. No, the ship reminded him he operated outside the law. It only took one screwup to knock his otherwise comfortable life off-kilter.

He looked over his shoulder. Heng was busy hitting on the yacht's female accessories. Heng had enough money that the women would allow him to delude himself into believing they found him desirable. Even if he didn't have money, just the fact Heng was Grachev's guest would ensure the Chinese gangster was treated with respect. If it weren't for the significant monetary advantages of their relationship, Grachev would do to Heng what he had done to that FBI plant.

Part of him was relieved to learn Davidov was out of the picture, but part of him grieved. Yuri had been with him for a long time, and it was really all Heng's fault. Heng killed his nephew's bodyguard, which probably led Davidov to believe Grachev would do the same to him, and so he gave in to the FBI. The day would come when Heng wouldn't be worth the trouble, and Josef would pay him back for Yuri on that day.

He heard a door open and glanced over his shoulder. Sophie sashayed out of the main cabin dressed in a flowing, red satin evening gown with a glass of champagne in her hand. It hadn't taken her long to get reacquainted with luxury. She sidled up to him and slipped her arm through his.

"When we get home, I sleep for a week."

"It's *I'm going to* or *I will* sleep for a week," Josef said. "You should spend less time watching Russian TV on satellite and watch the American TV; otherwise you're going to sound like a refugee the rest of your life."

"I speak better English if you let me talk to American people."

Josef looked away from her out into the darkness of the sound. "You can talk to American people when you know what to say and what not to say." He turned to look at her. "Right now you're too stupid to know the difference. Until you do, you talk to whoever I let you talk to."

Her arm slipped away from his, and she looked away. "If you hate me, why not send me home?"

Josef grabbed her arm and pulled her to face him. "You amuse me. But don't ever think of running. If you run, I'll make a phone call, and your sister and her kid get it. It's that simple. Now go to your room and go to bed. You've got a lot of work to catch up on when we get back. I may or may not be in later." He shoved her toward the cabin and returned to staring out into the darkness.

خطر

Ricky must have walked every street in downtown Seattle looking for the girl he bought the phone number from. When he reported to Tommy Woo that he knew where Michelle was and said he needed help tracing the address, Heng's right-hand man told him to forget it. She wasn't worth the trouble anymore.

That was fine with Ricky until Woo told him he still expected more years of service in exchange for losing her. Ricky tried to argue that if he had never found her in the first place, he wouldn't owe them anything. Woo slapped him across the face, making it pretty clear excuses would fall on deaf ears.

Now he had to find the street kid because she was his ticket to finding the address. He decided to double back to Westlake Center. The first time he went through, it was only six o'clock. Now it was closer to ten. Ricky's feet were starting to hurt from all the walking, but it seemed a mere nuisance compared to serving Heng any longer than he had to.

His search was made more difficult because he had to travel with crowds. Seattle police would still be looking for him, and it would be harder for them to pick him out of a group of people walking down the street. Now that it was getting late, the sidewalk traffic was thinning out and he no longer had that option. He just had to hope for the best.

When he got to Westlake Center, his spirits started to lift. A large group of teens were hanging around listening to an older man with a long, scraggly beard play a guitar. Ricky surveyed the crowd from the outer edge, and if he hadn't been in public, he would have wept for relief when he saw the pierced girl in the group.

Ricky moved around so he approached her from behind. He tapped on her shoulder, and she spun around.

"What do you want?" Scraggly guy stopped playing the guitar, and all eyes turned on him.

"I need to talk to you," Ricky said.

"About what?"

"You want to make money?"

Several of the guys in the group shifted to an aggressive posture. They'd clearly taken him wrong. Street kids tended to look out for each other, and he might as well have just propositioned their little sister.

She curled up her lip. "Get lost."

"I give you fifty dollars to make phone call, that's all."

She eyed him warily. "Phone who?"

The whole group watched him now.

"Can we talk alone?"

"I don't think so," the girl said. "I've heard of your kind grabbing girls off the streets. Get out of my face."

"I won't grab you. We will just walk a little bit away. Your friends will still be able to see you. A hundred dollars"—he took the money out of his pocket and held it in front of her—"that way you all can eat." He knew he was taking a chance. The kids might just decide to try to take the money.

Pierced Face chewed on her lower lip, looking at the money. "Okay. But two hundred bucks."

"Two hundred dollars just for a phone call? Too much."

The girl started to turn her back to him.

"Okay, okay, two hundred dollars."

"Deal," the girl said.

"We'll be watching," the guy with the scraggly beard said.

"Thanks," she said. She followed him about twenty feet from the group and then stopped. "This is far enough. Who do you want me to phone?"

"The girl who give you this number." Ricky held out the gospel tract he'd bought from her.

"Why?"

"Two hundred dollars. You need to know why?" Ricky held out his cell phone to her. "Call her. I need to know where she lives."

The girl looked at the phone for a couple seconds before taking it. "Cash first."

Ricky handed her the money, and she jammed it in the pocket of her ratty jeans.

The street kid dialed the number and put the phone to her ear. "Hi, is Roxanne there?" She looked up at Ricky and tapped her foot. "Hi, Roxanne. You gave me your number and said to call if I wanted to know more about Jesus. I want to know more. . . . Not on the phone; can we talk in person? . . . No, you don't have come out to Seattle, I've got a friend who'll drive me to your place. I have to get out of the city; I'm in trouble. Where do you live?"

The girl put her hand over the cell phone. "She won't tell me where she lives."

"Okay. Tell her you'll meet anywhere she want."

The girl spoke into the phone again. "Can we meet somewhere? I read what you gave me, and I really need to talk to someone. . . . No, I don't want to talk to a pastor here; I want to talk to you. You've been on the streets; I trust you. . . . Great." The girl started writing on the tract. "I'll see you soon. Bye."

She hung up the phone and handed the tract back to him. "She wants to meet me at her church in Bellingham. What do you want her for anyway?"

Ricky took the tract from the girl. "I don't want her. Just information."

But if she got in his way, he'd take her, too.

خطر

Jonathan pushed Hussein back down the stairs, grabbed the canister, and tossed it down into the dungeon. He released Hussein. "Help Omar out here before the gas suffocates him, then shut the door."

Hussein looked at him with confusion.

"Hurry up, or I'll just put both of you in there."

Jonathan looked at the wall. It was plaster. He fired a couple rounds up the stairs to make them think he was still planning on coming that way and to prevent another canister of tear gas from tumbling down. He hoped, as Bugs Bunny used to say, to exit stage right. At least he thought it was Bugs Bunny. It had been a long time since he'd watched cartoons, but that would all change as soon as their daughter was born.

Thoughts of Laura and their unborn child flooded his mind. Adrenaline once more coursed through his veins. He had to get home.

Hussein and Omar were both coughing when they came out of the dungeon. Omar looked weak and leaned heavily on Hussein. Hussein pulled the door shut to keep the tear gas away from them. Jonathan waved the machine gun at him. "Just stay put, and you'll live to see the end of this day."

Jonathan pushed himself up against the left wall and alternated fire at the opposite wall and at the upstairs door to confuse them about his plans. Plaster exploded as the bullets fragmented the wall. By the time he finished with the second clip, the wall looked like a moth-eaten garment. Kicking vigorously, he made a hole big enough to slip through. With the handgun ready, Jonathan slipped through the hole down into the other section of the basement, jarring his gimpy leg. He sucked in a deep breath and ignored the pain.

The basement was empty. High above, light from small windows streamed into the basement. Jonathan held back a curse. All the windows had bars on them. He looked about. There was another staircase leading to the next floor. He wouldn't have any more success with that route than the one he just abandoned.

Jonathan glanced about the dimly lit room looking for

any hope of escape. He heard another canister of tear gas bounce down the stairs and Hussein cursing at them in Arabic. Well, they knew he wasn't on the stairs anymore. He should've killed Hussein and left Omar in the room to die. What was the matter with him?

It was clear Jonathan wasn't getting out of this basement. He could surrender, but Hussein would probably carry out his threat and kill him. As long as he was alive, Jonathan had hope that somehow, some way, God would get him out of this mess.

There were worktables against the walls as well as a sink. The sink cried to his most basic needs. Keeping his machine gun ready, Jonathan limped over to the sink, put the plug in, and started to run the water. Next he took several gulps, never knowing water could taste so good.

Footsteps started down the stairs he had escaped from. Jonathan took the handgun and fired a round through the hole. The footsteps stopped. He yelled, "Hussein can drag Omar up the stairs, but if anyone comes down, I'll kill them." He didn't want to give them the opportunity to lob another canister of tear gas into the basement; it was bad enough with what drifted in from the stairs. The footsteps retreated, and he could hear Hussein half dragging Omar up the stairs.

As refreshed as a half-dozen mouthfuls of water could make him, Jonathan slung the machine gun over his shoulder and started pulling the heavy wooden tables to the far corner. The location gave him sight lines on the hole in the wall and the second staircase without exposing his back to a window. He set two tables in a vee shape for a makeshift fortress then kicked the legs off two more tables before placing the tabletops in front of the first tables. He knew one tabletop thickness wouldn't be enough to stop a high-powered bullet.

The water started to overflow the sink. Jonathan limped

over to the sink and turned off the tap. He plunged his head into the sink and reveled in the rejuvenating effects of the cold water and in washing the tear gas from his eyes. He pulled his head out and flattened himself against the floor when glass broke and bullets whizzed past him.

Jonathan unslung the machine gun and fired a short burst at the window, struggled to his feet, and awkwardly dove behind his makeshift fortress. Shots took chunks out of the concrete near the sink, but they couldn't get an angle to fire at the corner.

Jonathan set the machine gun to semiautomatic. He'd told Laura if anything went wrong to make contact on Wednesday. It was only Monday night in Bellingham. He needed to save his ammunition because it would be a long time before help came, if it came at all.

خطر

His phone rang, and Elijah Stone shook himself awake. Until the Corrigan issue was dealt with, he'd taken to sleeping on the couch in his office. He had no idea what the Sims woman had told McIntyre, which meant there was a wild card in play. Would McIntyre get involved, and if so, to what extent?

He reached above himself and turned on a table lamp. Still lying down, he picked up the receiver and put it to his ear. "Stone here."

"Sir, this is DeShannon in ops. We've got a development in Beirut."

Stone sat up. "What's going on?"

"A couple of terrorists have gone outside the building, and they're shooting into the basement. It may mean Corrigan is escaping."

Stone sighed. "This is terrible news."

"Sir?"

"It means he's definitely dead."

"I don't understand."

"DeShannon, if Corrigan tried to escape, he was outgunned ten to one, assuming he had a gun. No matter what we do now we can't save him, assuming it's him they're shooting at. The best thing now is just to gather intelligence so his death isn't in vain. When we get all the information we can, we'll pay those scum back for killing Jonathan in spades. Son, trust me, they're going to get a whole lot of hurt before this is over."

"Yes, sir," DeShannon said.

"Keep me posted."

"Will do."

Stone put the phone back on the receiver and shook his head before smiling. So Corrigan went and got himself killed. He picked the receiver back up and started to punch in Laura Corrigan's number. He was going to enjoy telling the woman her husband was dead. His finger paused before punching the last number. No, he wouldn't call until they had a body. Corrigan made a fool of him once before. He'd let the terrorists drag Corrigan's body through the streets, and then CNN could inform Corrigan's wife of his demise.

危险 خطر ОПАСНОТЬ

SEVENTEEN

Duncan McIntyre cruised up Interstate 5 in the car he had rented at SeaTac airport. The sun was just above the horizon, illuminating Seattle up ahead. He glanced at the clock in the dash. Just after five o'clock in the morning. Why was he even here? This wasn't his fight or his problem. Maybe it had something to do with his unrelenting itch for action. No, he could scratch that at Fort Bragg by schooling over-confident Special Force wannabes. He was here because if he didn't take care of this, Angie would try on her own, and there's no way he'd let that happen.

He wondered if Angie knew how much power she had over him. Only once before had a woman gotten close to him and she'd. . . He rubbed an escaping tear with his knuckles. Best not to think of that now.

He had first laid eyes on Angie in the cafeteria at CIA headquarters six years ago. He had no friends, and yet for some reason he wanted to get to know her, so he took the seat across from her and started small talk. She, of course, thought he was hitting on her, but romance was nowhere in his mind, and not just because eleven years separated them. Something about Angie tugged at his deepest self.

It took awhile, but they eventually became friends. Angie was probably using him during the early part of their friendship. She wanted to advance in the agency, and having a super-spy in her corner didn't hurt. Duncan didn't care why she wanted to be his friend, just that she was.

He looked at the Space Needle in the distance. He'd seen it on TV lots of times, but for some reason, it seemed more familiar than that. He'd never been to Seattle before—had he? Uneasiness had hit Duncan the minute the plane touched down at SeaTac, and the closer he got to the city, the worse it became. He turned his attention to the highway. The Tuesday morning traffic was still light, and he wanted to get past Seattle before rush hour started in earnest.

An hour and a half later, he turned off the highway and into Bellingham. As he traveled, the surroundings went from suburban to rural. He followed Guide Meridian Road out of Bellingham. Duncan saw Axton Road up ahead and turned left on the country road where the Corrigan farm was located.

So far all he had planned was a little reconnaissance. If Stone put a tail on Angie, he'd have one on Corrigan's wife. He needed to know how many agents had been assigned to her and whether there was some way of getting to the house without being spotted himself. He could, of course, incapacitate the agents, but that would alert Stone that he was up to something, although he had no idea what the something was yet. He hoped Corrigan figured that out before he left.

About a mile down the road, he passed an old Monte Carlo at the side of the road with some Chinese guy behind the wheel. Not likely a CIA agent but since the Corrigan farm was only a quarter of a mile away, he had to assume this guy had some interest in the place.

He passed the driveway of the Corrigan farm and observed an abandoned barn across from it. Crushed grass leading to the barn indicated someone had driven to it recently. In all likelihood, the agents were hiding in there. He continued on past the barn, confident the agents would note his license plate and have it checked. They'd get nowhere since Duncan had flown to Seattle using one of his own false identities, one not provided by the CIA.

From what he observed, he had two choices. One was to just drive into the Corrigan farm and not worry about the agents watching. The difficulty with that was his false identity was from Idaho. If these agents were anywhere near competent, they'd smell a rat when someone from Idaho just happened to visit the Corrigans.

No, he'd be better to approach the farm on foot through the tall grass of the adjacent hay fields, thus avoiding surveillance by both the CIA and the Chinese guy. It would mean getting wet and a lot of crawling, but Duncan crawled in wet places all the time. Since the farm on the left had already cut their hay, he'd have to approach from the Chinese guy's side. The truth was, getting there wasn't the problem; that would be convincing Laura Corrigan to trust him.

He could just see it now. *Hi, I'm Duncan McIntyre of the CIA. Now I know the CIA has deserted your husband in Beirut, but I'm a good CIA agent, and I really want to help. You can trust me.* Maybe he should've brought Angie instead of hiding her. A woman was more likely to trust a woman than some forty-nine-year-old guy covered in morning dew.

خطر

Roxanne checked the cinch on Duke one more time. The old gelding was perfect for a new rider. Duke was the poster boy of horses when it came to "been there, done that." Nothing would spook this old guy, and he had plenty of patience for a new rider. She looked back at Michelle standing close by. Her eyes were wide as saucers. They'd ridden in the corral yesterday, but this would be Michelle's first trail ride.

Roxanne had lent Michelle some of her clothes, and the Asian girl looked sharp, dressed in blue jeans and an avocado Western shirt. A cowboy hat would've topped her off perfectly, but Mom had insisted they wear helmets. Oh well, they could wear cowboy hats when they went shopping in the mall later to get Michelle some new clothes.

It took her mom half a day to figure out Michelle wasn't Connie's cousin, and she agreed to wait until Jonathan came home to decide what to do. Roxanne was relieved. No one seemed to know what Jonathan could do, but if anyone could do anything at all, it was he.

"Up you go," Roxanne said to Michelle.

Michelle inserted her left boot into the stirrup, grabbed a fistful of Duke's mane, just like Roxanne taught her, and hauled her slim frame onto the horse. Duke looked back at the girl and yawned.

Roxanne went over to Jonathan's horse, Phelan, who was tied to a hitching post. Phelan was only three years old and a completely different matter when it came to spooking. She needed a firm, experienced hand, and even then bad things could happen. Mom had reservations about letting her ride the buckskin mare, but Roxanne assured her they'd ride in the open where surprises would be few and far between.

Phelan's eyes were alert. Whenever Jonathan took her out on the trails, it was usually a wild romp, and she probably anticipated the same thing with Roxanne. She rubbed the horse's neck. "Sorry, girl, but it's going to be a bit slow today.

We're breaking in a new rider, and you're not all that experienced yourself."

Roxanne untied the horse and slipped a bridle over Phelan's head; she readily took the bit. Roxanne double-checked her own cinch and then pulled herself up into Jonathan's roomy saddle. Phelan snorted, and Duke snorted back. Rudy let out a couple sharp barks from the porch as if to say, *What about me?* "Sorry, Rudy," she called to the dog. Jonathan didn't want Rudy taken on trail rides; otherwise the German shepherd would get the idea wandering off was okay.

"Follow me," Roxanne said. She squeezed her legs slightly, and Phelan moved forward. Duke flicked his ears a bit indicating annoyance at not leading, but that was the extent of his rebellion. They started down the driveway through the tall pines. Roxanne shivered a bit until they emerged from the wooded area into the morning sun. It was going to be another hot one.

Roxanne gave Phelan slight rein pressure, and she turned to the left. "We'll go along the side of the road a bit."

"Road?" Michelle said.

Roxanne pointed to the strip of asphalt. "That's called a road or a street."

"Road or street," Michelle repeated.

Everyone in the family was enjoying teaching Michelle English, and she was making great progress.

"What happens with girl you tell about Jesus?"

Roxanne yawned deeply. "She never showed up. I think she was just playing a joke."

"Joke? Joke is funny. That is not funny."

Roxanne didn't realize how little sense the English language made until she had to teach it to someone else. "Sometimes a joke isn't funny. Sometimes it means a prank."

"Prank?"

"Doing something to fool someone."

"Joke, prank. I think I understand."

"Hang around my brothers long enough, and you'll understand the meaning of a prank."

"Brothers. You like having brothers?"

"Oh yeah," Roxanne said. She looked ahead at the older car parked beside the road. No one was in it, and she couldn't see anyone on foot up or down the street. "Looks like someone ran out of gas last night."

"Gas?"

"Stuff you put in a car to make it go." She pointed. "That's a car."

Michelle nodded, but Roxanne doubted she really understood the concept of gas and engines. At least in English.

"Let's go take a look," Roxanne said. She guided Phelan up the embankment to the road with Duke following. In the quiet morning, the horses' shoes clicking across the asphalt was the only sound to be heard. She guided Phelan around the car. "No dead bodies."

Michelle knit her eyebrows together. "Dead bodies?"

Roxanne chuckled. "In scary movies you always find a dead body near a car abandoned in the country."

Michelle whipped her head around, looking for an attacker.

"Don't worry, it only happens in movies. Real life in the country is much safer." Roxanne smiled. "Come on, let's keep going."

Roxanne guided Phelan back across the street and down the embankment. Phelan suddenly reared sky-high, and Roxanne slid back in the saddle. She pulled hard on the left rein, but Phelan took off like a rocket toward home. Roxanne pushed her boots into the stirrups, all the while trying to turn the horse around. Because the saddle was too big for her, she couldn't regain her seat. Phelan bucked, and Roxanne sailed through the air.

She crashed into the long grass. Air burst from her lungs, stars exploded in front of her eyes, and all the while she could hear Mom saying, "See, I was right about the helmet." Dirt from Phelan's hooves splattered her face as the spooked mare took off for home. "That's the last time I'm ever giving you a carrot!" she called after the fleeing animal.

She rolled over and looked up at Michelle, fifty feet behind her. The girl wasn't looking at Roxanne but off to the left. Roxanne followed Michelle's gaze. An Asian man stood in the long grass with a gun in his hand. He fired rapid Chinese at Michelle, and she slowly got off Duke. Unlike Phelan, the gelding ignored the man and turned his attention to the long grass.

Roxanne knew she should be scared, but the adrenaline coursing through her veins from being thrown dulled her common sense. "Who do you think you are?" she yelled at him.

He looked at her with open contempt then fired more Chinese at Michelle.

Roxanne looked at Michelle. "Do you know this guy?"

Michelle nodded. "Ricky. He works for the smugglers. I must go with him."

"Well, tell Ricky we're in the United States, and you're not going anywhere."

Ricky looked at her longer than was appropriate, then grinned. He waved the gun at her. "You come, too."

Roxanne shook her head. "In your dreams, buddy. Neither of us is going anywhere with you." She squinted her eyes and took a closer look at his face. "Hey, you're the guy who shot at my brother."

He waved the gun. "You come here."

Roxanne put her hand on her hip. "No."

Ricky rushed forward, grabbed Michelle by the hair, and jammed the gun to her head. "You come, or she dies."

The adrenaline evaporated, and Roxanne's knees weakened. Suddenly her mind was back in her bedroom in Seattle, being held down, helpless.

Ricky pulled back the hammer on the gun. "You come, or I shoot her."

"Okay, okay," Roxanne said, holding up her hands. "Don't hurt her."

"No," Michelle said. "You run. I don't care if he kills me."

"I care," Roxanne said. "You're my friend."

Roxanne started to walk through the long grass toward Michelle and Ricky, all the while praying that Jonathan would choose that exact moment to come home. Suddenly, viselike hands grabbed her ankles, and she crashed face forward.

"Stay down, and say nothing," a man whispered.

خطر

Duncan pushed down on the girl's back to emphasize his point.

"What are you doing?" the guy named Ricky shouted. "Get up, or I will kill her."

Duncan stood up and pointed his Glock 17 right at Ricky's face. The man's eyes widened with surprise. If he didn't have the gun cocked and next to the girl's head, Duncan might've just shot him and got it over with. The problem with cocked guns is they tended to go off, even if the shooter was already dead. "You kill her, and I'll kill you."

"Drop your gun, or I will kill girl. I mean it."

"Who are you?" the girl on the ground said.

Duncan figured she had to be Roxanne, Corrigan's adopted

sister. When he arrived at the farm, he was just going to go through the fields to the house, but the Chinese guy in the car bugged him. He hated unknowns and decided to watch the Chinese guy for a while. It paid off with a chance to give Laura Corrigan a reason to trust him. "Just shut up and stay down."

Duncan took a couple steps and put himself between Roxanne and the gunman. "How about you drop your gun, and I won't kill you?"

Ricky's face contorted in anger. "No. I have a hostage. You are a cop. You have to put gun down."

Duncan laughed, much to the shock of Ricky and the girl he held. "I'm not a cop, you fool. I don't care about law or procedure. All I care about is winning. The way I see it, if I drop my gun, you can shoot both girls and me. If I keep my gun, you can kill the girl but I'll get to kill you. That's close enough to a win for me."

"Are you nuts?" Roxanne whispered. "Put the gun down before you get my friend killed."

"I told you to shut up," Duncan said. "You have no idea how this game is played."

The gun shook in Ricky's hand. "I will kill her. No more warnings."

Duncan held his gun steady. "The instant you shoot, I shoot, and you die. I've been in eight of these standoffs. Four times the guy was smart; he put down the gun and lived. The other four times he was stupid, and I killed him. How about you? Do you want to live?" He waved his own weapon slightly. "Putting the gun down is the closest you can come to a win."

Ricky relaxed his gun hand slightly. "You will kill me the second I drop it."

Duncan shook his head. "Is there something about the air here that makes people stupid? I've made it quite clear you will die if you shoot the girl. If you put the gun down and for some reason I go back on my word and shoot you, you're no worse off. Maybe when you meet God, you won't have to answer for this girl's murder. But I'm not going to shoot you. In fact, I don't even care about you."

Ricky's eyes narrowed. "What do you want then?"

"The girls. As soon as you let her go, you can go. You're just an unlucky guy who got in the wrong place at the wrong time. My mission is to take these two girls."

Ricky looked like a lightbulb just went on. "You work for Grachev. He wants the girls?"

Josef Grachev. Duncan knew the name but had no idea what the Russian gangster's connection would be to Corrigan's sister and her friend. *When opportunity presents itself. . .* "Right. I work for Josef. Now put the gun down."

Ricky took his weapon away from the girl's head and lowered the hammer. "We work for same bosses."

"No kidding," Duncan said, lowering his gun but still ready to fire. "I wish they'd talk to each other so both of us aren't out here at the same time. I could've killed you." He looked at the girl. "Come here."

The Asian girl looked over her shoulder at Ricky.

"Go ahead," Ricky said to her.

The girl started walking toward Duncan. Duncan took a few steps so the girl wasn't in his line of fire anymore. He whipped his weapon up to firing position. "Drop your gun right now."

Ricky looked like a deer caught in headlights. "What?"

"Drop it now, or I fire!"

Ricky let the gun slip from his hand, and it fell to the ground. Duncan charged forward keeping the gun trained on Ricky. "Down on your knees—hands behind your head."

Ricky hesitated. "But we work for same bosses."

"I work for myself," Duncan said. "Down or die, your choice."

Ricky dropped to his knees.

Duncan found another gun tucked in Ricky's ankle holster. He put his gun to Ricky's head then noticed the two girls were holding each other, sharing a flood of tears while watching him. "Look away," he said to them, and they turned their heads.

"You say you will not kill me. You lied."

Duncan struck Ricky across the back of the head with the pistol, and the younger man crumpled face forward into the grass. He walked over to the two girls. Roxanne pushed her friend behind her, her shoulders thrown back and her chin jutting. "Before you try to take us, there's something you should know. One of my brothers is a CIA agent, and the other is a cop. They'll hunt you down, and when they find you, you'll never see a jail cell."

Duncan chuckled. "Well, aren't you tough?"

Her foot snapped toward his groin. Duncan grabbed her foot in midflight and resisted the urge to dump her on her bottom. He kept hold of it while she hopped on one foot trying to keep her balance. The Chinese girl charged from behind Roxanne with a flurry of fists. Duncan reached forward and grabbed the top of her head, keeping her at bay.

"Ladies, I'm not taking you anywhere."

He released Roxanne and pushed the Chinese girl back. She kept her fists at the ready. Duncan turned to Roxanne. "I'm a friend of a friend of Jonathan's. I need to talk to Laura, but the CIA is watching the house, and I don't want them to know I'm here."

Roxanne tilted her head sideways and looked past him. "You don't work for the same guy he does?"

"No."

"How do I know you're not lying, that this isn't some kind of trick?"

"Because if I hadn't come along, you two would be in the trunk of that car, on your way to a life I'd rather not tell you about."

"I already know about it," Roxanne said.

"Then you know what I saved you from. Now, go home and tell Laura what happened here. Tell her Jonathan is in trouble and I need to meet with her."

Roxanne straightened up. "Jonathan is in trouble. I knew something was going on. What kind of trouble?"

"I can't tell you. But tell Laura to bring whatever Jonathan gave her. I saw a coffee shop on the way through town, a place called Muffin Mania. Tell her to meet me there in two hours."

"What about the CIA guys? If they really exist, they'll follow her."

He smiled. "You don't trust anyone, do you?"

Roxanne shook her head.

"Good. Neither do I. I'll be inside when Laura gets there so they won't see me."

She nodded toward Ricky. "What about him?"

"You'll never see him again. Trust me."

危险 خطر ОПАСНОТЬ

EIGHTEEN

L aura pulled her car into an empty spot in front of Muffin Mania. There'd been a great debate on what to do back at the farm. Sandra voted for calling Danny. Roxanne made it clear she didn't trust the guy, but calling the cops would mean involving Michelle, and she didn't want to risk having the girl deported. Laura wanted to grasp at any hope of bringing Jonathan home and voted with Roxanne.

The man had told Roxanne one thing that Laura knew to be true. The CIA was following her. Shortly after turning on Guide Meridian, one of those government-type cars followed her. Laura had no skill in losing tails and didn't even bother to try. Instead she spent the whole drive praying, and now armed with that prayer, she got out of the car and entered the coffee shop.

Laura saw him sitting in the corner sipping a cup of coffee. He looked up at her as she approached. His attention shifted to her belly when she slid into the seat across from him. From the way the girls described him, he was bigger than life, but to Laura he seemed an ordinary guy except for his arms. They were knotted with muscles, and his wrists were abnormally large. The only distinguishing mark on his face was a scar on his forehead that disappeared into his military-style hair.

"You're pregnant," he said.

"Yes," Laura said. "Now, who are you and what do you know about Jonathan?"

He took a sip of coffee. "Coffee?"

Laura shook her head. "No. Now answer my question."

"Call me Paul. Your husband is being held in a building in Beirut by Hezbollah terrorists."

"I already know that," Laura said. "Roxanne said you're a friend of a friend of Jonathan's. Who's the friend?"

"I can't say."

"Then why should I believe you?"

"Because I just saved Roxanne's life."

"Roxanne thinks you might have staged that to win my confidence."

"That's ridiculous," Paul said.

"Maybe so, but I've had dealings with Stone and the CIA before. They've pulled off some pretty big schemes in the past to fool me. For all I know, Stone isn't sure if I have a way of helping Jonathan, so he established this ruse to find out."

Paul shrugged his shoulders and didn't display any of the signs of frustration she'd expect from a man telling the truth. "Stone has nothing to do with this. In fact, right now I'm working against Stone's interests."

"So say you. How do you explain the fact that the kidnapper's car is still parked out by our place? That tells me you two left together."

Paul smiled. "We did leave together." He dug into his

pants pocket and tossed a set of keys on the table. "There's a dark blue Crown Victoria at the far end of the lot. It has a Hertz rental sticker on the bumper. Take a look in the trunk."

Laura looked at the keys. Laura didn't care for trunks. Still, last night she had prayed God would do something to intervene. The next morning, this man showed up to rescue Roxanne. Short of an angel showing up with a signed letter from God, how much more did she need? She picked up the keys. "Okay, I'll take a look."

He took another sip of coffee. "I'll be right here."

When she stepped outside into the warm air, Laura was glad she chose to wear nothing more than a sleeveless top and shorts. The thing about being pregnant is you had to provide air conditioning for two. She dreaded to think what it would be like when she got further along. Paul had quite an observant eye. She was only starting to show.

Laura crossed the hot asphalt to the far end of the parking lot. The Crown Victoria occupied a lone spot twenty feet from other cars. She held the key at the trunk lock and stopped. Her hand had started to shake as memories of being trapped in a trunk flooded over her. She took a deep breath, inserted the key, and turned it. The trunk popped open, and she jumped back with her hand to her mouth.

خطر

Sam Perkins sat in the waiting area outside Arthur Conners's office. A secretary typed away, her eyes never leaving the computer screen. Sitting in the waiting room was the last place Sam wanted to be. The surveillance team watching Grachev's home reported that the Russian had come home. That meant none of the team watching Davidov was dirty. Only Ali could've betrayed them.

What he really wanted to do this morning was find Ali and drop in on Grachev, see how they reacted to each other. See if he could get any indication whether they knew each other or not. Deep down he hoped they didn't. He liked Ali. She was the kind of girl who could easily grow on a guy. But he had to remember that someone had put a bullet in Davidov, and no matter how he felt deep down, he had to think with his head, and his head said she was dirty.

But his morning wasn't unfolding as he planned. Ali didn't answer her phone, which looked bad—real bad—and then Conners called him in for a meeting. He picked up a fishing magazine, flipped through the pages, and put it down. "How much longer do you think Mr. Conners will be?"

The secretary glanced downward. "He's still on the phone. Would you like a cup of coffee or something?"

"No thank you," Sam said, and returned to learning more about the great fishing spots of the Pacific Northwest. He wished he'd never set foot in the Pacific Northwest. Life was fine being stationed in California. He'd planned on going back to California after handling the security detail on Jonathan Corrigan, but nothing ever went the way you planned.

Instead, the local office requested he stay and assist them on the Russian Mafia/Chinese Triad investigation. Big mistake. The next thing they asked was if he could recommend an agent from California who could do undercover work. They didn't want to use anyone local. Sam had recommended his good friend Paul Newberg, and now Paul was dead. Sam twisted the magazine in his hands. Maybe he should just put a bullet in Grachev and call it a day. Fight fire with fire.

"You can go in now," the secretary said.

Sam looked up. "Huh?"

"You can go in now."

"Oh. Right. Thanks."

Sam dropped the mutilated magazine and opened the door to Conners's office. Conners looked ready to rip someone apart limb by limb. He motioned with his hand for him to take a seat. Sam sat in one of the two cloth-covered chairs in front of the walnut desk.

"We've found our rat," Conners said.

Sam leaned forward hoping to hear any name other than Ali's.

"It's Marcoli, your partner."

Sam slumped back in the chair shaking his head. "I know I should feel angry, but I feel sick."

"That's to be expected," Conners said. "Finding out your partner is dirty is like coming home and finding your wife in bed with another man. It rips into the gut."

Sam nodded. "That pretty much explains it. So how did you catch her?"

"Phone logs. It seems Marcoli made four calls to Moscow, three before Davidov was shot."

"Who did she call?"

"Don't know yet. The Moscow phone company isn't exactly jumping to answer our request. It seems there's a *fee* for providing that kind of information. We're having someone from our embassy go to the phone company and grease the skids. Of course, Marcoli could just save us the trouble and tell us. I'm sure whoever it is, they're connected to Grachev somehow."

"Yeah," Sam said. "We just have to find her. I called her this morning, but she didn't answer her phone."

Conners smiled. "She may not have answered her phone, but she was home. As soon as I got the phone logs, I got a search warrant for her apartment. I was just talking to the guys who executed it. They found little Ali asleep in bed. They're bringing her in now."

خطر

The body in the Crown Victoria's trunk wasn't moving. Laura took a deep breath and stepped forward. An Asian man, who must've been the one who tried to kidnap Roxanne and Michelle, was hog-tied in the trunk. His face was badly bruised, and his lips were caked with dried blood. He was alive, but his respirations were quick and shallow. Laura slammed the trunk and stepped back.

She turned and rushed across the parking lot and back into Muffin Mania. Paul had gotten her a cup of coffee. Laura sat at the table and ignored it. "That man is dying. You've got to take him to a hospital."

Paul shrugged. "That man was going to take your sister-in-law and sell her into the sex trade. If he had succeeded, by this time tomorrow, Roxanne would be strapped to a cot somewhere being shot full of heroin to make her a willing addict. Who cares what happens to him?"

"I. . .um. . ."

"What's important is that you believe I'm not working with that guy. I'm on your side; I'm on Jonathan's side. Stone has no intention of rescuing Jonathan. I don't have much in the way of Middle East resources. I worked elsewhere. Jonathan, on the other hand, has plenty of friends in the Middle East. I'm hoping he left you with some way of contacting them."

Laura fingered the clasp of her handbag.

"Mrs. Corrigan, every moment we wait is another moment your husband remains in the tender mercies of the Hezbollah. You have to make a decision, and make it fast."

Oh, Lord, I hope I'm doing the right thing. Laura opened her handbag and dug out the piece of paper Jonathan gave her. She handed it to Paul.

He took it from her and looked at it. "An e-mail address. Did he tell you what to say?"

Laura shook her head.

"Then I guess we'll just have to send the truth to whoever this is and wait and see what happens. I'm surprised you haven't done so already."

"I was going to last night," Laura said, "but my security software detected the CIA watching my Internet service provider. If I had sent a message, they probably would've blocked it and gotten the e-mail address. I was going to use a friend's computer today."

"Well, knowing Stone, he probably tapped into not only your ISP but the ISPs of everyone you know. Even if you got the message through, he'd be waiting to intercept whoever responded. Out of curiosity, why does he hate your husband so much?"

"This might sound cliché, but I can't tell you for reasons of national security."

Paul chuckled. "No, I say it all the time. Tell me this: Is your husband a good man? Is he worth saving?"

Laura straightened and looked hard into his face. "Yes."

Paul put his coffee to his lips and sat back, considering her. "If this e-mail address goes to where I think it does, men are going to risk their lives to get him. Is he worth dying for?"

Laura looked into the man's eyes. "Jonathan promised me he'd never work for the CIA again. We've had a storybook life for the last couple years. Then Director Bolton shows up, and my husband breaks his vow. Why do you think he'd do that?"

Paul shrugged. "You tell me."

"Because whatever Bolton asked Jonathan to do, it was something only he could do, and it was important enough to leave his wife and unborn child. I think that makes him worth saving, don't you?"

Paul looked at the e-mail address again. "Good thing I brought my laptop."

خطر

Ali's eyes flashed when Sam followed Conners into the same examination room where they'd grilled Davidov. "What's going on here? They're throwing my clothes on the floor, ripping open my cushions, and they wouldn't even let me brush my hair." Ali pointed to her tousled mop.

Conners took the seat across from Ali, but Sam leaned up against the wall by the door.

"Yuri Davidov is dead," Conners said.

Ali's eyes widened, and she collapsed back in her chair. "What?"

"Nice try," Conners said. "It's been on every news station, but I don't think you needed the news to find out."

Ali leaned forward and pointed her finger at Conners. "I was sick yesterday. I spent the whole afternoon on the couch watching movies. After that I turned off the phone, went to bed, and stayed there until your troops started banging on my door. I haven't seen a TV, so no, I didn't know he was dead. But what I would like to know is, what's it got to do with me?"

"That's right," Conners said. "You called in sick yesterday. You don't look ill to me. No swollen nasal passages, no red nose or puffy eyes. It must've been a short-lived flu that kept you home the very day Davidov was shot."

Ali threw up her hands. "You think I had something to do with it?"

"Of all the people who knew where Davidov was, you

were the only one out of harm's way when the bullets started flying."

She folded her arms across her chest. "I wasn't the only one. You weren't there."

"I never knew the location," Conners said. "Besides, I've been cleared."

Ali looked up at Sam. "What about him? I suppose he's been cleared, too."

Conners nodded. "In fact, everyone who knew where Davidov was has been cleared except you."

"And were their homes invaded by storm troopers, too?"

"How they were cleared is of no relevance here," Conners said. "Our objective is to clear you, and the only way we can do that is if you answer our questions truthfully and help clear up some inconsistencies."

"What inconsistencies?" She crossed her arms again.

"Let's start with your illness. You obviously didn't have the flu or a cold. Why did you call in sick if you weren't sick?"

"I was sick, and I never told Perkins I had the flu. I just said I was sick."

"Fine. What kind of sickness did you have then?"

Ali looked away. "I'd rather not say."

Conners leaned forward. "Well, you're going to have to say. A material witness is dead, and right now all fingers are pointing at you."

"Just because I was sick."

"Not just because you were sick."

"Then what else?"

"Okay," Conners said. "Let's talk about yesterday. You said you unplugged the phone and went to bed. Why didn't you mention you made a phone call before going to bed? A phone call to Moscow."

Ali slumped back in her chair like she'd been struck. "You checked my phone records?"

"Yes, we did. Four calls to Moscow. Three before Davidov was shot and one after. It's not hard to connect the dots, Ali. You knew where Davidov was. Davidov's testimony would have put Grachev, a former KGB officer with strong ties to Moscow, in jail. You call Moscow, and Davidov dies. The day he's shot, you're sick, except you don't look sick. Tell us where we've gone wrong here?"

Ali bit down on her lower lip. Tears trickled down her cheek. "Fine. I'll tell you exactly where you went wrong."

Sam stepped back against the wall like Ali was a time bomb ready to go off. Her face was red, her shaking hands bunched into fists.

"It started in the shower," Ali said.

"The shower?" Conners said.

"Yeah, the shower. In case you haven't noticed, I'm a woman. While in the shower, I did a self-examination and found a lump on my breast."

Sam started to feel sick.

"I went to the doctor right away, and he scheduled me for a mammogram. It confirmed the lump, so yesterday I had the biopsy done, and it wasn't exactly a painless procedure. I couldn't even lift my arm to fire a gun."

Conners cleared his throat. "Fine. We'll have that checked out, but it still doesn't explain the calls to Moscow."

"Every woman who bothers to read the literature in their doctor's office knows family history is important when it comes to breast cancer. Family history is tough for me with both of my parents dead, so I called my grandmother in Moscow."

Conners held up a hand. "Wait just a minute, Marcoli. Your grandmother in Moscow? Your file says your parents were Italian immigrants. How did you end up with a grandmother in Moscow?"

"I'd rather not say."

"Well, you have to say. Right now you're a suspect in the murder of a federal witness. It doesn't get much deeper than this. Either you explain yourself, or I'll have to suspend you and take you into custody."

"Fine," Ali said. "I need a secure phone line, and only you can hear what I have to say."

Sam and Conners exchanged glances.

"A secure phone line?"

"Yes," Ali said, as if this were an everyday request.

Conners sucked in his cheek and tapped the table. "Okay, let's go. Wait here, Sam."

After fifteen minutes, Sam joined the agents observing in the room next door. It was a full hour before an agent knocked on the door and told Sam to go to Conners's office.

When he entered, a strained silence hung over the room. Ali was seated in front of the desk. Conners pointed to the free chair. "Take a seat, Sam."

He sat down and looked at Ali, but she turned her head away. She had her foot crossed over her knee, and it was tapping big time.

Conners folded his hands on his desk. "We have a difficult situation here." He turned to Ali. "I'm sure you're terribly hurt, and this new information certainly paints everything in a new light. The question is where do we go from here. I, of course, will respect the legalities of this situation, but the issue is whether you and Sam can continue to work as partners without him knowing what I know."

Sam tilted his head. "Knowing what?"

"I have been given information that clears Marcoli. It

comes from pretty high up." He turned his attention to Ali. "You've been hurt by all this, which is understandable, but if you take a step back, I'm sure you can see how we drew the conclusions we did. Are you able to put this behind you and carry on with the case?"

Ali nodded.

"Good."

He looked at Sam. "Now what about you? Can you work with her based on my say-so? All I can tell you is the information I received is compelling."

Sam looked over at Ali. So far she was one of the best he'd ever worked with, except for Newberg. But Sam hated secrets. "I will continue to work with Ali based on your word alone, sir. However, like you said, when a partner betrays you, it feels like catching your wife in bed with another man, because a partnership is a lot like a marriage. Well, in good marriages people don't keep secrets. If Ali doesn't want to trust me with this information, fine, but it can't help having an effect."

"Everyone keeps secrets," Ali said. "Even married people. But if the only way I can stay on this case is to tell you, I'll tell you."

Sam leaned back and considered her. She'd already proven she could watch his back, and whatever her secret was, it had to be deeply personal. "You tell me when you want to. In the meantime, now that we've got this matter cleared up, let's get out there and find a way to get Grachev."

Conners clapped his hands together. "Great. I'll call downstairs and have them release your weapon. Get to work." Conners reached for the phone.

"Just a minute," Ali said.

The receiver paused on its way to Conner's ear. "Yes?"

"Those guys destroyed my apartment. Who's paying for that?"

Conners grimaced. "I guess we are. Send me the bill, and I'll process it for payment. Will that do?"

"Yeah, it'll do."

He put the phone to his ear.

"One other thing," Ali said.

"Yes?"

"If everyone who knew where Davidov was has been cleared, how did they find him?"

Sam exchanged looks with Conners.

"Don't worry," Conners said, "I've got people working on it."

They got up and headed to the door. Sam held it for her as she passed through. They walked out into the hallway, and Sam touched Ali's shoulder. She stopped and turned to face him.

"Yes?" she said.

"The. . .um, biopsy. What did they say? You don't have. . ."

Ali's lower lip quivered. "They won't know for a while."

危险 خطر ОПАСНОТЬ

NINETEEN

Jonathan's eyes snapped open, and his heart raced. He heard something rolling across the floor. Hands over his ears, he flattened himself against the barricade and curled up in a ball. A flash of light and an explosion ripped through the basement. Chunks of steel ripped into the tables, splintering the wood. He reached for the machine gun and fired a short burst at the broken window.

He sat up, breathing hard and his hands trembling. The smell of gunpowder hung in the air. Jonathan had fallen asleep, and they'd taken the opportunity to throw in a grenade. The bars were too close together for a tear gas canister, but not a grenade. Sleep deprivation had finally gotten to him, and now that his body tasted sleep once, it would fight even harder to get there again once the adrenaline subsided.

He looked up at the windows. It was night outside, but the lights from the street streamed into the basement. He'd have to avoid those. Fortunately he'd spent his time in the basement well and managed to scavenge a box full of necessary materials for the move. The machine gun burst told them he was alive and ready to fight. They'd back off and formulate another plan, giving him precious moments.

Jonathan slung the machine gun over his shoulder and picked up the wood box. He was completely vulnerable if they chose to open fire at this moment. He gently stepped over the remainder of his barricade and walked ever so slowly to the hole he'd entered the basement from. The light coming in from the windows acted like some kind of security alarm system for his captors. They'd be watching from outside, and the darkness was his shield. If he accidentally stepped into that light, it would be all over.

He kept close to the wall, only stepping away from it when he passed the sink. Taking it slow and easy, he continued on to the hole leading to the stairway. Dead quiet indicated they were listening. A lack of flying bullets indicated they hadn't heard him move. He reached the hole.

Jonathan set the box down on a table he'd dragged under the hole earlier on. Moving that table cost him a dozen bullets of return fire while keeping them back. He gripped the edge of the table and shook it. It held firm so it hadn't suffered damage from the grenade.

Every little kid has a dream where they fall into a black hole. Looking at the deeper darkness of that hole, those childhood fears gripped him. Was the bogeyman on the other side? Except in his case, the bogeyman was Hussein with a broken nose and a vendetta.

Jonathan had a choice. With as much stealth as possible, he could go through the hole leaving them with the impression that he was still in the basement. However, if while he slept they'd moved to the stairs, he'd be dead before he got halfway through the hole. *Lord, any ideas since You know if anyone is on the other side of this wall?*

Silence answered back. Of course, silence. Everyone breathed at some point, except he didn't know how damaged his hearing was. Oh well, what choice did he have? Jonathan eased himself onto the table, slowly sucked in a deep breath, then stuck his head through the hole and listened. If someone was there, sooner or later they'd breathe; he just hoped he could hear it.

Jonathan waited until his lungs threatened to burst and then pulled his head out. Fighting the urge to breathe, Jonathan opened his mouth and slowly—agonizingly—exhaled. He took the next breath in at the same pace. After a minute, his lungs had enough air so he could move on.

Easing the box through the hole, he pushed it along the step and then slipped through after it. The upstairs door appeared closed, probably to keep out the odor of tear gas. That same odor probably kept them from trying an assault from the hole, and the same odor guaranteed the basement would be empty.

In a situation like this, it was hard to decide if there was a God in heaven. He'd certainly caught his fair share of breaks surviving, but he was still in the basement of a terrorist hideout, and the man who wanted him dead was head of the CIA. He found it more comforting to believe God was on His throne and the worst that could happen was they'd kill him. Then he could ask God personally what went wrong.

Jonathan picked up the box and gingerly worked his way down the steps, hoping to prevent any of them from creaking. He reached the door of the basement shelter and pushed it open, waiting for a creaking hinge to give him away; it opened smoothly. Jonathan stepped into the pitch-black room and set the box down. He returned to the door and grabbed the bars kept on the other side. After closing the door, Jonathan felt around until he found the brackets for the bars and set them in place.

He felt along the wall for the light switch and flicked it on. Jonathan blinked his eyes until they became accustomed to the light. The odor of tear gas was heavier here. He reached into the box and pulled out one of the water bottles. Moistening a cloth, Jonathan wiped his eyes with water. As soon as he finished preparing the room, he'd have to keep his eyes closed and breathe through a wet rag.

Jonathan slid the box to the far corner and emptied it. He picked up a chunk of steel bar he'd found and then turned the box on end. There were two vents covered by steel grates that supplied air to the room. Once they learned he was in that room, there'd be nothing to prevent them from sending tear gas down the vents. He planned on stuffing those grates with wet cloths to keep any tear gas out. The problem was it would also keep out any air. If he wasn't rescued in the next twenty-four hours, he'd have to surrender and hope Hussein was feeling forgiving.

خطر

Duncan pulled up to the back of Muffin Mania in the new car he'd rented. They couldn't very well travel around in his other rental with the Asian guy in the trunk. Besides, the CIA guys were sure to have noted it when Laura Corrigan opened the trunk. Duncan reached back and opened the back door.

Laura appeared out of the back entrance and ducked into the back of the car. She laid down on the seat, and he pulled away. He passed right by the CIA agents who were busy watching the front entrance. It wouldn't be too long before they went in the coffee shop to see what was taking her so long.

"Okay, we need a place with no questions asked and a telephone line."

"I know just the place," Laura said, and gave him directions.

To be on the safe side, Duncan did a few maneuvers to check for tails and then headed onto the highway. "You can sit up now," Duncan said.

Her face showed up in his rearview mirror. "Thanks."

"What's on your mind?"

"The guy in your trunk. He'll die in there. If not from his wounds, just from the heat and lack of air."

"I took care of him already."

"How?"

He shrugged his shoulders. "It's not important."

She sat back in the seat, her eyes staring at the back of his head. "You killed him?"

"It's not important. Rescuing your husband is." He pulled off the highway and found the motel Laura suggested. The Snowcap Motel had only one word that could describe it—flophouse. He looked in the rearview mirror at the refined lady in the backseat. "How would you know about a place like this?"

"It's a long story."

"Well, we'll probably have lots of time so you can tell me all about it." He parked the car in front of the office.

"I'll go in and register."

"Fine," Duncan said.

Laura disappeared into the motel office and reappeared a minute later. It didn't take long to register when one was paying cash. She got into the front seat of the car. "The one on the end has a phone jack."

"They don't all have phones?" McIntyre said.

She flitted a smile. "Apparently most of the patrons don't care."

Duncan pulled the car up in front of the motel room. They got out, and Laura unlocked the door and stepped in ahead of him. Duncan followed her into the room with his computer case. He felt like he'd stepped into the 1970s. He hadn't seen avocado carpet since. . .funny, he couldn't remember when, but he knew he'd seen avocado carpets sometime before the Vietnam War.

Duncan pulled the laptop from the case and placed it on the desk. He connected the phone line and hit the power, then stepped back and sat on the creaky bed. "You take it from here."

"Thanks," she said. Laura pulled up a chair and sat at the desk. Her fingers worked the computer keyboard like his fingers worked any firearm known to man. This lady was clearly in her element. The modem did its screeching thing, and she was on the Internet.

"I thought you just needed to use e-mail," Duncan said.

"I do, but first I have to get an e-mail account with my name on it. Whoever is on the other end of the e-mail address won't have a clue who Duncan McIntyre is."

Duncan stood up. "How did you know my real name?"

She turned and smiled at him. "You let me loose with your computer for two minutes. Don't worry, I've been keeping secrets for a long time now."

Duncan shook his head and dropped back to the bed. His name wasn't really a big secret now that he no longer worked undercover, but he liked to give it to as few people as possible.

She typed away at the computer for a couple more minutes. "Okay, I'm ready to go. What do you say to an anonymous e-mail address?"

Duncan got up and stood over her shoulder. "We have to assume that since Jonathan gave you this address, he trusts the person on the other end. You tell him the truth, but be careful how you do it."

Laura looked back at him. "What do you mean?"

"The National Security Agency has a bunch of computers at Fort Meade that pretty much monitor everything. If your e-mail goes by the wrong route, it'll be scanned and flagged unless we make sure certain keywords are obscured."

"Such as?"

"Well, you can be sure Stone has already notified them to scan for *Corrigan*, so break it up, misspell it. Do the same with *terrorists* and *Beirut*. Unfortunately, because whoever he is, he has to find this place, you'll have to put the address in correctly."

Laura returned to the keyboard and typed in the message. "What do you think?"

He looked over her shoulder. "Yeah, that should do."

She clicked SEND then turned her chair around.

"Do you have any idea who the recipient of this e-mail might be?"

Laura nodded. "Yes."

"Do you think he can help?"

"I'm sure he can help," Laura said. "I'm just not sure he'll be willing to after what happened last time."

خطر

Ali and Sam left the federal building and headed toward the pay parking lot. Her chest and shoulder still ached, but she wasn't going to tell Sam that. She had her gun and badge back and wanted to get back to work nailing Grachev. She hated Grachev with a passion, and now that he'd killed their only witness, Ali wanted to get at him even more.

They entered the parking lot, and she followed Sam to his reserved parking stall. "How much does it cost to park here monthly?" she said.

"Too much, but it beats circling the area looking for an empty parking spot."

He held the door open for her. The way she felt, Ali had no problem letting Sam be chivalrous. He closed the door and got in on the other side.

Sam looked over at her. "Seat belt?"

Ali shook her head. "Hurts."

"Oh, of course."

He looked straight ahead but didn't start the engine. "Uh, Ali—"

"Look, Sam," she said. "I can't tell you I'm okay with what happened, because I'm not. Just like you said it hurts when a guy catches his wife cheating, it hurts getting accused of cheating when you didn't. The logical part of me sees how you guys came to the conclusion you did based on what you knew. I only wish you'd bothered to talk to me before you destroyed my apartment and dragged me out of bed."

"That was Conners who did that," Sam said.

She tilted her head. "And if it'd been your call, would you have done it different?"

He shook his head.

"Well, what happened, happened. I'll get over it in time, but for now I'd like to move on and bury Grachev."

A smile crossed Sam's face. "That would suit me fine. Let's start by paying him a visit."

"To what end?"

"No better reason than to rattle his cage and see what falls out."

Sam started the car and pulled out of the parking lot. Ali watched the faces on the street. "I suppose if there was any news on that Chinese girl you would've already told me."

"Nothing. I think we can safely assume Heng has her."

"Maybe we should visit him after Grachev."

"Why not?" Sam said. "At the very least, we can let him know he's not been left out, that we've still got his bodyguard safely tucked away, and maybe hint we know more than we really do."

"Sounds like a plan."

They left the downtown core and worked their way out to the suburbs where the more wealthy people lived. Who said crime didn't pay? When they pulled up in front of Grachev's house, they found a mansion hidden behind wrought iron fencing and a security gate. Sam pushed the button to roll down his window and pressed the button by the intercom.

"Yes," a man's voice crackled.

Ali heard the whir of a security camera turn its attention to them.

"Special Agents Sam Perkins and Ali Marcoli, FBI," he said into the intercom. "We'd like to speak to Mr. Grachev." A minute passed.

"He doesn't want to see you," the voice said.

"We are on a federal investigation," Sam said. "We need to talk to him. Now, he can either invite us in, or we'll park in front of the gate until he comes out, and then we'll take him into custody and interview him elsewhere. It's his choice."

A minute later, the security gate opened, and Sam drove through. They traveled up a paved driveway bordered by hedges and maple trees. As they got close to the house, two German shepherds came out of nowhere and charged the car. They ran alongside and challenged it all the way to the entrance to the house.

A man with no neck and short hair stepped out the front door and called to the dogs. They broke off their attack, whipped to his side, and sat. Sam rolled down his window. "Is it safe to get out?"

The man held both dogs' collars and nodded.

Ali winced as she pushed open her door. She really could've used another day in bed. She fell in step with Sam as they walked up the marble steps to the front door. The two dogs kept barking as if to make sure Ali and Sam knew how unwelcome they were.

Inside the door, another broad-shouldered man dressed in blue jeans and a black T-shirt stood. "Follow me."

Ali and Sam followed the man through the entrance of the grandest house Ali had ever seen. Marble floors, two curved staircases, left and right, leading up to the next floor—the place was truly a mansion. The man opened a door and waited for Ali and Sam to pass through. "Please wait here."

"Must be the study," Sam said.

"Must be," Ali said, admiring the walls lined with books. Along the same wall was a gas fireplace with two love seats in front of it. By the full-length window stood an oak desk with a plush leather chair.

"Business hasn't suffered any."

"Not at all."

The door opened, and they both turned around. Josef Grachev entered, his perfect teeth in a broad smile. He closed the door behind him and walked up to them holding out his hand.

"I'm Josef Grachev," he said. "I'm told you wish to speak to me."

Sam shook Grachev's hand, but when he offered it to Ali, she just flashed him a tight smile. "I know who you are."

Grachev raised an eyebrow. "We've met?"

"Just at a distance."

Grachev nodded his head slowly. "I see." He pointed to

the love seats. "Well, let's sit down."

"Actually, what we have to say won't take long," Sam said. "We just dropped in to see if you had anything to say about the murder of Yuri Davidov."

Grachev sucked in a short breath and took a couple of steps back. "Yuri—dead?"

"Oh, please," Ali said. "As if you didn't know."

Grachev shook his head. "I didn't know. Yuri didn't show up for work about a week ago." He walked over to one of the love seats and rested against the back of it. "This is terrible."

Ali shifted to face him. "No kidding. So you admit he worked for you?"

"Why wouldn't I? He handled security for me."

"So let me get this right," Sam said. "Yuri Davidov handled your security, has been missing for a week, and you never reported him missing to the police. Why not?"

Grachev shrugged. "I just assumed he found himself a little honey and was enjoying himself."

"Oh," Ali said. "Did that happen a lot? It seems I'd want a man a little more reliable to handle my security."

Grachev held out his palms. "What can I say? He worked with me in Russia for years. He's a close family friend. Sometimes you have to tolerate these kinds of things." Grachev put his hand to his chest and looked at the floor. "Yuri dead; I can't believe it. How did it happen?"

"You know how it happened," Sam said. "He was in federal protection because he agreed to testify against you."

Grachev lifted his head with eyes wide. "Against me? For what?"

"Drugs, people smuggling, murder, plus a few miscellaneous felonies."

"Why would I get involved in crime? Did you know I was

in law enforcement back in Russia?"

Ali chuckled. "You were in the KGB. That's not law enforcement."

"I beg to differ," Grachev said.

Ali stiffened. "Differ all you want. Law enforcement doesn't include torture and murder."

"That is CIA propaganda. The KGB did a few regrettable things, but nothing so bad as was portrayed in the American media."

"If believing that helps you sleep at night, knock yourself out," Ali said. "Just be on notice that we don't appreciate you shooting our witness. We take it personally, and from now on we'll be watching you, and as soon as we catch you walking across the street against the light, you're going to jail."

Grachev jumped to his feet. "I had nothing to do with Yuri's death."

Ali stepped toward him. "You may not have pulled the trigger, but you gave the order."

"I did no such thing."

"Where were you the last few days?" Sam said.

"Here. I can get the house staff to verify that if you want."

"You never left home?"

"I went to a couple of my restaurants for dinner."

Ali smirked. "And I'm sure the staff there will testify to that?"

"Of course."

"Must be nice to own—what is it, a half dozen restaurants and just as many bars? Good cash businesses. Good places to launder drug money."

Grachev pointed to the door. "That's enough. Please leave."

Ali stepped in closer until they were inches apart. "I know more about you than you realize," she murmured in Russian.

Grachev's face reddened. "Get out!"

The study door whipped open, and a thick neck stepped in. "Don't worry," Sam said, "we're leaving."

Ali stepped back, flashed Grachev a smile, and made another comment in Russian that caused Grachev to grit his teeth.

"Let's go," Sam said.

Ali and Sam followed Grachev's thug through the house. A movement upstairs caught the corner of her eye. Ali looked up to see a stunning blond dressed in a gown that must have cost a week's salary watching from the rail above. Ali decided to take a shot in the dark.

She stopped, looked up at the woman, and spoke in Russian. "My name is Ali Marcoli, and you don't have to stay with that pig."

The thug gripped Ali's shoulder and gave her a little shove. Ali sucked in a deep breath and grimaced.

Sam spun, grabbed the man's hand, and bent back his wrist, dropping him to his knees. His face reddened, and he clenched his jaw. "Don't ever lay a hand on her again, or I'll break it next time." He released the thug's hand and stepped back. He took Ali's elbow. "Let's go."

They stepped outside, and the dogs barked and flashed razor-sharp teeth at them. A smug expression crossed the face of the man holding them. Sam released her elbow, and the next thing Ali knew, his weapon was in his hand pointing at the dogs. "Shut them up, or I'll shut them up."

The man's eyes widened, and he commanded the dogs to be quiet in Russian.

Sam holstered his weapon, and they walked back to the car. He held the door open for her. "You okay?"

Ali looked up at Sam and saw genuine concern. "Yeah."

Sam closed the door and got in on the other side.

"Thanks for sticking up for me," Ali said.

He looked straight ahead, glaring at the house. "Not a problem."

"So what next?"

"You and I go for coffee and trade secrets."

危险 خطر ОПАСНОТЬ

TWENTY

They found a quiet booth in a suburban coffee shop. The waitress filled two large mugs with coffee and returned to her magazine at a table.

"I'll start," Sam said.

Ali shook her head. "No, I'll go first. I should've told you about me a lot sooner than this."

"Okay, you first."

"First, I didn't learn to speak Russian in a couple of courses at college. Both of my parents were Russian."

"Somehow I'm not surprised. So why does your record say different?"

"My parents were scientists and secretly political dissidents."

"Secretly? How can you be a secret dissident?"

"With your mouth you tell people one thing, but with your heart you believe another. Unfortunately they didn't keep what was in their hearts to themselves. The KGB learned they weren't good party members, and they were *questioned*."

"Questioned?"

Ali looked down at her cup for a couple of seconds before looking back up at him. "Beaten."

"I'm sorry."

"Standard KGB protocol would've been to torture them until they revealed anyone else who thought like they did. Once they did, they would've been killed. But, because the work they were doing was particularly important, the KGB could only beat them. For over a year, they endured surprise visits from the KGB. They'd be dragged out of their home in the middle of the night, taken down to headquarters, and beaten."

Sam shook his head in disbelief. "How did they survive?"

"The CIA," Ali said. "An agent contacted them and offered to get them out in exchange for information. Mom was pregnant with me at the time, so they jumped at the chance."

"Hence the false identities."

"That's right."

"So you were born here?"

Ali nodded. "I grew up like most little kids thinking my parents were who they said they were."

"When did you find out differently?"

Ali took a sip of her coffee and then used a table napkin to dab her eyes. "When I was eight, I drew my mother a picture. In my mind it was such an exceptional piece of art I just had to show her. I thought she was upstairs in the bathroom putting on makeup, so I charged in the door. She was getting out of the shower." Ali sucked in a deep breath. "Her torso was covered in scars, burn scars."

"Oh no," Sam said. He reached across and took Ali's hand.

She nodded. "KGB torture. How do you explain away something like that to an eight-year-old? They had no choice but to tell me the truth."

"That must've been tough for you to take."

"It was. But at least once I knew the truth, they could tell me about my heritage and even teach me the language of my birthplace. It was kind of cool growing up having a big secret like that."

Sam released her hand and scratched his chin. "One thing I don't understand. Isn't standard procedure for the KGB to kill the relatives of defectors? Your grandmother is alive, right?"

Ali's fingers started to drum on the table. "Yeah, she is."

"Why?"

"She's the one who turned my parents in."

"Your grandmother turned in her own child?"

"Yep. Grandma was a good Communist and party member."

"Wow. Must've been hard to call her knowing that."

Ali's fingers stopped drumming. "I didn't know," Ali said. "I just found out."

"What?"

"All I ever knew about my grandmother was her name and that we didn't talk to her because then the KGB would know where we were. When I found the lump, I figured the Russians probably didn't care about the daughter of deceased defectors, and I found my grandmother's phone number on the Internet."

"It was listed?"

Ali shrugged. "With the iron curtain down, Russia isn't that secret anymore."

"She must've been shocked to hear from you."

"That would be an understatement. She wept on the phone and kept mumbling about how her prayers had been answered."

Sam lifted an eyebrow. "Prayers?"

"Apparently, somewhere between when she turned my

parents in and now, my grandmother found God. She's been praying for the chance to ask their forgiveness." Ali lifted the coffee cup to her mouth but didn't drink.

"And instead she found out they were dead."

Ali nodded and put the cup down. "Yeah. So she asked me instead."

"And what did you say?"

Ali started drumming the table again. "I told her because of the beatings my parents received, their health was never the same. That I lost my mother to cancer when I was fifteen and my father to a broken heart when I was eighteen."

"Whoa, you gave her both barrels."

Ali's jaw clenched. "You bet I did. Nothing better than being a teenage girl without a mother and then a father. I've been on my own since I was eighteen, and she says, 'Sorry I turned your parents in.'"

Ali grimaced. "She might've found God, and maybe it helps her, but I've still got this big empty place in my chest, and *sorry* just won't cut it. That's why I want to nail Grachev so bad. He's one of the monsters who did the KGB's dirty work. Maybe he even tortured my parents. In any event, all I want to see is Grachev swing from a gallows."

"But you've talked to your grandmother since that call. Conners said you made phone *calls* to Moscow."

Ali nodded. "Yeah. She said that even if I couldn't forgive her, she wanted to know what was happening, so she could *pray* for me. I figured it couldn't hurt and to be honest, as much as I hate her for what she did to my mom and dad, I had no one to talk to."

Sam took her hand again. "Well, you have me to talk to. Anytime you want. Okay?"

Ali's eyes glistened, and she nodded.

"And I've got some good news for you."

"I could use some," Ali said.

"Davidov isn't dead."

Ali straightened. "What?"

Sam explained the events surrounding Davidov's shooting.

Ali's eyes lit up. "So the doctor thinks he'll make a full recovery?"

"Other than blindness, yeah."

"So if it hadn't been for that breeze at the last second, he would've been dead?"

"Yep. It was just enough to offset the bullet's trajectory."

"Maybe Grandma is right. God works in mysterious ways."

"Lucky for Davidov if He does."

Ali bunched her right hand into a fist. "Let's go back to Grachev's house and drag his butt into jail."

Sam held up his hand. "Hold on, girl. Davidov is still in a coma, so all we've really got is a deposition, and we still have the problem with the container that was supposed to be full of drugs being full of people."

Ali slumped back in her seat. "Yeah, of course, you're right."

Sam's cell phone buzzed. He put it to his ear. "Yeah." He listened, flipped it shut, and looked at Ali. "Remember that mysterious ways thing?"

She leaned forward. "Who was it?"

"Conners. Bellingham police informed him that the Chinese guy who shot at Danny Corrigan was found in the trunk of a car—alive. He's in the hospital."

"The same Chinese guy who was trying to grab our refugee?"

"Yep."

Ali jumped up. "Then let's get going. He might know where she is."

Sam got up and tossed three dollars on the table. "I'm with you—partner."

خطر

Ali reached for the door handle when Sam parked the car in the parking lot of St. Joseph Hospital in Bellingham.

"Let me get that," he said.

"I'm not an invalid, just sore."

"Well, you'll heal faster the more you rest your arm," he said while getting out of the car.

Sam came around and opened the door for her. Ali had to admit it felt nice even if she was being untrue to her semi-feminist roots. "Thanks," she said and stepped out into the late afternoon heat. She was thankful she chose to wear a light jacket, cotton blouse, and blue jeans.

They walked through the emergency entrance. The waiting room had half a dozen people in it and a young nurse in her early twenties manned the desk.

"Been a long time since I've been here," Sam said.

"When were you here last?"

Sam looked away for a second. "Believe it or not, it is classified."

She touched his arm to stop him and stepped closer. "It was you, wasn't it?"

He stiffened. "Me what?"

"You shot Corrigan. I remember he stayed in the Bellingham hospital for a day or so. Why else would you be here?"

Sam's Adam's apple bobbed up and down. "We were both on the LA terrorist detail, and when he was shot, I came up here to handle his security."

"You're hedging."

"I've told you everything I can."

"Fair enough, but you must've felt sick when he was shot."

Sam shook his head and smiled. "Ali, you've gotten all you're going to get. Now, let's get back to the business at hand."

"Right, boss," she said and followed Sam to the nursing station.

They both produced their identification, and Sam said, "You've got a John Doe here under police guard. We need to see him."

The nurse flashed her blue eyes at Sam and smiled. "I'll let them know." The nurse picked up her phone, continuing to look at Sam.

"Thank you," he said.

Ali looked at Sam for a reaction, but there was none. The nurse wasn't Hollywood material but pretty enough most males would at least smile back. She'd noticed in their time together that he seemed to be immune to feminine charm and managed to keep his eye on the road no matter what was walking down the sidewalk.

A solidly built man in his late thirties with short dark hair and humorless blue eyes, approached them from the hall leading to the emergency case rooms. His sports coat flapped open as he walked, and his sidearm could be seen. He extended his hand. "Detective Ted Brock, Bellingham PD."

Sam shook it. "Special Agent Perkins, Special Agent Marcoli."

Brock shook Ali's hand then turned to Sam. "Mind if I see some ID?"

"Absolutely not," Sam said. They both produced their IDs again.

"Follow me," Brock said.

They followed the detective through the emergency room to a door where two uniformed officers stood at alert. Brock nodded, and one of them opened the door for them to pass into a private hospital room.

An Asian man with a bandaged head occupied the lone bed with IV tubes running into his arm. A matronly nurse sat at his bedside. His leg was in a cast and hung at a thirty-degree angle from the bed. His right arm boasted a cast and rested across his chest. His face was bruised, lips swollen, and blackened eyes closed.

"What a mess," Ali said.

"Yeah," Brock said, "and that's just what you see."

"What else is wrong with him?" she said.

"He's got three cracked right ribs, four missing teeth, and a skull fracture. He's also dehydrated."

"What happened?" Sam said.

"We got an anonymous tip to check out a car at Cordata Place. It was eighty-five degrees outside when we found this guy curled up in the trunk."

"Any idea what his name is?"

"All he'll tell us is his first name: Ricky."

"What made you connect him with the shooting at the Seattle police officer?" Ali said.

Brock chuckled. "At first we thought we'd found a Seattle cop. He had a Seattle police badge identifying him as John Wang in his pocket. When we called them to tell them we had one of theirs in hospital, they told us they don't have a John Wang and they'd get back to us. Ten minutes later, they phoned back and told us this guy was wanted for shooting at a Seattle cop and the FBI was also interested. You guys got here first. Do you know who he is?"

Sam shook his head. "No, but we know who he works for." Sam looked over at the nurse. "We'd like to talk to him."

She crinkled up her forehead. "He's unconscious."

"Uh-huh," Sam said. He walked over to Ricky's bedside.

"Ricky, FBI, time to wake up."

Ricky didn't stir.

Sam gripped Ricky's elbow and squeezed.

Ricky's eyes popped open. "Ow!"

The nurse shot to her feet. "What are you doing?"

"I figured he was faking," Sam said. "When someone's sleeping, there's usually eye movement under the lids."

"Not always," the nurse said. "That's just during the dream phase."

Sam shrugged. "I guessed right this time. Could you please leave the room?"

"No. He's a very sick man and requires twenty-four-hour monitoring."

Sam motioned for the nurse to follow him to the door out of earshot of Ricky. He whispered into her ear by the door; the nurse nodded and left the room. Sam returned to Ricky's bedside, and Ali took up position where the nurse had been on the other side. Sam turned to Brock. "You might not want to stay."

Ricky's eyes widened. "Why might he not want to stay?"

Perkins looked down at Ricky. "Fewer witnesses the better."

"I don't know about this," Brock said.

"Don't worry," Sam said. "We won't kill him, at least not deliberately."

Brock sucked in the corner of his lip and nodded his head. "I understand. Take your time." The Bellingham detective left the room.

Sam sat on the edge of the bed bumping Ricky's broken leg. The Asian man winced. "Sorry, I'm a bit clumsy. So, how did you end up in the trunk of a car in Bellingham? Heng usually kills bumbling subordinates."

"Bumbling subordinates?" Ricky said, mispronouncing the words.

"Screwups," Ali interpreted. "He usually kills anyone who

works for him and screws up. Why didn't he kill you?"

Ricky shook his head. "Not sure. He does not work for Heng."

"Who was it then?" Perkins said.

"A white guy. That's all I know."

"One of Grachev's guys?" Ali said.

"Do not know."

"You don't have to be scared of Grachev and Heng," Perkins said. "If you cooperate with us, we'll protect you."

"I do not know who he is," Ricky said. "Never see him before. Maybe works for Grachev, but don't know."

Ali sat on the bed bumping Ricky's ribs with her knee. He grimaced.

"Oh, sorry," Ali said. "I thought your left ribs were cracked."

"He tell you right ribs," Ricky slurred through his fat lips. "I hear him tell you."

"Sorry," Ali said. "I must not have been paying attention." She moved her knee closer to his ribs. "So, if you can't tell us who put you in this hospital bed, why don't you tell us where the girl is?"

Ricky's eyes strained to look at her knee without moving his head. "What girl?"

She bumped his ribs. "Don't mess with us. The girl you were trying to kidnap in Seattle with that fake badge. We want to know where she is."

"Don't know," Ricky said.

Sam rested his fingers on the rope holding up Ricky's leg. "Are you sure? We're only going to ask the question one more time."

Ricky's eyes shifted to Perkins's fingers. "Really don't know. White guy knocks me out, and then I wake up in the trunk. He must have them."

"Them?" Ali said. "Who's them?"

"Two girls. One white girl, and Michelle."

"Michelle, that's the Asian girl's name?" Ali said.

Ricky nodded, still watching Perkins's fingers. "Michelle was staying with the white girl. She a preaching girl in Seattle. That's where she meet Michelle."

"What did this girl look like?" Sam said, stroking the rope.

"Pretty, dark hair, tall."

"You wouldn't happen to have a name?" Sam said.

Ricky nodded. "Roxanne."

"So if this Roxanne met Michelle in Seattle, how did you end up in Bellingham?" Ali said.

"Because Roxanne lives in Bellingham," Sam said.

Ali looked up at Sam. "You know her?"

He nodded. "Let me guess," he said to Ricky. "You followed them to Bellingham."

"No," Ricky said. "Roxanne give her phone number to street kid. I get street kid to phone her. They make up meeting place in Bellingham. I go there, wait for her to show, then follow her home."

"Why is this Michelle so important to you?" Ali said.

"I find her when she leave ship," Ricky said. "Then she get away. I have to pay for her now."

"So you went to Bellingham to get her back?" Sam said.

"Yes."

"And when you tried to grab her, this white guy intervened?"

"Yes," Ricky said. "He comes out of nowhere."

Sam laughed and shook his head. "You poor idiot. Of all the girls in the world to kidnap, you had to pick that one. You're lucky he just beat you to a pulp."

"I take it you know who did this?" Ali said.

Sam nodded. "Yeah, the same guy we were talking about

on the way in here."

"No kidding." She looked down at Ricky. "You're lucky to be alive."

"So, you protect me—right?"

Ali and Sam looked at each other. "He can corroborate she was on the ship," Ali said.

Sam nodded. "It all helps." He put his hand on Ricky's leg, and the man winced again. "It's your lucky day, Ricky. You just became a material witness. We'll protect you until you go to jail."

Ricky's eyebrows lifted. "Jail?"

"You shot at a Seattle police officer and tried to kidnap two girls. Your testimony is helpful, but not crucial. We'll keep you alive, but that's all we're promising for now." Sam looked up at Ali. "Let's go collect Michelle."

危险
خطر

TWENTY-ONE

S am turned the car into the Corrigan farm and navigated down the driveway until he came to the Corrigans' large log house. Chained to the garage was Jonathan's new dog, making threats Sam knew the dog could carry out.

"Nice animal," Ali said.

"Just don't try to pet him."

"No danger of that."

Sam parked in front of the steps leading up to the verandah and front door. Ali opened her door before he had a chance to say anything.

"It's okay," she said. "Now that we're starting to get some breaks, I'm feeling a lot better. I can even visualize Grachev sitting behind bars."

"Me, too," Sam said.

As they walked up the steps, the front door opened and Sandra Corrigan stepped outside.

"Sam," she said, "how nice to see you. And who's that pretty woman with you?"

Sam glanced over at a blushing Ali. He certainly couldn't disagree with Sandra's assessment. Ali was pretty. "This is my partner, Ali Marcoli."

Sandra Corrigan knit her eyebrows together. "Partner? Oh, I thought. . . This isn't a social call, is it, Sam?"

He shook his head. "No. I need to talk to Jonathan."

A shadow passed over her face. "Jonathan isn't here. He's out of town."

Sam cocked his head. "Are you sure?"

"Yes. He's not here."

"Uh, we have information to the contrary," Ali said.

"No, we don't," Sam said. "If Mrs. Corrigan says Jonathan isn't here, he isn't."

"Then who. . . ?"

Sam looked at Ali and shook his head. "I don't know." He turned to Mrs. Corrigan. "We need to talk to Roxanne."

Sandra Corrigan straightened her shoulders, making a formidable opponent. "Why? What's she done?"

"It's not what she's done," Sam said, "it's what she knows."

"Then what does she know?"

"We believe she knows the whereabouts of an Asian girl," Ali said. "This girl is crucial to an investigation we're involved in."

"I'll ask her when I see her."

"Is she home?" Sam said.

Sandra Corrigan looked at him, but her mouth didn't move. Sam remembered Jonathan saying his mother had trouble even shading the truth. No answer was as good as a yes.

"May we come in and talk with her?" Sam said.

Ali jabbed his arm and pointed toward the horse barn. "Sam, look."

He turned his head just in time to see Roxanne's head disappear around the corner of the barn. "Roxanne!" he called out.

"I'd like you to leave our property right now," Sandra said.

Sam looked back at Sandra. She had her farm-woman arms crossed and looked like she was prepared to throw him off the property if need be. "Sorry, Mrs. Corrigan, but this is too important." He turned to Ali. "Let's go."

He broke into a jog to the barn. Ali followed him at as quick a walk as she could manage. When Sam reached the barn, he stepped inside. Not a soul to be seen. He went back out. "Go around the other side," he said to Ali. Sandra Corrigan was close on Ali's heels.

Sam went around the opposite side of the barn to Ali, and they met at the back. "See anyone?"

She shook her head.

"I'm ordering you to leave our property. You have no search warrant, so get off."

Sam appraised Sandra Corrigan. Any other time he'd visited, she treated him like a long-lost son; now her eyes smoldered and her jaw twitched. She reminded him of a bear protecting her cubs. "Mrs. Corrigan, we don't need a search warrant to talk to someone, especially if they run from us. Roxanne isn't in trouble, and neither is the Asian girl."

"I don't care. Go."

"Let's take another look in the barn," he said to Ali.

Sandra Corrigan blocked his path, but Sam stepped around her, and Ali followed him to the entrance of the barn. Half a dozen stalls lined the right, and bales of hay were stacked to the left. Sam jerked his head toward the stalls. "Stay by the door."

Ali nodded.

Sam opened each stall in turn, and the only evidence he found was of horses.

"They must've run into the bush," Ali said.

"Satisfied?" Sandra Corrigan said, her foot tapping like a rock-and-roll drummer's.

He looked at the stack of hay bales arranged in step fashion so they could be climbed to get to the top. "No."

Sam climbed up the bales until he reached the top. He noticed one row seemed to be out of line. He crawled over and laughed. "Don't you look a mess."

Roxanne shot him a venomous look. Wedged between the row of hay bales and the barn wall, she and Michelle were covered in hay. "You're not sending her back. She's my friend."

"I have no plans on sending her anywhere," Sam said. "We just need to talk to her. Now climb down from there."

Sam climbed down from the stack of two hundred or so bales with Roxanne and the Asian girl following. When they got to the bottom, Roxanne stood with her weight shifted to one side and looked ready to rip his throat out. Michelle looked like a rabbit caught in a snare. Sandra rushed between the girls and placed an arm around each of them.

Ali joined Sam and stood at his side.

"Is that the girl you saw in the water?" he said to her.

Ali nodded.

"I don't suppose you speak English as well as Chinese."

"I speak English," the Asian girl said with a heavy accent.

"Good. What's your name?"

"My name Michelle."

"My name *is* Michelle," Roxanne said.

"My name is Michelle."

"Definitely the same girl Ricky was after," Ali said.

Michelle tensed. "Ricky! Ricky here." She moved behind Sandra Corrigan.

"No, no," Sam said. "Ricky can't hurt you. He's with the police."

Michelle relaxed a bit but stayed behind Sandra Corrigan.

"Michelle, don't you remember me?" Ali said. "I helped you save that boy in the water."

Michelle moved from behind Sandra a bit and looked at Ali closely. "I remember. Boy is okay?"

"Yes," Ali said. "He had to go to the hospital, but he's okay. Now we need to know something about the container. Were you in the same container the whole trip over from China?"

Michelle cocked her head. "Same?"

"Too bad Laura isn't here," Roxanne said. "She speaks some Chinese."

"One container," Ali said holding up a single finger. "Were you in one container all the time?"

Michelle shook her head. "No. Two containers. Before we get here, we go into clean container."

Sam looked at Ali. "That's what we needed to know."

"What do we do now?" Ali said.

"Not send me back! Not let Ricky get me!"

Sandra Corrigan tightened her arm around Michelle. "Don't worry, you're not going anywhere. You're going to stay with us."

Sam took a deep breath and exhaled slowly. "Actually, Mrs. Corrigan, that decision belongs to the INS, but you have my word we'll do all we can to get them to grant her status."

"I don't care what you or the INS say. This girl isn't going back. They tore her from her home, forced her to live in a container, and then tried to make her into a prostitute. If she goes back, they'll kill her. This farm is where Michelle stays."

Sam held out his hands. "Like I said, we'll do our best."

"Well, Samuel Perkins, your best might not be good enough. When Jonathan gets home, he's going to take care of this. This country owes him plenty, and it's about time it paid him back."

"I hope you're right, but in the meantime, we have to take

her into protective custody."

"And just what does that mean—jail?"

"Sort of. We take her to a secure facility where she'll be safe."

"Safe from whom?"

Sam shook his head. "Some pretty nasty people."

"Then send people to guard her here."

Sam shook his head. "We tried that before—remember? You know how hard it is to secure this place. It's better we take her somewhere else."

Sandra Corrigan shook her head. "You're not going to stick her in some cage. She's already spent enough time locked up."

"She can stay with me," Ali said.

Sam looked at his partner. "I'm not sure that's such a good idea."

"What choice do we have? I agree with Mrs. Corrigan. We can't cage her up after what she's been through, and honestly, Sam, I need a rest—if you know what I mean."

Sam did understand. Ali would heal from the biopsy quick enough, but she still had to deal with the fears jangling in her head. Looking after Michelle would give her something to occupy her mind. "Okay, she can hide with you, but not at your place. I'm sure he knows where you live."

"Which makes it the last place he'd look. Besides, there's only one way in."

"And only one way out."

"Still better than being in the middle of nowhere. At least if something does go wrong, help is only minutes away." She put her hand on his arm. "Sam, you'll have to trust me on this one."

"Okay," he said. "Is that all right with you, Mrs. Corrigan? Can Michelle stay with Ali?"

"Only on one condition. You swear you will not let them send that girl back before Jonathan returns."

"I promise."

"No," Sandra Corrigan said. "You swear. That's an oath between you and God. Not something lightly broken."

Sam put up his hand. "Okay, I swear I won't let anyone send Michelle back until Jonathan has a chance to do something."

"We've got another problem," Ali said.

"What's that?" Sam said.

"If Ricky found Michelle here, they're going to know she was here. I suggest everyone leave the farm until this matter is resolved."

Sandra shook her head. "This is a dairy farm. We can't just leave."

"Then I think we need to make Michelle's arrest public," Ali said. "We have to make it clear that she's not here; otherwise they'll come looking."

Sam started to open his mouth to object, then realized that Ali was right. Grachev would probably learn via Heng that Michelle was at this farm. There was nothing to keep secret anymore. Taking attention away from the farm was the number one priority. "Okay, we'll get the INS to announce they caught her and will be deporting her."

Sandra stiffened.

"Just for pretend," Sam said. "We'll probably let the news shoot some footage of her being taken into custody, but Ali will be with her all the time."

"Just remember your oath," Sandra said.

"I will."

Ali turned to Roxanne. "Something I'm curious about. We know Ricky attempted to kidnap Michelle, but someone stopped him. We thought it was Jonathan, but he's out of town. Who was it?"

Roxanne shook her head. "I don't know, but the guy had

ice water in his veins."

"Did he say or do anything after he rescued you?"

Roxanne shook her head. "No. He just knocked the guy out and told us to go home."

"That's all?" Ali said.

"That's all."

Ali looked up at Sam and lifted her eyebrows.

"Probably one of Jonathan's CIA buddies," Sam said.

"Yeah, probably."

خطر

It was getting dark outside and still no response to the e-mail. Laura had spent the whole day cooped up in the stuffy motel room with Duncan McIntyre. Their conversations were pretty much one-sided. He asked lots of questions but never said anything about himself. They passed most of the day watching television or playing cribbage. At the moment, McIntyre was sizing up his cards.

Laura looked at the door. "Doesn't look like he's coming."

McIntyre set his cards down on the rickety kitchen table. "Considering we've been in this room all day, and I haven't harmed you or given you any reason to believe I'm not on your side, why don't you share with me who *he* is?"

Laura shook her head. "I'd like to, but I can't. I signed something."

McIntyre folded his arms across his chest and leaned back in his chair. "Really? What kind of thing?"

"The kind of thing where everyone agrees to shut up about something because everyone did something wrong, and as long as everyone shuts up, everyone gets to live their life without trouble."

McIntyre grinned. "So that was Corrigan?"

"What?"

"The Bellingham mess. The reason Stone resigned. You must be the key girl."

Laura straightened in her chair. "How do you know about that? Only those involved knew."

"I was involved. I was involved in trying to find the key."

"You?"

"I speak Russian. The key might've been Russian-based. You've got to admit the language symbols make for a tempting base."

"So you worked for the CIA then?"

"In a manner of speaking."

Laura threw her cards down and jumped to her feet. "You are working for Stone. You—you. . ." Laura fought to keep her language civil.

McIntyre held up his hands. "I am not working for Stone. I am loosely attached to the CIA, but most of my work is with the military. If I was working for Stone, you'd be, uh, elsewhere."

Laura backed away from him toward the door. "I can't believe you. I can't believe anything the CIA says. You guys tried to kill me."

"You have to trust me, Mrs. Corrigan. I am your husband's best hope of ever returning home."

Oh, Lord, Laura thought. *What do I do? What can I do?*

Three solid raps sounded on the door, and Laura jumped away from it. A gun appeared in McIntyre's hand, and he rushed forward and pushed her down beside the bed. What was it with spies and shoving her down beside the bed?

Keeping low, McIntyre shuffled to the door, reached up, and slid the chain lock off. He looked at Laura and whispered. "Ask who it is."

"Who is it?" Laura called to the door.

"It's. . ."

McIntyre yanked the door open and sprung out the door. Laura heard bodies crash together, and grunts followed. Less than fifteen seconds later, McIntyre appeared holding his gun to the head of a slightly built man with fine features. It was Ruben Abrams, an Israeli spy.

"Mrs. Corrigan," Ruben said with his slightly Mediterranean accent, "this is no way to greet a friend."

"Is this who you thought it would be?" McIntyre said.

Laura nodded. "Yes." The last time she'd seen Ruben, he'd been holding a gun on her and Jonathan.

McIntyre released Ruben and slipped his gun in behind his back.

Ruben turned around to face McIntyre. "And who might you be?" he said.

Duncan pushed the door shut then held out his hand. "Duncan McIntyre. Sorry for the rough stuff. We've been having some trouble."

Ruben shook Duncan's hand then looked over at Laura. "Trouble? What kind of trouble?"

Laura climbed up from beside the bed and pointed to the kitchen table. "Why don't we all sit down?"

"Certainly," Ruben said.

The two men followed her to the table and sat.

"So," Ruben said, "what kind of trouble?"

"CIA trouble."

"Why am I not surprised?" the Israeli said. "Jonathan was such a good spy before he met you."

Laura tensed. "What is that supposed to mean?"

Ruben flashed a disarming smile. "Oh, don't get me wrong. I think he is a better man since he met you. He's just a lousy spy because now he has divided loyalties, a dangerous situation for any spy. Isn't that so, Mr. McIntyre? No ties is best."

"I imagine so."

"So what has happened?"

"CIA Director Bolton convinced Jonathan to go on one last mission. Jonathan wouldn't tell me what the mission was or even where he was going, but he also wouldn't promise he was coming back. I received a call from Director Stone yesterday. Jonathan has been taken by Hezbollah in Beirut, and they're demanding ransom."

Abrams's forehead creased. "This is not good. Stone hates Jonathan. It's like having the fox arrange security for the chickens."

"We have information that confirms Stone has no intention of getting him," Duncan said. "He could've prevented the capture, and he could've mounted a rescue operation by now. There's a carrier nearby with Special Forces guys who were good to go. They've been ordered to stand down."

Laura tilted her head. "You never told me that."

"Mrs. Corrigan, I never tell anyone more than they need to know. Mr. Abrams needs to know; you had enough to worry about."

Again Laura found her hand resting on her belly. *Oh, Lord, I don't want to raise this child alone.* She took a deep breath to keep the threatening tears at bay.

"I'm not sure what I can do," Ruben said to McIntyre. "I work for the Israeli government, that I will not deny, but my assignment now is to keep an eye on terrorists working out of Canada. I have little to do with Middle East operations."

He turned his attention to Laura, and he held up his right hand. Two of the knuckles were knurled. "I was a concert pianist before Jonathan did this to me. Now I can only play in bars, though I do get rave reviews. I'm not sure how big a favor I owe Jonathan."

"You weren't a concert pianist," Laura said. "You were a

killer using it as a cover. And at the time Jonathan did that, you had a gun on us. What did you expect him to do?"

Abrams shrugged. "Anything but break my hand."

"Jonathan didn't tell me everything about his days working in the Middle East, but I know he saved your life on at least one occasion. A couple broken knuckles don't make up for a saved life."

Abrams shrugged again. "I can't argue with that. You are right of course, I do owe Jonathan my life, and that is why I have come. But I assume what you want me to do is have the Israeli Defense Forces rescue Jonathan?"

"That's right," Laura said.

"I am only a spy, not a military commander. I can recommend, that's all. To be frank, unless it's in Israel's interest, they are unlikely to do anything."

Laura slumped in the chair, and a couple of tears managed to breach her defenses.

McIntyre's hand rested on her shoulder. "Just relax." He turned to Abrams. "It is in Israel's interest."

Abrams leaned back in his seat. "How?"

"First, Corrigan saved more than just your butt. I've seen the file. He provided intelligence that led to the interception of several suicide bombers. Israel owes him plenty."

"Those are past deeds. You are asking the IDF to attack Beirut. We get lots of bad press when we do that. My government will need a good reason."

"Humph," McIntyre said. "I thought helping out a friend would be reason enough. Well, how's this? Jonathan has intelligence on some kind of proposed terrorist attack. As much as Stone hates Corrigan, I doubt he'd let that kind of intelligence go unrecovered if it had to do with an attack on the U.S. Since Stone is willing to let Jonathan rot, the intelligence must be for some other country." McIntyre put his fingers to his cheeks. "I wonder what country that could be?"

"Israel," Abrams whispered.

"It could be Israel. Now Hezbollah has him, and I know you don't like them. Can you make something happen or not?"

Abrams chewed on his lower lip. "You know exactly where he is?"

"We do."

"Give me the location. I'll see what I can do."

خطر

Jonathan lay prone on the floor with the machine gun in front of him. They'd long cut off the power, so he was in total darkness. The last time he'd heard anything was the gunfire coming down the stairs and then through the hole into the other basement. That ended quickly when they realized he wasn't there.

Their next step was to put tear gas down the vents. By keeping the cloths blocking the vents wet, he neutralized that attack. There was only one way in, and that was through the door. If Hussein was half as smart as Jonathan suspected the terrorist to be, he'd realize it would cost half a dozen men to come through the door.

No, Hussein was doing what Jonathan would do. Wait it out. Sooner or later, Jonathan would run out of air. Although he tried to keep as relaxed as he could and keep his respirations slow, already the air was becoming stale. His original estimate of twenty-four hours might have been optimistic.

He stood and stretched in order to keep his muscles limber. After the bullets were gone, he had every intention of fighting until they killed him. Something bad was on its way to Seattle, and he'd do whatever was necessary to get free.

危险
خطر
ОПАСНОТЬ

TWENTY-TWO

Josef Grachev jumped out of bed, making his exit particularly noisy so that he'd wake up Sophie. She moaned but made no sign she intended to join the living.

"Get up," he said. "You have work today."

"Let me sleep," she said in Russian.

Josef slapped her on the rump, none too tenderly. "Look. You had a day off yesterday. Now get up and remember—speak English."

Sophie bundled the duvet around herself and rolled to a sitting position on the bed. "I am up."

"You better stay up. I've got a meeting this morning, and then it's off to work for you."

She nodded her head but made no effort to move.

"I'm warning you, Sophie, if you're not ready when I am, more than your butt will be sore."

"I will be ready," she said.

Josef hit the shower, dressed, and then headed for the dining room. The smell of fried bacon and scrambled eggs filled the house. His lawyer, Ray Kuhl, was already at the table sipping orange juice and dressed to take on the world.

"Good morning, Josef," Kuhl said. "Sleep well?"

"Yeah. It's nice to sleep in a bed that isn't moving with the ocean." Josef took the seat across from Kuhl. He poured himself a glass of orange juice from the pitcher on the table. A thick-necked man entered from the kitchen. "Would you like to be served now?" he asked in Russian. A lot of Josef's inner circle was ex-KGB, including those who served his food.

"Sure."

The thick-necked server reappeared carrying plates stacked with bacon, scrambled eggs, pancakes, French toast, hash browns, and regular toast. Josef was never sure what he wanted to eat in the morning, so he had the kitchen staff make everything. Wasting food was a luxury he never had back in Russia. The server retreated to the kitchen and closed the door. No one would enter until Josef told them to. His staff was very careful not to hear what they shouldn't, because the penalty for knowing something you shouldn't was severe.

"So," Josef said, "where are we? Any problems?" He scooped some eggs onto his plate, followed by a half dozen strips of bacon.

"For the most part—no," Kuhl said. "There's been no notice given to the grand jury concerning you. Prosecutors are busy with other things. The FBI's case seems to be at a standstill." Kuhl went for French toast with hash browns.

"Good. You said 'for the most part.' I don't like that phrase. What's wrong?"

"Have you been watching the news?"

"Yes."

"Did you see the story about the illegal Chinese girl caught in Bellingham?"

"Sure. What does she have to do with me?"

"I talked with Heng. He says she was in the container that was dumped in the ocean."

Grachev put down his fork. "Really?"

"Yeah."

"It doesn't matter anymore, does it? Davidov is dead, so even if this girl was willing to testify the containers were switched, without Davidov her testimony is useless."

"If he's dead."

Grachev tilted his head and looked at Kuhl. "Why would you say that? The second man says the sniper got a head shot. Our other guy followed the ambulance to the hospital and saw the body."

"He saw *a* body," Kuhl said. "Remember, he never really got a good look at the face."

"Still, a bullet to the head. If Yuri is alive, it's only as a member of the vegetable garden."

"I agree," Kuhl said, "but one thing bugs me."

"And that would be?"

"I've got a source who says after the INS arrested her, they handed her over to the FBI, and she hasn't been seen since. Why would they do that unless—"

Suddenly Josef wasn't hungry. "She was of use to them."

Kuhl nodded.

"Meaning Davidov might be alive and have a vocabulary greater than a carrot stick?"

"I'm afraid so."

"Well, we can't leave this to chance," Grachev said. "I'll have my guy track her down."

"I know it's more work, but I suggest you don't kill her if you don't have to."

Grachev lifted an eyebrow. "Really? Why?"

"There's a wild card out there. Whoever took out Heng's guy isn't FBI or Heng's or ours, but he's very good. We need to know who he is. The girl might know, and if she doesn't, whoever's guarding her might. At this point, information is more valuable. We can always kill her later."

"Yes, you're right, of course. I'll make it happen."

"I think you need to go back to the freighter," Kuhl said. "As a precaution."

"Can't. It moved on up to Canada."

"Well, there's always the yacht."

"Yeah," Josef said, "there's always the yacht."

خطر

Ali heard a sharp sound. She rolled off the couch to the floor while grabbing her gun from underneath the pillow. In one motion she flicked off the safety, pulled back the hammer, and poked her head around the couch aiming at the door. It was closed with all locks in position.

"Sorry to wake you," Michelle's voice sailed over the couch from the kitchen. "I make breakfast to surprise you."

Michelle's feet padded over to the couch, and her child-like face peered down at Ali. Ali slowly put the hammer back in place and flicked on the safety. "It's okay. I should be up anyway." Her chest burned, reminding her it wasn't up to full duty yet.

"Not right for you to sleep on couch. Guest should sleep there."

"No," Ali said, "you're a witness, which means I sleep by the door." She climbed up off the floor. "So, what were you going to make for breakfast?"

"Scrambled eggs. Mrs. Corrigan teach me to cook scrambled eggs and toast, but I burn toast all the time."

Ali picked up her holster from the coffee table, slipped it on, and put her gun in it. "Let me help you then." The two women went into the kitchen where a carton of eggs sat on the counter, and a bowl and a whisk rested on the floor. "I take it that's what woke me up."

"Sorry." Michelle shrank away from her like she expected to be hit.

"Hey, it's no big deal. I drop stuff all the time." Ali picked the whisk up and rinsed it in the sink. "Why don't you crack the eggs into the bowl? I want two."

Michelle relaxed and began the task of breaking the eggs. The girl handled them like a professional short-order cook. Ali dug a frying pan out from beneath the stove. Truth was, she did little cooking at home, preferring to eat out. Financially Ali was doing all right. Her parents left her with a good chunk of money. Money that would never fill that empty void of not having them. She squeezed the handle of the frying pan wishing it were Grachev's neck.

"You okay?"

Ali realized she was grinding her teeth. She forced a smile to her face. "Yeah. Sorry, I was just thinking about something."

"Something bad?" Michelle said.

"Yeah, something bad." Ali put the frying pan on the stove and turned on the heat. She opened the fridge and found a lump of butter. There was a carton of milk two days past expiry. She wouldn't be able to show Michelle the secret to great scrambled eggs.

Working in tandem, the two women managed to put together a breakfast of eggs and toast. Ali would've loved to enjoy the sunny morning by having breakfast out on the balcony but didn't dare risk it. The curtains would stay closed, and the two of them would stay out of sight.

Ali carried the plates into the little dining room, and Michelle followed with glasses of water. They sat across from each other. Ali picked up her fork to dig in, but Michelle bowed her head and started to whisper.

"What are you doing?"

Michelle ignored her for a few seconds then looked up and smiled. "Praying."

"Oh," Ali said. "I didn't think China was big on God, being a Communist country and all."

"Many believe in God in China. You believe in God?"

"Not really," Ali said.

"Why not?"

Why should I? Ali thought. *Because my parents thought wrong, they were tortured and died young, leaving me alone. Now I might have cancer.* "No particular reason."

"I can tell you about Him if you want. He loves you; He loves me."

"Uh, He loves you?" Ali said. "Aren't you the girl who was sold by her parents to smugglers?"

Michelle nodded. "Yes."

"If God loved you, I think you'd deserve a better fate."

"Fate?"

"If God loved you, bad things not happen." *Great, now I'm starting to talk like Michelle.*

"Bad things happen to everyone. God does not make them happen. He try to make them good. My parents sell me, yes. But ship not sink. Many go on ships that sink, and they die. I think I come to America to look after children, but smugglers want me to"—Michelle took a deep breath—"be with men for money. I run away from smugglers, and Roxanne find me and take me to her home. Her brother will help me stay in America. I meet you, a friend. What is bad is now good, yes?"

A grin forced its way to Ali's mouth. "You could look at it that way."

"I think in container I will die, but no. God help me. He always find way out for us if we listen to Him. Missionary come to my village, say we go to bad place when we die because we break God's laws. No matter how good we try to be, it never be good enough. No hope, he said. Then he talk about Jesus, God's Son. He say Jesus step between us and God. Die for us, take our punishment, so God will forgive us."

"And your point is?"

"No matter how bad it look, with God always hope. He sees. He knows."

Ali scooped a mouthful of eggs with her fork. "Well, Michelle, that's great you have something to believe, but it's not for me."

"Why not?"

"It just isn't. Now eat up. We've got a hard day of watching TV and playing board games ahead of us."

خطر

Sam rode down the elevator of the federal building after a meeting with Conners. Everything was starting to come together. Grachev would be behind bars soon.

He headed outside into the late morning foot traffic of downtown Seattle. Sam covered the short distance to the parking garage on foot and got into his car. Ali had phoned earlier and asked him to pick up some food. Preferably food that could be cooked in a microwave. After stopping off at a market, he went through a convoluted set of turns that included a short stint down Interstate 5 before heading to Ali's building.

By the time he got there, the lunch crowd was in full swing. He parked about four blocks away covering the rest of the distance on foot. Checking for tails in the busy foot traffic was next to impossible, but he felt confident no one could've kept up to him in the car.

He entered the lobby of the building carrying four plastic bags of groceries, and the doorman, an elderly gentleman with snow-white hair, approached him.

"Can I help you, sir?"

Sam looked down at the frail man. The only thing this guy would be good for would be to call the cops. "I'm here to see Ali Marcoli."

"Please wait, and I'll call up," he said.

The doorman retreated to his desk near the elevators and picked up his phone. He spoke briefly into the phone and then hung it up. "Tenth floor."

Sam rode up the elevator to Ali's apartment. He found her door, put down a couple bags of groceries, and knocked. He stood by the peephole so she could see him.

"Are you alone?" she called through the door.

"Just me, myself, and I," Sam said. That was the code she gave him on the phone. There was always the chance Grachev might capture him and use him to get in the apartment. If he said anything other than that, Ali would call for help.

He heard three dead bolts and two chain locks click before the door opened. Ali smiled and brushed her hair back from her face.

"Say, we're dressing informally these days."

Ali looked down at herself. She wore sweatpants, a Sonics T-shirt, and a shoulder holster. "Standard slumber party issue. Come on in."

Sam entered the apartment, and Ali snapped shut all the locks. He'd never been in her apartment before. In the living room, he saw a light tan couch and a walnut rocker facing a cartoon movie on a flat screen TV. The walls were white with a hint of pink. All the drapes were closed, but he imagined that from the tenth floor she'd have a good view. Michelle walked out of the kitchen with a glass of milk in her hand.

"Hi!" she said and headed to the couch.

Sam looked at the TV then at Ali. "*The Lion King?*"

Ali shrugged. "She's never seen it."

"No kidding."

"There's a lot of new things for this girl."

"Can we talk—alone?"

"Sure," Ali said and turned to Michelle. "You stay put. Don't open the door or go near the windows."

Michelle nodded, but her eyes were glued to the screen.

Ali looked at him and shook her head. "It's like having a five-year-old living with you. Let's go to my bedroom."

Sam followed her down a short hall and into the bedroom. Ali closed the door behind them, and they faced each other. He felt awkward standing alone with her in this particular room and moved toward the curtains. He parted them. "Wow, you've got a balcony off your bedroom. How do you afford a place like this on what we make?"

"I have no vices, and my parents left me money," Ali said.

"Nice."

She moved to the bed and sat on the edge of it. "So, what's happening?"

"Great news. Davidov is awake."

"He can talk?"

"Oh yeah. He's all there, and according to the doctor, he's furious. We won't have any trouble getting his cooperation."

"So what are we waiting for? Let's get Grachev."

"Conners wants to hold off. A judge has granted us a bunch of wiretaps. It would put the final nail in Grachev's coffin if we could find his accountant, the one who figured out the marked money."

"Why?" Ali said. "What more do we need? We've got Davidov who saw the murder, and we've got Michelle who can clear Davidov on the containers."

"The U.S. Attorney is worried Grachev may get off with murder two."

Ali straightened up. "How? He stabbed an FBI agent to death and threw his body into the sound."

"We're weak on premeditation. If we can get the accountant, we can nail down premeditation. The fact is, Ali, I not only want to get Grachev, I want to kill him. He killed my partner. If we get premeditation, we get first-degree murder, and the death penalty is on the table. Closure for me is Grachev getting the needle."

Ali considered him. "Yeah, that works for me, too."

خطر

Stone clicked the mouse button to scroll down the reports he read on his computer screen. The world was pretty much in chaos, so his job situation was secure from a workload point of view. From a family point of view, the outlook wasn't so bright. Lunch still sat heavy in his stomach. He never should've agreed to meet his wife for lunch. He should've insisted on dinner so that the whole workday didn't end up ruined.

They'd barely started their salads when Shelly opened fire. She demanded a fixed date that he would be leaving the agency. He tried to mollify her with words like "as soon as a replacement could be found, but until then he had to put his own wishes aside." She didn't buy it.

Shelly fired accusations at him, true accusations that he was glad to be back and had no intention of leaving. Of course, he defended himself with more lies, and that's when she let loose the missile. He was to tell the president he had thirty days to find a replacement because she wanted their retired life together back again. If he were still director of the CIA after thirty days, Shelly would continue with her retired life—alone.

It was like she punched him in the gut. They'd been married thirty-one years, and their union had borne no children. Shelly was all he really had in the world besides his job. Elijah needed to talk with the president to see what his intentions were regarding him. If the president intended to make the appointment permanent, he'd have to call her bluff. If she wasn't bluffing, well, at least he'd still have a job.

Stone continued reading about the religious tensions in Nigeria. If Nigeria weren't an oil-producing nation, they would not even be on his radar. His intercom buzzed.

He pushed the button. "Yes."

"Director of Operations Lavigne to see you," his secretary said.

"Send him in."

The door opened and Lavigne entered, closing it behind him.

"Have a seat, Rich," Stone said. "What's up?"

Lavigne sat in one of the chairs and crossed one of his long legs over his knee. "The Corrigan situation is fast slipping out of control."

"How so?"

"Our guys in Bellingham lost Laura Corrigan, and we suspect she may have met up with Duncan McIntyre."

If his wife threatening to leave him felt like a punch in the gut, McIntyre getting involved felt like a kick to the head. "Is this confirmed?"

"No, just a suspicion. Our guys observed Mrs. Corrigan

look in the trunk of a car. After she left, they checked it out and found a badly beaten Asian man. The work looked like McIntyre's, and, of course, she disappeared after that."

"Okay, let's assume McIntyre's involved. He's got friends, but not enough to launch a rescue mission in the Middle East. What's he up to?"

"No idea."

"I wouldn't put it past him to jump on a plane to Tel Aviv, then sneak into Beirut and try to rescue Corrigan himself. Obviously he doesn't know Corrigan is probably dead."

"Well, at least that would take care of the McIntyre problem," Lavigne said.

Stone leaned forward and pointed his finger at Lavigne. "I'm sorry if I gave you the wrong impression about McIntyre. He's not expendable. He may be a thorn in the side at times, but his loyalty is unquestioned and his service unsurpassed. If McIntyre is spotted anywhere near that building, intercept him at all costs and take him into custody. Failing that, send in everything we have to assist him." Stone put his hand down and sat back in his chair.

"Sorry, Director, I thought with what he did to our guys—"

"He didn't do anything we didn't train him to do," Stone said. "You don't train a dog to attack strangers and then kick it for doing so."

"Yes, sir."

"So that's it?"

"No," Lavigne said.

Stone felt a headache coming on to match his churning stomach. "What?"

"Well, Corrigan might actually be alive. The terrorists have made another demand. They say al Qaeda has offered a million dollars for Corrigan. We have twenty-four hours to double that amount, or they'll hand him over to al Qaeda. Al Qaeda will execute him publicly and drag his body through the streets then post the video on the Internet."

"Or they might just be trying to get some cash out of us for a dead body."

"What do we do, pay the ransom just in case he's alive?"

"Yes, but not because he might be alive."

"Why then?"

"What do you think the terrorists will do once they get the money and give us nothing in return?"

"They'll all go back to the building."

"That's right," Stone said. "We'll have the whole terrorist cell in one place whooping it up over how they duped the stupid Americans. That's when we give them a little surprise."

"We send in the Special Forces?"

"No, we send in an F-18 and blow the building to smithereens. Kill them all."

Lavigne smiled. "When do you want to do this?"

Stone looked at his watch. "It's getting dark now in Beirut. Since we're attacking from the air, we might as well do it at pre-dawn to minimize the risk of collateral damage. Get one of our guys in to laser the target, and we'll have an F-18 hit in the morning."

"Our intelligence says that building has a bomb shelter in the basement."

"Tell them to use a Daisy Cutter. That'll break through anything. Once that baby hits, there won't be anything left but charred remains."

"Yes, sir," Lavigne said and started to leave.

"One last thing," Stone said.

Lavigne paused. "Yes?"

"See if we can get them down to a million and a half."

危险 опасно
خطر

TWENTY-THREE

THURSDAY, JULY 11, IN LEBANON

Sergeant Steve Germano was positioned on the roof of the building across the street from the Hezbollah outpost. He could hear the rumble of the F-18 clearing the target area. He had to wave the jet off when a school bus appeared at the head of the street. When the smoke cleared, there'd be no question the U.S. hit the building, and a bunch of dead kids wouldn't play well on CNN.

A bunch of dead kids wouldn't play well on his own conscience either. He'd done some pretty despicable things since joining the CIA from Special Forces, but he had a line, and killing civilian children was where it was drawn. As it turned out, the bus only had a lone driver when it passed, but even an empty bus got bad press.

"Thumper, this is Bambi," he whispered into his microphone. "Target area is clear. I have painted the target, and you are clear to take it out."

"This is Thumper," the pilot's voice crackled in his earpiece. "Instructions understood. Flower, do I still have a green light?"

Flower was Langley, where Director Stone was overseeing the operation personally. Germano wondered if the director knew Flower was the skunk in the Bambi movie.

"Thumper, the light is green. You are cleared to terminate the target with extreme prejudice."

"Affirmative."

Germano could see the afterburners light up the early morning sky when Thumper made his turn. In most cities, a fighter jet screaming across the sky would attract attention, but not in Beirut. The Israelis did it all the time, and if any militia got it in their head to open fire, they'd give the Israeli pilot the excuse he was looking for to ram a missile down their throat.

All in all, this was an easy mission for Thumper. Acquire the target, drop the bomb, and return to the carrier in time for breakfast. Germano's job might not be so easy. The local militia, after getting over the initial shock of a crater where a building used to be, would start looking for anyone who looked like an Israeli or American. Once that bomb hit, he'd be gone before the dust settled.

"This is Thumper. I'm lined up with the target and have acquired. Land values are about to drop in this neighborhood."

Germano kept the laser steady on the building. He'd keep it there until Thumper told him to duck. He was so close to the target he wanted to have his head behind the wall at the roof's edge when the concrete started flying. Thumper would warn him just before impact.

Germano heard a familiar sound then looked to the southern sky. The sun was just breaking over the horizon.

"Good morning, Beirut," Thumper said.

"Wave off!" Germano screamed into his microphone. "Wave off!"

The morning sky rocked with the sound of afterburners kicking in. The F-18 corkscrewed vertically into the sky.

"Is the package gone?" shouted Germano. "Is it gone?"

"Negative, Bambi," Thumper said. "But I've never come so close."

"What's going on?" Flower barked. "Why did you wave him off?"

The heavy *whump-whump* of helicopter blades enveloped him, as three choppers roared over him and descended in front of the target building. Commandos poured out of the choppers, before they pulled up and hovered over the building.

"It is the Israelis," Germano said. "They are attacking the target."

"What? Are you sure?"

"Yes, sir. There are choppers and commandos. What do you want me to do?"

"Get out of there!" Flower said.

Oh, great, Germano thought.

"Stay put," another voice came over the earpiece.

"Who's that?" Flower demanded.

"This is Walt. Keep your man in place."

Germano breathed a sigh of relief. Walt was code for the admiral in charge of the battle group in the Mediterranean.

"Why?" Flower said.

"Because the Israelis are going to shoot at everything that moves. Take a nonaggressive stance, Bambi, and pray they realize whose side you're on."

"Yes, sir," Germano said.

He put down the laser and laid his rifle down beside it. Another chopper flew in from the south and hovered over his position. Germano put his hands over his head and prayed like he'd never prayed before. A man in combat fatigues with his face blackened stood on the landing gear of the chopper and looked at him through binoculars. He waved at Germano, then the chopper moved to the building across the street, dropping off the man and five others before going up in the air again.

"This is Bambi," he said into the mouthpiece. "The Israelis have identified me as a friendly."

"Bambi," Walt said, "stay put. I'm sending a Blackhawk in for you."

"Thank you, sir."

An explosion ripped through the still morning. Germano peeked over the lip of the edge and saw the door to the building had been blown apart. Commandos were throwing flashbangs in.

"Flower."

"Go ahead."

"Something's wrong."

"What?"

"The Israelis are using flashbangs."

"So?"

"If it was an attack, they'd be using frags. This isn't an attack; it's a rescue. Who are they rescuing?"

"Oh," Flower said.

"What does 'oh' mean?" Walt said.

"One of my agents was in there. We thought he was dead."

Walt's voice boomed in his ear. "Are you saying an American CIA operative is in that building, and we almost bombed it?"

"Like I said, our intelligence said he was dead."

"Looks like Israeli intelligence has one up on you again. Bambi."

"Yes, sir."

"Keep your head down. Cavalry's coming."

خطر

Jonathan heard the muffled sound of an explosion upstairs. He double-checked that the machine gun was cocked and got ready to fire. What were they trying now? Why didn't they just wait until he passed out from lack of oxygen instead of taking the risk of losing men?

Gunfire. What was going on? His heart started to race, and tears streamed from his eyes. "Oh, Lord, please let it be."

The gunfire upstairs lasted for about two minutes, then all went silent. It had to be a rescue, but did the silence mean he'd been rescued, or that the rescuers were all dead? All Jonathan could hear was his own breathing. Finally footsteps thumped down the stairs. Three solid raps sounded at the door.

"Corrigan, are you in there?" a man's voice called through the door.

Jonathan stood with the gun ready. Who was it? U.S. Special Forces or a terrorist who spoke English like an American? Maybe everything upstairs had just been a charade to get him to open the door. Maybe there'd been no gun battle and the floors were littered with shells from blanks fired in the air while bearded terrorists laughed at their ruse.

"Corrigan, my name is Duncan McIntyre. I'm with the CIA. We're here to rescue you. Open up, 'cause we can't stay long."

Jonathan angled himself away from the door, so if they shot through the door at his voice, he wouldn't be hit. "How do I know who you are? You could be anyone."

"Yeah, but we're not anyone."

"Prove it."

"Your wife's name is Laura, pretty with copper hair and green eyes."

"Public knowledge," Jonathan yelled at the door.

"She's pregnant and just starting to show."

"Easy to find out," Jonathan said.

"You made a tape for your unborn daughter before you left."

Tears leaped to his eyes. Jonathan felt through the dark, until he found the door and yanked it open. Duncan McIntyre grabbed him and started pulling him up the stairs.

"Lebanese militia are on their way here," McIntyre said. "As far as the Israelis are concerned, their mission is over. Let's not impose upon their hospitality."

"Israelis? I thought you were CIA. Why are we using the Israelis?"

"Because Stone is an idiot. Your wife contacted Abrams, and he set this up. By the way, he wanted me to tell you the score is even. Now come on."

Jonathan awkwardly ran up the stairs after McIntyre. They entered the hallway, which was riddled with bullet holes and bodies. Hussein's body was slumped against the wall, his lifeless eyes staring at the ceiling. "Prisoners! Why didn't you take prisoners? These guys have information we need."

McIntyre turned and looked back at him. "We can't take prisoners if they keep shooting at us, can we? Now come on." They rushed through the hall to the building's main entrance. Half a dozen Israeli commandos stood by the open door. "Stay back," the one with a radio said.

"What's going on?" McIntyre said.

"Lebanese militia have blocked us in on both sides. So much for a quick in-and-out."

خطر

Germano watched with horror. Matters were going south fast on the Israelis. Several jeeps filled with Lebanese militia converged on them from both sides of the street. The Israeli choppers opened up with heavy machine gun fire, and the militia answered back with rocket-propelled grenades.

The choppers had to pull up and away to avoid the RPGs. A dozen commandos were on the street taking position behind cars and firing back at the militia with light arms. This was going to be a massacre. The jeeps had heavy-caliber weapons mounted on them.

Germano spoke into his mouthpiece. "Walt, this is Bambi. The Israelis are pinned down by Lebanese militia. Their choppers have been driven back with RPGs. How long until the cavalry arrives?"

"Did you say Lebanese militia?" Walt said.

"Yes."

"Sorry, son, I can't send them in to fight the Lebanese."

"Why not?"

"Because we're not at war with Lebanon."

"Sir," Germano said, "the Israelis are going to get slaughtered trying to save our guy."

"Don't worry," Walt said, "I've got an idea. Thumper, I need you to go down Main Street. Go supersonic. That should be enough to get them to back off. We've picked up the Israeli tactical frequency. We'll warn them about your arrival."

"And if they don't back off?"

"I'm a pretty good card player."

Germano ducked down behind the ledge of the building. The F-18 could be heard ripping in from the west. Its jet engines weren't at full throttle because it had to keep its speed at subsonic. Germano spotted Thumper banking to the north and then making a 180 to come down the street in front of the building. He covered his ears.

Just before the Lebanese militia, Thumper hit his

afterburners, breaking the speed of sound. Glass shattered up and down the street, and Germano could see militia grabbing their heads and ducking. A wall of wind struck him as the F-18 approached him and a blast of heat hit him as it passed. Thumper pulled up, nearly toasting one of the jeeps.

The F-18 corkscrewed again and cruised above the city. The militia returned to firing at the pinned-down Israelis.

"They're not giving up, sir," Germano said into his mouthpiece.

"Were they able to fire when the F-18 came through?"

"No, sir, it really rattled them."

"Then I suggest you cover your ears, son."

"Why?"

"Take a look to the south."

In the distance he could make out another jet. As it grew larger, Germano made it out as an F-14. It hit its afterburners, and again all combatants were ducking with their ears covered. The jet pulled up, and Germano saw another F-14 coming from the other direction.

"Sir," Germano shouted into his mouthpiece. "It's working, but we can't keep this up all day."

"Sure I can," Walt said. "But don't worry, I've got another card up my sleeve."

For ten minutes, jets took turns screaming down the street, effectively shutting down all warfare on both sides. The Lebanese militia wasn't stupid. They knew if they took a shot at the jet fighters the rules of engagement would kick in. American forces were allowed to return fire if fired upon.

Thumper blasted through again, but no F-14 followed. It was quiet, but only for a second. Appearing out of side streets, two sets of Blackhawks took up position behind each militia group, firing a short burst of machine gun fire over their heads.

The Blackhawks would be under orders not to shoot at the militia, but the militia didn't know that. Deciding the better part of valor is to live to fight another day, the militia gunned their jeeps and fled down side streets. Walt's bluff paid off.

خطر

The Israeli commandos broke into a cheer. "The air show is finished," the radio operator said. "We can go now."

Jonathan followed Duncan out into the street. A Blackhawk hovered just above the ground.

McIntyre turned to the Israeli radio operator. "Thanks for your help. I'll let your people know what we've learned."

The Israeli nodded and ran to his own chopper. Jonathan followed McIntyre into the Blackhawk, and it lifted off into the air. Six Special Forces members all stared at him as if trying to decide if he was worth saving. A seventh man occupied the cabin of the chopper, and though dressed in black fatigues, he wore no insignia. He straightened up when he saw McIntyre and saluted. "Colonel McIntyre."

McIntyre looked at him and grinned. "Germano, good to see you. I heard you'd come over to the dark side."

"Colonel McIntyre?" Jonathan said. "I thought you were CIA."

McIntyre shrugged. "Yeah, well, I kind of get around. Now, where would you like to go?"

"The carrier. I have to get to a secure line in a hurry."

خطر

Stone slumped in his chair like he'd just gone ten rounds with Mike Tyson and Tyson hadn't been gracious enough to knock him out, but instead played with him the whole fight. Lavigne sat across from him.

"What are we going to do?" Lavigne said. "We nearly bombed one of our own agents. A retired agent who happens to be a national hero, at that. And how do we explain the Israelis going in for him?"

"I'm not sure we have to explain anything."

"How so?"

"What did we really do wrong? Our intelligence said he was dead. We saw them shooting in the basement; we had every reason to believe they'd killed him then. If they hadn't, why didn't the terrorists produce Corrigan after we paid them?

"Now how he survived, we'll have to ask him, but no reasonable observer would come to any other conclusion than the one we did: He was dead. It only made sense to take out the terrorist cell.

"As for the Israelis, who said they went in for Corrigan? As far as I'm concerned, their operation was independent of ours, and it was just unfortunate they collided. Good thing for them we were in the area, or they would've gotten their clocks cleaned."

Lavigne tilted his head. "Uh, the ambassador to Israel is going to ask them what they were doing there. I doubt they're going to say it was an independent mission. It's clear McIntyre found some sort of leverage to get them to act. Why should they say anything different?"

Stone made a tent with his fingers and tapped his chin. "Because the Israelis always need something. They must have a shopping list. We just need to find out what is on it and trade it for their cooperation."

"What about McIntyre? What are you going to give him?"

Stone folded his hands together. "Nothing. I doubt McIntyre will say anything."

"Why wouldn't he?"

"Because McIntyre is a simple yet complex man. He just wants to get the mission done and do what's right for the country. Right now we're in the darkest part of our history, fighting an enemy who doesn't fight fair. Duncan knows I'm a director who doesn't believe in the fair fight. He knows I'm the man for this time in history. Taking me down hurts America, and Duncan won't hurt America."

Lavigne half grinned. "Surely you don't believe that?"

Stone nodded. "Oh, I do. Sure, Duncan is probably going to want a private moment with me, scream at me a bit, but he'll do what's right. I have no doubt."

"I hope you're right for both our sakes," Lavigne said.

Stone's intercom buzzed. He pressed the button. "Yes."

"You need to go to the operations room, sir. Jonathan Corrigan is calling on a secure link."

Stone and Lavigne exchanged glances. "Now the party begins," Stone said.

خطر

Jonathan inhaled the coffee, savoring the smell while he waited for Stone to come on the monitor. Only Duncan McIntyre was in the room with him and out of sight of the camera. The ship doctor wanted him to go to the infirmary and get checked over, but he had to tell Stone what he'd learned before the ship carrying the terrorists got anywhere near the West Coast.

As much as he wanted to wring Stone's neck for trying to kill him, Jonathan was glad he was reporting to Stone and not Bolton. Stone would do what had to be done and ask for permission later. Maybe it was for that reason Jonathan had decided to do nothing about Stone leaving him to hang out to dry. Getting that ship was number one priority, vendettas number two.

The monitor flickered, and Stone's face appeared.

"Jonathan, I'm so glad to see you alive."

"Yeah, right," he said. "Let's get this out of the way first, just so there's no misunderstanding later on. If we were in the same room right now, I'd smash you in the nose so hard you'd be breathing out the back of your head."

Stone's eyebrows lifted, and he moved back a bit. "Corrigan, you're out of line."

"And so are you," Jonathan said. "The protocol was to send in the Apaches at the first sign of trouble. You didn't do that, did you?"

He could see Stone swallow. "Well, no, I didn't, and for good reason."

"And what would that be?"

"I knew they wouldn't kill you because they'd want to get information out of you. Since you've been out of the loop for a while, I knew you had nothing to give them. I felt it was more important to find out who these guys are and gather intelligence. Sooner or later, when they knew you had nothing to tell, they'd want to trade you, and that's when I was going to get you out. I didn't think you'd mind."

Jonathan set his cup down before he threw it across the room. "Oh, and just where did you get that idea?"

"From you."

"Me?"

"Sure. Maybe you've suffered a memory loss or something, but my recollection of you when you worked as a field agent was the more dangerous the better. Whatever needed to be done to protect America was okay with you. Well, considering today's enemies, I just assumed that still stood. You were willing to sacrifice your life before, so what's changed?"

"Aw, give it a rest, Stone," Jonathan said. "Before I was a

single guy. Now I'm married with a child on the way."

"All the more reason to take a dangerous assignment. Each of us fears the next attack will harm our loved ones; I assumed you to be no different. I'm sorry if I misunderstood."

"Oh whatever," Jonathan said. "We're not going to get anywhere with this. The significant thing is I have some important intelligence we have to act on right away."

Stone's face grew in the screen as he moved closer. "What have you got?"

"My source worked on the docks. He saw six men with a three-foot-by-six-foot wooden crate board a Russian container vessel. He identified two of them as Hezbollah, and they were all armed. None of them got back off the ship. They talked about seeing the needle in space, so I think we can safely assume the target is Seattle. They've been at sea for almost four weeks."

"What was the ship's name?" Stone said.

"He couldn't read it because it was in Russian, so he checked the harbormaster logs. No ship was logged in that berth."

Stone scratched his chin. "Well, this would be disturbing information indeed if your source wasn't dirty."

Jonathan leaned forward. "What?"

"Your source. I believe you call him Petra. Well, after you were taken, we kept an eye on him. The terrorists were shaking his hand, slapping him on the back, and even gave him your escape car. You were duped, Corrigan."

Jonathan shook his head. "No way. Emile is as solid as they come. He's a Christian; he wouldn't lie about something like this."

"Really. Then tell me why he's still alive. If he'd given you anything at all, they would've shot him and his family. He's alive and well in Beirut, and I hear his son even joined Hezbollah.

Hardly sounds like a guy who's on our side."

"Maybe that was their plan. If they killed Emile, it would have validated his information. They let him live so we would believe the information was just a ruse to capture me. This is a serious threat, Stone."

"Okay, let's go on the assumption the information is correct. They had you; why keep a traitor alive? The information was contained. Which brings me to another question. Did they ever ask you what he told you?"

"No," Jonathan said.

"Did they torture you?"

"Just rap music and lights."

"So they didn't try very hard. No drugs, no beatings."

Jonathan shook his head.

"See. You had nothing, and they knew it. All they wanted you for was money. In fact, before the Israelis hit the building, we were negotiating your ransom. We paid one and a half million to get you back. When they didn't produce you at the exchange point, we knew you were dead. That's why I ordered an F-18 to demolish the place. I was just a little ticked off, and I wanted to send a message of what happens when you kill one of our agents."

Jonathan had to admit Stone was good. If he didn't know the man was a professional liar, he could almost believe him. Besides, he knew something Stone didn't; he knew Emile. "I don't care how it all looks. I know Emile, and he wouldn't lie to me. He saw what he saw, and we're dealing with a smarter-than-average bunch of terrorists here. They've gone to a lot of trouble to protect this mission; it's that important to them. They were dedicated enough to fight the Israelis to the death rather than be captured and forced to corroborate Emile's information."

Stone looked away for a second. "Okay, Jonathan, this is

the reality of the situation. We get literally thousands of threats a day of terrorist attacks. We don't have unlimited resources, so we can't check them all. We have to prioritize and go after the ones that look most promising. Yours doesn't look that promising.

"What we have here is your buddy Emile joined Hezbollah. If you'll think back, you gave the Israelis a lot of intelligence on Hezbollah, and the Israelis acted with extreme prejudice against them. These guys don't like you, and they found a way to lure you into their backyard. Nothing more than that happened."

Jonathan shook his head hard. "You're wrong, Stone. This is a bona fide threat. I know it in my gut, just like when I met Harrison McIvor in Istanbul I knew he was up to something. I wasn't wrong then; I'm not wrong now."

Stone took a deep breath. "Do you even realize as it is we only search 3 percent of the containers that land at our ports? What do you want me to do? Pull every agent off what they're doing to search containers? While they're chasing your red herring, a real attack might get through."

"I don't want you to search the containers," Jonathan said. "By that time, it'll be too late. I want you to get the navy to board every Russian ship anywhere within three hundred miles of our coastline and search it."

Stone shook his head. "Oh, that's not going to happen. Not with what you've got. The Russians would go through the roof."

"Then you're going to ignore this?"

"No," Stone said. "I'll notify the navy and the Coast Guard to be on a higher alert, but I'm not boarding every Russian vessel approaching our shores. I don't have enough evidence to use that much manpower. Now why don't you go home to that nice wife of yours and take a rest?" Stone's picture flickered away.

Jonathan turned to McIntyre. "What do I do now? I know the threat is real. Go to the media?"

McIntyre shook his head. "No. With the new laws regarding homeland security, they probably wouldn't report it and you'd go to jail. Don't be too discouraged just yet. This has to do with Russians, and if there's anything I know, it's Russians. There'll be someone waiting on the other end for this ship. They shouldn't be too hard to find."

"What makes you say that?"

McIntyre grinned. "Unlike the FBI, a suspect's constitutional rights mean nothing to me. I can convince almost anyone to tell me what I need to know."

危险 опасноть
خطر

TWENTY-FOUR

FRIDAY, JULY 12

S am took the exit off Interstate 5 into Bellingham on his way to the Corrigan farm. The place was well guarded. In spite of Sandra Corrigan's objections, he had two men assigned to watch the place. Those two agents discovered the CIA agents hiding in the barn, and so now all four were watching. Still, he wanted to check for himself because he'd rather face anything other than Jonathan's wrath if something happened out there.

He passed a donut place, but instead of the usual visions of cream-filled donuts dancing in his head and torturing his resolve to eat better, he found Ali occupying his thoughts. When she announced she might have breast cancer, his stomach churned. When Grachev's man grabbed her shoulder, rage boiled up in him.

Both of those incidents could be marked down to the closeness partners feel for each other. But when he was in her apartment, talking to her in her bedroom, he felt something he had never felt for a partner—strong attraction. Not a surprise he'd never felt it before, considering she was his first female partner.

He sighed. Sam and women had been an elusive combination. He wasn't exactly the easiest guy to look at, and up until two years ago, he carried more weight than was considered attractive. He could dream, but he wasn't even in the same ballpark as Ali. Her kind of guy would be younger and a lot more buff.

A car shot out of a parking lot in front of him with a child in the front passenger seat. Sam jammed on the brakes and swerved right, his antilock brakes allowing him to steer for a clear part of the sidewalk. His seat belt cut into his shoulder as the car bounced over the curb and lurched to a stop. A bang with a hissing sound followed. The tire must've blown. Sam looked after the car to get its license number, but it'd cut into another lane, and he couldn't get it. He muttered a few choice words, flipped his emergency lights on, and got out of his car.

A small group of people gathered around and stared. A tall, gangly teenager with a goatee and wearing a muscle shirt shook his head. "I wouldn't have swerved. I would've nailed him. Taught the jerk a lesson."

"Good plan," Sam said. "Then instead of a flat tire, I'd have smashed up the front end and have some little kid's blood on my hands."

"Huh?" Goatee said.

"There was a kid in the passenger seat. I would've T-boned the car and probably killed the kid. You got any more great ideas?"

"Uh, no."

"Didn't think so."

Sam walked to the front of the car and surveyed the damage. The tire was flatter than a pancake. He walked to the passenger window while he took his cell phone out of his belt clip. The number for the manufacturer's roadside assistance was on a decal. Sam punched it in and requested they come help him change his flat. Sure, he could do it himself, but why bother when help was only ten minutes away?

Sam sat on the fender while he waited for the tow truck. He ignored the stares of passersby and instead enjoyed the warm sun. Washington State was on its way to setting some kind of record for consecutive sunny days. If the wiretaps bore fruit and they found the accountant, Grachev wouldn't be enjoying the weather much longer. The thought of giving Grachev a choice between hanging and lethal injection brought a smile to Sam's face. Newberg was a good man. He deserved better, and Grachev deserved worse.

Sam saw the flashing yellow lights of the tow truck as it pulled up behind his car. A tall, bulky man wearing coveralls climbed out of the cab of the tow truck. He had a flattened nose and salt-and-pepper hair. He walked up to Sam.

"Hi, my name's Jerry." A broad smiled crossed the man's face. "Looks like we had a little boo-boo."

Sam nodded. "Guy cut me off. Tire needs to be changed."

"Not a problem," Jerry said. He bent down and looked behind the wheel. "Actually, you need more than a tire change."

"What?" Sam said.

"The tie-rod is bent. You must've hit the curb hard."

Sam rubbed his shoulder. "Yeah, I did."

"I'll have to tow it to a shop and get it replaced. Got any place you prefer?"

"The nearest dealership, I guess."

"You got it. You mind just moving it off the sidewalk onto the road? It'll be easier to hook up, and you can't do any more damage to it than you've already done. You'll find the steering a little awkward."

"Sure," Sam said. He got into the car and backed it off the sidewalk. Just like Jerry said, the steering was awkward. He looked up at Jerry, who was scratching his head. He bent down and picked something up. Sam got out of the car, and Jerry held an electronic device toward him.

"I don't ever remember seeing one of these on a Buick before," Jerry said.

Sam took it from him, and his stomach started to do flip-flops. Now he knew how they'd been able to track him. Why the FBI's scans for electronic devices didn't catch it was a question for another day. He'd been to Ali's apartment, and anyone watching him with the groceries would put two and two together. Sam pulled out his identification. "Sorry, Jerry, but I need your tow truck."

خطر

Michelle was a fast learner when it came to the American monetary system. Currently she owned three-quarters of the real estate on the Monopoly board, and Ali had just landed on Boardwalk.

"I get much money for that, right?"

"Yes, you do."

"How much?"

Ali looked at the board. If she mortgaged everything, she could pay the rent, but there'd be no way to pay the money back. "You win."

Michelle clapped her hands. "I own everything?"

"You own everything."

"Play again?"

"Sure."

A solid knock sounded at the door. Ali looked at it. The doorman Arnie never let anyone up unannounced. She pulled her gun from its holster. "Michelle, get in the bedroom and remember to do what I told you."

Michelle's eyes were like saucers. "What wrong?"

"Just go."

Michelle scurried from the kitchen to the bedroom. Ali approached the door with her gun in hand. "Who is it?" she called through the door.

The door exploded open. Ali fired three shots at the stocking-faced man who charged through, each thudding into his bulletproof vest. He was on her, grabbing at the gun before she could adjust her aim higher. As they tumbled to the floor, Ali drove her knee into his groin. He grunted but held on to the gun with both of his hands. He was in too close for a throat punch so Ali did the next best thing. She grabbed his trachea and squeezed for all she was worth. Her attacker gagged and tried to pull his head away.

Another pair of hands pulled her hand away from the attacker's throat while a shoe stepped on her gun hand. She had to let the weapon go. A handcuff was snapped onto her gun hand.

"Flip her over," a raspy voice said.

She had to give Michelle time. When the first attacker started to get up so they could flip her, Ali brought her knees up to her chest and slammed two feet to his midsection. He grunted heavily and staggered backward. She tried to kick at the man to her left, but he managed to keep out of the way.

"Aren't you a wild one," the attacker holding her handcuffed hand said. His gloved fist smashed into her face, and her head exploded in pain. Ali became woozy, and they flipped her over and cuffed her hands behind her back. She heard the hammer of a gun being pulled back.

"Now stay put," the raspy voice said, "because bringing you

in alive is optional. Go get the other one from the bedroom," he said to one of his men.

Three of them stood over her, while a fourth stocking-faced man walked to the bedroom door with a battering ram—the same type the FBI used on a drug dealer's door. No wonder her door locks didn't hold. The attacker checked the door, but it wouldn't yield to him. Michelle had locked it like Ali told her to. He slammed the battering ram against it, and the door frame cracked as the door popped open.

He entered the room and Ali smiled as she heard him swearing and tossing furniture around. The thug walked out with a chain ladder in his hands. "She must've used this to go down to the next balcony."

"That's right," Ali said, her voice a little slurred, "and the cops are on their way. Run now, and you might have a chance to get out of the building before they surround it."

"Shut her up," raspy voice said.

The thug put down his battering ram and pulled a strip of cloth from his pocket. He bent down beside her, and Ali turned her head away. She clenched her teeth shut but eventually yielded before he ripped her lips off trying to get the cloth in place. She winced as he yanked it tight.

"Pull her up," Raspy voice said.

Hands grabbed her arms and pulled Ali to her feet. The room spun a bit, and she stumbled. An attacker each took an arm.

"Let's go," he said.

Raspy voice pointed a silencer-equipped gun at her head. "Remember, bringing you in is optional. Any trouble and you'll get one of those nice funerals they give dead cops."

They shoved her down the hall toward the fire escape. Even if there were anyone home, which on a weekday in a downtown

Seattle apartment building was unlikely since everyone worked downtown, Ali wouldn't try to attract attention. These guys would just kill anyone who tried to help her. She'd just have to let the cops handle this one. It would be a switch being the hostage and not the hostage rescuer.

Raspy voice pushed open the fire escape doors, and they went down the concrete stairs one level. He opened the door and looked down the hallway. "All clear," he said.

What were these guys doing? It was nine floors to the bottom.

They went down the hallway until they came to the door of the apartment directly below Ali's. Ali couldn't believe it. Even with the cops coming, they were going to try to retrieve Michelle. They already had one hostage too many for Ali's liking.

Raspy voice stepped ahead of her to try the door handle. She snapped a kick at his gun hand, and the weapon flew free. The second kick got Raspy voice's knee, and the third his face as he crumpled.

The two men holding her were too shocked to know what to do. Ali back kicked, hitting the guy with the battering ram in the groin. She fired a side kick to the knee of the guy holding her right arm. He dropped but instead of letting her go pulled her to the ground. The second attacker fell on her legs. Ali could hear footsteps coming to the door. *Oh no,* she thought. *They've heard the commotion. Keep the door closed. Just wait for the cops.*

It opened, and a man stepped out holding a gun. Ali looked up at him with wide eyes. He looked at the melee on the floor and shook his head. "Bring her in," he said.

They yanked Ali to her feet and shoved her into the apartment. It had the identical layout to her own. Michelle was on the couch gagged and hands cuffed. She looked up at Ali with eyes wide and body shaking.

The man who opened the door grinned at her. "I think you'll find we're smarter than your average thugs. We made sure we blocked all avenues of escape. Now I think we should all go before someone notices your doorman is missing."

Ali heard footsteps thumping in the apartment above her. The man looked up at the ceiling and cursed.

"Well, it looks like we might be here awhile. Keep an eye on her while I go onto the balcony and listen."

خطر

Sam drove the tow truck up onto the sidewalk in front of Ali's building. Six Seattle police cars and an ambulance were already there. An ambulance. His heart broke out in a pace like a racehorse. Ali. Was Ali hurt?

Flashing his ID, Sam charged past the cop at the door into the lobby of the apartment building. Two paramedics were wheeling a stretcher toward the door. He stumbled to a stop beside it and nearly wept when he saw it was the doorman and not Ali. The old guy had an oxygen mask on and a nasty bump on his head. His eyes were closed.

Sam dug out one of his cards and shoved it in the paramedic's shirt pocket. "I want to be informed as soon as this guy wakes up. Got it?"

"Yeah," the paramedic said.

He ran over to the elevator and pressed the button. His foot was like a jackhammer on the floor waiting for an elevator car to come downstairs. Eventually it arrived, and Sam pressed the button for the tenth floor. His foot continued tapping all ten floors up. The door opened, and he burst out and jogged to the entrance of Ali's apartment where another Seattle cop stood. He flashed his badge and entered.

A six-foot-four cop with Dumbo ears approached him. "Sorry, Sam, we didn't get here in time."

"What have you got, Danny?"

"Broken door, three shell casings," Jonathan Corrigan's brother said. "Signs of a fierce struggle in the bedroom; that's about it. We've got the forensics people on their way."

"Let me see the bedroom."

"Actually, we're preserving it as a crime scene."

Sam pushed past Danny. "There won't be time for forensics to solve this one. We've got six hours at best."

He entered Ali's bedroom and felt sick. Just yesterday it'd been neat, tidy, and feminine with Ali's stamp all over it. Now it looked like a bomb went off. The bed turned over, dresser on its face, the contents of the closet on the floor. Danny stood beside him.

"Quite a mess," he said.

"This isn't a struggle," Sam said. "This is a search. But a search for what? Michelle is all they wanted."

"Who's Michelle?"

Sam looked at Danny. "A material witness in another investigation. For now that information is on a need-to-know basis. Okay?"

"Sure."

He opened the balcony doors and stepped outside and looked at the city below. His heart had slowed down now, the adrenaline easing out of his system. Although he was anxious to find Ali, he was able to stand back and use his training to think this through.

He left the balcony and with Danny in tow went back to the entrance of the apartment. The doorjamb hung from a couple of nails, and the door was caved in where a battering ram hit.

"Okay," Sam said, "they used a battering ram which means Ali didn't get much warning." He looked at the shell casings on the floor about six feet from the door and then at the kitchen table. "They must've just finished a game of Monopoly."

"How do you know that?" Danny Corrigan said.

"One player has most of the money and property, and there's no men on the table. When I played, the loser cleaned up. Since Michelle is from a Communist country, we can assume she'd suck at Monopoly and Ali won, meaning Michelle was at the table cleaning up. After a long game, Ali would be on her feet so when they crashed the door she was standing."

Sam knelt down and picked up a shell casing with the end of a pencil. "Nine millimeter. That's the right caliber for Ali's personal gun. She got three shots off."

"Which no one heard," Danny said, "because there's no one home during the day."

Sam nodded. "Exactly. But there's no blood. There's no slugs in any of the walls or hallway, so she didn't miss. What did she hit?"

"They were probably wearing vests."

Sam nodded. "Yeah, that's probably it. She's standing near the door stretching, it crashed, she grabs her sidearm and starts firing at the largest target, the chest. Three shots are gone before she realizes he's got a vest on. By then he's on her, and it's too late to go for the head. I pity the guy who was first on her."

"Why?" Danny said.

"Because getting on top of Ali would be like jumping a cougar. She'll have done maximum damage. I'll bet it took three or four guys to subdue her." He looked at the bedroom door. "So while they were occupied with Ali, Michelle must've hightailed it into the bedroom and locked the door."

"And they used the battering ram to open it up."

"Yeah," Sam said and walked back into the bedroom. "But why did she come in here? There's no way out. Why not try for the open door while they're busy with Ali? Ali must've told her to come in here for a reason."

Sam poked around the bedroom and then went back out on the balcony. He looked up. Even with his height he couldn't climb to the next one up. Danny came out and joined him. He looked down.

"Long jump," Danny said.

Sam put his hand on the wrought iron railing. He looked down and then noticed the scratches about two and a half feet apart on the rail. "She didn't jump, she climbed down to the next balcony."

"How?" Danny said.

"Ali must've had one of those chain ladders people use for emergency fire escapes. Michelle went to the apartment downstairs!"

خطر

Raspy voice charged out of the bedroom of the other apartment. "They've figured it out," he said. "Let's go."

He stepped up close to Ali and put his gun to her temple. "I'm not kidding when I say we don't have to bring you. You're bonus, no more. Some bonuses aren't worth having, so if you cause trouble, I won't even hesitate to pull the trigger. Now let's go."

Two men grabbed each of Ali's arms and the same with Michelle. They scurried out of the apartment and down the hall to the furthest staircase. In spite of the fact they'd chosen to work for a Russian crime lord, these guys were smart. The police would be sure to come down the nearest staircase. She thought to struggle but somehow believed Raspy was telling the truth. Besides, the Seattle police would have all exits to the building blocked so there was nowhere they could go.

In the lead, Raspy pushed open the door to the stairs, and the two women and the six men went through. They tried to run down the stairs, but neither Michelle nor Ali could keep their balance with their hands cuffed behind their backs. Still, they kept up a good pace. The closer they got to the ground floor, the more Ali smiled on the inside. There was nowhere for these guys to go.

She looked back when they passed the entrance to the ground floor. The parking garage had no way of escape but up. Were they thinking they could sneak out in a car, or were they just going to go flying out and hope to outrun the Seattle police? There were so many patrol cars in the downtown core it would be an effort in futility that would only result in a smashup.

They reached the bottom parking level, and Raspy motioned for them to stop. He opened the door and entered the garage. A moment later, he came back. "It's clear. Let's go to plan B."

Ali and Michelle were herded into the parking garage, but instead of being taken to a car, they went to the door of the building's physical plant. One of the thugs took the battering ram and smashed the door in. They went inside where the powerful motors hummed that were responsible for pumping the water up the high-rise. Electrical panels lined the walls to deliver electricity to the apartments. What did these guys have in mind? Hide out here?

They walked to the back of the room where the large sewage pipes came from above and down into the concrete. Near the pipes a hinged steel plate with a padlock keeping it closed was inset in the floor. Ali groaned against the gag.

Raspy turned to her and smiled. "It's only the storm sewer, but we'll still need a shower after we're done." He fired three rounds at the lock, and it broke off. He pulled the plate up, and a dark hole with a ladder leading down greeted them. "Down we go," he said.

Ali shook her hands forward and mumbled. There's no way she or Michelle could climb down the ladder handcuffed.

Raspy took a deep breath, then nodded to his partner. "Take their cuffs off." He held his gun level with her face. "Just give me an excuse."

The man unsnapped her handcuffs and then did the same for Michelle.

Raspy pointed to two of his men. "You two go first, and then we'll send down the women."

The two thugs descended into the hole, and then Raspy pointed at Michelle. "You next."

Michelle looked at Ali, trembling. Ali nodded that she should do as they were told.

A thug took Michelle's arm and guided her to the hole. With one last look at Ali, she descended into the darkness.

Raspy waved the gun. "You next, and remember, no problems."

Ali sat on the edge of the hole, put her feet on one of the steel rungs of the ladder, and began climbing down. Because of the dry spell, the air was just cool and slightly damp. Below her she could make out the flashlights of the two thugs watching Michelle. There would never be a better time.

Ali dropped the last eight feet, landing on one of the men. His flashlight skittered across the concrete floor. "Grab the light and run!" she screamed against the gag, hoping Michelle figured out what her garbled scream meant.

While on the man's back, she drove her fist into the base of his neck, and he convulsed. A boot caught her in the ribs, and Ali tumbled off him but rolled onto her feet. The other flashlight was in her eyes. Michelle's footfalls retreated behind her. Good. As long as Michelle got away, she didn't really care what happened now.

She could hear the thug pulling a gun out of its holster. It was a trick that really only worked in movies, but she decided to give it a try anyway. Ali dove forward planting her hands on the concrete, swinging into a handstand with recoiled legs and kicked upward. The man howled as her feet caught him under the jaw.

Feet thumped onto the concrete as Ali rolled into a sitting position.

"You are way too much trouble," she heard Raspy say, and the tunnel exploded into light.

危险 ОПАСНОТЬ
خطر

TWENTY-FIVE

FRIDAY, JULY 12

Jonathan let McIntyre drive them back from the airport. The doctor said he had a slight hearing loss, would experience dizzy spells for a while, and better not drive.

That McIntyre was an enigma would be an understatement. He defied Stone and yet convinced the director to get a military plane to transport them directly to Bellingham from Tel Aviv, so they could start hunting down what Stone referred to as the "phantom terrorists."

McIntyre got intelligence on some of the big players on the Russian scene in Washington State. Their primary interest was a guy named Grachev. CIA had information that the FBI wanted this guy in the worst way and he was involved in some kind of deal with the Triad to do people smuggling. People smuggling meant ships; ships meant terrorists.

"Turn here," Jonathan said.

"I know the way," McIntyre said and turned the car onto Axton Road. Home was just minutes away.

"You're going to keep this short, right?" McIntyre said.

As much as Jonathan wanted to fall into Laura's arms and die there, reunions would have to be cut short. They had no idea what route this ship took or when it could arrive. Time was the enemy.

"Just long enough to kiss my wife and then get everyone on their way up to Canada."

"Now you understand that I don't work by the usual rules," McIntyre said. "I'm a results-oriented guy. The way I see it, there's a genuine terrorist threat, so as far as I'm concerned, constitutional rights are something to be dealt with after we neutralize the threat. Are you okay with that?"

Jonathan grinned. "We're not that different. Don't worry, whatever it takes, I'll be right there beside you. Turn here."

McIntyre turned the car into the wooded driveway and pulled up to the house. Rudy went ballistic straining at his chain. Jonathan popped open the door to the car and got out. The dog's threats of destruction turned to barks of greeting, and his tail wagged his whole body.

The door to the house opened, and Laura flew out. Jonathan's heart surged in his chest and he walked toward her with wide-open arms. Laura threw her arms around him and pressed her head against his chest.

"I don't believe it," she said through tears. "It's you. It's really you."

Jonathan buried his face in her hair, blinking back his own tears. He took a deep breath of her scent and nearly collapsed with pure joy. He eased Laura's face back from his chest and kissed her tenderly. It was a kiss where time stood still, neither of them wanting to break it off. McIntyre clearing his throat shattered Jonathan and Laura's paradise.

The mission. There was a mission, and his desire to just fall into his wife's love and forget everything that had happened would have to wait. He had to get them out of here. He eased her back, and before he could say a word, Laura broke off the embrace and hesitantly walked up to McIntyre.

"I. . .you. . .God bless you," she said, and threw her arms around him. "You got him out of there."

McIntyre gingerly put his hands on Laura's back and looked to Jonathan for help. He reminded Jonathan of tough guys who hold a baby for the first time and are afraid they'll break it. "I had help," McIntyre said.

Laura stepped back and wiped her tears with the back of her arm. "I don't care. You brought him back. That's all that matters." Laura returned to Jonathan and wrapped her arms around him. "I'm afraid if I let you go you'll disappear."

Jonathan's mother filled the doorway and lifted her hands into the air. "Praise God," she repeated over and over, as she charged down the stairs and wrapped both of them in a hug.

She planted a huge kiss on his cheek. "I just knew He'd bring you home. I just knew it."

"Jonathan!" Roxanne's voice called from the direction of the horse barn.

He turned in the direction of the voice. She was running and was already halfway to him, and he hadn't heard her footfalls. He might be getting hearing aids long before his time.

Roxanne skidded to a stop, and her eyes went directly to McIntyre. "You. You really are a good guy."

"Yeah," McIntyre said.

"So you really saved us that day? It wasn't just some kind of trick?"

McIntyre shook his head, and before he knew it, Roxanne had her arms around him. "Then I never thanked you." Once again he had that helpless look.

"Let him go, Roxanne," Jonathan said. "I've got something important to say."

Roxanne stepped back from McIntyre, and everyone's attention was on Jonathan. He looked over at the house and saw Alice McIvor stand in the doorway. "Alice, come over here. You need to hear this."

"I can hear fine from here," Laura's mother said.

"Fine." He turned to his mother. "You all have to leave the farm and go up to Canada."

There was a chorus of whats and whys.

"I can't tell you why," Jonathan said. "All I can tell you is I want everyone to pack up and drive to a place called Prince George and stay at a place called Esther's Inn. It's about eight hours north of here. You can't tell anyone you're leaving."

His mother's hands started to shake. "Jonathan, if you know something that means we have to go that far away, what about Danny? I should phone him right away."

"Already done, Mom. I called him from the airport. He's on his way here. Don't use our phones for anything. The CIA will still have them tapped. That goes for cell phones and e-mail, too."

"What about you?" Laura said. "Aren't you coming?"

Jonathan took her face in his hands. "I can't. McIntyre and I can stop this."

She started to open her mouth, but he put his finger on her lips. "Don't say anything. I have to do this."

"But—"

"Don't."

She formed a frown and placed her head against his chest and held him.

"What about the cows?" his mom said. "They'll die if they're not milked."

"We've got farmhands; let them take care of them."

His mom shook her head. "Jonathan, if what's coming is

so terrible you want us to leave, I'm certainly not going to leave Billy and Ida here while we flee to safety."

"Then let the cows die."

"No, not getting milked is a horrible way for a cow to die."

"Fine, then I'll kill them before you go."

Laura's grip tightened around him. "Jonathan, if it's that bad, shouldn't we be telling everyone? At least our friends, our church?"

He shook his head. "Can't. The more people you tell, the more chance it'll get out, and there'll be widespread panic. More people could die fleeing from the threat than it might kill on its own. We don't even know the exact nature of the threat or when it's going to hit, if it hits."

"Wait a minute, Jonathan," his mother said. "You're going to kill all our cows, and you don't even know what we're running from, or if it's even going to hit?"

"I know enough that I don't want any of you around here. It's that simple."

"Maybe for you, but I'm staying with the cows."

"No, you're not; you're getting out of here."

She folded her arms across her chest. "Son, you're not big enough to make me. I've been on this farm since the day I married your father. I'm not running from an 'if,' and I'm certainly not going to kill our livestock for a 'maybe.' "

"Neither am I," said Roxanne. "If Mom stays, I stay."

"No," his mom said. "Everyone else is going."

"You can't handle this place alone," Laura said. "I will stay, too."

Jonathan eased Laura back. "Not in a million years. I'm big enough to throw you on a plane if I have to."

"This is my home, too. I'm not running."

"Me, either," said Roxanne.

"See what you started, Mom. Now everyone wants to stay."

"I'll stay with her," Alice McIvor called from the door. She walked down the steps and stood next to his mother. She looked at Laura. "You, young lady, are going. You don't just speak for yourself anymore; you speak for your unborn child, too." A tear trickled down her cheek. "Besides you, that baby is all that's left of your father in this world."

"Mom—"

"Mom nothing, Laura. You're going."

"What about Michelle?" Roxanne said. "We can't leave her behind."

Jonathan looked at McIntyre. "Is that the girl who was with Roxanne when you took out the Chinese guy?"

"Yeah."

"She was forced to come here on a ship," Roxanne said. "God sent her to us for protection."

"Fine," Jonathan said. "Where is she? I'll go get her."

"Sam has her," his mom said.

Jonathan raised an eyebrow. "Perkins? Why does he have her?"

"He said she's a material witness in some case involving Russians."

Jonathan and McIntyre exchanged glances. "Think it might have something to do with our problem?"

"We are looking for Russians," McIntyre said. "We should talk to this Perkins fellow."

"Okay, we'll go see Sam and find out where this Michelle is and get her to safety."

"Don't be lying to me, Jonathan," his mom said. "That girl is under my protection. You get her to safety—promise?"

"Promise. Now everyone get packing. We're heading off to Seattle." He put his hands on Laura's arms to release himself, but she tightened her grip.

"No," she said.

"Laura, I have to go."

Alice McIvor stepped over and put her hands on Laura's shoulders. "Honey, let him go."

Laura released him and whipped around. "Don't be so anxious to see him go die, Mother."

Alice McIvor stumbled back like she'd been punched. "That's not what I meant."

"Yeah, right." Laura put her hands on her hips and trembled. "You. . ."

Jonathan put his hand on Laura's shoulder and turned her around. He took her hand. "Come with me."

They walked over toward the barn and stopped when they were out of earshot. He turned to her and took her other hand. He looked into her emerald eyes and took a deep breath to keep his composure. "I have every reason to believe we're going to get these guys, but"—he swallowed—"but there's always the chance."

Her lower lip trembled. "I know."

"If that happens, your mother is the only blood relation you'll have left. I need to know everything will be okay with you two."

She looked at the ground. Jonathan touched her chin and lifted her face to him. "Will everything be okay?"

"Yeah," she said, her voice scratchy. "Everything will be fine."

He looked into her face. "You know I love you."

Her eyes became pools. "I know."

"And I love our daughter. You'll tell her, right?"

She threw her arms around his neck and squeezed until he choked. "I'll tell her." She let him go. "Now go before I change my mind."

Jonathan pried his feet from the ground and walked back

toward the group. He stopped at his mother. "You won't change your mind?"

She shook her head.

Jonathan kissed her on the cheek. "Then Duncan and I will just have to get them, that's all."

"That's right, son, you get them. You do whatever you have to do."

He turned, and Roxanne stood in his way. "Be careful," she said, then threw her arms around him and kissed him on the cheek.

He started to walk to the car with McIntyre when a voice stopped him. He turned to face Alice McIvor.

"Jonathan," she said, "I understand now why you did what you did. Please come back."

Jonathan smiled at her. "Count on it."

He got into the car. Duncan started the motor, turned around, and headed back out the driveway. He didn't dare look back.

Jonathan dug a pay-as-you-go cell phone he bought at the airport out of his pocket. Stone wouldn't be able to trace it to him. He punched in Perkins's cell number.

"Yeah," a gruff voice said.

"Sam, it's Jon."

"Hi, Jon. What do you want?"

"A girl named Michelle was staying with my mom. You've got her, and I want her."

"Sorry, can't."

"Can't, or won't?"

"Doesn't matter which. She's part of a case, and I'm not at liberty to give details."

"Would it have anything to do with a Russian named Grachev?"

Silence. "What do you know about Grachev?"

"Lots. Now where's Michelle?"

"Meet me at FBI headquarters in Seattle. I can't talk about this over the phone."

"Okay," Jonathan said. "Just make sure this Michelle is there."

"Yeah, sure," Sam said.

Jonathan hung up the phone. "He's not saying, but something's wrong. We're to meet him at FBI headquarters in Seattle."

"Okay," McIntyre said. "By the way, how could you do that back there?"

"What?" Jonathan said. "Leave my family? What choice do I have? We've got no clue what's in that crate. It could be anything from guns to something catastrophic."

"Actually," McIntyre said, "I was talking about letting your mother stay behind. If it'd been me, I just would've went in the barn and killed all the cows."

"I thought about that, but she'd stand in front of them before she'd let me shoot them. Besides, she won't stay."

"She won't?"

"No. When Danny arrives, he'll throw her in the van. He'll be the one who stays, and for that reason alone I'm going to do whatever I have to, to find out where the ship that has that crate is. No one is going to hurt my little brother."

خطر

Sam stood by the metal detector arch at the entrance to the federal building and waited for Jonathan. His foot tapped rapid-fire against the floor. Inside he was a sea of emotions. Like a tide retreating, he dreaded trying to explain to Jon that they'd lost Michelle. Like a tide roaring in, he just wanted to get out and find Grachev and wring the mobster's neck until he told him where Ali was.

And then there was the churning of a whirlpool in his gut. He loved Ali. Sure, she'd never know, and it didn't matter. She was more than a partner to him, and if they didn't find her alive, then that whirlpool would just suck him to the bottom of the ocean.

The main doors opened, and Jonathan walked in with another man at his side. The guy was late forties, normal build with salt-and-pepper hair and an easygoing walk. Sam waved to Jon, thankful for something to distract him from his own internal hell.

Jonathan walked through the arch, and the detector went off.

A hulking security guard stepped in Jonathan's path and held up his hand. "I'll have to search you, sir."

"It's okay," Sam said. "He's with me."

The other guy walked through setting off the detector.

"He's okay, Sam," Jon said. "He's with me."

The guard looked at Sam.

"He's okay, too. Come with me, guys."

Sam headed to the elevator with Jonathan and his friend in tow. They only waited a couple of moments before the doors opened, and they entered the elevator alone. "So, who's your friend?"

"Sam Perkins, meet Duncan McIntyre, Central Intelligence Agency."

Sam shook McIntyre's hand. His grip was restrained, like he could crush every bone in Sam's hand if he wanted to.

"Nice to meet you," McIntyre said.

The elevator came to a stop, and Sam led them down the hall to Conners's office. His secretary looked up from her typing as they entered the waiting room. "Go right on in," she said.

Sam opened the door to find Conners barking on the phone.

"Tell that judge a kidnapped FBI agent is all the probable cause we need. I want warrants not just for his lawyer's office but for anywhere Grachev breathed. Tell him if he doesn't do it and we don't get her back alive, everyone will know who was preoccupied with constitutional rights. Got it? Good." He hung up the phone and looked at Sam, shaking his head.

"You believe this? The judge says we have no direct evidence linking Grachev to Ali's kidnapping, so he won't issue a warrant to search the lawyer's office. If anyone knows where Grachev is, that guy does. He's just as dirty as his client." He looked at McIntyre, then Corrigan.

"Mr. Corrigan, I recognize you from the newspaper picture. Great job down in California. Who's your friend?"

McIntyre stepped forward and offered his hand. "Duncan McIntyre, CIA."

Conners shook it then pointed to the two chairs in front of his desk. Sam pulled a third chair over from the wall, and the three men sat across from the SAC.

"So, Sam tells me you CIA guys have intelligence on Grachev."

"We do," Corrigan said. "But first I'd like to see Michelle."

Conners looked at Sam and frowned. "How much can we tell these guys?"

"Everything," McIntyre said. He threw his identification on Conners's desk. "I'm also attached to Homeland Security. You can't get clearance any higher than mine, and quite frankly, there are things I can do that you can't. So fill us in. What's going on?"

Sam looked at Conners, and his boss nodded.

He turned to Corrigan and McIntyre. "We've been track-ing the movements of Josef Grachev because we suspected he'd formed an alliance with the Triad. They supply him with drugs, and he'd supply them with freighters to smuggle people in. It was a sweetheart deal. Grachev accesses the high-quality Asian narcotics, and the Triad doesn't lose half their human cargo to the sea.

"My partner, Ali, and I were on a stakeout listening to the bugged apartment of Triad boss Billy Heng's nephew. There was a card game going on between Billy's nephew, Tony Heng, and Yuri Davidov."

"Davidov?" McIntyre said. "He's Grachev's right-hand man. If he was there, then this alliance must've been extremely im-portant to Grachev."

"It was," Perkins said. "Before the alliance they were kill-ing each other, and although Grachev's guys are smarter and tougher, Heng had more bodies to throw at the war. Peace benefited Grachev.

"Unfortunately, or fortunately, depending on your point of view, during the card game Davidov caught Tony Heng cheat-ing. Tony went for his gun; Davidov was faster and killed him."

"So you were able to turn him?" McIntyre said.

"Thanks to Billy Heng, yes."

"Really," McIntyre said. "How?"

"We caught Davidov and one of Heng's bodyguards, Jimmy Lo. The other bodyguard floated up on the shore. Since we needed to know if it was self-defense, we used Heng's throw-away policy on inept bodyguards as leverage to get Jimmy to tell us what really happened in exchange for protection from Heng. Heng even tried to sneak a phony lawyer in here to threaten Lo. Ali. . ."

Perkins swallowed. "Ali went to law school. She spotted the

guy as a fake, and it gave us even more leverage to convince Davidov and Lo their bosses were going to kill them first chance they got. They both agreed to testify, but Lo didn't really know anything we didn't already know. Davidov was the prize."

Sam took a deep breath. "Six months ago, we had another agent working undercover in Grachev's organization." He looked at Corrigan. "You met him, Jon—Paul Newberg. He was there the night we raided the McIvor home. A good man and a good friend."

"Past tense?"

"Yeah. We found his body on the beach. He'd been stabbed multiple times." Sam bunched his hands into fists. "We knew Grachev killed him, and with Davidov we could prove it, except Davidov wouldn't give us anything on that until we gave him a new identity."

"So what does this have to do with Michelle?" Jonathan said.

"I'm coming to that. To prove his good faith, Davidov gave us the number of a container with drugs in it. When we raided the ship, the Russian crane operator dumped the container into the water. Ali noticed a sewage hole in the bottom of the container and jumped in after it. It was full of illegal immigrants, and if it hadn't been for her, they would've all died."

"Kind of destroyed Davidov's credibility," McIntyre said.

"Yeah. How could we go to court with a witness who gave us wrong information that nearly led to several deaths?"

"Did he?" Jonathan said.

"No, the drugs had been moved from the container and people put in it. This is where Michelle comes in. None of the Chinese would tell us anything without them all being allowed on American soil to claim refugee status. INS wouldn't go for it. Michelle was one of the few who escaped, and since Ali had seen her in the water, we could prove she was in the container. Michelle was willing to testify they'd been switched."

Corrigan took a deep breath. "But you don't have her, do you?"

"No," Sam said. "We had a security problem."

"What kind of problem?"

"Davidov was shot by a sniper when we were moving him from the safe house to be relocated."

"So much for your case," McIntyre said. "How did they find him? Someone from the inside or a tracking device?"

"At first we thought we had a traitor in our midst, but everyone checked out. All the vehicles were examined for tracking devices, and nothing came up. We really had no idea how they found him until I got cut off in Bellingham and went up over the curb."

"Huh?" Corrigan said.

"A tracking device fell off."

"But you said—"

"It wasn't your typical tracking device," Conners said. "We sent it to the lab. It had an electromagnet on it that could be released by remote signal. Whenever they wanted to follow Sam, they'd put one on, and then when they found what they needed to know, they'd make it drop off so we wouldn't find it later. Right now we have microcameras in Sam's car to see if we can find out who did it."

"Michelle was staying at Ali's apartment," Sam said. "I'd been there with groceries. Grachev's men must've figured it out and went after them. They were well organized to the point where they broke into the apartment below Ali's as well to block off any route of escape down the balcony. We searched the building, and it turns out they went out the storm-sewer system."

"I take it you've paid Grachev a visit," McIntyre said.

"Oh yeah. That's the first place I went. He seems to have gone out of town."

"Any idea where he is?" Corrigan said.

"Somewhere offshore. Although there's no record of him owning one, we know he has use of a yacht."

"So, you just find the yacht, and you find Michelle and your partner," Corrigan said.

"We wish it were that easy," Conners said. "You've seen the weather. There's over three hundred yachts floating around out there. Just the process of checking them would tip Grachev off, and we can't take that chance."

"You're afraid he's going to kill his hostages," McIntyre said.

Conners nodded. "Now, we've told you our story, how can the CIA help us?"

McIntyre grinned. "Well, the way I see it, you have one solid lead—his lawyer. We just need to talk to him."

"That's why we're waiting for the warrant," Sam said. "We want to go in there hard, tear the place apart. Hopefully we can find something in his records that we can use as leverage to get him to give Grachev up."

McIntyre stood, and Corrigan followed suit. "Well, it's been nice talking to you, gentlemen."

"What?" Conners said, standing. "You said you could help."

"Sorry," McIntyre said. "Sounds domestic. Can't get involved." He looked at Sam. "Mind walking us out?"

"Hey," Sam said. "What gives here?"

"Just walk us out, Sam," Jonathan said.

Conners sat down slowly. "Yeah, Sam, just walk them out."

Sam looked at his boss, and then it hit him. "Sure, I'll walk them out."

Sam led them out of Conners's office, and no one spoke

until they were in the elevator.

"The lawyer's name is Ray Kuhl," Sam said.

"What's his address?" Corrigan said.

"I'm coming with you."

"No, you're not, Sam. You're an FBI agent. You can't come."

Sam looked at Jonathan. He forced himself to breathe slowly. "Ali is my partner. When we walk out of this elevator, I'm not an FBI agent, and I won't be again until Ali and Michelle are safe. I'm coming."

"Fair enough," McIntyre said. "Your badge could come in handy. Just don't go all law and order on us later. There's more at stake here than just your partner. As far as we're concerned, Grachev is a foreign threat, and that means the gloves are off."

McIntyre looked at Corrigan. "As soon as we get out of this building, we're going to call Stone. The only way we're going to take this yacht without everyone getting killed is with a couple of teams of your old buddies."

"Stone won't do that based on what we've got."

"Don't worry," McIntyre said. "After I talk with him, he will."

危险 خطر
ОПАСНОТЬ

TWENTY-SIX

Ali's head pounded, and she felt like vomiting. So she wasn't dead after all. She must have a bump the size of a goose egg on the back of her head. Her hands were cuffed behind her, and even her feet were bound. So they'd finally figured out she could use her feet as easily as her hands.

She was on a bed, quite a comfortable bed. Ali blinked her eyes a couple of times to clear them and saw three small round windows lining the wall. The bed rocked gently, which meant she was on a boat. She sucked in a short breath. Sam said they killed his other partner on a boat. Was this some kind of twist of fate that Sam was about to lose his second partner that way? *Oh, Lord, please, no.* Hmm, little Bible-thumper Michelle must be wearing off on her.

Then again, considering her situation, praying might not be a bad idea. She was bound, at sea, and being held captive by a man who would give no thought to killing an FBI agent, or his own people for that matter. If there were ever a time to start talking to God, now would be it.

At least Michelle was safe. Or was she? Ali's back was warm. She flipped herself over and looked into the worried eyes of Michelle.

"I pray for you," Michelle said. "I afraid you die. Lots of blood. Your beautiful hair ruined. Pretty lady with sore face come in and clean. I talk to her, but she not speak English."

Ali smiled to reassure the frightened girl. Michelle was only a teenager, torn from her own land, and yet she was doing remarkably well. Maybe there was more to this God stuff than Ali gave credit.

"What happened?" Ali said.

"I get lost; they find me. They blindfold me, and we walk in tunnels for while, go up ladder, and then I put in car. We drive for a bit, then get on boat."

"This boat?"

"No. Small boat, noisy motor. We in water for long time, then go on this boat and put in here. You sleep long time."

Ali heard a dead bolt and looked to a door that must adjoin to the next cabin. It opened, and the striking blond who Ali saw at Grachev's home looked in. Her right eye was blackened and her bottom lip swollen.

"Are you okay?" she said in Russian. Her voice was soft with a hint of genuine concern.

"I've felt better," Ali replied in Russian. "You don't look so good yourself."

"You speak same language?" Michelle said.

"Yes," she said.

"So," Ali said, switching back to Russian. "My name is Ali Marcoli. What's yours?"

"Sophie."

"So, Sophie, what happened to you?"

Sophie shrugged. "I did something to make Josef unhappy."

"You made him unhappy, so he beat you. What did you do?"

Sophie looked away. "I can't say."

"Well, whatever it was, he can't do that to you. This isn't Russia. This is the United States. We put men who abuse women in jail. You should go to the police."

Sophie stepped in the room and pointed at Ali's bound hands. "You are the police, and look what he did to you. No one can escape Josef. He does as he pleases."

"No, he doesn't," Ali said. "He's a criminal, and right now he's scared. Why do you think he's on this boat? He's afraid of getting arrested. He's running."

Sophie shook her head. "He's not running."

Ali lifted an eyebrow. "He's not. Then what's he doing?"

"He says he's just taking care of a problem, and we'll go back home."

That sent chills up Ali's spine, but she couldn't show weakness. "And when he gets you back home, he'll just beat you again. Men like him never stop, Sophie. The beatings will just get worse until the day he kills you, and then we'll find your body washed up on shore like we did that FBI agent. Help me get out of here, and I'll protect you."

Sophie shook her head. "Your INS will just send me back to Russia. I'm not here legally. Even if you could protect me, he'll just have my family in Russia killed. No one can save me."

"That's not true. Right now the FBI is looking for me. When they find us, Josef is going to jail. If you help me, I'll make sure you can stay."

Sophie chewed on her bottom lip. "No. They'll never catch him."

Sophie crossed the room and sat on the edge of the bed. "Do you like movies?"

"Huh?"

"I'm not allowed to talk to anyone but Josef's men, so I watch a lot of movies on TV. Josef doesn't mind, because it helps me to learn to speak English. If he caught me talking to you in Russian, he'd be angry. I'm supposed to use English all the time, but it's so nice to talk to someone in my own language. So, do you like movies?"

"Some," Ali said. What was this woman on about? Of course. She was lonely, and this was her first chance to talk to another woman and in her own language.

"I saw this movie, but I don't understand it."

"Which one?"

"It was called *A Tale of Two Cities*."

"Never heard of it."

"It's old. It was in black and white. Josef likes me to watch the older movies because the English in them is better. Not so many swear words."

"So what didn't you understand?"

"The movie takes place in England and France during the French Revolution. In the movie there's this lawyer who's in love with a girl. He's a drunk, but after he falls in love with her, he stops drinking. She likes him, but as a friend."

Kind of like me and Sam, Ali thought, *only in reverse.*

"The girl is in love with a young man, and she marries him. They even have a baby together. The young man has to go back to France, and he's captured and sentenced to death. The lawyer goes to France to rescue the young man. He gets into the prison and switches places with the young man. He ends up dying in the young man's place." Sophie shrugged her shoulders. "Why would he do that? He could've just let the young man die and then got the woman he loved. This makes no sense to me. Does it to you?"

Ali chewed on her lip for a second. "Not really. He died

for the husband of the woman he loved?"

"What you talking about?" Michelle said. "Please, I want to talk, too."

Ali looked at Michelle. Why not? She related the story to Michelle. "Do you understand why?"

"Sure," Michelle said. "It is story of Jesus. He love us, but we not love Him; we love this world. We are all in France. We all going to die. Jesus love us too much so He switch places with us. He die for us, so we don't have to die."

"Huh?" Ali said. "What are you on about?" She looked over at Sophie, and the attractive woman had a distant look in her eyes. "She said. . . ," Ali started in Russian.

"I understood her," Sophie said in English. "It make sense to me."

The main door to the cabin opened, and Josef Grachev filled the door frame. "What are you doing in here?"

"I–I. . .was checking on her injury," Sophie said in Russian.

"Don't lie to me, Sophie. I warned you. Get to your room. I'll deal with you later."

Sophie scurried to the door, glancing over her shoulder at Ali, terror filling her face. She pulled it shut behind her, the lock snapping shut.

Grachev looked down at her. "So," he said in Russian. "You want to be Sophie's friend, do you? Hoping maybe if you're nice to her she'll help you escape, is that it?"

"No," Ali said back in Russian. "She just came in, looked at my bandage, and asked if I needed to go to the washroom. Then you barged in, and yes, I do need to go."

Grachev snorted. "Tough." He turned and headed toward the door.

"Don't you touch her," Ali said.

He stopped and looked at her, grinning. "Oh, you hardly

look like you're in a position to do anything."

"I won't be in this position forever."

"No," Grachev said, "you won't be. I'll be back for you later."

خطر

Jonathan took the lead when he and McIntyre passed through thick glass doors and entered the main reception area of the law offices of Kuhl, Carey and Butterfield. Perkins stayed with the car they'd parked in the alley behind the building. Truth was, Jonathan wanted to keep Sam away from as much of the illegal stuff as he could. If they stopped the terrorists, likely everything they'd done would be forgiven, but if not, well, it'd be nice to have a friend on the outside.

The middle-aged woman at the reception counter looked over reading glasses when they entered. She sized them both up before returning her attention to Jonathan.

"May I help you?" she said.

Jonathan leaned on the counter and smiled at her. "Hi, we're here to see Mr. Kuhl."

The woman typed at her computer. "Do you have an appointment?"

"No." Jonathan pulled out Sam's badge from his windbreaker and showed it to her, making sure he kept his thumb on the picture. "But I don't think we need one. Get him, please, but don't tell him anything other than someone called Joel is here and he won't say what it's about."

The secretary bristled. "I'll do no such thing."

"Fine," Jonathan said. "We'll get him ourselves."

The woman started to reach for her phone, but Jonathan grabbed her wrist. "Believe me when I say your loyalty to your boss, while admirable, is misplaced. Warn him, and there'll be consequences for you, too. Which way to his office? Left or right?"

"Left," she said.

Corrigan released her hand. "Remember, don't warn him."

The woman nodded her head and rolled her chair to get as far from him as she could.

Jonathan looked at McIntyre. "What do you think?"

"She's lying."

"That's what I think."

They crossed the short distance to the hallway that ran perpendicular to the entrance and turned right. "Probably in the corner office," McIntyre said.

"His name is first on the letterhead," Jonathan said.

They charged down the hallway to the corner office. A solid oak door with Kuhl's nameplate on it was closed. McIntyre pushed the door open, and Jonathan followed him through, closing the door behind him. Kuhl was behind his desk with two young men dressed in wannabe big shot lawyers' suits sitting in front of him.

Kuhl jumped to his feet, and the two lawyer wannabes turned their heads. Jonathan flipped open the badge. "Ray Kuhl, come with us."

Kuhl put his hands on his hips. "Excuse me?"

"Come with us," McIntyre said. "How hard can that be to understand?"

The two wannabes stood and took a position between their boss and Jonathan and McIntyre. They both looked fit, and if you removed the suits, they'd even look formidable.

"We don't have time for this," McIntyre said. He darted forward, and his hand flashed to the throat of the wannabe on the right. The man grabbed his neck and dropped to his knees choking. The other guy threw a punch, which McIntyre ducked and then came in with an uppercut. The lawyer crumpled.

"Okay," Jonathan said. "Are you coming without a fuss or not?"

Kuhl was white, and his hands trembled. "What am I under arrest for?"

"Who said you were under arrest? We told you to come with us. Now come, or be carried out."

"Who—who are you guys?"

"We're the really nasty branch of your government," Jonathan said.

"Then if you're with the government, I've got rights."

McIntyre crossed over to the lawyer, grabbed him by the neck, and slammed him facedown onto his own desk. "When it comes to terrorism, no one has rights."

"Terrorism? What are you talking about?" Kuhl said as McIntyre cuffed him. Jonathan cuffed the other two lawyers to the desk then gagged them.

McIntyre looked over at Jonathan. "This guy isn't going to keep quiet on the way out. Plan B?"

"Yeah," Jonathan said.

McIntyre stood Kuhl up and from behind nestled the lawyer's neck in the crook of his arm and squeezed, closing off the blood supply. Kuhl slumped to the floor.

"Night-night," McIntyre said.

Jonathan moved to behind the desk and took Kuhl's right arm while McIntyre took the left. "How do we explain this on the way out?"

"We don't," McIntyre said. "By the time they get over their shock and call the cops, we'll be gone."

"Then let's go."

They dragged Kuhl to the door, Jonathan opened it, and then they continued dragging him down the hall past the offices of his employees. Lots of heads turned as they passed, and Jonathan just kept flashing Perkins's badge. When they entered the reception area, the secretary jumped to her feet, flew around her desk, and blocked their path.

"You put him down. I've already called the police."

Jonathan and Duncan kept on moving, and the woman had to jump out of the way or be steamrollered by them.

"I hope you're in good shape," McIntyre said. "Because I think we should take the stairs, just in case the cops are on their way up. It's only six flights."

"I can handle it."

They took a right and dragged Kuhl down the hall to the door leading to the stairs. McIntyre pulled the steel door open, and they dragged Kuhl through and started down the stairs. Kuhl's feet made a rhythmic thump as they bounced on each step.

"His feet sure are going to be sore," Jonathan said.

Kuhl stirred. "Hey, what's going—"

McIntyre's elbow silenced him.

Jonathan was drenched in sweat by the time they got to the ground level. The abuse in Beirut combined with the wounds from a couple years before took their toll.

"You going to make it?"

"Yeah. Don't worry about me."

They leaned Kuhl against the wall. "I'll make sure the way is clear," McIntyre said.

"No," Jonathan said, "let me do it."

"Why you?"

"Because I'm still a hero in these parts. Lots of cops recognize me and are more likely to believe what I say."

"Okay."

Jonathan pushed open the stairway door and stepped into

the hallway. He walked toward the elevators, and sure enough, there were a couple of cops standing there. He doubled back and checked the route leading to the door to the alley. The route was clear, but the door wasn't. It had one of those bars that would set an alarm off if it were opened. It was to be used for emergency purposes only. Well, this was an emergency.

He returned to the stairway door and opened it, only to face McIntyre's gun. The CIA agent lowered it.

"Well?" McIntyre said.

"Clear to the back. The door is alarmed, so I couldn't check to see if Perkins is still clear."

"We'll have to chance it. If worse comes to worst, we can see just how far your celebrity status will take us."

They each grabbed an arm and pulled Kuhl out of the stairwell and down the hallway to the back door. Without missing a beat, they hit the bar setting off the alarm. Perkins had the dark blue Crown Victoria borrowed from the FBI parked right by the door. As instructed, he popped the trunk open but didn't look their way. He would truly be able to say he saw nothing.

Jonathan and McIntyre heaved Kuhl into the trunk, then slammed the lid. Jonathan got into the front seat with Perkins while McIntyre crawled into the back. Sam floored the accelerator just as two Seattle cops appeared at the door. Perkins hit the lights and siren.

"What are you doing?" Jonathan said.

"One of the ways of avoiding being chased is to look like you're chasing someone." He flipped open his cell phone and punched in three numbers. "Police," he said. "This is Special Agent Perkins of the FBI. I am in pursuit of a green Windstar van. I observed an unconscious man being dragged into it. Please advise Seattle police to join pursuit. I'm now going west on Tenth in a dark blue Crown Victoria." Sam listened for a second. "No, I didn't get the plate. . . . Good."

Sam flipped his cell phone shut, and then turned off his lights and siren and turned east on Tenth. "Looking for the van should keep them busy for a while. Where to?"

"Somewhere quiet."

Sam guided the car through downtown Seattle and headed to the docks. At the security gate, he flashed his badge and they drove right through.

"Park the car between some containers and then take a walk," McIntyre said.

Perkins shook his head. "No. This scum knows where my partner is. I want to be in on this."

Jonathan put his hand on Perkins's arm. "No, you don't," he said. "Trust me. Getting information is what McIntyre does. Just stop the car between some containers, and you and I go for a walk."

Sam chewed on his lip but nodded his head. He drove the car among the containers until they were out of earshot of dock employees. Sam parked the car, and the three men got out. There was muffled shouting and banging coming from the trunk.

McIntyre pulled a long piece of cloth out of his pocket to use as a gag. He looked at Jonathan. "I'll give you a shout when I'm finished."

"Right," Jonathan said. "Come on, Sam, let's go."

Perkins followed him, and he could hear the trunk opening, Kuhl screaming obscenities, and then a dull thud and a moan. Sam started to look back, but Jonathan grabbed his shoulder. "Don't."

They rounded the corner, and Sam stopped. "Jonathan, I've been playing this by ear with you, but I have to know, who is this guy, and why are you two so willing to help the FBI retrieve an agent?"

Jonathan looked into the eyes of his friend. Sam had really gone out on a limb for him—if he couldn't trust this man, he couldn't trust anyone. "I just met him a couple days ago myself."

"What?"

"He rescued me from terrorists in Beirut."

Sam cocked his head sideways. "Beirut? What were you doing in Beirut?"

"I went there to follow a lead about a terrorist threat. I got my information but was captured before I could communicate it to the agency, for all the good that would've done."

"Excuse me?"

"Another story, another day." There was no point in telling Sam that their own government left him to rot in Lebanon. "McIntyre led the mission to rescue me. He's a well-experienced and well-respected field agent of the CIA. Once I was debriefed, the agency assigned him to assist me in neutralizing the threat."

Sam took a step back. "Let me get this right. You tracked down a lead on a threat in Lebanon, and that brought you back to Seattle to track down Josef Grachev. What kind of threat is this that Grachev would be involved?"

"It's not so much that he's involved, but that he may have vital information on the source and timing of the threat."

"Such as?"

"Such as where a certain ship that stopped off in Lebanon and picked up six men and a wooden crate is."

"And why would he know?"

"Because it's a Russian freighter, and it's headed here."

Sam slumped back against the container. "Is Seattle the target?"

"Maybe."

"So you're not really helping me to find Ali, are you?"

Jonathan shook his head. "No. She would be a secondary mission objective. Getting Grachev—alive—is the primary."

"So if you get him, are you going to let me question him as to Ali's whereabouts?"

Jonathan looked away for a second. "Sam, I'll do all I can to rescue your partner; you have my word on that. Remember, she's with Michelle, and before I left, my mother made me swear I'd bring Michelle back. I can't do one without the other." He put his hand on Perkins's shoulder. "Okay, partner?"

Sam nodded. "Okay."

"You can come back now!" McIntyre shouted.

They rounded the corner of the container, and Kuhl was slumped against the back wheel of the car. As they drew closer, Jonathan could see his face was pale, his eyes were glazed and blood was flowing from his nose and mouth. "That didn't take long."

McIntyre grinned. "It seems Mr. Kuhl isn't ready to die for his client."

"So, where's Grachev?" Perkins said.

"We're right. He's on his yacht."

"Great, which one?"

McIntyre held up a cell phone. "Whenever Mr. Kuhl needs to see his client, he calls him on this cell phone, and Grachev gives him the GPS coordinates. In exchange for his life, Mr. Kuhl has agreed to make that call and get us the information."

"Then let's go," Sam said.

"When it gets dark," McIntyre said.

"Ali may not have until dark. Get him to make the call now."

McIntyre shook his head. "We wait until dark. I've requested two SEAL teams, and they'll be here in a few hours. If they were to assault in the daylight and Grachev's men decided to fight, there'd be a bloodbath that would not only jeopardize our mission but could result in your partner being killed."

Sam looked at Jonathan with pleading in his eyes.

"He's right, Sam. Remember that I was a SEAL. If we had to go during the daylight, invariably bullets started flying. Night's the best time. The water is warm right now. The chopper will drop them with submersibles, and they'll be able to sneak up on the yacht undetected. With those parameters, the SEALs will be able to take the yacht with minimal bloodshed."

"You guys just better be right," Sam said. "Because if I lose Ali, there'll be plenty of bloodshed."

危险 خطر ОПАСНОТЬ

TWENTY-SEVEN

Ali rolled over when the door to the cabin opened and two muscle-bound men dressed in black pants and T-shirts stepped in. Both men had flattened noses and blinked their eyes. They had to be ex-boxers. The one on the left probably learned to fight in response to taunts about his pimples. His face was covered in acne scars.

Grachev likely figured the best way to handle a kickboxer was with boxers. He was right. She didn't want to tangle with either of these guys if she didn't have to.

Scarface walked over to the bed and pulled a large knife out of his pocket. He flipped it open and leaned toward them. With a single swipe, he sliced through the bindings on Ali's feet. He did the same to Michelle.

"You are to come with us," he said with a Russian accent.

Ali rolled to the edge of the bed and sat up. She held her cuffed hands toward him. "Not until you take these off and let us go to the bathroom. Neither of us can hold it much longer."

Scarface looked at his partner and told him to go ask Grachev if it was okay, in Russian. The man returned a moment later. "Josef say okay because nowhere for you to go, so behave, or we tie up again. Got it?"

"Got it."

Scarface pulled out a gun and pointed it at Ali while his partner unlocked her handcuffs. He released Michelle, as well.

"Bathroom down hall."

"You go first," Ali said to Michelle.

Michelle nodded gratefully and went with Scarface's partner. A few minutes later, she returned looking quite relieved. Ali walked out of the cabin with Scarface's gun in her back.

"You need help?"

Ali looked over her shoulder. "You want to sing soprano in the church choir?" she said in Russian. "One more remark like that, and you will."

Scarface let the gap between them increase to four feet. Ali used the small washroom and looked for anything she might be able to use as a weapon. Nothing presented itself. Fact was, most of the fight was out of her. They were on a yacht at sea. Where could she go? Her only hope was rescue, or God. Michelle spent most of her waking time whispering prayers in Chinese. At first it bugged Ali, but after awhile she took comfort in Michelle's soft whisperings, hoping Michelle was right about God and she was wrong.

Ali opened the flimsy door, and Scarface leered at her when she exited. If she knew for sure that he wouldn't pull the trigger, it would be worth nailing him one, just to take the smile off his face.

He waved his gun. "That way."

Ali walked along the corridor and opened the door to a large stateroom. They passed through it and entered the deck on the back of the ship. The night air was warm and quiet, which meant no other vessels were nearby. The tantalizing smell of barbecuing chicken reached her nostrils.

Michelle was already there, seated at the end of the yacht. Sophie was dressed in jeans and a light cotton top, looking gorgeous. Including Scarface and his partner, four muscle-bound men stood off to the right looking as threatening as they could.

Grachev stood in front of a barbecue wearing slacks and a dress shirt. He turned when she stepped onto the deck.

"Ah, Ms. Marcoli," he said. "Care to join us for dinner?"

"I'd rather throw your rear end in jail. Have you any idea how much trouble you're in, kidnapping a federal agent and a witness under federal protection? The only light you're going to see for the rest of your life will be a 40-watt bulb hanging in your cell."

Grachev waved a pair of tongs with a chicken breast wedged in them at her. "That's just it, Ms. Marcoli. I don't know how much trouble I'm in. You see, I thought everything was all right. Yuri could have told lies about me that you might believe, but then he got killed in that unfortunate accident. My world seemed to be all right; then you people take this girl into protection. Why would they do that, I asked myself."

"Because some jerk smugglers were going to force her into the sex trade. We needed her to get to them."

Grachev put the breast back on the grill. "Yes, I thought that as well. But I heard rumors that Yuri gave you some misinformation on a container with drugs. That misinformation almost caused a bunch of poor immigrants their lives. Of course if the immigrants were put into a different container before reaching port, someone might believe Yuri was actually telling the truth."

"Yeah, they probably would," Ali said.

"But it seems the immigrants won't talk without a deal, and the INS won't give a deal. The only person who could help you out was this girl." He pointed his tongs at Michelle. "I heard she wasn't exactly grateful to get a new start in a new land. I also heard she's the kind of person who might just talk when they shouldn't."

He flipped all the chicken breasts. "So, I thought, if Yuri is dead, why do you care about this particular girl? What if you found a look-alike, and he's the one who's dead? I could be in a bad situation. So, I thought it would be nice if we could sit down to a nice dinner and talk about just what the FBI does know."

"Why don't we sit down and discuss what form of execution you want? I understand Washington State gives you a choice between lethal injection and hanging. I'd prefer you picked hanging."

Grachev's jaw clenched, and he took a couple steps toward her and waved the tongs. "Don't push me."

"Okay," Ali said. "Maybe we can talk." She casually moved over to Michelle. "Problem is, I really want to get out of this alive, with Michelle. It doesn't look like you're willing to do that."

"Oh, but I am. If Davidov is alive, then I'm headed for a warm, non-extradition country. You confirm that for me, then I let you two go."

"And why would you do that?"

"Because killing a federal agent and witness can motivate the FBI to chase harder than they normally would. I don't need them to have that kind of motivation."

"Okay," Ali said, "he's alive."

Grachev nodded his head. "I thought as much. Where are they keeping him?"

Ali chuckled. "You've got to be kidding."

"I'm not kidding. You could be lying about him being alive, just so I'll let you go. Tell me where he is, we'll check it out, and if he's truly alive, then you and the girl can go."

"I don't know where he is," Ali said.

Grachev's jaw tightened again. "Yes, you do. Now no games. Tell me where he is, or"—he whipped a gun out from behind his back and pointed it at Michelle—"or I will kill this girl. Yuri is a scum criminal. Whose life is really worth saving? His, or this poor innocent girl who's done nothing wrong?"

Michelle jumped to her feet and stood beside Ali. "Tell him nothing. I die, it okay. I just go home."

"What is she talking about?" Grachev said.

"She's talking about Jesus," Ali said. "You know, the guy who got crucified a couple thousand years ago for the sins of mankind. A guy you're not likely to see after they execute you."

Grachev waved the gun. "If anyone is going to be executed, it won't be me." He pulled back the hammer.

The door to the stateroom opened, and a tall man in a captain's uniform appeared and whispered into Grachev's ear. Grachev looked at his watch. "You're right. He is late. Something's wrong. Get the boat moving."

The captain disappeared back into the stateroom. Grachev turned his attention to Ali. "I will not waste time with you. Where is Davidov?"

Ali gripped Michelle's arm. There was no doubt in her mind Grachev meant to kill them. Whatever the captain said, it changed everything. The yacht's motors started up, and the boat started to move. Michelle said there was always a way with God. She hoped her young friend was right.

"You promise not to kill us," Ali said. "You swear on your mother's grave."

Grachev held up his right hand. His gun hand. "I swear."

Ali twisted and pushed Michelle into the water. She jumped from the boat, and a gunshot followed her. The back of her right leg burst into pain, and then the whole leg went numb. She hit the briny water and let herself sink. Bullets whizzed through the water above her. Even if the bullets didn't hit her, with one leg, how long could she swim?

خطر

Sam's gut churned more than the water below the blades of the helicopter. To avoid detection by Grachev, the helicopter had to stay out of earshot. The SEALs deployed half an hour ago in their submersibles. All he could do was wait. Jonathan, of course, wanted to go but couldn't because of his leg. Instead, his friend spent the time with his head bowed. McIntyre, in spite of the objections of the SEAL commander, went along with the teams.

Perkins's radio crackled to life. He and Corrigan exchanged glances.

"We've surfaced and have the boat in sight." It was the voice of Lieutenant Zimmer, the commander of the SEAL team. "We're fifty yards off her bow. There's light and people at the stern, so we'll have to board from the aft side."

More painful silence. Curses filled the radio. "The yacht has started to move. It's coming right at us. This is going to be fun."

More silence.

"We've lost the spook," another voice came on.

"Why am I not surprised," Zimmer said. "We'll look for him later. Run the submersibles full-out, parallel with the yacht, and try to board. Oh, this just gets better and better. We have shots fired off the back of the boat. I think someone might've gone in. Do we do anything about the man overboard?"

Jonathan's voice came over the earpiece. "Negative. Get Grachev alive. That's the primary objective."

Sam snapped his head up and stared at Jonathan. "That could be Ali. Tell them to help her."

Jonathan's eyes were wide with regret. "I can't, Sam. They need every man they've got to do this mission."

"Forget the mission," Sam said.

"We're on board," Zimmer's voice crackled. "Let you know how it turns out."

Perkins's heart pounded. Ali could be in the water, wounded. He leaned toward Jonathan as if to talk to him. Jonathan leaned toward him, and Sam punched him flush in the face.

Corrigan fell back, and Sam was on him in a flash. He grabbed Jonathan's weapon and charged to the cockpit of the chopper. He pressed it to the pilot's head. "Take us in, now."

The pilot jerked around. "Are you kidding? No way. Not until our guys are clear."

"Then prepare to die," Sam said.

"Fine, shoot me," the pilot said. "I'm not going to do anything that could cause one of our guys to get killed. We all go down in flames, pal."

Sam gripped the gun until his knuckles turned white. He had to do something. Anything.

The pilot touched his earpiece to hear better, and then the chopper surged forward.

خطر

The bullets stopped, but Ali couldn't get enough kick with one leg to push herself to the surface. Her lungs ached for air, and she fought the urge to open her mouth. Once the seawater got in her lungs, she'd die a horrible death. If only she could pass out before that happened.

A hand grabbed at hers. It was small and feminine. Michelle had come back for her, but there was no way slight Michelle could ever pull her up. Ali tried kicking, but they weren't gaining any ground. Suddenly lips were on hers. Ali opened her mouth, and Michelle blew air into her lungs, then swam away.

God bless you, Michelle, Ali thought. *You're a real fighter, aren't you?*

Her lungs started to burn again, demanding she let the air out. Ali burned up a lot of oxygen trying to slow her descent by kicking and pulling at the water. Michelle arrived again and gave her air.

A couple of minutes passed, and just when her lungs were about to explode, Michelle came again and gave her air. The girl was tiring, and the intervals were getting longer. Ali grabbed Michelle's head and turned it left to right to tell her she wanted Michelle to stop. She didn't want them both to drown. Michelle swam away again.

She let herself sink. Ali closed her eyes and let her thoughts drift back to happier times. Times when she thought she had a normal life and normal parents. Her dad helping her to ride a bike. . .her mom letting her help bake cookies. Ali wanted to cry, but that would mean opening her mouth and letting the seawater fill her lungs. No, the plan was to pass out before that happened.

She thought about Sam. Decent guys like him were getting rarer all the time. He'd take this hard. She would be the second partner he'd lost to Grachev. When she told him she might have breast cancer, he really cared. With time Ali wondered if they could've been more than partners.

Bright light filtered down through the water. Huh, maybe

all those prayers of Michelle's had done some good. So an angel was coming to take her to heaven at the request of her young friend. Wait a minute, that couldn't be right. Michelle had made it clear no one went upward until they gave themselves to Christ. Ali had never done that.

The brightness intensified. Her lungs demanded she let the air out. Ali was only seconds from meeting her Creator. *Jesus, I know this must sound phony since I'm just about to die and all, but I don't want to face God without You. Take me to be Yours. Take me now. Take me home.* Ali closed her eyes and opened her mouth. The remaining air in her lungs escaped into the ocean that would be her grave.

Powerful hands gripped under her arms, and lips forced themselves onto hers. An angel with lips? It couldn't be an angel; Michelle had come back. No, it couldn't be Michelle. The lips, they were a man's lips. Ali opened her mouth, and he blew air into her lungs. She opened her eyes but could not make out his face. A powerful light dropped from his hands and descended into the blackness below. He pulled her upward.

Ali started kicking her one leg and pulling at the water with her hands, helping her rescuer as much as she could. Her lungs started to scream for air again. They broke free of the surface, and Ali filled her lungs with glorious air.

The roar of a helicopter overhead deafened her. The water shoved them about with the prop wash and flares lit up their position. She turned to her rescuer and started to weep. "Sam," she sobbed.

"Thank God I found you," he said, tears in his own eyes.

Two life preservers splashed into the water beside them. Sam helped her put hers on before hanging onto his own. He wrapped his arms around her, and Ali cried into his shoulder.

خطر

Sam sat next to Ali in the chopper. A medic had already stopped the bleeding and put her on an IV. Sam held her hands and looked into her glazed eyes.

McIntyre moved beside him. "How is she?"

"She'll be fine," Sam said. "I thought Grachev was the primary objective."

"He was," McIntyre said. "I just missed the boat, so to speak, and saw a couple of women go into the water. I knew it'd be a long shot finding them, so I lit the flares hoping the chopper would find us. With the spotlight on that chopper, I figured they'd have a chance of being found."

"You figured right," Sam said. "I owe you one."

McIntyre looked down at Ali, his eyes moist. "You don't owe me anything. I couldn't let it happen again." He wiped at his eyes and shuffled over to the open door of the chopper where Corrigan waited.

The chopper slowed to a hover. They were over the yacht. They still had to interrogate Grachev, and Sam wanted to do it personally, not just for Newberg, but now for Ali, too.

He lightly touched Ali's cheek. "I'll see you later."

"Hurt him bad," Ali murmured.

"I will," Sam said and joined Jonathan and Duncan by the door.

Jonathan rubbed his cheek.

"Sorry about that."

Jonathan smiled. "I would've done the exact same thing."

The three of them were lowered by hoist to the yacht. A SEAL met them on the deck, and they followed him to a spacious cabin just off the stern deck of the boat. Inside, eight crew members were bound and leaning against the wall. Sophie Lebedev was sitting in a chair with a SEAL standing over her.

Grachev was bound to a chair with a smirk on his face.

Grachev wouldn't be so smug in a second. Sam pulled out his gun, rushed across the room, put his knee on Grachev's lap, and jammed the gun in his face. He heard all the SEALs' weapons cock. "You tried to kill my partner, and now I'm going to kill you!"

The smirk vanished. "He's nuts! Get him off of me!"

"Sam, don't!" Jonathan shouted.

"Why not? He killed Newberg, and he tried to kill Ali and Michelle. This guy is scum. He deserves to die."

Jonathan moved closer to him. "Sam, I need him."

"Back off!" Sam said. "I'll splatter him all over the floor if you come any closer."

"I'm a U.S. citizen," Grachev said. "I have rights."

"So did Newberg, and you killed him!" Sam got off Grachev and holstered his weapon. The tension in the room dropped 100 percent. "Now, it makes me sick to do this, but I'm going to offer you a deal."

Grachev's face was pale. "What kind of deal?"

"The U.S. Attorney was going to ask for the death penalty for the murder of Newberg, but in exchange for you pleading guilty to the murder of Newberg and telling Corrigan what he wants to know, we'll waive the death penalty."

Grachev laughed and smiled. "You can't prove I killed anyone."

Sam lifted an eyebrow. "Really." He dug into his pocket and showed a soggy picture to Grachev. "It's a little wet, but I think you can make out who it is holding yesterday's paper. He's even waving to you, although I don't know why he isn't using all his fingers. I think Yuri is upset that you tried to kill him. He's telling us everything we want to know."

"He's just one man. That's not enough for a murder one conviction."

"I think it is, especially since you tried to kill him," Perkins said. "But we've got Kuhl, too." He pointed to McIntyre. "Seems after speaking with our friend over here, he decided he'd rather make a deal than protect you."

Grachev's smile faded. "No, I don't believe you."

Sophie Lebedev stood up. "They have me, too."

"Sophie! Sit down and shut up!"

Sophie curled her lip up in a sneer. "You not order me around anymore. I not afraid of you. You not all powerful. Look at you. Tied like a dog, your men tied like dogs. You try to kill my friends; you hurt me. I not count your dirty money anymore. I not keep your secrets."

"Remember your family, Sophie. I have a long reach."

Sophie stiffened and stepped back.

McIntyre stepped forward and talked to Sophie in Russian for a minute then turned to Sam. "I'll get the State Department to contact the Russians. State will have the Russians put her family into protective custody until we can see about bringing them over here."

Sam turned to Sophie. "What secrets?"

"He kill FBI agent. He stab him to death. I saw it."

"Even if it were true," Grachev said, "and it's not, it could've just been a fight gone bad. Manslaughter."

Sam scratched his chin and looked at Sophie. "What did you mean about counting his dirty money?"

Sophie looked at McIntyre and spoke to him in Russian. McIntyre grinned.

"Seems Grachev has Sophie enter all the serial numbers of the money he takes in into a computer." McIntyre turned to Grachev. "Why would you do that?"

"I know," Sam said. "So if a cop ever uses drug money that's passed through his hands before, Grachev will know. It's how he discovered Newberg, and this gives us premeditation. It's murder one. Now, do you want to make a deal, or do you want the death penalty? Your choice."

Grachev looked at Sophie, McIntyre, Corrigan, and then Sam. He cursed. "I'll take my chances in court."

McIntyre looked over at the commander of the SEALs. "Clear the room. I need to talk with Mr. Grachev alone."

خطر

Sam and Jonathan sat in the bridge of the yacht by themselves while McIntyre *talked* with Grachev.

"Ever want to own something like this?"

Jonathan looked around the bridge. "Not really. I had my fair share of boats in the SEALs. I like solid ground now."

"Me, too."

They let the time pass in silence until the door to the bridge opened and McIntyre stepped out. "Is the deal still on?"

"You mean no death penalty?" Sam said.

"Yeah."

"You can't get him to talk otherwise?" Jonathan said.

"Probably, but he is former KGB. He's tough. I might end up killing him in the process."

"Then why is he interested in taking the deal now?" Sam said. "What changed his mind?"

McIntyre grinned. "It seems Grachev was unaware his ship picked up some terrorists in Lebanon. Looks like the captain might be making some money on the side. I told him that if he didn't talk, I'd make sure he was in Seattle until whatever happened, happened, and he could go down with us all. He didn't like that idea. He likes the idea of life in prison better."

"Sure, the deal's on."

"Great," McIntyre said.

"Did you learn anything at all?" Jonathan said.

"Oh, sure. He knows what ship we're talking about, and it's more than seven days from port. Once he gets a signed, sealed, and delivered document, he'll give us the exact location along with a whole bunch of other interesting stuff. From there we'll have a SEAL team board it, take the terrorists prisoner if possible, and find out what they were bringing in. It should be simple."

"It's not that simple," Jonathan said. "I've still got an asset in Lebanon who risked his life to give us this information. The only thing keeping him alive is the terrorists want us to believe his information is useless. Once you take out that ship, they'll kill him and his family. I have to go back to Lebanon and get him out."

McIntyre shook his head. "No, you don't. Now that this threat is confirmed, Stone is going to be like putty in our hands. He's going to want to be able to take credit for this, and the only way he can do that is if you and I say he was in on it all along. If you can live with that, I can get him to go get your guy and his family. Can you live with it?"

"I can live with it."

"Good. Then it looks like everyone will get what they want," McIntyre said.

EPILOGUE

Jonathan's biochemical warfare suit crinkled as he turned and surveyed the similarly dressed team of SEALs lining the walls of the chopper. McIntyre was up front talking to the pilots.

It took them two days to find the Russian freighter drifting five hundred miles south of the position Grachev gave them. Thermal scans both by satellite and helicopter showed no signs of life. Since no one abandoned ship at deep sea unless it was sinking, they prepared themselves for the worst.

McIntyre plodded back and took the seat next to him. "We're almost there. We'll sweep the ship and then you can come on board. Okay?"

"Okay," Jonathan said. With his bum leg, he'd hinder the team if it turned out the terrorists had managed to thwart the scans and a firefight broke out.

McIntyre gave a thumbs-up, and a petty officer slid the door to the chopper open. The SEALs all slipped on their headgear and fastened it to their suits. McIntyre left the helicopter first, followed by eight SEALs armed with machine guns. Jonathan moved to the open door and listened on the headset as the SEALs broke into teams of two and worked their way through the ship, signaling what areas were clear.

"This is McIntyre," a voice crackled. "We've found something in cargo hold one. Everyone stay put for now. Corrigan, we need you here, and make sure your suit is zipped up. Myers, go back to the LZ and lead Corrigan here."

"Yes, sir," a voice answered.

"Be right there," Corrigan said, his stomach starting to churn. Why the concern about his suit? He pulled on the suit's headgear, and the petty officer manning the hoist helped him fasten it. They clicked the hoist to his harness, and Jonathan slipped over the side of the chopper and descended to the freighter. The heavy boots of his suit clunked onto the freighter's deck as one of the bulkhead doors opened and a silvery apparition waved to him.

He unfastened the tether and started toward the bulkhead door. Jonathan felt like he was in some kind of end-of-the-world movie. SEALs moving around a ghost ship dressed for biochemical warfare.

He followed Myers through the ship and down to the cargo hold. McIntyre and two SEAL members were looking down at the floor. Jonathan gagged when he saw what they saw.

Sprawled on the steel floor were two Middle Eastern men, their decaying skin covered in open sores. Littering the floor were fragments of wood and chunks of stainless steel.

"What happened?" Jonathan said.

"Cut your radio, and follow me," McIntyre said.

Jonathan turned off his radio, and he and McIntyre stepped about fifteen feet away from the other SEALs. They put their face shields together.

"The crate exploded. Must have been booby-trapped,"

McIntyre said. "But I don't think we were the target."

"You don't think this was an accident?"

McIntyre shook his head. "I think the operation was a success."

"I don't follow."

"Whoever sold them the bioweapon never intended for it to reach the U.S. They intended to take out the terrorists. Now who do you think would've done something like that?"

Jonathan groaned. "CIA."

"You bet. Since I don't know of any op like this—black or not—my guess is we've stumbled across a rogue operation."

"That explains a lot," Jonathan said. "I thought Petra's son gave me up to Hezbollah, but obviously a group in the CIA has been working against us all this time. Probably the same people who interfered with the FBI's investigation."

"Now the question is," McIntyre said, "just how many more terrorist groups have they targeted? What have they given them? I've never seen anything like this"—he nodded toward the bodies—"so it's ours, and experimental, or it's something our intel hasn't discovered yet. Either way, what happens if a target group figures it out, disarms the bomb, but still has the bioweapon?"

"This isn't over yet, is it?" Jonathan said.

"Not by a long shot."

ABOUT THE AUTHOR

Andrew Snaden is a writer and an accountant who lives on a farm in Prince George, British Columbia. His other books include the acclaimed *Betrayed* and *Face Value*, both cowritten with Rosey Dow. Andrew also writes articles for magazines such as *On Mission*, *The Evangelical Beacon*, and *Live*. He and his wife have one daughter.

Visit the author's Web page at www.andrewsnaden.com for group discussion questions.

If you enjoyed

TRAITORS

check out these gripping suspense titles from Barbour:

Chayalocha

by Shane Johnson
ISBN 1-59310-051-5
Discover what happens when an innocent
man meets an ancient evil bent on possessing
him—as it has possessed others throughout
history.

abduction

by Wanda L. Dyson
ISBN 1-58660-812-6
Detective JJ Johnson and Zoe Shepherd
attempt to find an infant, stolen from her
crib in the dark of night—and uncover a
history of missing children.

Each for only $8.97

AVAILABLE WHEREVER BOOKS ARE SOLD.

If you enjoyed

TRAITORS

check out these gripping suspense titles from Barbour:

BENEATH THE ICE
by Alton Gansky
ISBN 1-58660-674-3
Engineer Perry Sachs is in for the adventure
of a lifetime after agreeing to excavate a
mysterious object hidden three miles
beneath the Antarctic ice.

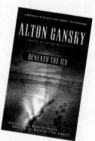

OPERATION FIREBRAND: DELIVERANCE
by Jefferson Scott
ISBN 1-58660-677-8
When a handful of refugees—risking their
lives trying to escape North Korea—is
intercepted by the Communist Chinese,
Team Firebrand must fight back.

Each for only $8.97

AVAILABLE WHEREVER BOOKS ARE SOLD.